DARLING WILDFIRE

A RED RABBIT NOVEL
Kraven's Story

DEVYN RIVERS

Everyone sees what you appear to be,
few really know what you are.

MACHIAVELLI

For my darlings who like to play with fire,
And the ones who love Kraven as much as I do.

A WARNING

May contain spoilers.
If you don't have triggers, go in blind.

This book contains scenes that may be
disturbing to some readers.
Your mental health matters.

I want to draw special attention to the following triggers.
These are the _only_ warnings. Proceed with caution.

Death of a child by violence occurs in Chapter 28 & 67
Harm to a child (knife wound by an adult) occurs in Chapter 67

These are open door scenes and are extremely important to the story,
but if you need to skip them to protect your mental health, you can
move on to the next chapters. This book **DOES NOT** contain descrip-
tive scenes of underage sexual abuse or animal abuse of any kind.

This story includes
sexually explicit scenes, morally gray themes
and the following tropes and triggers:

Revenge, Friends to lovers, MF, MFM (main characters), MFMM, MM - bi awakening (secondary characters), Military/ Armed Forces & Law Enforcement (SWAT), Antihero/villain, Russian Mafia, Kidnapping, Why choose, Knife play, HEA, Sexual assault/rape of a main character, Rape, Non-con/ dub-con, Sex trafficking, Suicide, suicidal thoughts and suicidal attempts, Violence, Blood, Killing, Gore, Gun Violence, Military Men, Branding, Non-con bondage, needles, Scars, Captivity, Electrocution, Torture, Whipping, PTSD, Anxiety attacks, nightmares, Genital piercing, War Themes/Military deployment, Grief and Loss, Death of a sibling, Death of a friend, Discussions and Themes of Death, Psychological abuse, Drugging and Rape while drugged, severed body parts, harm to a child (knife wound by an adult), MM sexual abuse, child death

AUTHOR'S NOTE

This is Theron North's story.
Or as you know him: *Kraven.*

It is dark. It is sad. It has extremely disturbing themes.
While this is partially a romance—there is a happy ending—and while there are plenty of steamy, spicy scenes, this book is not your classic dark romance novel. Also, while we all love Kaelin and Graham—and they are definitely important to Kraven—in the grand scale of Kraven's life, he has not known them for very long. Please keep this in mind. Overall, I recommend going into this story with an open mind because Kraven is not always who he seems to be.
But this is the story he wanted me to tell.

One thing is for sure—he is a sociopath, he is a villain, and he is one of my absolute favorite characters.
So without further ado...
He has a message for you:

"I thought we would relive old times.
I hope you haven't forgotten; you're mine.
—no one can break you like I can.

You're a wildfire, darlin'
—a goddamn wildfire."

When the Fox hears the Rabbit scream he comes a-runnin',
but not to help.

THOMAS HARRIS

PROLOGUE

Who am I if not a hunter?

I don't want to think about what I'll do after this. I've spent the last decade wreaking havoc around the world in preparation—destroying, building and killing—a lot of killing. For most people that would be the part that would get to them, but not me. At what point do you start considering yourself the reaper? At what point do you give in to the god complex of holding a life in your hands? Sometimes literally—I've held a bleeding heart, still beating, after I've torn it from my enemies chest.

At what point do you consider yourself evil?

Those are the questions your humanity is supposed to answer, but unfortunately that was stripped from me long ago.

What happens to a man when that's gone? I'm afraid I'll know the answer when all of this is over. That's what they don't tell you—no matter how deep into the shadows you go, the fear of losing yourself follows.

Even the dead and the dying fear the darkness.

Who am I if not a hunter?

Maybe I'll live long enough to find out.

But first...

One last hunt.

One last dangerous game.

PRESENT DAY

His desire for revenge had not forsaken him.

COUNT OF MONTE CRISTO

1

THERON

NEW YORK CITY

I looked out over the dark bay from my vantage point in my office and took a deep breath as excitement and anticipation filled me. The skyline sparkled with lights from the docks and the nearly full moon illuminated the water.

It was time.

Everything I'd built, everything I'd accomplished, it all led up to this.

The patience, the hard work—literal blood, sweat and tears—forged into the foundation of everything I'd done the last decade.

Anything to accomplish my goal. *Revenge.* Oh, and what an addictive drug that was. Ever since I'd escaped the hell that was *Atrox Gaming Inc.*, my blood had raged with the lust for complete annihilation of the one who had taken everything from me.

Vetticus. My rage for him festered. It dug under my skin and grew into something alive, with a monstrous hunger for vengeance not easily sated and impatient for action. But I didn't need to suppress it any longer. It was time to unleash everything I'd meticulously built and passionately cultivated.

It was the beginning of the end. *The last game.*

I looked down at my phone clutched tightly in my hand as my five team members around the world checked in. Five kill shots that would set everything in motion. As the last team let me know they were in position, I typed out the two words that would help bring about the retribution I longed for and the peace I knew would come after. Two words that would incite justice for not only myself but all the people I'd lost in the process of getting here.

My thumb hovered over the button. The clock changed to the top of the midnight hour. And I lit the fuse.

2

ATLAS

DUBAI

end it.

Send it.
I glanced at the text from North out of the corner of my eye; it was go time. The hot sun beat down on me from where I lay on the top of a terracotta tiled roof but I hardly noticed, too wrapped up in the man sitting in my crosshair. He was seated at a busy cafe, sipping an espresso, his tailored suit at complete odds with the local garb. He stuck out, which told me he didn't have a care in the world—he thought he was untouchable. Two bodyguards stood a few feet away and while they were dressed like the locals and trying to blend in, they weren't doing a very good job of it.

Sweat beaded on the man's forehead and I could feel my own sweat dripping down my face as I made one last adjustment, and with a squeeze of the trigger I set one part of the bigger game in motion.

The man dropped, a dead shot straight through his eye and then I was up and running as the cafe descended into chaos. I jumped a few rooftops before sliding my gun under my robes and dropping into an alley where a bike rested in the shadows. The motor rumbled to life, and I took off through the city, merging into traffic and leaving the crime scene behind.

Exhilaration rushed through me—this is what we'd been working towards for the last ten plus years and five bullets into the five board members of *Atrox*, had just set everything in motion.

Part of me wished it would have been Vetticus in my sights but that would have been too easy. Plus, he was a hard man to find and trust me, we'd tried. We'd found his company but he was always doing everything by proxy and so the plan was to incite him to act—to draw him out.

Although, even if we could find him, a quick and unexpected death was not what that bastard deserved, and not what we had planned. He had taken so much from me—from North and Nyx too—and after the horrors we'd all gone through at his hands, we were about to make the bastard regret it all.

Despite all of that, the thought of Nyx brought a stupid smile to my lips, hidden by my face covering but still there all the same. We'd found each other in the darkest of places and I wouldn't have survived it all without him. It was strange not to be on a mission together after all these years. I was eager to get back home where he'd stayed behind with North.

Leaving the traffic behind, I pulled the bike onto a small airstrip on the outskirts of the city where a jet was waiting. A familiar face appeared at the doorway and Lachlan descended the steps, an unlit cigarette held between his lips.

"Successful hunt?" He asked as we clasped forearms in greeting.

Lachlan Frey, our Austrian ex-Jagdkommando—Austria's Special Forces, and one of the most unhinged people I knew besides maybe Nyx and North. He hid it all behind a sunny disposition but I'd known him since the beginning of everything, when we went to Austria for our first job after escaping Vetticus' clutches. This man may look like a blond surfer, especially now that he kept his hair long, but his eyes gave him away—dark blue pits of chaos and death.

I pulled the bullet casing from my pocket and tossed it to him as I went to board the plane.

"Wouldn't settle for anything less," I said over my shoulder.

"Aw a souvenir. How sweet." Lachlan lit the cigarette and went to do his walk around. "Oh, and text your boyfriend will you? He's been bugging the shit out of me!"

I chuckled and entered the cabin, pulling my rifle case from an overhead bin and pulling off the local robe in favor of jeans and a black t-shirt I'd stashed there too. Then I sat down and shot off two quick texts—the first one to North.

> **Me**: Confirmed.

Then to Nyx:

> **Me**: Stop bothering Lach

> **Nyx**: Tattletale.

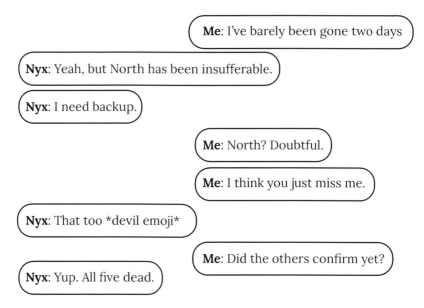

Me: I've barely been gone two days

Nyx: Yeah, but North has been insufferable.

Nyx: I need backup.

Me: North? Doubtful.

Me: I think you just miss me.

Nyx: That too *devil emoji*

Me: Did the others confirm yet?

Nyx: Yup. All five dead.

A smirk pulled at my features and I muttered an excited *fuck yeah*. We'd just waved a huge red flag at the bull and now just had to wait for him to charge. It wouldn't take long for Vetticus to find out it was us behind the kills—it was kind of the point seeing as we were hoping to draw him out.

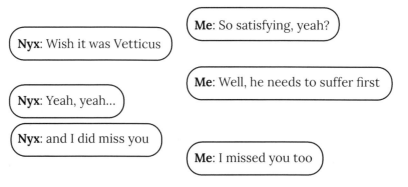

Me: So satisfying, yeah?

Nyx: Wish it was Vetticus

Me: Well, he needs to suffer first

Nyx: Yeah, yeah...

Nyx: and I did miss you

Me: I missed you too

I heard Lachlan board the plane and the door get pulled shut behind him. "Wheels up in two!" He called out.

Me: We're taking off. Be home soon.

Nyx: Can't wait

Nyx: *black heart emoji*

I smiled as I put my phone away and turned to my gun, taking it apart to clean. Even after ten years, I was still stupidly in love with that man. I was looking forward to the day we didn't have Vetticus' shadow haunting us at every turn.

3

NYX

A tlas and Lach are on the way home," I said.

North turned away from the window in his office. He nodded but I could tell he was distracted as he came and sat down behind his desk. He leaned back in his chair and stared out at the cityscape, illuminated brightly by the full moon. I sank down into one of the plush chairs in front of his desk.

"When do you think we'll hear from him?" I asked.

My nerves were all over the place now that we'd initiated things. This had been the plan all along but it was one thing to plan for a decade, and another for the time to arrive to actually execute that plan.

North didn't answer for a long moment. I couldn't figure out what he was thinking but that was nothing new so I waited him out.

"Hard to say."

"I would be really surprised if he hasn't tried to find you at least once since we escaped," I scoffed.

"I'm not hard to find."

"You're also not easy to find," I smirked.

North finally turned to me and a ghost of a smile slid across his face as he inclined his head in agreement. His calculating eyes fixed on me, those gray depths always so efficient at seeing past my walls. He was the only person, besides Atlas, that I could be transparent with. Abruptly, he stood and walked over to his minibar, pouring out two glasses of whiskey. He came over and handed one to me.

"Are you going to tell Kaelin?" I asked.

I figured if I beat him to the personal stuff, it would delay the inevitable discussion of how I was feeling about all of this. He sat down in the chair next to mine and took a sip before answering, humoring my deflection.

"No."

"No?" I raised my eyebrows. "What about Graham?" He took another sip, looking like he was maybe making this decision at this exact moment. "I mean, you've thought about this already right?"

"Of course I have," he scoffed.

"It's okay to be worried—"

His gaze sharpened on me and if it wasn't for our years of friendship a lesser man probably would have backed down under such a forceful warning stare but I wasn't such a man.

"She kind of showed up in your life at—shall we say—an inconvenient time," I continued.

Something resembling a growl of agreement escaped North as he looked away with a frown.

"The less she knows, the better," he grumbled.

"That's what they always say, and it never seems to be true," I muttered before burying my face in my glass, inhaling whiskey fumes as I took a large sip. The burn was welcome and did wonders to steady my nerves. Not for the first time in the last two days I wished Atlas was around to help me talk sense into North. He was always better at it than I was. I tended to stir up North's volatile side whereas Atlas tempered it all down with reason.

"I'm going to ask Graham to join the team," he said.

I wasn't surprised about that although I'd thought it would happen a lot sooner. I'd been on the Red Rabbit job which was where I first met him. He was a solid guy who I'd gladly have at my back again and I knew North trusted him explicitly now.

"Then he'll need to know all of it," I stressed. "What's your hesitation? I understand Kaelin, but him?"

North sighed. "I haven't had to tell someone the full story in a really long time," he admitted. "Most of the team has been with us since the beginning—West, Lach, Knight—even Knox, Tex and the Volkov brothers joined a few years in."

He had a point. Everyone was already aware of just how deep into the shit we were. He'd found Kaelin under false pretenses and I'm sure, even now, she had no idea what kind of man he really was. The last few years had put more of a strain on him and it wasn't just from the revenge against Vetticus.

"She could probably help us with the other thing," I said carefully.

Kaelin was already a touchy subject with North and I wasn't looking to fight tonight especially by bringing up another sensitive subject. He made a noncommittal sound in the back of his throat, staring out the window again.

"She's going to find out about—"

"Enough," North said quietly. "We are so close, Nyx, so fucking close."

Regardless of whether he was talking about Vetticus, or the other thing—excitement rushed through me. I couldn't help the dark smile that curled my lips at the thought of getting my hands on Vetticus on my terms, playing our game. The anger and hatred for him hadn't lessened over time, it only made my resolve to rip him apart piece by piece more of an intense primal urge.

My gaze dropped to my left hand that was missing my pinky finger—a constant physical reminder of the pieces of us Vetticus had taken and the scars he'd inflicted.

"I've thought about this moment for a really long time," I admitted and when he met my eyes with a smirk of his own, I went on. "And it feels better than I imagined."

He held his glass up. "Cheers to that, my friend."

4

THERON

ONE WEEK LATER

Mine.
The word slid across my mind, almost seductive in the way it lingered, as I saw Kaelin enter the office and head past reception. Those green eyes landed on me and not for the first time I cursed Cooper for ever taking away the fire that burned there. Now she was unleashed, untamed and undeniably mine. Graham noticed where my attention had gone and turned from where he sat sprawled in a chair in front of my desk.

"Do you think she followed the instructions?" He asked.

We watched her walk down the hall in a tight black dress that went to her knees. The neckline was high and it wasn't revealing or inappropriate but somehow she still made it look sinful. She wore her hair down in loose waves and I loved watching her walk in heels. Especially when they were the red bottoms I'd bought her last week.

"Are you hoping she did or she didn't?" I asked dryly.

Graham scoffed but didn't get a chance to answer before she pulled the door open and walked in. The smile on her face made me want to kiss her breathless and then do naughty things to that mouth.

"Hey gorgeous," Graham drawled.

"Hey sexy," she said. She went over to him and leaned over to kiss him. Graham slapped her ass as she straightened and she walked around the desk to me.

"Darlin'," I smirked at her, wrapping my arms around her waist.

I yanked her to me, enjoying the small gasp as her hips collided with mine.

"Hi, T," she breathed.

She was so soft and I brought my lips to hers. My hands dropped lower to her ass and I squeezed her through the fabric, loving the small sounds of enjoyment she made as she plastered her body against mine. I pushed her against the desk and my kiss dropped to her neck, nipping lightly. She tilted her head to give me better access. I hit a button and the glass walls of my office transformed into tinted panes, sealing us inside a bubble of privacy. Another locked the door.

"Did you follow my instructions?" I murmured against her neck.

"Why don't you find out," she said.

She met my gaze with a coy smile and my hand slid up to her neck.

"Do I need to warn you about what happens if you didn't?"

I turned her around and pushed her down over the top of my desk. My other hand ran up her leg, dragging the hem of her dress up until I pushed it over her ass. I groaned at the sight of her—she was perfection—and she'd followed my instructions. She wasn't wearing panties and I kicked her ankles apart a bit further so I could see her pretty pussy teasing me between her legs.

"Are you wet already, love?" I asked. I brought my hand down and spanked her. She jumped and dipped her head in pleasure, her hands digging into the wood.

"Yes—what was that for? I followed your instructions?"

"That's cause he knows you like it," Graham answered. He was relaxed back in the chair, stroking the bulge in his jeans as he watched.

"She did follow instructions," I said to him.

The small jewel of a butt plug peeked through her ass cheeks. I ran my hand over where I'd spanked her and pulled her cheeks apart so I could see the plug better.

"Come here," I said to Graham. He got up and walked over and hummed his approval at the view. He slid his finger down the plug and across her pussy.

"So fucking pretty," he murmured. I sat down in my office chair and pushed it back a bit.

"Take out his cock, darlin'," I said.

She stood up, and Graham pulled her in, kissing her intensely for a long moment. He slid the zipper of the dress down her back, giving me a show of revealing her skin inch by inch. Graham turned and sat on the edge of my desk with her between his legs as he slowly slid the dress off her shoulders.

As he pushed the dress down her body, her scars came into view, like cracks that were fused back together. I knew every single one of them because I spent any second I could tracing them—kissing them—making her believe they did nothing but show me how strong she was.

Something broken could be beautiful, and she was my masterpiece.

Graham pushed the dress the rest of the way off and she stepped out of it, standing before us in only her heels. I unzipped my pants and pulled my cock out, already hard, I stroked up and down my length, watching Graham's hands run back up her body. He tangled his fingers in her hair and pushed her head down towards his cock where he'd pulled down his pants and boxers just enough to free it.

Kaelin bent at the waist, pushing her hips back towards me to give me an even better view. Graham groaned as she took him into her mouth and his hands gathered her hair up in a ponytail, gripping it in his fist as she moved up and down his length. I saw his eyes darken as he watched what she was doing.

"God, I love your lips wrapped around my cock, pretty girl," he gasped.

I ran my hands over her hips and leaned forward to kiss her ass, then sank my teeth into her skin. She moaned around his cock and his eyes flashed to me to see what had elicited her reaction. I pushed her legs further apart and ran my hands up the backs of her thighs so my thumbs just grazed her pussy. Kaelin shivered and Graham cursed softly. His hand on her head got more forceful and he took control, fucking her mouth until all I heard was the sloppy sounds she was making.

Graham pushed her head down, sliding all the way back into her throat and held her there. His eyes were hooded as he watched her choke on him and he didn't let up. She squirmed from lack of air, gagging on him.

"You're okay, baby, fuck," he gasped.

When he finally pulled her back up, she pulled in a big breath through her nose before he pushed her back down again. She pushed her hips back towards me and I knew she was aching for someone to touch her. Her hand drifted between her legs and I grabbed it and pulled it behind her back.

"I don't think so, gorgeous," I said darkly. "You love choking on Graham's cock don't you? She's soaking wet for you, man."

Her pussy was glistening with her arousal. I heard her choke on Graham's cock again as he held her down and I knelt between her legs, watching the wetness pool and begin to drip from her pussy. I blew on her and goosebumps broke out over her body. Graham pulled her head up, letting her breathe and the moment he shoved her back down again, I licked her from her clit all the way to the plug. They both moaned.

"Fuck, do that again," Graham gasped. He let her take a breath and pushed her down again, holding his dick down her throat. I sucked on her clit and she squirmed between us as she ran out of air.

"You're doing so good—I love when you choke on my cock."

Graham started up a ruthless pace, fucking her face, and I licked her clit in quick strokes of my tongue. Between my tongue and sucking Graham's dick, she was soaking wet and shoving her hips down trying to ride my face. The whimpering sounds coming out of her mouth were enough to make Graham pant and my cock to leak.

Graham pulled her up by her hair and I heard his cock pop free with a wet sound as she gulped in air. He held her head up, her curls spilling through his fist, watching her grind on my mouth as she moaned and panted.

"Damn, you're beautiful riding his face like that," Graham said huskily.

Her legs started to shake and I knew she was close by the little sounds she was making. I slid two fingers into her pussy and a few strokes pushed her over the edge. She cried out as she came, riding my face. I pulled away and she collapsed towards Graham with a moan. He kissed her softly before pushing her gently into my arms as I got to my feet. I captured her lips in mine, kissing her hard, letting her taste herself on my lips and tongue.

"I'm going to fuck you while you choke on him, darlin'." I said against her lips. "Bend over."

Graham's other hand was teasing her nipples. I ran my tongue across her parted lips and pushed her facing Graham again. He kissed her as I fisted my cock and ran the head through her wetness, teasing her clit.

I met Graham's eyes and in silent agreement he pushed her head down on his cock at the same time I slid inside her, pulling a groan from all three of us. We started fucking her slowly in unison—as I'd pull out, he'd lift her head up and then we'd both sink back inside her. I watched her hand drift once more between her legs, needing more and I quickly grabbed both of her wrists and pinned them behind her back with one hand.

I spanked her hard with the other. "Naughty girl—not listening." She moaned in protest around Graham's cock and he threw his head back in pleasure. "Keep your hands behind your back."

She obeyed and I reached down and tugged at the butt plug, watching it pull slightly out and then sink back in. She shoved her hips back towards me, impaling her hard on my cock. She let out a frantic moan and I smirked.

"Your ass is needy, baby girl," I said breathlessly.

I pulled on the plug again and her pussy tightened around me. I groaned and set a steady pace. Each time I pulled out of her, I tugged the plug out slightly. Her legs started to shake again and I could feel her get close.

"Are you going to come all over my cock, darlin'?" I panted.

She whined in answer, moving her hips as much as she could against me. I continued playing with the plug but brought my other hand around to her clit and she screamed around Graham's cock, making his hips buck.

"Come for us, baby," he groaned. "Come on T's cock like a good girl."

A moment later she shattered and I slammed my hips into her, feeling her contract again and again around my dick. My eyes closed and I tipped my head back, letting her orgasm wash over me. I slowed my pace as she came down and her hands came to rest on the desk on either side of Graham's hips. He caressed her face as she caught her breath, kissing her gently on the cheek and then her nose.

"I'll never get over watching you come like that," he said darkly.

She moaned in answer, still too breathless to answer.

"I want you to fuck me in the ass," she said to Graham.

I smirked and gave her a gentle smack. I remember a time I told her I'd have her begging to have her ass taken. I liked being right. I pulled her to me and picked her up in my arms. She kissed me, sucking at my bottom lip, as I walked us over to the couch in my office and sat down against one arm with her straddling my hips. I pulled her down on my chest and she greedily slid her wet pussy along my cock, seeking friction.

"Baby girl," I groaned.

I ran my hands up and down her back, watching her face as she took pleasure from me. Graham came up behind her and I saw the moment he grabbed the plug and started playing with it. From the look on his face, he was going to tease her for a minute. I pulled her hips down so my cock lay against her pussy but when she tried to move, I held her still. She moaned in frustration and her head fell back on her shoulders at whatever Graham was doing. I loved watching the pleasure play across her face. She showed you everything in these moments and I soaked it all in. I ran my thumb across her bottom lip and she sucked it into her mouth, gently running her tongue over it and looking at me with sultry eyes full of sin. My cock twitched and I saw the smirk in her eyes when she felt it.

She moaned around my finger as Graham pulled the plug free and tossed it aside. My thumb popped from her mouth as Graham pushed her down against my chest. He must have grabbed the lube from my desk because I heard the cap pop and I saw in her eyes the moment he pushed his head against her opening. There was always a flash of initial fear and wariness that took over the pleasure. She was so close to my face, her breathless pants caressed my skin.

"Just relax, darlin'," I murmured.

I lined my cock up and slid into her pussy at the same time Graham pushed further into her ass. She moaned and tensed up until he rubbed a hand down her back and I felt him slide all the way in. It didn't matter how many times we did anal, she always doubted herself in the beginning. We sat like that, buried deep inside her, letting her adjust.

"Please," she whimpered.

I loved when she begged.

"What do you need, darlin'?"

"More—fuck me—please," she said breathlessly.

Graham's cock slid against mine through her walls as he pulled almost all the way out before sinking back in and we both groaned. Kaelin tightened around my cock and her eyes were hooded, lips parted in pleasure. Her body was plastered to me, her hands digging into my hair and she brushed her lips against mine as we shared air. I moved my own hips and soon we found a rhythm, fucking her slowly and driving her towards the edge.

"You take us so well, beautiful," I panted, tangling my hands in her hair.

"Fuck, you both feel so good," she gasped.

We picked up the pace and the sounds she made were driving me wild. I was so hard inside her, drowning in all the sensations. Everytime Graham and I pushed inside her she tightened around us, making us groan and soon we were all lost in the moment. Her hands had a death grip in my hair and she brought her lips to mine in a searing kiss that nearly tipped me over the edge. I felt the moment she became overwhelmed with pleasure and she cried out as we drove her into a state of heightened bliss. My hand slid down between us and the moment I touched her clit she buried her face in my neck, shoving her hips back to take both of us harder.

"Yes, yes—" she chanted under her breath and then she was coming.

She tightened around me over and over again, pulling me with her as she cried out in pleasure. It hit her hard and seemed to go on forever and my own release roared through me, sending me to join her. My hands twisted in her hair, holding her face above me as I watched her lose control. It was my favorite thing—to watch her come apart like that. To see her reduced to nothing but pleasure and feel the energy rolling between us in waves was like a drug—potent and addicting.

I felt Graham shove inside her and curse as his own orgasm raced through him a moment later. He collapsed to one side of the couch, his lips against her shoulder. She rested her forehead against mine, eyes closed as she caught her breath. When she opened them, the green was alive with gold and it took my breath away. I saw the vulnerability in them and I felt the words on the tip of my tongue—everything I've been longing to say to her but couldn't. I kissed her and brushed a curl behind her ear. She turned to Graham and kissed him, then grinned at both of us.

"That was amazing," she breathed. Graham chuckled and gently pulled out of her causing us all to moan at the loss. He growled low in his throat and we both looked back at him.

"Now that is a sexy view—hold still." He walked over to his pants and pulled out his phone then came over and snapped a picture. He turned his phone towards us with a smirk. My cock was half buried in her pussy, cum leaking out around it while her ass was dripping Graham's cum. My cock twitched and I ran a hand over my face.

"Jesus—put that away before I'm hard again."

"I'll send it to the group chat," he said.

Kaelin laughed and slowly slid off me.

"Let's get you cleaned up, pretty girl," Graham said. He held out his arms and swept her up, kissing her on the forehead before heading to the private bathroom I had adjacent to my office.

I let them have a moment before I stood up and walked into the bathroom. Graham was in the enclosed toilet area and Kaelin was still gloriously naked at the sink. I wrapped my arms around her from behind and she smiled and sank back into me, looking at me in the mirror. She ran her hands over my biceps and I nestled into her neck, kissing her softly.

"I'll never get enough of you, baby girl," I said.

"Good," she murmured, looking pleased. She half turned in my arms and brought her hand to my face, studying me with a soft look I'd started to see occasionally in the more intimate moments between us.

"You make me really happy, T," she said.

I smiled darkly at her and her eyes lit up.

"You make me happy too," I said—and it was true.

5

GRAHAM

So, I looked into *Northern Tactical*," Kaelin said.

She dragged her brush through a deep blue and applied it to the canvas in front of her. She'd been working quietly on the sky for the better part of an hour. I'd come to see her at her studio and after fucking her on her paint table—one of my favorite things to do—I'd relaxed on the couch with my computer, doing some work while I watched her work her magic.

"You know it's a global enterprise, right?"

"Yeah," I said warily.

She turned to look at me. "Did you know Theron isn't mentioned anywhere online in association with *NorTac*? It's all very vague. In fact, Theron North technically doesn't exist."

"I'm sure he has his reasons," I said. She made another few adjustments to the painting before starting on another color combination, tweaking the blue already on the pallet.

"Why the sudden interest? You know North won't like you snooping around."

"I didn't hack into anything—" she said dryly, flashing me a quick smile. "Nothing West would notice anyway. I'm just curious. Who is Theron North, you know? He hasn't really told us anything about himself and it's been over a year. Shouldn't I know more about him by now?"

"I mean, we know each other pretty intimately don't you think?"

She laughed. "That's true. I don't know, I know your skeletons, and I guess I just hoped he'd want to share his by now."

"Not everyone wants to talk about their past," I said gently. "You and I just went through some traumatic survival shit which expedited our sharing."

"True," she said, tilting her head at the painting but her brush had stalled, indicating she was lost in thought. "I think he's hiding something."

I barked out a laugh, and when she turned, she raised her eyebrows.

"What's so funny?"

"Sweetheart, of course he is. Men like that have secrets."

"I don't like secrets," she grumbled.

I stood up and came over to her, wrapping my arms around her. She set down her paints and turned into my arms, looking up at me.

"He cares about you and would do anything to keep you safe," I said. "Isn't that enough?"

She sighed. "He's just never who I think he is. One minute he's aggressively taking what he wants from me in the Warren—and then the next, he's in my kitchen, making me coffee just the way I like and asking me how I like my eggs—I don't know. He's just so confusing sometimes."

I chuckled. "Our relationship isn't normal. I mean, if it was, I probably should be more upset about what he did to you in that place. Instead all I can think about is how he kept you safe. In his own way—but safe all the same." I kissed her on the forehead. "He'll share when he's ready."

North was a mystery but you could always tell a lot about a person by the people they surrounded themselves with and North's men were top tier. Their skills alone would have been impressive, but it was the loyalty they demonstrated that was next to none and unlike anything I'd ever seen. They looked at North as though he was a god and if I was being honest I was starting to look at him like that too, and I hadn't even known him for very long. There was a ruthlessness and precision about him that demanded you sit up and take notice.

I knew from bits and pieces of conversation that Nyx and Atlas had been with him the longest. I didn't know their story, they were tight lipped about it and would say only that they met under dark circumstances. But that was pretty much all of our stories—if I knew one thing, it was that darkness followed all of us. As much as I wished that didn't include Kaelin, I knew the shadows followed her too.

"We're going to go through some CQB drills today—"

I stood in front of a group of ten men, ranging in age but all military. North had made me an instructor at *Northern Tactical* so I spent my days teaching NorTac contractors everything they needed to know to be successful out in the field. North owned the entire building which meant he'd outfitted it to his specifications. This included several floors of just kill houses where the floor, ceilings and windows were all bullet and sound proofed for live ammunition drills. The building also included floor plans ranging from clearing houses and office buildings, all the way to even a full setup of a desert town—sand included. It was a marvel I'd never seen before and the soldier in me still geeked out every time I got to run drills on any of those floors.

Then there were the gun ranges, both for handguns and rifles, classrooms and of course the offices which sat on the top floors of the building and held panoramic views of the city and the bay beyond. Basically, North had more money than god but that was to be expected when you ran one of the largest military contracting companies in the world and a bit of legal, and also illegal, arms dealing on the side. The entire basement of the office building was an armory that would put most military stockpiles to shame. Nyx and Atlas had walked me in to show me around and I'd been struck speechless so badly Nyx hadn't been able to stop laughing.

The three of them had slowly been inviting me deeper and deeper into the fold but it was still frustrating to know in my gut Kaelin was right—North was hiding something—I just didn't know what it was and I didn't like not being prepared for something that would probably impact me, and definitely Kaelin, when it all came crashing down.

After class, I hung around and talked to a few of the guys and then headed off to the gym showers—because of course he also had a full gym and locker room too—and ran into Nyx finishing up a workout.

"Hey man," Nyx grinned. "A few of us are going to Elysium tonight if you want to join."

I groaned. "Last time I tagged along I was hungover for days afterwards."

"Yeah, Lach never knows when to stop," Nyx chuckled. "Damn Austrians."

"Is Atlas back?" I asked.

"Yeah, I'm dragging him along too," Nyx grinned.

"Good—I've been meaning to tell him how insufferable you've been with him gone," I teased.

"You too?" Nyx groaned. "Traitor. Lach already tattled on me. You guys make me sound like some lovesick puppy."

I raised my eyebrows, a grin pulling at my lips at the apt description.

"Okay, okay," Nyx laughed. "So maybe I don't know what to do with myself when he's gone—whatever." He threw his gym towel at me before putting on his shoes. "So you coming tonight or what?" He asked.

"Nah, Kaelin is making dinner—I think she wants a date night with the three of us because we've been so busy over the last few days."

"Ah, to be a fly on that wall," Nyx smirked, winking at me as he grabbed his gym bag and slung it over his shoulder.

I laughed. "Hey, you just have to ask the boss, and I don't mean North."

"Funny, North said the same thing."

I'd gotten the feeling they'd all shared women before, although Nyx and Atlas were in a relationship with each other—cue the lovesick puppy reference, even though that failed miserably to describe the way they looked at each other. It was more like two gods sending smoldering waves of passion crashing between them at any given moment. It was enough to knock anyone close to them off their feet—even someone as straight as me. Maybe because they were both two extremely masculine men—rugged, violent and vicious— and it was fascinating to see them come together with all that power—I shook my head. North and I weren't bi but there was no denying we loved the power exchange we got during sex and part of me wondered just how hot it could get if the five of us were in a room, maybe with North directing—*fuck*.

"It's hot to think about isn't it?" Nyx smirked, and I looked over to see him watching me with a smug expression on his face. He headed towards the door. "Say hi to Killer for me," he called over his shoulder, using the nickname Knight had coined for Kaelin when he'd come along with Cal to rescue us in the woods.

Neither of us had realized it in the beginning, but having North around also meant we'd see a lot of his personal TAC team. Some of them were quiet and evasive, like the Russian Volkov Brothers, but others like Nyx, Atlas and Lachlan were really hard not to like. Even West, North's tech genius, was fun to be around—that is whenever he decided to come out of his cave.

But I knew Kaelin was right—North was hiding something—something his entire team knew about and was executing behind the scenes. I was okay with not knowing, for now, but when shit got hot—and I knew it would because it's North—I was going to need to know. I just hoped he'd be forthcoming but again, knowing North, I'm sure it wouldn't be that easy.

6

THERON

W"hat is this?" I came out of Kaelin's study holding a copy of an email. She looked up from where she was making dinner. Graham wasn't at the house yet and it was just the two of us.

She raised her eyebrows. "Snooping again?"

"How long have you been getting death threats?" I demanded.

She had the nerve to wave her hand in the air like it was no big deal and went back to chopping up a potato.

"I get them occasionally," she said vaguely.

"Did this start before or after the Warren?" She looked up at my tone and frowned as she studied the way I was clutching the paper.

"Since before—"

"When were you going to tell me?" I demanded angrily. I pulled out my phone and opened my messages.

She shrugged. "I didn't think it was a big deal. Nothing has ever happened. What are you doing?"

"I'm texting Viktor," I said.

I'd put the Volkov Brothers—Viktor and Konstantine—on Kaelin's security detail during the Red Rabbit job and hadn't taken them off since. The paranoid side of me wanted her watched at all times so something like Cooper couldn't happen to her again. Especially now that I'd put things in motion to end a decade long revenge plot, I didn't know what dangers lay ahead—I just knew they would come and I wanted to be as prepared as possible.

"Why are Viktor and Kon still around?" Kaelin asked. "I thought they were only staying with me while you took down Cooper?" I walked over and slammed the paper down on the counter, pushing it towards her.

"Because of things like this," I growled. "Death threats might not start as a big deal, but they sure as hell can turn into one."

"Yeah because—" She stabbed the knife at the paper. "'I'm going to slash your tires you dumb bitch'—is really concerning."

She leaned her hip against the counter and casually pointed the knife tip at me, giving me a look like I was overreacting which just pissed me off more.

"I've traced some of the emails—they're just from unhappy suburban housewives who don't have anything to do but browse the internet looking for arguments." I ran a hand over my face and shook my head. It was harmless housewives now, but it could be Vetticus later.

"How are you so nonchalant about this after everything that's happened?"

I saw the confidence falter briefly. I knew the shadows lingered just beneath the surface.

"I just don't want to think about it, okay?" Kaelin snapped. "If I think about it too hard or too often, it makes it hard to function."

She went back to chopping, but she was glaring at the vegetables now, the knife coming down harder than necessary. Sometimes it was easy to overlook the trauma she'd gone through because she was so damn stoic and stubborn. She hid her distress almost too well. As soon as we'd come back from the Red Rabbit op, I'd pulled her from her ridiculous self-defense classes she'd been taking and put her through a rigorous, although condensed, military training. She'd hated every second, but it'd made Graham and I feel better. We were still making her take a class at the office once a week and after the initial hell week we'd forced her through; she was begrudgingly starting to enjoy the tactical practice, not to mention she excelled at the gun range. So much so, she asked to go several times a week.

"Okay, then I'll take care of it," I said, running a hand over my face. "I need you protected."

"You've said that," she interrupted. "What does that even fucking mean?"

"It means I need to know every possible place a threat can come from."

"That's not an answer—" she sighed. "I don't know what you want, Theron," she said. "You can't keep me locked up in this house, under guard, like I'm one of your possessions instead of a human being." I walked over and trapped her against the counter bringing the knife to rest between us.

"What I want—is you." She shivered at the darkness in my tone, her pupils dilated, filling her vibrant green eyes with black. "I don't want anyone to take you from me, but I can't be prepared if you don't communicate."

I hadn't factored her into the plans that were in motion because it caught me completely by surprise when I found her in the Warren. All I knew was I had to make her mine and fuck everything else. But now 'everything else' was here, and I hated thinking about something happening to her again. Except the truly terrifying part was I couldn't guarantee her safety. Everyone around me had already signed up for the risk we were putting ourselves in, knowing that shit was about to hit the fan in a spectacular way.

"It goes both ways," she said. "I hardly know anything about your life, but something is going on—I can feel it."

"I need you to trust me."

"And I need *you* to trust *me*," she insisted.

"I can't trust someone who '*doesn't want to think about it*,'" I said. "In my world, negligence gets you killed." I pushed closer to her so the blade sat against my neck and her breathing picked up.

"And I'm in your world now? Is that it?" She breathed.

I hadn't expected to have someone I cared about in my life during this time. Nyx and Atlas were different—they'd gone through hell with me and suffered at Vetticus' hand just as much as I had—so while I cared for them, they wanted this as badly as I did and were willing to see it all come down around us. I knew Nyx and Atlas wanted me to tell her everything, but there were so many moving pieces—and part of me didn't want to show her the man I really was because I didn't know what would be left after this was over. But none of that could tame the possessive beast inside me—maybe I should let her go, or give her the choice, but when it came to the people who belonged to me, I'd never been rational.

"You're mine, baby girl," I growled. I skimmed my knuckles across her jaw. "Or did you forget?"

"You won't let me," she said, her eyes fluttering at my touch.

"That's right," I murmured. Her eyes dropped to my lips, and this time I couldn't hide the smirk as I watched her defiance bleed into desire. I pressed even closer, bringing my lips down near hers. I felt the sting as the knife bit into my skin.

"Would you be able to kill a man like this?" I asked softly. A small trickle of blood ran down my neck. I watched her eyes drop and her lips part in a gasp when she noticed she'd cut me. She went to pull her hand away, but I placed my hand over hers on the hilt and held the blade where it was.

"It's different from shooting someone," I murmured.

I lifted my chin and made her push it further into my skin.

"Theron," she hissed, her eyes going from the blood to my eyes and back again. I could see the conflict happening—she didn't know if she should be afraid or turned on.

I liked it when she was both.

"It's more intimate this way," I continued. "You feel everything—the resistance at the first contact with the skin before it breaks. The scrape across every muscle—the jarring sensation of hitting a bone—It takes more force than you'd think."

I dipped my head and brushed my lips against hers—not quite a kiss.

"You have to mean it," I whispered. "You have to really want to kill someone." I kissed her then, softly at first and then my other hand went to the back of her neck and pulled her closer, my tongue caressing hers. I groaned into her mouth as the knife slid down my neck, cutting me more and she hissed against my lips in protest.

I let her move the knife then, following her hand and helping her guide it behind us to the counter where we let it drop. Then her hands were around my neck and the kiss grew heated. I lifted her up and set her on the counter, stepping between her legs. I ran my hands up her thighs, taking the shirt with me until it bunched around her hips.

We came apart breathless and then a dark look settled over Kaelin's features that sent a thrill racing through me. She ran her thumb through the blood, smearing it, then leaned forward and slowly licked the entire length of the cut she'd made. My breath caught, and I groaned—almost instantly getting hard.

"Kaelin," I growled, but it was a breathless sound—half warning, half prayer.

My fingers dug into her thighs as her tongue skated across my skin. I yanked her back by her hair and she looked up at me with the most devilish smirk I'd ever seen on her lips smeared red with my blood. It was one of the hottest things I'd ever seen in my life.

I pulled her mouth to mine, and the kiss was hungry as our hands grabbed at clothing. I tore her shirt off, tossing it down before she pulled mine off and ran her fingers down my chest, humming in pleasure as her eyes took me in.

I let her eyes travel up my body and when they settled on mine, her breath caught at whatever she saw there. My hand caressed her breast, teasing her nipple and she arched towards me. I dipped my head and took her other nipple in my mouth, sucking on it before dragging it through my teeth. The moan she made went straight to my cock. I straightened and met her eyes again as I traced my fingertips up her chest and then closed my hand around her neck. Her eyes flashed and her breath caught as I stepped closer to her, bringing my lips right over hers. I tightened my grip and the way she looked up at me—with a lustful darkness mixed with pure trust, made those feelings surface again. The ones I wanted to put words to but couldn't.

I pushed her back to lie on the counter and dragged her legs over my shoulders before I trailed kisses down her inner thigh, watching her face while I did. I kissed everywhere but her clit until she was writhing under me and looked down with a frustrated pout on her pretty blood stained lips. I chuckled against her pussy and ran my thumbs up her center before parting her and licking her clit in slow teasing strokes. She threw her head back and her legs fell open giving me more access.

"You taste amazing, darlin'," I murmured before picking up the pace. I could eat her pussy forever—she'd tap out before I ever would. I heard the alarm deactivate as I slid two fingers inside her. She was soaking wet and gasped my name as I rubbed the spot that drove her crazy. Her legs shook and then she was coming, crying out and arching her back as she let herself go. She pushed her hips against my mouth and I didn't let up until I felt her slowly come back down.

"Looks like I got home just in time," Graham smirked. "Early dinner?" I looked up to see him leaning against the entrance to the kitchen.

"More like dessert," I said. I kissed Kaelin's inner thigh as she caught her breath. She craned her head to see Graham, and a sated smile appeared on her face. She held out her hand to him.

"Fuck—I don't know how you guys expect me to stay clothed when you show up to the house in tactical gear."

Graham chuckled and walked over to where her head rested near the edge of the counter. He was still in all black, with his leather shoulder gun holsters on. He planted both hands on either side of her head and leaned over her.

"Well, that's just it baby girl—we don't." He dipped his head and kissed her. When he pulled away, he raised his eyebrows.

"Why do you taste like blood?" He asked.

"Oh, T was teaching me how to hold a knife," she said dryly. He looked over at me, and I saw his eyes dip to my neck, and everything clicked.

He chuckled. "I see." He kissed her again, his hand sliding down to tease her nipple. She arched into his hand. He straightened and ran his thumb over her lips.

"Are you going to join?" Kaelin asked.

"I have to shower first, beautiful," he said. He kissed her on the forehead and disappeared into the bedroom. Kaelin sat up and I lifted her into my arms, carrying her over to the couch. I set her down and spun her, bending her over the back. I did quick work on my jeans and soon my cock was pressed against her pussy. I didn't hesitate but slammed inside her making us both groan in pleasure. I grabbed the couch and set a relentless pace that left us both panting. I slid my hand around to her clit and slowed down just enough to bring her to the edge then backed off. I did that a few times until she was whimpering and begging.

"Fuck—please, please—oh god—"

She tightened around my cock and I picked up the pace again, rubbing her clit in quick strokes until she came loudly, pushing back against me as she let the pleasure sweep her away. I pulled out of her.

"Kneel," I demanded gruffly.

She sank to her knees before me and looked up through her lashes before taking my cock deep into her mouth. I grabbed her hair and pushed her further, making her eyes water. I set the pace, fucking her mouth until she had tears streaming down her cheeks. I pushed her down and held her on my cock, making her gag. When I pulled her back, drool ran from her lips and I ran my thumb through her tears.

"Beautiful and mine," I murmured darkly. "Say it."

"I-I'm yours," she gasped, looking at me with an intensity that had me sinking into her throat again. I groaned when she swallowed around my cock. I pumped into her throat a few more times before my release blazed through me and I held her head down so I came deep in her throat. I released her and she swallowed around her gasps of air.

"Such a good girl," I growled.

She was still catching her breath, but she smiled a soft smile at me, a pleased look on her face. I pulled her up into my arms and sealed my lips over hers, kissing her gently. I brushed my knuckles over her cheek.

"I mean it," I said. "You're mine."

"And *you* are mine," she said, putting her hand on my cheek. Her eyes searched mine for the feeling I saw reflected in hers. Sometimes I wished I could know what she saw when she looked at me like that.

The touch sent heat rushing through my body, settling in the vicinity of my heart. The fierce urge to protect her bubbled up, hot and violent, but there was something else too—something that went beyond just the physical attraction and possessive hold I had on her. It was a feeling that made words I hadn't spoken in decades linger on my tongue.

I couldn't go there though. Not when everything I was about to do was going to cast my world into chaos. Everything was coming to a head in a way that made a rush of adrenaline take my breath away.

I was so close—to revenge, to getting back what I lost—to finally having peace through the retribution I, and everyone involved, deserved.

I pulled Kaelin to me in a fierce kiss that said all the words I couldn't voice, hoping in some way she'd understand, while knowing she deserved more.

The blaring of the kitchen timer broke us apart.

"Go take care of Graham," I said, giving her ass one more squeeze for good measure before moving towards the kitchen to finish dinner. I watched her head towards the bedroom, then down at the bloody knife in front of me on the counter.

I'd bleed for her, that was for certain. But the one thing I couldn't do felt much more dangerous than sliding a knife across my skin.

7

KAELIN

Still glowing from my orgasms with Theron, I walked into my bathroom and stepped into the shower with Graham, my arms sliding around his waist.

"Hi, gorgeous," he said, turning in my arms.

I watched the water run down his skin and between the valleys of his abs. Even with all their scars, I thought my men were stunning. The way their bodies told a story tripped something primal in me—an urge to mark them as mine the way the world had marked them.

We didn't speak as I wrapped my arms around Graham's neck, meeting his smoldering gaze through the steam. He grabbed the backs of my thighs and lifted me into his arms, his cock already hard between us. I ground my hips against him and he growled against my lips as his tongue slipped into my mouth.

I dragged my fingers through his hair, trying to pull him closer and with a quick adjustment of my hips, we joined in an effortless motion. I was already wet and ready for him, his delicious length stretching me even after everything Theron and I had done. I moaned against his lips, gasping in air as the kiss turned heated. I bucked my hips against him, wanting to feel him move. He shoved me against the tile wall, driving deeper. His mouth attacked my neck, making me arch into him at the sensation of his teeth scraping across the sensitive area under my jaw.

"Those sounds you make drive me crazy," he panted, dragging my ear between his teeth. "Touch your clit for me, princess."

My hand skated down his chest between us and settled on my already swollen clit. I knew I wasn't far away from coming again. A few quick circles and my breath came faster, molten heat pooling inside me as I met Graham's dark eyes watching me hungrily. His movements slowed, and he tilted my hips to ensure he hit that spot inside me that made my eyes roll back in my head and my lips part.

"Just like that," I gasped breathlessly. The edge roared towards me, sharp and steep and all-consuming like the shadows raging in his eyes before our lips met and I shattered in his arms, my cry swallowed up by his tongue against mine. My release triggered his and with a groan of pleasure and a curse, he buried his face in my neck as he came, his teeth biting into my neck, claiming me in all ways.

As we came down, catching our breath, he carefully dropped my legs, only for them to buckle under me. He chuckled and steadied me, gently moving a strand of wet hair stuck to my cheek.

"Too much for you, baby?" He asked, a wicked gleam in his eyes.

I scoffed, but it came out more like a contented hum and I knew a stupidly satisfied look was on my face from the smug way Graham was looking at me.

"It's never enough," I breathed.

"I know," he answered, sharing the same breath as he brought his face close to mine and softly kissed me.

It didn't take us long to clean up and after taking a few minutes to dry my hair and throw on another oversized t-shirt; I headed out to the kitchen to see Graham already there pouring drinks for us as Theron finished setting the food out on the counter. We never ate at the table, preferring the bar that was part of the center island instead.

"How are your exhibit pieces coming along?" Theron asked as he handed me a plate.

"I have one left to finish and then they'll be ready," I answered, accepting a glass of red wine from Graham. I took a sip before setting it down in favor of getting food. I'd recently been attempting to sell some of my paintings and a few months ago a friend of mine secured an entire wing of a gallery showing for me. It was a huge opportunity to sell some of my pieces and get my name out there. It had taken me forever to come up with a theme but eventually I'd settled on one.

"I've seen some of them," Graham said. "It's going to be really incredible to see them hanging up and properly lit."

I nodded, nerves getting the better of me at the thought of having my intimate art shown to strangers. It was one thing to put a painting in an auction or something for charity; it was another when people bought it of their own accord.

We sat down to eat and talked of other things, only to quickly dissolve into laughter as Graham told a work story. It was amazing to me the transformation of these two when it was just the three of us. For a moment in time, the weight of the world seemed to lift from their shoulders. Theron's eyes weren't so broody, Graham's brow not as furrowed and both were quick to laugh, a sound I had come to adore from both of them. It never lasted long enough, those moments where the world fell away and we were just us, but they were the times I cherished more than anything.

I knew their lives were dangerous, dark and violent. That was never something I was going to make them change. My world revolved around the same thing in a way, while I didn't have any direct line to the violence, I helped feed it—creating tools for men like Theron and Graham to use to achieve their directives. We lived in the grey and I never knew if one day they wouldn't come home to me, so while I hated the thought and loathed living in a world without them in it, I held these moments close to my heart and buried them deep in my soul so if ever there was a time we weren't together, I'd still carry them close to me.

We were almost done eating when Theron's phone went off. Usually he didn't check it during dinner but I watched his eyes slide to where it sat across the kitchen. The text notification went off again.

Then again.

Finally, as his phone started to ring, he got up and retrieved it. The look that came over his face was absolutely terrifying because of the way he completely shut down his emotions, his eyes going dark and dangerous as he frowned down at whoever was trying to reach him.

He grabbed his leather shoulder holsters and his jacket before coming over and kissing me on the cheek.

"I have to go. Don't wait up, darlin'," he said.

I'd never seen him like this except maybe when he came in, guns blazing, to take out Cooper when he was here. It just reinforced my suspicion that something was going on—something big, that didn't have anything to do with normal *NorTac* operations. Our earlier conversation hadn't gotten anywhere and had dissolved into sex as usual and while I was okay with how things were right now, I knew in my heart I was going to need more from him. I didn't like thinking of myself as one of those women who wanted to 'fix' a man, but I had hoped to know more about Theron at this point. He was intimate, giving and protective but there was a line he wouldn't cross even though I swore I could see the emotions I wanted him to vocalize in his eyes when he looked at me.

Theron grabbed the keys to his Aston Martin and met Graham's eyes over my head. Something passed between them, so brief I couldn't tell what it meant, before Theron turned and left.

"What was that about?" I asked.

"I'm not entirely sure, but I don't think it's good."

8

THERON

I called Nyx back the minute I settled into the Aston and took off towards the house my team used as a home base, or as we called it—Alpha One.

"He made contact," Nyx said as soon as the line connected. "A recording was found by the night guard at *NorTac*."

"On my way."

I gripped the wheel tightly, preparing myself to hear Vetticus' voice again after so long. Even though we'd been preparing for this, it still felt strange to finally be drawing him out. Our attempts to track him over the years had varying degrees of success. Years after we escaped, we'd sent a drone into the mountains and found the estate where he'd kept us but it was abandoned and run down. The nearby maps were all disassembled, gone, like they'd never existed but in our minds.

It took us years to relocate *Atrox* headquarters and once we did, I took my time planting people within his supply lines. Sleepers waiting for the time when I was ready to strike. Like us, it seemed as though Vetticus was licking his wounds and regrouping. He did everything in the shadows, or by proxy and even if we'd wanted to simply assassinate him, it would have been nearly impossible to get to him.

Twenty minutes later I pulled through the gates of the house. It was more like a compound with guards and state of the art security on sprawling acreage. There was a gun range, training room and I'd converted the basement into an interrogation room complete with a few holding cells. There were also rooms for all of the men on my team if they chose to live there, which most of them did. *Northern Tactical* had teams around the world, but these men were my inner circle and personal crew. Any operation I went on or anything that I oversaw myself, they were who I called.

I walked into the house and saw the glow of computer monitors in the war room. It was really just a living room we'd converted into a debriefing space. A big butcher block table took up the center of the room with one wall full of computer monitors. The wall across from it was a floor to ceiling pane of glass that was also a touch screen where we pulled up our electronic evidence boards. When not in use, it looked into an enclosed and private atrium in the center of the house.

At this time of night, the place was quiet. Only West and Nyx were at the table sitting in front of West's computer. West Lockwood was my tech genius and resident hacker. He was also an amazing tactician and sniper although these days he rarely saw the field because I needed him behind the computer. He'd been around since the beginning. He was one of Nyx's Navy buddies and soon after our escape, Nyx contacted him asking if he wanted in on a job we had planned—the first job, Austria. After that, he decided to stay.

"Show me," I said, not bothering with a greeting as I walked in the room.

West nodded and threw his laptop screen up on a monitor. He pulled up an audio file and hit play.

"*Kraven, Kraven, Kraven—*" A voice I hadn't heard in over a decade came through the surround sound speakers filling the room. I gripped the chair back in front of me until my knuckles were white. "*My fearless hunter...look at you. Look at what you've become!*" He chuckled. "*I'm quite proud of you, my friend, honestly.*"

There was a long pause and then he sighed dramatically. "*But everything must come to an end. Remember when I told you once that I knew you'd run? Do you remember what I said after that?*" Another pause. "*I said, our reunion would be extra sweet. Being away from you for this long has killed me, but I knew we'd find each other again, eventually.*"

He chuckled. "*You've run from me for long enough—I'm coming for you— I'm coming for it all. And when everything has crumbled to dust and you're kneeling in front of me in the ruins, I'll remind you, again, who you belong to.*" The pause was so long, I thought he was done but then his dark laugh whispered through the room. "*I can't wait to meet your new playthings—and say hello to Phantom and Reaper for me. Their deaths will be your punishment for ever thinking you could leave me.*"

The recording ended, and no one spoke.

I took several deep breaths trying to control my visceral reaction to hearing him again. Having him threaten Atlas and Nyx took me back in time to the room I still visited in my nightmares.

"You can imagine how upset it makes me when I think about losing you."

Vetticus tilted his head at me, looking annoyed that I wasn't speaking to him, even though I rarely did. The cuffs bit into my wrists restrained behind my back and I stared off at a point across the room.

"Do you even know where we are?" He asked. "Do you have any idea?"

I turned my head to look at him then, my lip curling in displeasure. "Does it matter?"

He chuckled. "No, I suppose it doesn't. You're going to try it, regardless. Every time you take out a camera, I wonder to myself if this is it—is this when I'm going to have to kill you?"

He walked over to where I sat in a chair across from him and ran his hand across my face. I leaned away from him in disgust and looked anywhere but up at him.

"I hope it doesn't come to that. You know how to keep me on my toes and it surprisingly is something I love about you," he murmured. "I'm actually looking forward to hunting you down though. Our reunion will be extra sweet."

He leaned closer and his grip tightened on my jaw, turning my head towards him and forcing me to meet his eyes.

"And just so you know. When I catch you—and I will—I'm going to take great pleasure in torturing Phantom and Reaper in front of you and then killing them slowly..."

"North," Nyx sounded like he'd been trying to get my attention.

"Call the team in," I said.

The team would assemble in the morning, until then I knew I would never be able to sleep with his voice in my head and the memories thrashing to the surface, so I did the one thing that always settled my nerves—I went downstairs to the shooting range. It was a large soundproofed, industrial space under the house with five lanes. I grabbed a few boxes of ammo and my .45s.

"Who are you?"

"I go by Vetticus—recruiter, trainer, sponsor...I wear many hats."

My memories were running wild as I loaded up a few clips. Nyx appeared and leaned back against the partition, shoving his hands into his pockets, he watched me quietly.

"You good?" I asked him, glancing up briefly before resuming my loading.

"Yeah, I showed Atlas," he said before falling quiet again. I finished loading and pinned up a target before sending it out into the range. I shoved a clip into the gun but still felt him staring at me.

"Spit it out, Nyx," I grumbled.

"I saw your face out there—and you had the 'North is going to do something stupid' look."

I frowned at him before throwing on protective eyes, then tossed him a set of noise canceling ears before donning my own. They allowed us to hear each other clearly but muffled the gunfire.

"A recruiter for what?"

"Atrox Gaming," he said.

"Never heard of it."

"That's intentional," he smirked. "One of those private, invitation only things."

"Well, I decline whatever this is," I said.

"Unfortunately, it doesn't work that way."

"I'm going to follow the plan."

Sometimes I hated how well Nyx and Atlas knew me. None of us could hide from the other—but then again, that was my fault because when we'd started to descend into the madness of the nightmare, I'd made it very clear that hiding wasn't an option. We would face it all head on, together. They'd taken the order seriously and to this day it was something we held each other accountable for.

"That's what you say now, but hearing his voice after all this—"

I cut him off by unloading the entire clip rapid fire at the target, my anger surging. I ejected the clip and turned to him.

"I'll do what I need to do," I growled. "This has been over a decade in the making—you really think I'll do something reckless to endanger that?"

I shoved another clip aggressively into the gun.

Nyx shrugged. "And Kaelin?"

"Nothing changes," I snapped, still irritated.

"Are you ever going to tell her how you feel at least?" Nyx asked.

He looked like he was trying to hide a smile which just pissed me off more. I unloaded the clip again, unable to hold back. When I ejected the clip this time, I slammed it down on the table.

"Can you be brave for me, baby?"

"I love you..."

"I don't do love," I said harshly.

Nyx raised his eyebrows and scoffed. "That's not what I see."

I rounded on him angrily and he just raised his hands in surrender but still looked amused. I turned back and started reloading the two clips, trying to center my thoughts.

"Have you heard from Deathwing recently?"

"No," I said flatly.

Now was not the time to think about the fact I hadn't heard from Deathwing in months. If I thought about that situation now...no, I told him I'd trust him to execute and while it was the hardest thing I'd ever done, I'd honor my word. I pushed all of that away for now.

"I'm just saying, shits about to get heavy and she's involved—" he said, giving me a pointed look. "You need to tell her what she's getting into or you need to leave."

I slammed the gun down. "Nothing is going to stop me from finishing this," I said in a deathly calm tone. "Nothing. I warned you all in the beginning and by staying you understood the sacrifices I would make if it came to that."

I didn't want it to come to that. But they all had to understand there were no lines I wouldn't cross and no corner of hell too deep that would stop me from killing the man who had ruined my life and taken everything from me.

"Don't you think you should give her that choice too?" Nyx asked. "Who knows, maybe she can actually help us. I'm just saying, if you plan to keep her, she should know what you're willing to sacrifice to end this."

When I didn't answer right away, he shook his head and turned to go.

"Honestly, I hope you grow a pair and tell her because I've never seen you this way with a woman," he nudged me with his shoulder and smirked. "I kind of like it. She and Graham are good for you."

Once he left, I unloaded clip after clip at the target until it was a shredded mess. But I wasn't seeing the paper outline, I was seeing Vetticus and his lust filled eyes and the smirk that always set my teeth on edge. His voice cut through the gunfire and it was his hands I was shooting as they reached for me, or Nyx or Atlas—I knew what I was getting into and yet I still wasn't prepared for what it actually felt like to hear him stake a claim on our lives again.

But this wasn't his game anymore.

It was *mine*.

And I knew it was only going to get a whole lot worse before the end.

9

NYX

Atlas was waiting for me when I emerged from the basement.

"Is he good?" Atlas asked. I scoffed and shook my head as I walked past him towards the kitchen.

"What do you think?"

I needed coffee—preferably something stronger but coffee was already brewing. I stood in front of the coffee machine, listening to it grumble to life. Atlas' hand snaked around my waist as he reached for mugs above my head. He set them down and then jumped up to sit on the counter. His hand curled around the back of my neck, drawing my attention to him.

"It brought it all back for me too," he said.

My lips curled in disgust and anger. Even knowing I'd feel this way wasn't enough to stop the emotions from storming viciously to the surface.

"Hearing his voice again was—" I shook my head. "It's like no time has passed."

"I'm worried about him," Atlas said quietly, and I knew he was talking about North. "He has someone important to him again right when everything is about to go off."

"Shit timing is what that is," I grumbled.

Atlas pulled me in to stand between his legs and I leaned into his touch, letting it calm the rage and ease the tightness under my skin. The shadows inside me were eager for release and when my eyes clashed with Atlas' I saw the same darkness reflected there. The storm was here, and we were ready.

His eyes darkened and the air between us turned electric as his fingers brushed against the back of my neck, teasing me closer. My hands drifted up his thighs to his hips and under his t-shirt, heat spreading through my body as I touched his bare skin. His hand pulled me closer, but before I could claim his lips in mine the way I wanted to, I saw Lachlan out of the corner of my eye as he came into the kitchen.

"Oh, sorry," he said, but he had a smirk on his face.

"No, you're not," Atlas said easily.

"No, I am—sorry I didn't wait another two seconds so I could watch," he teased. "Last time was hot."

Lachlan hopped up on the counter across from us and I turned, pushing my back against Atlas' chest as his arms snaked around me and I rested an elbow against his thigh, unable to hide my grin. We'd met Lachlan in Austria shortly after our escape and he'd quickly become one of our best friends which to us, meant we may or may not have hooked up in various capacities over the years.

"Saw North downstairs shredding paper," he continued. "Did Vetticus make contact?"

"Yup—he wants a team briefing in the morning," I said.

The noise of the coffee machine cut through the air, struggling to dispense the last bit of coffee into the pot. I left Atlas' embrace and grabbed it, pouring it into the two mugs.

"Coffee, Lach?"

"Sure, I won't be able to sleep with North prowling the property."

West walked in. "I smell coffee," he said. "Anyone know how I can get an IV of this stuff?"

"You could Google it," Lachlan said dryly.

"Ha ha," West said sarcastically. "I should probably just put a coffee machine in my office."

"If you did that we'd never see you—you'd never leave your cave," Atlas stated.

"That's kind of the point," West grinned, accepting the mug I gave him. At this point I'd need to brew more since apparently none of us were planning on sleeping. "How are you guys doing?"

"Ready—impatient," I said.

West nodded. "It feels like just yesterday we were all coming together for the Austria job although I'm sure it has felt much longer for you guys."

Lachlan groaned. "Don't remind me of Austria."

"Homesick?" Atlas teased.

"Low blow," I laughed as Lachlan flipped him off.

"You're still not over that?" West asked.

"More accurately—not over her," I joked.

"What ever happened with Mads?" West asked. "She just disappeared after the job."

"Maybe because Casanova over here wouldn't leave her alone," Atlas grinned.

"Say what you will, but that was one of the best nights of my life," Lachlan sniffed, pretending to look down his nose at us.

"That tends to happen when North gets involved," I laughed.

"You guys and your threesomes," West said, shaking his head.

"It was more than a threesome actually," Atlas supplied with a smirk, winking at West and making him blush. He was completely straight and a little shy when it came to his sexuality. I thought it was endearing even if we liked to tease him about it.

"At that point, I think it's safe to call it an orgy," Lachlan laughed.

"Where was I?" West asked incredulously.

"You were off counting the gold I imagine," I said. "Or maybe you were asleep?"

"I highly doubt I would have been able to sleep through all of that," West laughed. "It's much more likely I was off being the responsible one."

West's phone dinged, and he saluted us with his coffee before disappearing off to his cave again. Lachlan jumped down from the counter.

"I'll go notify the troops," he gave us one last lingering look. "You two finish what you were about to start earlier."

And just like that, it was just Atlas and I once more in the now quiet kitchen. Even though they'd interrupted, I cherished every moment I had with our friends. Atlas and I shared a look between us and I knew he was thinking the same—we didn't know who would come out of this alive, all we knew was that none of us were going to leave unscathed and that wasn't a pleasant thought to have.

Later that morning, I walked into the war room to see all nine members of the team present. It was an eclectic group we'd pulled from various parts of the world during the last decade. Each one brought a mastery of their skills to the team and all were hardened warriors. All of them were ex-military but their backgrounds didn't matter to us, their loyalty and skill set did.

I went around greeting a few of them before I settled in one of the high back armchairs near the couch. All we were waiting for was North.

A few moments later he walked through the double doors, looking much calmer than when I'd seen him last night although I knew him so well I could still see the tension lining his jaw and the way his fingers kept flexing as though they wanted to be wrapped around a gun—or someone's neck.

He looked around at each of his men before coming to stand next to my chair, then nodded to West. I steeled myself to hear Vetticus' voice again, making eye contact with Atlas who was across from me, leaning up against the wall near the door.

"*Kraven, Kraven, Kraven...*"

The recording filtered through the room, once more Vetticus' silky voice surrounded me and the nausea crept up. My hands dug into the arms of the chair and I fought to keep my mind in the present. Atlas' eyes drilled into mine. If I didn't know him as intimately as I did, I wouldn't notice the flicker of his eyes as Vetticus said our call signs or the way he folded his arms across his chest to hide the tremor in his hands. I knew he wished they were wrapped around Vetticus' throat.

I let out a breath as the voice died away, forever a ghost we had to endure. North looked around the room at the grim faces of his team—they all knew what the recording meant but it was like seeing the objective at the end of a mission, the proverbial light at the end of the tunnel. Everything we'd all been working towards was finally culminating to this moment of totality.

It'd been a long road.

"Phase one is complete. I want security tightened everywhere," North said. "Things are going to move rapidly now. We've eliminated *Atrox's* board members. This week we are taking out the four architects of the maps. He will most likely try to isolate me by going after all of you so stay vigilant. Remember the goal is to draw him out and this—" He gestured to the recording. "Is a good sign."

He looked around the room.

"You know our story—" he gestured to Atlas and I. "—and why we want vengeance. But—Nyx reminded me last night that there is such a thing as free will—" the men laughed softly at that. "So even though I warned you all at the beginning what you were getting into, apparently, I should give you the choice again," I said dryly.

"Fuck, Nyx, really?" Tex groaned.

His real name was Cruz Beckett, but everyone called him Tex. He was one of our team leaders. A huge black man from Texas who wore cowboy boots and a wide brimmed hat whenever possible.

"Why are you making' him go all sentimental on us?" He asked around a grin.

"Are you doubting our life choices?" Lachlan chimed in. "I'm offended personally."

"Whoa," I held up my hands in defense and glared good naturedly at North. "I was talking about Kaelin, not all of them."

"It's about time something happened around here," Sakari said. "Half of you got to have all the fun in the Warren, while the rest of us had to stay home."

North had found Sakari Tanaka in Japan and I was convinced he was a samurai reincarnated. He was usually quiet and subdued but I knew he was itching for action as he casually flicked a throwing star between his fingers.

Knox chuckled. "I think you have your answer, North. We're all in, nothing's changed."

Knox Ashford was sprawled in an armchair, looking every inch the Marine he was, even though he was long retired. His wife, Macy, had been the first person we encountered when we escaped. Macy told us Knox was missing in action and after the Austria job, North made it his mission to find him. It took a few years, but we found him in some shithole prison in Syria and busted him out. A year later, he showed up at NorTac with Macy in tow, and he's been around ever since.

North nodded. "Tex, work with Atlas and get your team ready to take out the architects—"

We spent the next hour going over logistical planning on our contingency plans and what teams would lead what. North predicted Vetticus would try to take down as much of NorTac as possible, except this was what we'd been planning for and this was why North had wanted to create a global empire. He wanted to become a force that would take great effort to destroy.

And he'd done that.

Now, he was dangling himself in front of Vetticus, waiting for him to bite. As the meeting wrapped up, North looked once more around the room.

"Remember what I said—do not underestimate him," he waved his hand. "Dismissed." Everyone filed out and went their separate ways except for me and Atlas.

"How does it feel?" Atlas asked. North shook his head and sat down heavily in a chair.

"I've been patient for so long and now all I want to do is go out there and end it." He looked up at both of us, studying me then Atlas where his attention sharpened.

"I'm fine," Atlas said. "It was just strange to hear him again after all this time." North nodded, and I felt Atlas steel himself next to me for what he was about to broach next.

"You need to tell Kaelin and Graham," he said.

Speaking to North like that would usually earn someone a quick temper and a fist to the face, but North just met Atlas' gaze with a dangerous look, his jaw clenched in irritation.

"So I'm hearing," he murmured.

"If not Kaelin, then definitely Graham," Atlas continued. "You're going to have him join the team anyway, so he needs to know what he's actually signing up for."

North made a noncommittal sound in the back of his throat.

"Anything else?"

"Yeah, either go get some sleep or go get laid—you look like shit."

North barked out a laugh, and the tension left his face. He stood up and as he walked passed; he put a hand on Atlas' shoulder, his eyes brimming with darkness.

"You order me like that again, I'll have Nyx edge you so badly you'll be begging me to let you come."

Atlas stiffened, and I heard his breath catch.

"Jesus," I muttered, adjusting myself as a thrill went straight to my cock. Don't tempt a masochist with a good time.

"Understood?" North growled.

Atlas' eyes darkened with a challenge as they met North's and it looked like he was seriously debating whether or not to provoke him. Like myself, his cock was trying to decide for him, obviously remembering all the other times North directed in the bedroom.

"Yes, sir," Atlas said, his voice throaty.

North's attention jumped to me briefly before he left the room and I ran a hand through my hair as Atlas remembered how to breathe properly.

"Fuck me—" Atlas muttered. "Whenever he does that—" He couldn't even finish a sentence.

I smirked and stood up, pulling him with me.

"Come on—I think it's time you followed your own advice."

"What? Get some sleep?" Atlas teased even as his eyes hungrily drifted over me, making me bite my lip to stop myself from attacking him right that second.

"Yeah—sleep," I winked and pulled him behind me to our bedroom, planning on doing everything besides that.

10

THERON

I was yards from the porch of the lake house when the man turned. I put a bullet in his head and took the stairs in one leap. Crouching down, I grabbed the dead man's AR and ammo, then carefully opened the back door and edged inside. I cleared the living room and heard hushed voices from the kitchen. There were two men standing on the other side of the island.

I stepped out and pulled the trigger.

I dropped both men before I had to lunge for the cover of the island as the gunfire drew a man in from the family room who walked in spraying bullets. I stayed low and went around the island, watching his reflection in the oven. I leaned out and fired, hitting him in the leg. He went down, and I quickly stepped out to finish him. I headed for the doorway of the family room when a man rushed in.

I grabbed his gun before he could fire point blank and slammed my elbow into his face just as arms wrapped around me. I backed hard into the wall, turned my gun and fired into his stomach. His grip loosened, and I lunged forward tackling the other one into the family room.

I lost my gun in the scuffle and dodged to the side as he came at me with a knife. I met his attack with a sharp hit to his neck and sent him crashing backwards into the coffee table. I moved for the gun at the same time as the other man and once I grabbed it; I twisted onto my back and shot him in the face as he fell forward onto me.

I shoved him off and heard movement upstairs as the floorboards creaked. Fear cut through my adrenaline as I made my way up the stairs, clearing the hallway and each room along it. I saw that the master bedroom door was cracked and headed towards it. Dread seeped through me.

I pushed open the door.

A bloody hand reached for me, and screams filled my ears.

I woke up abruptly, sweat coating my forehead and my chest heaving as I took in several deep breaths. I looked at my hands, already knowing they wouldn't be covered in blood like they always were in my nightmares but still feeling like I needed to wash them clean again and again. I lay there looking up at the dark ceiling, catching my breath. The dreams were always similar and always ended the same—with blood and death—a horrifying reminder of my failure.

I got out of bed, careful not to wake Kaelin and Graham. I pulled on my boxer briefs and a t-shirt. It was a warm night as I made my way out to the back patio. I nodded to Konstantine who was on night duty and he disappeared respectfully around the side yard as I sat down heavily in a chair.

Even after all these years the nightmares still found me often. Usually they fueled my fire for vengeance—reminding me of every reason why I was doing this. But then there were nights like tonight where I just wished it was all over.

My elbows were braced on my thighs as I leaned over, head in my hands. I heard the sliding glass door hiss open, and I straightened to see Kaelin come out in one of my shirts. She hesitated once she neared me. I knew the way the shadows were falling on her face that she couldn't see mine very well.

"Did I wake you up, darlin'?"

She shook her head. "Are you okay?"

I sighed. "I will be."

I held out my hand to her and pulled her into my lap. I wrapped my arms around her with a sigh and leaned back in the chair, burying my face in her hair. We sat like that for a while. Her heartbeat helped to steady mine, and I focused on the smell of the damp earth and how her warm body felt against me. She sat up straighter and turned towards me as she ran her fingers across the scar on my face. She worshiped mine the same way I worshiped hers.

"Do you want to talk about it?" She asked quietly.

I took her hand in my own and brought it to my lips, kissing her knuckles and then shook my head. I could feel her disappointment but how could I possibly tell her everything? It was daunting. The past was this deep abyss of dark memories and trauma.

It was my burden—my curse—my punishment.

She still didn't know why I'd really been in the Warren, or why I couldn't immediately get her out of there. Instead, she knew things like how I took my coffee in the mornings and what my favorite cologne was. Intimate things but not the sum of things that made up a person's soul. Once she knew the truth, there was no taking it back.

But I couldn't let her go—she was in my blood now. She was my obsession.

"You're still so much of a mystery," she whispered before she leaned forward and kissed me.

When she stood up, she went to walk back into the house but stopped and put a hand on my shoulder.

"I don't love you any less not knowing, but I still wish you'd tell me what's going on." She squeezed my shoulder and disappeared back into the house. I groaned and leaned back in the chair, looking up at the meager spread of stars above, dim due to the light pollution of the nearby city. That was the closest she'd ever come to saying I love you.

Love.

I didn't know much about love anymore—just obsession. Maybe I was getting the feel for it again. The memory of what it felt like so long ago was like a whisper of a word on the tip of my tongue. It was elusive and when I tried to reach for it; it disappeared. I knew I'd experienced it once but everything I loved was brutally taken from me again and again until I stopped associating the word with anything.

After a few minutes, I went back inside, but I knew I wouldn't be able to go back to sleep so I went into Kaelin's office and did a few hours of work. My men were taking out Atrox's architects in two days and I needed to ensure the execution was flawless. There was no room for error now that the end was in sight.

The three of us stood in Kaelin's bathroom finishing getting ready for the day. Graham was buttoning up his shirt, and I was brushing my teeth when Kaelin let her robe drop to the floor of her closet that we both had a perfect view of in the mirror.

"Unless you want to stay here all day, you better put some clothes on," Graham said, his fingers stalling on the last few buttons. With my mouth full of toothpaste, all I could do was groan an agreement. Her laugh made me smile and she quickly pulled on a black dress and walked out to stand between us. Graham finished his buttons and then slowly dragged her zipper up her back.

My teeth brushed, I turned and ran a hand up her thigh.

"Panties?"

She smirked at me and her breath caught as my fingers found my answer between her legs. Brushing her pussy I teased her clit with a light touch. Her lips parted and Graham planted a kiss on her neck. She groaned in frustration and closed her eyes.

"I wish I didn't have a meeting this morning," she moaned.

"Cancel it," Graham said, his teeth finding her ear making her shiver.

"Can't," she said breathlessly.

My finger slipped inside her, feeling her wet heat. I added another finger, hooking them just enough to make her breath catch. Graham nudged her legs apart and his hand traveled up the back of her thighs until I felt two of his fingers join me inside her.

"Oh fuck," Kaelin whimpered.

"Do you like both of our fingers inside you, gorgeous?" He murmured.

Her hands landed on my chest, gripping my shirt tightly.

"Yes," she breathed.

Graham pressed forward, pushing her closer to me as I leaned back against the counter, sandwiching her between us. His other hand curled around her neck. Her dress rode up her thighs until it bunched around her hips and her breathing picked up as we continued our slow strokes.

I pulled my fingers from her and rubbed her clit with her arousal, slow circles making delicious sounds escape her lips. I pressed my fingers back inside her, my thumb resuming on her clit. Her hips shifted as we quickly worked her into a panting mess.

I met Graham's gaze over her shoulder, his pupils blown, probably similar to mine. A slow smile slid across his lips and together we increased the speed slightly eliciting a breathless curse from Kaelin.

She opened her eyes and I looked down at her, running my thumb over her lips. Her eyes jumped to Graham's in the mirror and he tightened his grip around her throat.

"Fuck—" she gasped. I could feel her nearing the edge.

"You're strangling my fingers, princess," he growled in her ear.

"You going to fall apart on our hands, darlin'?" I rasped, watching her closely.

I loved how she bit her lip as the pleasure overtook her and the moans she made, throaty and breathless. She stood on shaking legs, gripping my shirt in a death grip as together, Graham and I sent her over the edge.

We held her between us as she cried out, bucking and grinding down on our hands. Her pussy pulsed around our fingers and I reveled in how fucking gorgeous she looked falling apart.

Kaelin leaned back against Graham, looking at me through hooded eyes as she caught her breath. He released her throat, caressing her jaw before planting a kiss on her neck and removing his fingers. I followed suit and brought my fingers up to my lips, sucking off her come. She watched me and hummed her approval.

"Fuck, that's hot," she murmured.

I pushed my fingers into her mouth and she closed her eyes as she sucked the rest off.

Graham licked his fingers and pulled her head around and kissed her. I watched his tongue dive into her mouth, letting her taste herself there. They pulled apart and Kaelin fixed her skirt before running her hands over my now wrinkled shirt. A sexy blush tinted her cheeks and I pulled her into me.

"Don't worry about it, beautiful," I said.

She gave me a sheepish smile before I kissed her deeply, holding her face in my hands, wishing I could stay home with her all day instead of going to work.

I headed out to the kitchen and poured coffee into to-go mugs, throwing a spoonful of brown sugar into Kaelin's and handing it to her as she walked in a moment later with Graham behind her.

"Thank you—" she kissed me again. "I know this last year has been crazy, are you two still okay with everything? All of this?" She gestured to the three of us.

"We're good," Graham said, taking his coffee mug from me with a wink. "We've talked—exchanged threats—"

Kaelin hit him lightly on the arm as he passed by to grab creamer from the fridge. He chuckled and looked back at her.

"It feels right to be together—I'm sure North will agree—" Graham nodded at me. "No sense making you choose or pushing one of us out when quite frankly, none of our lives are normal. I don't think I would do well with conventional—you?"

I looked over at Graham and raised my eyebrows like it wasn't even a question.

"I think you both know the answer to that," I said dryly as I threw on my shoulder holsters, checking both guns. Kaelin smiled and nodded, kissing Graham before walking over to me and putting a soft hand on my jaw, pulling my attention to her.

"I can't imagine my life without either of you right now, so don't go doing anything stupid to take you out of it."

Before I could reply she turned her head seeing movement in the backyard. Viktor was crossing the back patio on a rotation.

She sighed. "Not that I mind having all the eye candy around all the time—and the twins and I have grown close—but is this really because you're—just being...cautious?" She treaded lightly around the word I knew she wanted to use: paranoid. "Or is there something else going on? I know this can't be just because of those death threats."

"I own one of the largest security companies in the world," I said. "That's just what happens when you date the boss, darlin'."

I could tell she didn't really believe me as she moved towards the door and grabbed her keys, jacket and purse.

"You know I could just hack into your stuff and find out myself," she said over her shoulder.

I could tell on her face when my eyes took on a dangerous look, and I slowly advanced on her until she was backed up against the wall. Her eyes flashed and her breathing picked up but she submitted with a sultry look on her face. I knew she enjoyed pushing me and I'd be lying if I didn't enjoy it too.

"Is that a threat?" I murmured.

My hand came up to her neck and I tightened my fingers ever so slightly.

She leaned into me. "It's a promise," she whispered, those fierce green eyes alight with a smoldering fire.

"You're lucky I like your fire, baby girl," I said against her lips.

"So you've said." Her hands trailed up my chest, and then her lips pressed against mine.

Kaelin finally made it out the door after throwing both of us a kiss over her shoulder. I waited until I heard the garage door shut behind her before I turned back to the kitchen and finished prepping my guns.

"Is that really why Viktor is still here?" Graham asked. "I understand not wanting to involve Kaelin. But I'd like to know what's coming so I can help protect her—and you," Graham added, smiling slightly.

While Graham and I weren't romantically involved, I couldn't ignore how hot things got in the bedroom between the three of us and with that intimacy, a mutual trust and friendship was growing along with a fierce need to protect what we had. I'd said I was going to invite Graham to join my personal *NorTac* team, but that would involve telling him everything and it was a very long and very dark story. We all had skeletons in our closet, but mine were very much still alive and dangerous.

Before I could answer, my phone lit up on the counter showing a call from Nyx. I hit accept and put it on speaker, looking over the island at Graham.

"Yeah."

"Fish just received a suspicious package at the docks. It's addressed to you," Nyx said.

"Tell him to stay away from it—how far out are you?"

"Thirty at least," Nyx said.

"Alright—meet me there." I disconnected the call and stared at Graham, debating for a moment. "You're right—something is coming," I said.

If I didn't have time to tell him, maybe I could just show him. It was a stupid evasion of the inevitable but it was all I could do right now. I grabbed the keys to one of the *Northern Tactical* blacked out SUVs and tossed them to Graham.

"The only ones who know are the guys on my team."

"Is this your way of inviting me to join the inner circle?" He asked with an amused smile. "Cause it's about damn time."

We walked out to the vehicle and climbed in.

"Had to know you were serious about things—I know Cal has been hounding you to join him."

"I hope you know where I stand now," Graham said.

"I do," I nodded. "My personal team is not involved in the everyday *NorTac* ops. They work for me in a different capacity."

Before I could go on, my phone rang again. I watched Graham's eyebrows raise at the name that appeared but he didn't comment as I hit accept, pushing the call through the car speakers.

"Demetrius," I greeted.

"Theron—remember when we first met, and you told me there may come a time in our relationship where you'd need to call in your favor?"

"I'm listening," I said.

"I think this might be it," Demetrius said cryptically.

"What happened, D?" I demanded, not liking the man's tone.

"Come see me at the club as soon as you can," he said. "We need to talk."

The call disconnected. Graham glanced at me out of the corner of his eye.

"Russian mob?"

I gave him a quick grin. "We go way back."

Fish was standing in the doorway of his mobile office as we pulled into the docks. Fish was the dockmaster and privy to all *Northern Tactical's* imports and exports that went through this city.

To the public, *NorTac* was a legal private military company specializing in security and protection details. It was a global enterprise with teams all over the world. On the other side, I dealt in the illegal arms business selling military grade weapons to the black market, and some governments, all over the world.

Fish played a big part in making sure customs didn't discover anything they weren't supposed to see and ensured the products were received and stored in the appropriate containers to await pickup and distribution by my staff.

Graham parked the SUV, and we climbed out to see Fish currently staring with apprehension at a package that sat out in the open in front of the office building. I stopped a comfortable distance from the package, tilting my aviators slightly to look at Fish.

"Fish."

"North—Is it a bomb?" He asked immediately.

"Unlikely," I said. "Go inside."

While Graham walked around the perimeter, looking through the spaces between containers and up into any spot a sniper might sit, I surveyed the package. I was pretty positive it wasn't a bomb, Vetticus wouldn't escalate to that quickly, but it didn't hurt to be safe. I pulled out my gun, aimed at the box and pulled the trigger.

Graham turned abruptly at the sound and headed back over once he realized it was me. I crouched down over the box and saw blood oozing out of the bullet hole. Across the top was 'To Kraven' written obnoxiously large in black sharpie. I took my knife and opened the box, revealing a bloody mess inside.

"What the fuck—" Graham muttered.

Inside was a bloody heart with a knife through the center pinning a note to the organ. I stared at it for a long moment, jaw tight at the message. I gingerly pulled the bloody paper from the knife and pulled my lighter from my pocket, holding the flame to the corner.

I dropped it at the last second before the fire took the rest of the note and the ash cascaded to settle in the gravel at my feet. I heard tires squeal behind me and as car doors opened; I rose and turned abruptly, motioning Graham to follow.

We headed back towards the SUV as Nyx, Atlas and Lachlan jogged towards us.

"Get rid of it," I said as we passed Nyx. "Have West pull all security footage."

"Where are you going?" Nyx asked.

"Demetrius wants to see me," I said over my shoulder.

This time I climbed into the driver's seat and pulled out of the docks a little too aggressively, causing the tires to scream around the first corner, giving away my irritation. Graham was silent all the way to the freeway before he spoke.

"Who sent that?"

Silence.

"His name is Vetticus."

"Why didn't you show the note to Nyx?"

Silence again.

"Nyx will understand the message without the note."

I tapped the steering wheel with a finger, trying to control the intense anger at the sight of that note. I didn't want Nyx and Atlas to see it—the heart alone would be enough of a message for them. Besides, the note was for me. It was him claiming me all over again—ensuring I remembered who I belonged to.

You are mine.

No.

Not anymore and I was going to make damn sure he never touched any of us again.

A short drive later we pulled up to Elysium. The club sat in the bustling downtown area on a trendy street filled with restaurants and a vibrant nightlife. It was the perfect mix of a high end speakeasy with a gentlemen's club undertone. We used it to launder the money from our illegal dealings and had several around the world. This one turned into Nyx and Atlas' special project and I had to admit they'd done a fantastic job. So much so, Demetrius came to me once it was done and asked to have offices there. I wasn't lying when I told Graham we went way back—Demetrius was one of my longest clients, turned business partner and now friend.

I led the way through one of the back hallways into the main space. Demetrius was leaning against the bar, looking every inch a mobster. He was wearing a tailored gray suit with his tattoos spilling out from under the cuffs and onto his hands. He turned as we approached, a smile breaking up the intensity of his features.

"Theron, my friend," he said. He was a handsome man around my age, with carefully styled black hair with a gray streak running along one side and a muscular, six foot four frame. There were three deliberate knife scars that ran through one eye, turning it white, while the other was a whiskey color that looked nearly gold.

"Demetrius," I said, smiling and clasping his hand before embracing him. Stepping back I gestured to Graham. "This is Graham Wolfe. Demetrius Volkov."

"Ah, another wolf—" He said, amusement in his eyes as he extended his hand to Graham. They shook hands as Demetrius gave him a once over.

"Theron told me all about your adventures and how you got Kaelin out of the Warren. Nasty business."

"It was," Graham answered. "Volkov—are you related to Viktor and Konstantine then?"

Demetrius nodded. "Viktor and Kon are my brothers. Theron has a habit of collecting misplaced soldiers if you haven't noticed."

Graham looked over at me. "So Kaelin was being protected by the Bratva while we were on the Red Rabbit job?"

"Indeed, she was in good hands," Demetrius said in amusement.

"So, why'd you call me, my friend?" I asked.

Demetrius' face fell, and he gestured towards the back. "Let's go into my office."

I followed Demetrius upstairs and down a narrow hallway before we entered a spacious office. Once seated in leather chairs in front of his desk, Demetrius handed me a manila envelope with 'Kraven' written in sharpie.

"This was dropped off here last night," he said.

Anger immediately flared when I pulled out a stack of photographs. I handed a few to Graham.

"What is this?" He growled when he saw what they were.

"You can see why I'm concerned," Demetrius said.

I pulled out my phone and dialed West, putting him on speaker.

"Yeah, boss," he answered.

"Pull up Kaelin's work cameras," I demanded.

While I waited, I turned to Graham. "Call Nyx."

Graham dialed his number and put that call on speaker as well.

"Yeah," Nyx answered.

"Nyx," I said. "I need you to go to Kaelin's office."

I took a picture of the photo I was holding in my hand and texted it to him.

"On my way. What happened?"

"He knows." After a moment I heard him curse as the images came through.

"What do you want to do?" He asked.

I handed Graham the pictures. The top one was of Kaelin sitting at her desk at work, while the one behind it was of her and I in the backyard of her own house. The others I held in my hand were of Nyx, Atlas and a few other team members.

"North?" Nyx snapped. "He knows about her now."

"Let me know when you're at the office."

I slammed my finger down on the end call button just as West came back on the phone.

"She's in a meeting in her conference room," he said.

Relief coursed through me.

"Do not let her out of your sight," I said to West.

"Will do, boss."

I hung up and turned to see Demetrius studying me curiously, then he nodded and sat back.

"It's him, isn't it," Demetrius stated. "The one you've been preparing to go after all these years."

I nodded.

"My brothers are in those pictures—I'm even in one," he said, tossing a few of the photos onto his desk. "He knows our association."

I shoved the pictures back into the envelope and tossed it back onto Demetrius' desk.

"He's making a point he can get to anyone close to me," I growled.

Even knowing something like this was coming, it didn't help calm the possessive fury of seeing an intimate moment between Kaelin and I captured by that asshole.

"We need to talk about how he was able to take a picture at Kaelin's house and access her work cameras," Graham said. "We need to have her tighten that up."

"We'll head over there after this," I said.

"So—are you going to ask me?" Demetrius asked, his hands steepled in front of him on the armrests and a sly look on his face.

When I didn't answer right away, Demetrius chuckled, looking amused.

"Come on, T," he said with a knowing smile. "I know the only reason you took over as my supplier all those years ago was for this moment. Hell, I'd even go as far as saying that's why you saved my brothers in Syria if we want to go back that far."

My brooding look lasted a moment longer before I smirked. "It worked didn't it?"

"You're lucky you've grown on me," Demetrius said fondly. "Well, go ahead—let me hear it."

I barked out a laugh. "Demetrius, I'm calling in my favor."

He chuckled. "I thought you'd never ask. I have to say, ten years is a long time to owe someone. I'm ready to even the score."

"After this I'll probably owe you," I admitted.

"I'm looking forward to it," he said. "So what's the plan?"

An hour later, we were back in the SUV driving towards Kaelin's office.

Graham was quiet for the first part of the drive, no doubt trying to process everything we'd just discussed in the office. When he finally did speak, it wasn't what I expected.

"Syria, huh?"

I looked at him briefly.

"Yeah, one of the first *NorTac* ops we were hired on to guard a gas refinery in Syria. We were attacked by a group of Russian special ops. When the dust cleared, we'd taken a few hostages—"

"Viktor and Konstantine?"

I nodded. "I had heard of the Volkov brothers and their associations with the Russian mob. Back then, Demetrius was a new *Pakhan*, the big boss, so I saw an opportunity to get in their good graces—they run deep in illegal arms and I needed to get my foot in the door in a big way. I staged a breakout and let the brothers go. When I came back, I got rid of the Russians usual supplier and approached them. Demetrius wasn't happy obviously—almost killed me—" I chuckled at the memory. "His brothers showed up just in time and told him who I was—"

"Wasn't saving your life repaying you saving theirs?"

I smirked. "I told them all of that was independent and that one day I would call in my favor to them. They could either shoot me right there, or become a client. I gave them a commission rate and also cut some of their costs—basically gave them a deal they'd have been stupid to refuse."

"So now you're calling in your favor."

"Yup. Demetrius and I grew pretty close after that and our businesses cross over sometimes. He has a lot of contacts in Russia where we have a lot of accounts. He also helps run the clubs. Our teams help each other out and Viktor and Kon kind of latched on to me after we reunited after Syria so when they're not needed with mob business, they're with me."

"Powerful friends," Graham mused.

"In order to go after Vetticus, I needed to have money and power. I wasn't going to risk going in with just Nyx and Atlas. Too emotional, not enough support—too much margin for error and failure," I gripped the wheel. "It's not an option to fail."

"So I have to ask—are you using Kaelin for her *Phox* connections then? She's pretty powerful in the military contracting world."

I knew he'd ask me some variation of this question at some point because I knew what it must look like.

"No, my feelings are genuine. I didn't know who she was in the Warren—I found out *Phox* was involved early on but of course, didn't know Kaelin's association—"

"Wait, *Phox* is involved?"

"Yeah, they supply *Atrox*, Vetticus' company, with military drones."

That was a detail few knew about. I'd discovered invoices going back years and when I looked into it, it turns out, Kaelin was behind the design of the military drones Vetticus now used in his games. She didn't know of course—Atrox was just a client out of thousands—but now, Vetticus knew about our connection and I hated to admit it, but she was a weakness I wasn't anticipating in all my years of planning.

"Fuck...does she know any of this?"

"No."

"Have you told her anything?" He sounded annoyed.

I pulled into the underground parking garage at the *Phox* offices downtown and pulled into a spot next to Kaelin's Tesla. I turned off the car and turned to Graham.

"Look, I practically just met you and Kaelin. Sure, this has all been hot and heavy and I-I care deeply for both of you," I said, stumbling slightly over the declaration of feelings, not sure how to word what I felt. "But I will do whatever is necessary to accomplish what I set out to do. That means being careful with information and being careful with a life I wasn't expecting to have to watch out for."

"Do you love her?"

I stepped out of the car before answering. He met me around the side of the SUV.

"I'm not sure if I know what love means anymore," I said honestly. "Where does obsession end and love begin?"

He shrugged. "I can't answer that. Maybe they're one and the same."

I nodded. "I would burn the world for her—but I also know there is a deep darkness inside me that is driven by retribution and fed by vengeance. I have obligations—" He looked grim. "It's complicated. I will do whatever I have to do to accomplish what I've spent the last decade putting into place."

All I knew was I needed to end this. I was just hoping Kaelin and the other people I'd come to care for were still around when the dust settled.

"She knew what she was getting into," I continued. "She knows what kind of man I am."

"The dangerous kind," Graham agreed.

"Who plays dangerous games."

11

GRAHAM

My mind was still turning everything over as we stepped into the elevator. Even though I sat through North and Demetrius' planning session, I still didn't have the full picture of what was going on. All I knew was that Kaelin was in some photographs she shouldn't, and North had a crazy stalker after him. I knew it was deeper than that but I couldn't see exactly to what extent—yet. I fully intended on finding out though.

"How are you going to get her to lock the cameras down tighter without telling her why? Can't West do it?" I asked as we rode the elevator up to the executive suites on the top floors.

"Yeah, he could. Just easier if she does it," he answered.

The doors opened up into a large lobby with a receptionist desk on one side and a wall of glass offices along the far wall. Everything about the building was spacious, expensive and high tech. I followed North as he walked purposefully past the reception desk. The woman stood up behind it.

"You can't—" North completely ignored her. She hurried to try and intercept him. "She's in a meeting!" The woman insisted.

North fixed her with a glare and she froze, paling slightly, then he kept walking. I smiled at the woman, trying to ease the anxiety clearly on her face.

"We won't interrupt her," I said firmly. "We'll wait in her office."

The conference room glass was currently blurred out, signifying a meeting was in place. I walked past it and entered her office to see North already looking around.

"You could be nicer to Maeve," I said with a chuckle. "She's terrified of you."

"She should stay out of my way then," he said distractedly, looking up at the camera in the corner of Kaelin's office. Her office was simple but with small feminine touches here and there—like the vase of white flowers on the coffee table and the accent pillows on the couch. There was a massive painting she'd done on the wall across the room from the desk but the other wall was all windows and looked out over the sprawling city scape and further out to the bay.

"I think she has a better view than you do," I said.

North scoffed and glanced briefly out the bank of floor to ceiling windows. We both did a quick walkthrough of the room but didn't find anything out of sorts. I sat down on the couch, arms stretched out across the back while North went and sat down in front of her computer.

Before I could start in on all the questions I had, Kaelin walked in.

"This is a nice surprise," she said, smiling at both of us. "I only have a few minutes until my next meeting though."

"Plenty of time," North said. His gaze swept over her hungrily. She went over and sat down on his lap and he pulled her in to kiss her. Their kiss got so hot and heavy I got lost in it for a minute and had to adjust myself as my cock hardened. She pulled back breathlessly, her eyes searching his before she looked over at me.

"So what brings you guys here in the middle of the day?" She asked.

"West was poking around and he doesn't like how lax your security is on your camera feeds," North said, jumping straight to the point.

She blinked and her eyebrows shot up as she looked at North again.

"Why was West *poking around*?" She asked, lingering on the words as though they offended her. She looked at me and then back at North again and sighed. "This is related to our conversation earlier isn't it?"

"We just want to make sure you're safe everywhere, gorgeous," I said, because regardless of why or what was happening, keeping her safe through it all was paramount and something we both agreed on.

"Then why don't you tell me what you're keeping me safe from," she said, her eyes narrowing as she looked back at North, already knowing he was the reason for all of this. "Because I can guarantee, those death threats you found are not coming from anyone capable of hacking into my camera feeds."

North just fixed her with a look and she sighed and gestured to her computer. He scooted the chair up with her still on his lap so she could reach her keyboard.

"Call West," she said, her voice resigned.

"Good girl," North murmured and I watched his eyes darken in approval. Kaelin visibly shivered at his tone. I loved watching her visceral reaction to us, it would never not turn me on. North pulled his phone out of his pocket and dialed West, putting it on speaker in front of them.

"Yeah boss," he answered.

"I'm with Kaelin. You're on speaker."

"Hey Killer, what can I do for you?"

"I heard you were 'poking around' my video surveillance," she said dryly. "Since you seem to have done a diagnostic on the weaknesses already, I thought I could save myself some trouble and just loop you in—"

They started talking in heavy tech terms and North watched Kaelin's fingers travel quickly across the keyboard as she coded.

"And save me a backdoor or T will kill me in my sleep," West said.

Kaelin laughed. "I'm half tempted to kick you out and make you hack in all over again."

West groaned. "Please don't."

"So why the increased security?"

West fell silent. "We're a private military company who specializes in security and protection—unfortunately, you're dating the boss and that means you get the brunt of his obsessive attention to detail. You know he means well. He cares about y—"

"Okay, sounds like we're done here," North interrupted.

"Bye West!" Kaelin got out before he hit the end call button. Kaelin looked over at North and smirked, kissing him on the cheek. She still looked a little annoyed, but then her eyes shuttered and she squirmed in his lap. I couldn't see his hands but I knew what he was doing just by watching her face flush.

"See, that wasn't so bad," North murmured.

"You can't fix everything with sex," she tried to argue, but it wasn't very convincing.

I chuckled. "I beg to differ."

"Me too," North said, running his nose over the curve of her ear. He growled against her neck.

"I should ban you from ever wearing panties," North muttered, and I assumed his fingers had found their way under her skirt.

"Theron, I have a meeting in—" She looked at the computer clock. "Two minutes."

"In fact, I'm putting that policy into effect immediately," North said, ignoring her comment. "Take them off."

"Theron..." She stood up and looked over at me but I just shrugged. I bit my lip and raked my eyes down her body.

"I'd do as he says, princess."

Kaelin narrowed her eyes at me first then turned back to North, seeming to assess whether he was serious and if she wanted to risk whatever he'd do to her if she didn't listen.

"Don't make me ask again," he said, his voice dangerously low.

Fuck. I loved when he did that. The way he commanded her was provocative and dangerous.

Her hands slowly crept under her dress, and she pulled her panties down. They only got as far as her thighs before North pulled his knife out and quickly sliced through both legs, pulling the ruined clothing away from her body and stuffing it into his pocket. North spun her around and pulled her back onto his lap, throwing her legs wide over his.

"Fuck, I have to start my meeting," Kaelin protested.

"Then start it," North murmured in her ear.

His hands traveled up her thighs as he slid the chair forward so she could access her keyboard.

"That's not a good idea," she mumbled but I saw her eyes shutter and he must have found her clit.

"Do it, darlin'," he said. "Graham, come here."

When I got around to the other side of the desk, I saw North rubbing circles on her clit as she pulled up her teams chat app and hovered the mouse over the "join" button. He looked up at me with a devilish look in his eyes and his lips crept up into a smirk.

"Edge her," North said with a wicked gleam in his eyes.

"Okay, you guys have to be quiet," Kaelin hissed.

I knelt down between their legs and ran my hands up Kaelin's thighs. I heard the mouse click and then chatter came out of the speakers.

"Hey everyone—" Kaelin said. I kissed up her thighs.

"We have a lot to talk about today—"

Kaelin's eyes nervously met mine briefly as I hovered close to her pussy.

"First, I want to bring up the Gallagher project—"

She maintained eye contact with me as I slowly brought my mouth to her clit, then she closed her eyes and took a deep breath.

"Where are we with that one?" She asked.

My tongue started the slow pace I knew would work her up. Her hands gripped the arms of her desk chair.

"Okay, but you're figuring that roadblock out, Josh?" Kaelin asked, cutting off one of her people. "Are we still on track for the deadline?" She squirmed in North's lap but he held her thighs firmly with his hands. As he watched me, one of his hands snaked its way up her side and under her shirt.

"Good—" The word came out a little breathless. "Bill, did we fix the bug—in the new release?"

Her eyes closed and her lips parted slightly as I continued licking her pussy. One hand slid along her opening where she was quickly growing wet. Someone must have said something she didn't like because her eyes snapped open and sharpened briefly.

"Okay, but Bill—why is that team of developers taking so long? Do we need to re-evaluate—" Bill interrupted her and I slid two fingers into her pussy. She slapped a hand over her mouth to cover up a moan as I hooked them and rubbed that perfect spot.

"I want a status report—by end of day," Kaelin managed. "I want to remind everyone about the communication protocols. Comments are essential—" She closed her eyes again and a look of pleasure flashed across her face before she could speak again. "I need to be able to go in and get the info I need."

She grew wet around my fingers and she subtly pressed her hips against my mouth. North kissed her neck, amusement on her face as she was now visibly flushed and close to panting in his lap.

"Lily, I have a few meetings this week regarding that—I'll look into it," Kaelin said in answer to someone's question.

"We need to get back to the design team regarding the Titan project," Kaelin said. "What are some issues you're all seeing with that and are the notes complete for the meeting tomorrow?"

It must have been an in depth topic because she threw her head back against North and mouthed a few curse words as she squirmed. An audible gasp escaped her lips but no one seemed to notice. North caught my eye and gave a subtle nod to let her come and my tongue and fingers worked her closer. A moment later she sat back up, slammed her finger down on the mute button and looked down at me. Her breathing was erratic and she let out a whimper. I could tell she was close.

"Oh god," she moaned. "Yes—yes..." Then she was coming. North slammed a hand over her mouth as she got loud.

"Come all over his face, pretty girl," he growled in her ear as he held her through the aftershocks. My mouth didn't let up until I felt her start to come down. I withdrew my fingers, covered in her come and stuck them into my mouth, licking them off one after the other.

"Kaelin—" A voice had her jumping towards her computer. She was flushed a pretty pink and her eyes were glazed as the pleasure continued to run through her in the afterglow.

"Yes, that looks good," she said.

I smirked and got to my feet. My hand snaked into her hair and pulled her up for a quiet kiss. I could tell she wanted to sink into me but another person demanded her attention in the meeting. An annoyed look crossed her face.

"I feel like there's some room for improvement there—"

North stood up and smoothed her skirt down. He pulled her in for a kiss too before we quietly left her office, leaving her to the rest of her work day. We got to the elevator when our phones both went off with a text.

"Jesus..." I muttered.

North pulled it up and he rubbed his hand over his jaw. "Damn."

It was a picture of her sitting back in her office chair. Her legs spread, one propped up on the chair with a perfect view under her skirt.

"I like the no panties rule," I smirked at North as he chuckled and pocketed his phone.

"Me too."

I followed North through the front doors of Alpha One and met Nyx in the War Room.

"I thought you were going to *Phox*?" I said.

"The team is in position," Nyx reported to North first then turned to me. "I sent Atlas. He's posted up across the street."

"Wait—position for what?" I asked. It sounded suspiciously like a job was in progress.

"They're taking down the architects of the maps today," North explained.

"Maps?"

"Vetticus would have maps designed for the games. Think of Call of Duty maps—like that but real life," Nyx answered. "We took out the board members, now the architects—we're working to cripple *Atrox*."

"I see," I grumbled. Except I was still lost.

"Why not just take Vetticus out?" I asked.

They both turned to me with equally blank expressions on their faces. It was North who finally raised his eyebrows and fixed me with a look.

"You of all people should understand," he said flatly.

I guess he was right. I didn't know the extent of what Vetticus had done to them but it was something bad and North was right—I knew revenge intimately and I knew sometimes people deserved more than just a bullet.

"How can I help?" I asked.

"I want you to join Tex and his crew on their job," North said. "I'm having them hit a few warehouses this week."

I nodded. "Alright—where?"

"One is here. The other two are Rome and Canada. They hit the local one tomorrow night."

12

ATLAS

I opened the door to the vacant apartment and deadbolted it behind me. No one lived here—it was rented through a false name by *NorTac*. We had it just in case a situation like this ever came up with Kaelin—North always tried to be prepared. I shoved the kitchen table in front of the window, pulled the curtains almost all the way shut and readied my rifle.

From the backpack I carried, I pulled a few monitors and hooked them up on the floor tilted up so I could see them, then brought up the *Phox* security feeds West had forwarded to me. All was business as usual.

I pushed the comms unit into my ear. "Report in."

I laid down on my stomach on the table and trained my sights on Kaelin's office building. On top of surveillance of Kaelin's building, I was in charge of the architect job, and the team was getting into position now. This time I wasn't one of the snipers delivering a kill shot but I was okay with that. We were lucky that two of the architects were local. I'd sent Knox and Tex to deal with those while Sakari and Lach were abroad in London.

"Getting into position now," Knox's voice crackled in my ear.

"This bastard is either doing blow or taking a really long shit," Tex grumbled. "I'm in position though."

I chuckled and dialed in my own settings, scanning the street and entrance of the all glass atrium that made up the two-story lobby of Phox corporate.

"Target locked in," Sakari said.

"All dialed," Lach drawled.

I looked at the time on my phone.

"Fire when ready," I ordered.

As I waited for them to report the job done, I thought about the message Vetticus had sent—both the recording and the bloody heart. It had been jarring to hear his voice again after so long and I'd be lying if I said it didn't bring back the nightmares of being in that place. I'd nearly lost my mind when

I heard him mention Nyx's call sign and what he planned to do to him—to us—if he ever got his hands on us again. I didn't care about myself, I cared about Nyx and subjecting him to all of that—again.

The three of us had almost not made it out and now part of me worried at how opening up old wounds would impact us. I was ready to end it all. I was tired of looking over my shoulder, always expecting Vetticus to come jumping out of the shadows, but I wanted to end it for North and Nyx too. I wanted North to stop feeling like the responsibility always rested solely on his shoulders. He'd carried the weight of it in captivity and during the games, and I'd seen the toll it took on him. I was looking forward to the day he didn't have to carry it anymore.

"Target eliminated," Sakari chirped.

One down.

I saw Kaelin on the video feed talking to her receptionist. She'd been a surprise addition to our lives in the best way, even if it was the worst timing. I wanted North to be happy with her and Graham and I knew he wouldn't be able to do that until the threat of Vetticus was gone and until he'd found—

My thoughts were interrupted by Lachlan in my ear.

"Confirmed," he said. "Headed back to the jet."

Two down.

My phone went off with a text from Nyx:

Nyx: Status?

Me: Hi to you too

I was teasing, but we also had spent very little time together the last few weeks as we readied everything and put our plans in motion. To say I missed him would be putting it lightly.

Nyx: Hello to the love of my life

Nyx: Soulmate—my great love....

He followed the message with a shit ton of emojis I didn't bother looking at. I chuckled and dialed his number, putting the call on speaker.

"Shit head," he grumbled as he answered on the first ring.

I laughed. "I should tease you more often—I like when you lay it on thick."

"That's what she said—or he said," Nyx quipped. "Now come on, update me. North is hovering." I heard a scoff from the background and smiled, picturing North's irritation.

"Sakari and Lach are confirmed," I said. "Wait—"

Nyx stayed silent as I heard Tex report in. "Confirmed—asshole made me wait long enough—and just in case you were curious, he was doing blow."

"Yes, we were all waiting with bated breath," Lach laughed.

"Confirmed—only Tex would be this invested in his target's bathroom habits," Knox said, coming over the line and the last to confirm his kill.

I laughed. "Copy that—text when you all are en route. Over and out."

"What's so funny?" Nyx asked.

"Tex just being Tex," I said. "All kills confirmed."

"Perfect," Nyx said. "Graham is coming to take Kaelin to dinner tonight so once he shows up, come back to Alpha One. We'll meet you there."

"Copy that," I said. "See you then—soulmate."

"Too much?" Nyx said, his voice dripping with amusement. I could practically see his smirk on the other end of the call.

"Never—I love you."

Nyx laughed softly. "Love you too."

13

GRAHAM

ROME, ITALY

Wolfe—you're with me," Tex said. "Sakari, Knox—around back."
We were stationed a block away from the warehouse in Rome, ready to cripple the last of three warehouses Vetticus used to house *Atrox* inventory. Over the last week I'd helped Tex and his crew take down the others. They were quick jobs—in and out. We'd take out the guards, rig explosives and light the entire thing up.

Tex and I crept towards the structure and split off from Sakari and Knox. I stood at Tex's shoulder, scanning the area while we waited for the other two to get into position around back. There was one guard having a smoke near the door, illuminated by the soft glow of the street light nearby.

"In position," Sakari said over comms.

"Copy—let's go," Tex said.

He motioned to me and we jogged towards the front door as soon as the guard had his back turned. Tex came up behind him, wrapped his arms around his head and twisted savagely. He carefully set the dead man down and I gripped the handle of the door. He nodded and I pushed it open. We worked our way inside the warehouse. It was quiet and dark. We systematically swept the first few areas. I saw two men standing around near some pallets talking. Tex signaled to sneak up close to them but gunfire rang out in the warehouse giving up our element of surprise.

I raised my gun and took out one of the guards while Tex shot the other one. With lethal precision we took out all the guards and regrouped in the middle of the warehouse space. Sakari dumped a large duffle bag at his feet and started pulling out explosives.

Tex shoved a canister of gasoline into my hands and I went off to one of the far corners. At first I thought the gasoline was excessive since we were rigging the entire thing to explode, but these men were nothing if not thorough. Plus, they liked to watch the show afterwards and gas plus explosives definitely was something to see.

I sloshed gas around the space, dragging my face covering up over my mouth and nose to avoid the fumes. Even so, it reeked of gas by the time we were all backing out the door.

"Want to do the honors with this one?" Tex handed me a box of matches.

I took them and struck it, watching the flame burn bright. I may not know what it all meant, but this was in my blood. Chaos, destruction—delivering vengeance to the people who had wronged the ones I loved.

I dropped the match and hesitated briefly, entranced by the flame. So beautiful, yet destructive.

Then Tex was grabbing me by the vest and hauling me away. We ran a few blocks where we'd left the SUV and piled in. Sakari pulled out an electronic device and pushed a few buttons.

A moment of delay and then three explosions in quick succession rumbled and we saw the fireball explode up into the sky as the building went up in spectacular fashion.

"Boom," Sakari said.

He always looked way too excited to blow things up.

I went with Tex later to pick up food. I only had a few hours before I had to fly back to New York for Kaelin's art show. This week had been nonstop and I was exhausted. But it was the good kind of exhaustion I always got from a job successfully completed. Still, I was looking forward to showing Kaelin just how much I'd missed her this week. Plus, I couldn't wait to see her in whatever stunner she was going to wear to her gallery showing. Tex pulled me back from my thoughts that were progressively getting dirtier by the minute.

"Thanks for the help this week," he said. "I'm glad you're on board."

"How'd you fall in with North?"

"I was working for this other security company, on a job—escorting some foreign ambassador—when shit went down. Like, shit hit the fucking fan," he emphasized. "I ended up getting taken with the ambassador and held for what was the longest twenty-four hours of my life. The fuckers ended up decided I wasn't useful to them so they took me out to the yard with two others in my crew and started executing us."

He shook his head. "Straight up, on our knees, bullet in the brain type shit. They killed the other two men and the gun was leveled at me next. I was ready for the end, man. I was convinced that was it. And then North was there."

Tex chuckled. "I used that opening to attack the gunman. Took him down with my hands behind my back—killed him with just my legs. Got my hands in front of me and started helping them clear the place. But man, North and his crew came in and basically annihilated everyone in what felt like minutes. It was the most spectacular display of military precision I've ever witnessed. They worked so seamlessly together—North was a beast—" Tex grinned at me. "Nyx came up to me after. He cut me out of the zip ties and said, '*Need a clean pair of panties, dude? That was a close one.*'"

I laughed with him because that sounded just like Nyx.

"North came in from outside: '*That your handiwork out there?*' I nodded and Nyx held up the zip ties. '*Took them all down with his hands tied too, boss.*' North looked me over then nodded. '*You want a job?*' Naturally I accepted on the spot and that was that. Been with him ever since. He's one of those men who is ruthless—I mean, he has to be a psychopath or something—but he cares about the men around him. I wouldn't want to cross him, that's for sure. He's a dangerous man who I owe my life to many times over at this point. He'll have my loyalty until the day I die."

Everyone seemed to have similar stories about North. I'd seen first hand the way he operates during the Red Rabbit job and getting to work beside him then I knew what Tex meant. Tex was right but at the time I thought North's edge came from a disregard for everything. Turns out, it wasn't that at all. He cared about his people and his people only and he would protect them at all costs and dole out retribution in the process.

"North is a complicated man," I muttered. Tex's laugh rang out as we grabbed the bags of burgers and headed back to the car.

"Truer words have never been spoken, my friend. He is that."

"So, what about Sakari?" I asked.

"Sakari we found while on a job in Japan," Tex said, his smile dropped and he grew solemn. "It's not really my story to tell honestly but he was in a bad situation and when we found him—" Tex shook his head. "Somehow he'd fought his way through the building he was in—and like the ninja he is, he was up on a damn roof. North, Atlas and I had followed him up there just in time to watch him take a hit I was sure had killed him. North was about to get the same treatment when out of nowhere, Sakari sends one of his throwing stars into the guy and saves North's life."

Tex looked at me as he started the car. "After that job, you best believe North had us training in martial arts for months. He doesn't like close calls."

We drove the rest of the way in silence, each of us lost in our own thoughts and when we finally pulled back up to the safe house, Tex turned off the car but didn't get out right away.

"Look, I know you've just joined the club, and while I wasn't at the Red Rabbit job, I heard about it—" he shook his head. "What's going on with all of this—it's definitely not my place to disclose—but I've seen the way he looks at Kaelin and the way he talks about what the three of you have going on—" Tex grinned. "It's important to him. But so is this and he won't be able to move on until it's over."

I nodded. "I know."

And I did know. Intimately.

Revenge was not something you could set aside and move on from until it was over. There wasn't a high road. There wasn't the option to forgive, forget and move on. It was a rage and a compulsion that simmered and eroded everything inside you until it was your entire existence—it was in every breath, every action, every thought.

But the problem was, with that consuming you, it was easy to lose yourself. By the time it was over, there was no telling who you'd be when the dust settled. And that was what I was worried about: who would he be when this was over? And would there be anyone left to care?

14

THERON

It was the night of Kaelin's art show. I'd gotten held up at work so I was meeting Kaelin and Graham at the gallery. Nyx and Atlas would be there too—Kaelin had invited everyone actually—even Viktor and Kon, but I needed them to watch Kaelin's house. She'd seemed a little annoyed when I'd told her as much but had simply pursed her lips and decided not to push things.

It was a black tie event and as I stepped through the doors into the crowd milling about the artwork, I was transported back to the gala where I'd first laid eyes on Kaelin after months of not knowing if she was alive or not.

I stood across the room, my eyes automatically finding her in the crowd. Even if she hadn't been wearing a red dress, I would have been able to find her, that's how much she dragged me into her orbit. The dress hugged her like a second skin and I let my eyes drift over her hungrily as I sipped my whiskey.

There was a slight tremor in her hands and a tightness around her mouth whenever she spoke to someone, but otherwise she seemed to be in her element here. Or she was hiding things well, which I'd seen her do first hand and the more I watched her the more I was convinced something bad had happened in the Warren after I'd left. She was too jumpy—her confidence a thin barrier when before it had been a force to be reckoned with.

Still, she was stunning and I wanted nothing more than to grab her and take her out of here. But I had somewhere else to be. I'd only come over here to sneak a look at her quickly to satisfy the ache that had settled in my chest ever since I found out she was alive. I had no intention of letting her see me—yet—but it was as though she was drawn to me in the same way as I was to her because suddenly her eyes clashed with mine.

It was like a direct hit to my senses.

We both stood frozen and her eyes widened as a myriad of emotions flashed through them—shock, disbelief, wariness...was that excitement?

Then her glass slipped through her fingers and shattered the moment. As soon as her eyes left mine, my breath rushed back to me and a rumble of irritation ran through me. I threw back my remaining whiskey and walked out before I did something I didn't have time for—like go up to her.

Then I'd never leave because this time, once I had her in my arms, I wasn't going to let her go again.

Tonight she was wearing a silver dress that shimmered and fell from her curves like liquid quicksilver. Again, my eyes immediately settled on her. She was laughing at something someone said and I marveled at the contrast between this event and the gala—she looked vibrant tonight.

Confident, proud...happy.

Just like the gala, she seemed to feel me watching her and her eyes swept the room to land on me. This time, instead of shock, her gaze sharpened into that calculating self assurance I loved to see on her. Her lips pulled into a slow seductive smile and as I walked over to her, she slowly took me in from head to toe, no longer paying attention to anyone around her. I stepped to her side and my arm snaked around her, pulling her into me.

"Hello, darlin'," I said quietly.

My other hand took her chin gently but firmly between my fingers and planted a lingering kiss on her lips, full of possession as I claimed her in front of everyone. This time, I wanted the world to know she was mine. She kissed me back, her fingers lightly grazing my jaw in affection.

"You look incredible," she said.

"So do you," I said. "Now where's this artwork of yours?"

She took my hand in hers and led me over to where one half of the room was dedicated to her paintings. Kaelin stopped in a spot where I could see her entire work on display and I realized they told a story as you progressed through the series. Most of them were massive pieces, elegantly lit to create more drama. They started out dark, morbid even, with intense storms of dark colors. That part of the room seemed more shadowed, like her paintings were absorbing all the light in the space. Gradually things lightened until the other end of the room was bright, full of redemption, courage and victory.

"Darlin' this is—" I shook my head, running my attention over the entire thing again. I turned to her and whatever she saw on my face made her breath catch and I watched the hopeful apprehension fade into pride. "I'm so proud of you."

It was like the words made her light up from the inside out and a smile appeared on her face and stayed there. Before she could say anything, Atlas walked up with Nyx in tow.

"Kaelin, you are incredibly talented," Atlas said. "I've been to a lot of gallery showings and I've never seen something quite like this."

"You should be proud of yourself," Nyx added, kissing her on the cheek.

"Thanks guys," she said, an adorable blush tinting her cheeks pink.

"Come on, I want to look at this side again," Atlas said, nudging Nyx before he walked off to get a closer look at one of the paintings.

Nyx winked at Kaelin. "He's like a kid in a candy store—he won't stand still. He's loving being around all this art again—thanks for inviting us."

"It never crossed my mind not to," Kaelin grinned, giving Nyx's arm a squeeze.

I watched Nyx walk up to Atlas and put an arm around his waist. A burst of pride swept through me. All of us had come so far to be here like this. They deserved a night to relax and be happy even though I knew it wouldn't last. We still had a lot to do before this was over.

For the next few hours we celebrated Kaelin. I let her lead me through the entire series, explaining her vision and then she was pulled away for a bit to socialize only to come back a short time later, flushed and vibrant.

"I made a sale," she breathed, the green in her eyes a vivid burst of color. I'd never seen her so radiant. Graham congratulated her and Nyx and Atlas reappeared to toast her. She was all smiles after that and as the night wound down, it became apparent she was going to sell most of her paintings and come away with a few key contacts.

She was rambling on about one commission she'd been approached about when suddenly her words cut off abruptly and she was staring at someone over my shoulder; her face growing paler by the second.

I heard a voice that set my teeth on edge.

"Well, well, well—Kraven, you didn't tell me you took your rabbit out of the Warren."

"What are you doing here?" Kaelin snapped, her voice shaking slightly along with her hand that was choking the life out of her champagne glass.

I turned to see Greg Mahoney, looking crisp in a suit, his eyes lazily sweeping Kaelin from head to toe before settling on me. His hand was outstretched and forcing a smile onto my face I shook it.

"Greg," I said, working hard to keep the irritation from my tone. "I didn't know you were into art."

"I'm not really, but one of the artists here is a friend of mine." His attention returned to Kaelin. "You are full of surprises my dear—if I had known who you were in the Warren..." He reached out a hand to touch her and I casually stepped to intercept it as Kaelin stiffened next to me.

"You know I charge for that," I said lightly, even though my blood was running hot and I wanted to rip his hand from his body for even daring to try and touch what's mine. His face hardened as he looked back at me. We stared at each other for a long moment before Mahoney shook his head, a suggestive smirk pulling at his lips.

"And here I thought we were friends, Kraven," he said casually.

"Friends?" Kaelin choked out, seeming to have found her voice again.

Mahoney ignored her, his attention still fixed on me as he studied me with renewed interest and a wariness I hadn't seen on his face since the beginning.

Fuck. I couldn't have him questioning our friendship now—after all the work I'd put in. I huffed a laugh and slapped a hand on his shoulder, breaking the tension and stepping between him and Kaelin as I directed him away.

"Come on—*friend*," I said. "I need a drink."

I didn't look back but walked with Mahoney to the bar, ordering a whiskey before turning to him.

"Kaelin doesn't know I'm still involved with specific dealings," I said. "I'd like to keep it that way." Mahoney studied me a moment longer and then I saw the questions fade away and he grinned knowingly.

"I get it. I do wonder though—I heard the Warren was destroyed. Specifically in an attack." He let the words hang in the air between us.

"Do you know by who?" I asked.

Mahoney shrugged. "Rumor is there's a new savior in the game—haven't gotten a name yet. But I will."

He spoke with his usual calm assurance and I knew it was true. Greg Mahoney always got what he wanted sooner or later. I would have to warn Deathwing his cover was wearing thin.

"So how did you acquire her if you didn't save her?" He really wasn't dropping the Kaelin thing, and I saw his eyes drift to her again. She was standing with Graham across the room, her posture tense and those green eyes alive with fury as she glanced over at us every few seconds. Graham was speaking to her, leaning down near her ear, but it wasn't doing anything to calm her down.

"I just got lucky," I said evasively. He was quiet for a moment then turned to me and lifted his shoulders as though he was shrugging the whole thing off.

"Well, if you ever feel inclined to share her again—I'll gladly pay."

I chuckled and nodded. "I'll keep that in mind."

We both took a drink. "How was your trip abroad?"

"Profitable," he said. "Come by the club tomorrow, I could use your help with the inventory."

My eyebrows raised in surprise and skepticism. "Where's Palmero?"

Mahoney never let anyone help him with inventory for an auction except his partner in crime, Alex Palmero.

"He's around. But your advice ended up being crucial on this last sourcing trip and I don't enjoy being in debt to someone."

"I didn't know advice between friends came at a price," I said.

"Everything has a price," Mahoney countered dryly. "Even between friends, as you just demonstrated."

He finished his drink and set his glass on the bar behind him.

"Enjoy the rest of your night," he said. "Tell your rabbit it was truly a pleasure to see her again."

I nodded curtly and watched him walk off through the crowd. Only once I watched him disappear through the main doors did I walk back over to Kaelin and Graham, steeling myself for the storm I could see gathering around her. Nyx intercepted me before I made it across the room.

"What the fuck was Mahoney doing here?" He demanded.

"Hell if I know. I want West to look into it," I said.

I hated secrets and I wanted to know whether Mahoney had been telling the truth about knowing someone here or if he'd been following me. If he was following me, it meant his trust in me was in question. I didn't completely believe that all of a sudden he was ready to include me in helping him with inventory when for the last three years, he'd only let himself and Palmero touch that aspect of his business. I couldn't afford to lose all the ground I'd made with him.

I was too close. Deathwing was too close.

"Kaelin recognized him," Nyx stated, a question in his eyes.

"It's worse than that," I sighed. "I let Mahoney have a go at her in the Warren."

Nyx stared at me and then chuckled. "Oh boy, have fun with that one."

I continued on towards Kaelin and Graham who were both eyeing me with varying looks of displeasure. Kaelin's was more violent and as soon as I stopped in front of her she opened her mouth to speak but nothing came out. She shut it and then tried again.

"What the fuck, Theron!"

"I didn't know he'd be here," I said.

"You're friends with him?" Her voice was quiet, accusatory and dripping with hurt.

"It's complicated—"

"It's a yes or no question," Kaelin breathed.

I took a step towards her and she took a step back, running into Graham's chest. He was frowning at me as his hands went to her shoulders to steady her. My jaw clenched at her avoidance and I stepped up in front of her, my hand going to her throat.

"I might have shared you with him in the Warren," I growled. "But I want to make it very clear he is never going to touch you again."

"I don't know you at all, do I?" She murmured, the hurt now dominating over the anger. She sagged back against Graham. "I want to go home."

"I'll drive you—" Graham started to say but she shook her head.

"No, I want to be alone tonight," she said firmly.

I let my hand drop from her neck but I didn't step away. Graham released her shoulders and she slipped out from between us. A low sound of displeasure escaped me as I watched her walk away.

"Does this have to do with Vetticus?" Graham asked.

I could feel his eyes drilling into the side of my face as I watched Kaelin leave.

"No," I said shortly. "It doesn't."

15

KAELIN

I drove the entire way home in silence.

This should have been one of the best nights of my life having accomplished something I'd never dared hope for until recently. But instead it was overshadowed by seeing *him* again.

Greg.

Remembering how Theron had shared me at the lounge that night, allowing Greg to have his way with me, made my face heat even now. And to find out Theron was friends with him!

I was pissed.

I pulled up to my house, bent on tearing off my dress and digging into some pity party ice cream, when I immediately knew something wasn't right. Usually Viktor or Kon met me in the driveway but it was eerily empty. Even though I questioned why Viktor and Kon were still watching over me, I'd gotten attached to the twins when Theron had left them behind on the Red Rabbit op as my bodyguards. They'd been like my two identical shadows ever since and despite the annoyance of not having my home to myself, I'd gotten used to them being around.

I didn't pull into the garage but parked in the driveway and grabbed my gun from the glove compartment. When I'd left this morning, Kon had been there so I knew it would be Viktor tonight. I unlocked my front door and stepped inside. There was a light on in the kitchen, but that was normal. I checked the room near the door and then advanced my way into the house.

I made it around to the kitchen where the french doors to the patio were wide open and Viktor was lying just outside bleeding from a gunshot wound to his shoulder and a nasty gash on his temple.

"Viktor!" I rushed over to him and knelt by his side.

Before I could do anything, I heard the gate slam on my side yard and heavy footsteps. I pulled my gun and leveled it at the corner, only for Kon to sprint into view. He held up his hands at the sight of me but I'd already lowered the weapon.

"Hurry!" I said as Kon rushed over. "I just got home and found him like this."

"He was on the phone with me when it happened," Kon said. "I called Nyx already." He quickly cut Viktor's shirt off, making sure that was the only gunshot wound and did a quick field dressing. By the time he was done, I heard my front door open and Nyx was there, his gun also drawn as he quickly took in the scene.

"Are you okay, baby girl?" He asked.

I nodded, holding Viktor's hand as Kon dressed the cut on Viktor's head. I was nauseous thinking about anything happening to Viktor. My thoughts strayed back to when I'd first met him and Kon and how over the month they were my bodyguards, I'd slowly broken down their tough outer walls.

"Tell me about yourself, Viktor," I said.

I hated the silence as we drove to my therapy appointment. He never let me take my car and always made me sit in the back of the blacked out SUV.

"Not much to tell, ma'am," he said gruffly.

"I told you—it's Kaelin," I said automatically.

Theron had been gone for two weeks, and I'd been trying to get through the wall of Russian muscle. All I knew was that he was a twin—something I discovered by accident I might add—and Russian. In two weeks, I'd only heard them speak a handful of words and two complete sentences. One sentence had been when he'd introduced said twin—Konstantine—and the other sentence was the one he'd just said.

"Were you born in Russia then?" I pressed.

Silence.

I couldn't tell him apart from his brother unless I was staring at their faces and then I could see the different scars they had. Even some of their tattoos were identical although I could only see the ones on their hands and occasionally forearms.

"What brought you to the states?"

Silence. That was how all my questions were usually answered. Even if I asked him something as mundane as what he preferred on his pizza—silence. So naturally I'd made it my goal to get him to crack. It was something to keep my mind off the fact my men were about to go after Cooper and put themselves in danger.

"Do you have any other siblings?"

Silence.

I crossed my arms and sat back. I'd exhausted all my questions for the drive because a moment later we pulled into the office complex where my therapist practiced. The SUV pulled to a stop, and I didn't bother opening my door as Viktor came around and did it for me. The first time he'd driven me, he'd made it very clear I was not to get out of the car until he came and opened the door for me.

"Thank you," I said, like I always did.

Not even a nod. Cool.

I dreaded therapy recently because with the appearance of Cooper came the resurgence of my nightmares. It was always the same dream—I was walking into my house after the gala and Cooper was there, standing over the bodies of Theron and Graham. The feeling of despair and agony in those dreams was so strong I would wake up not being able to breathe.

In those dreams there was no one coming to save me and even though I tried, I couldn't save myself and Cooper would always drag me away and out of the house, presumably to go back to the Warren but I always woke up before I could find out where he was taking me. For that I was grateful.

I came out of therapy in a bad mood and feeling like I was on the verge of crying. I hadn't had a hard session like that in a while and we'd spent most of the hour pulling back layers until my edges felt exposed and raw. Sometimes I wasn't sure if it helped to talk about my trauma or just hurt more but today had drained me. Viktor was waiting for me and opened the door, then we were off.

The phone rang, and he answered it through the car speakers.

I could tell it was Konstantine by his voice but they spoke quickly in Russian. It didn't sound like either man was happy but then again, it could be the language.

Nope, Viktor was definitely scowling more than usual as he barked something to Konstantine.

They hung up the call, and I watched us deviate from the usual path home. A short drive later, we pulled up in the back lot of a club called Elysium. I'd never been inside before but I'd heard it was a trendy speakeasy with gentlemen's club vibes.

"Do you own the club?" I asked, looking at the building that was on a side street in bustling downtown. It was obviously popular as the parking lot was packed with cars on a Friday evening.

"Something like that," Viktor answered.

I looked at him in the rearview mirror.

"What does that even mean?" I asked irritably.

He met my eyes, probably taken aback by my tone. I was usually polite and friendly but I wasn't in the mood for riddles.

"It's North's establishment," he said, parking the SUV. "My family helps him run it."

"North owns a nightclub?" I mused, looking back out at the building.

Viktor got out and opened my door. I followed him through the back door of the club where the vibrations of the bass from the music slammed into us but instead of heading towards the main floor, he took a set of stairs up to another hallway and opened one of the doors. It was an empty office.

"Sit," he said, pointing to a couch. "Stay here."

I scowled at him. "I'm not a dog."

He ignored me and left.

The office overlooked the club so instead of sitting; I walked over to the floor to ceiling wall of windows. They were tinted on the other side so no one could see in, but I looked out over the sea of people. It was part nightclub, part lounge with different levels, floors and VIP areas. Several bars dotted the space with a massive circular one in the center. It was beautiful, modern and sleek with industrial touches while still maintaining a cozy and intimate atmosphere.

This early in the evening it was mostly people having a cocktail after work so while the music was intense, the crowd looked lively but not as much of a club atmosphere as I was expecting.

I figured North was involved with private military companies, not nightclubs, but then again, I knew next to nothing about him. I didn't think I'd ever see him again after he left me in the Warren.

I hoped I would—at one point, in the darkest times, I'd fantasized heavily about him coming to save me—but he never did. Instead, it had been Graham that'd come back from the dead to get me out. Theron said he'd tried, but that Cooper said I wasn't there so he must have reached out once I'd already escaped.

I didn't blame him for not coming sooner, but I was interested to know why. A man like him had money, power and influence but when he hadn't immediately tried to get me out, I doubted what I meant to him. I was something he'd purchased for a set amount of time. I meant nothing in the grand scheme of things.

What made me think I was anything special to warrant a rescue attempt? Especially since it would have had to be dramatic and dangerous with Cooper not wanting to let me go.

These were all questions running rampant in my head. The one where I thought I wasn't worth being rescued by Theron was what was messing with me the most and I hoped once he came back, it wouldn't be like that. I wasn't a sex slave, and I didn't want to be treated like one—no matter how mind blowing the sex actually was.

I lost interest in people watching and realized I had to pee. I bit my lip, debating on whether to leave the office or try to wait for Viktor to come back. Finally, I couldn't wait any longer and poked my head out of the office door. There didn't look to be any bathrooms along the hallway, so I headed back towards the stairs we'd used to come up here.

I reached the bottom and found the bathroom. When I came back out, two men were stumbling out of the men's restroom. One of them fell heavily against me and I shoved him off as he mumbled an apology.

"Hey gorgeous, can I buy you a drink?" The second one asked, leaning into my personal space.

"Nope, I'm good, thank you," I said, trying to go around him and head back up the stairs. His arm went around my waist and before I realized what I was doing, I turned and punched him squarely in the jaw.

We both cursed at the same time. He stumbled backwards, his lip cut, while I shook out my hand with a hiss. Punching someone hurt. I hadn't meant to react that way but the Warren weighed heavily on my mind and I'd just reacted. The man I punched cursed at me angrily and he and his friend stepped towards me. I backed up a few steps, glaring at them.

"Fuck off," I snapped.

"Bitch," he hissed and tried to grab me.

I kneed him in the groin and he fell forward into me, sending me stumbling backwards into another door. Unfortunately, the door was being opened at the same time I hit it and I fell through the doorway with the two drunk men on my heels. By some miracle, I kept my feet under me but the one I'd kneed wasn't so lucky and fell onto the ground in front of me. I punched the second guy, again, and his nose started running blood. He stumbled against the wall clutching his face and that's when I heard the low rumble of a laugh from behind me. I turned to see ten pairs of eyes fixed on me.

"You are every bit as lovely as I imagined you'd be, Ms. Bennett."

A tall, handsome man around Theron's age stood up from where he was seated around a table. He had black hair with a gray streak but it was his eyes that were truly captivating. He had scars running through one of them turning it white and the other was the most beautiful shade of gold I'd ever seen. He had his sleeves rolled up revealing tattoos and with a flick of a heavily ringed hand, two of his men forcefully escorted the drunk men out.

"I've been eager to meet the woman who finally caught North's attention," he continued, looking at me in amusement as he made his way around the table and stopped in front of me. "Your name precedes you of course but I must say you are much more captivating in person."

His energy was similar to Theron's, nearly oppressive with an aura of power and danger. But I didn't feel unsafe and so when he reached for my hand, I let him take it. He raised it to his lips but stopped just short and instead pulled a handkerchief from his pocket and gently placed it over my knuckles that I realized were lightly bleeding. He carefully wrapped my hand in the cloth, his eyes never once leaving mine. He kissed my fingers and let my hand drop.

"My name is Demetrius Volkov," he said.

"Pleasure," I murmured.

"I wish I had the time you deserve, my dear, but unfortunately you caught me in the middle of important business."

"I apologize—"

He held up his hand with a smile. "The interruption was worth it." He winked at me and then his eyes shifted over my shoulder and I turned to see Viktor scowling near the door.

I left the room feeling Demetrius' eyes on me until the moment the door closed behind Viktor and I.

"I told you not to leave the room," he growled.

"I had to pee," I sniffed. "It wasn't my fault two of your patrons were drunk out of their minds this early in the evening."

The drive home was silent as usual and when we got back to the house, I waited patiently in the entryway while he swept the house and made sure everything was clear. I went into the kitchen and untied the cloth around my hand. It hurt—quite a bit. Punching someone was not glamorous even if it had been satisfying. I grimaced when I put my hand under the water to wash the cuts.

"Let me see," Viktor said, suddenly beside me with a bottle of hydrogen peroxide and some bandaids. The cuts weren't bad and only one even needed a bandaid.

"Demetrius is my older brother," he said after a moment.

"Seems like a cool dude," I muttered dryly.

Something rumbled through Viktor that sounded suspiciously like a laugh.

"You're Bratva, aren't you?" I said. When he didn't answer right away I scoffed. "Viktor, I stumbled into a room full of Russians who look like textbook mobsters. I don't need to know what you were doing, but I know mob business when I see it."

A ghost of a smile flickered across his face and he looked at me and nodded.

"Yeah—Demetrius is the Pakhan." It didn't surprise me that Theron would have powerful friends so the fact he was close with the leader of the Russian mafia just had me nodding in understanding.

I tilted my head, studying him. "How did you get in with Theron?"

"Kon and I owe him our lives," he said.

He grabbed an ice pack from the freezer and handed it to me. I hoped he'd continue but after he watched to make sure I put the icepack on my knuckles, he left to do his usual rounds of the property. As I watched him cross the back patio, I wondered what I'd gotten myself into that Theron would have to leave someone behind to watch me. At first I thought it was just a precaution against Cooper, but now I was pretty sure it had nothing to do with that and everything to do with Theron's own enemies.

Viktor's eyes fluttered open and before he could freak out, he noticed my hand in his, then his eyes quickly looked around at his surroundings and he cursed in Russian before meeting my gaze.

"Are you okay, *lisichka*?" he said, groaning as he sat up.

I nodded. Shortly after the scene at the club, the twins had started calling me by my name after I'd snapped at them for the hundredth time, then soon after Theron returned, they'd started calling me *lisichka*, or "*little fox*." When I'd asked about it, they said it was because I was tricky like a fox, escaping from Cooper, and a play on the company I worked for. I thought it was adorable.

Kon and Nyx pulled him to his feet and helped him through the house out to Kon's waiting SUV, talking quietly about what happened.

I walked into the house behind them and went to close the french doors, only to see someone had spray painted something across the inside. I backed up to see the full picture and my body froze in shock. Blood roared in my ears making me lightheaded. I clutched the back of the couch as I fought to keep breathing.

Someone had spray painted a giant red crosshair across the doors leading to my back patio. Nyx came up behind me and grabbed my shoulders, making me startle so violently he had to catch me as I stumbled.

"Whoa, easy, pretty girl," he said. "Just breathe—Graham and North are on their way."

I was getting lightheaded and my chest felt tight as I struggled to breathe. I sank to the ground of my living room and Nyx followed as I clutched at him, needing some sort of anchor in the storm that suddenly had me flailing in fear. He pulled me to him, murmuring words I hardly heard. When I finally calmed down, I couldn't tear my eyes away from the french doors leading out to my backyard. Nyx helped me to my feet but I couldn't bring myself to let go of his hand.

"Who—who did that?" I asked.

Before Nyx could answer, I heard a door slam, startling me again.

"Where is she?" I heard North demand loudly before he appeared and pulled me roughly into his arms, his eyes going over my head and turning absolutely murderous. Graham was right behind him, looking equally furious and my own anger surged. I pushed away from North, taking a step back to glare at him.

"Who did this?" I demanded.

"We'll take care of it—"

"That's not what I fucking asked," I snapped. "Something is going on and I need to know right now."

His eyes darkened, and he took a step towards me, only for me to take another step back and I shook my head viciously.

"No. No—you do not get to brush this off," I said, my voice rising as my panic crept up. "What the fuck is going on, Theron?"

"Kaelin—" Graham stepped up beside Theron and my eyes jumped to him, glaring equally as hard.

"Do you know?" I fumed.

His mouth snapped shut and his face grew stoney. I felt slightly unhinged as my gaze flickered back and forth between the two men I trusted to keep me safe and for the first time doubt crept in because they'd failed. Someone had been in my house and shot Viktor.

What if I had been home too?

"Is anyone going to tell me what's going on?" I said. "Who shot Viktor and what the fuck is that?" I waved over my shoulder at the spray paint. When neither man spoke, I rounded on Nyx and he held up his hands and shook his head sadly.

"I'm sorry, Killer—" he said. "This isn't my call."

"This is why you were so upset over the death threats," I said, my voice shaking with anger. "Because you knew something like this was going to happen."

Theron didn't even have the decency to look guilty. In fact, his face was so emotionless I couldn't get a read on him at all, it was like he'd completely shut me out.

"You told me you didn't want to think about these things," North said.

"This is different and you know it!"

He didn't answer.

"Get out," I hissed.

If they weren't going to tell me anything, then I didn't want to be around them. Their silence and lack of trust in me cut deep. When neither of them moved, I threw my finger towards the front door. "Get the fuck out of my house!" I screamed.

"Kaelin—" Graham tried to take a step forward and again I took a step back, my legs hitting the couch.

"I said get out! If you aren't going to tell me what the fuck is going on—get the fuck out. I don't want you here."

Graham looked hurt, but he nodded and turned to Theron who was still looking at me with expressionless eyes. They flickered beyond me to the doors and I saw his fists clench at his sides, the only tell that he was internally churning with emotions I couldn't gauge. Graham came up even with Theron and I heard him say something low in his ear.

Theron's mouth twitched as though he wanted to snarl something back but he refrained and without a word, he turned and left with Graham close behind. Something slammed into my heart so hard I was momentarily breathless. He left instead of telling me what was going on. He just…left…and that hurt more than I realized it would.

Tears choked me as they pooled and threatened to fall. Nyx was still standing nearby, guilt written all over his face. He reached out to me but I held up a hand to stop him just as a rogue tear escaped down my cheek. Before I could have a full on meltdown, I stormed off into my bathroom and locked the door, barely holding back a sob as I slid down the wall and broke apart.

I was right.

Theron wasn't trying to protect me from my enemies—he was trying to protect me from his.

16

THERON

I stood in Kaelin's driveway with Graham pacing angrily beside me. The fury had calmed, only to be replaced by the never-ending loop of seeing the hurt on Kaelin's face when I wouldn't tell her what was going on. Even worse, seeing the betrayal in her eyes as I left. Viktor came over, pain etched on his face as he grasped his freshly bandaged shoulder.

"It's my fault—"

I held up a hand. "Viktor, go home and get yourself checked out by Doc," I nodded to Kon hovering behind him. Viktor looked upset and angry with himself and opened his mouth to argue but I cut him off again. "We knew this was going to get rough—this is no one's fault. Get that out of your head because I need you focused, understood?"

He stood a little straighter and nodded curtly before leaving with Kon.

"You need to tell her," Graham growled, drawing my attention.

"I don't *need* to do anything," I said coldly, my anger flaring and needing an outlet as our eyes clashed.

"North—" It was Nyx. He came up, looking between us with a frown before holding out a folded piece of paper. "This was stuck to the door." I held Graham's gaze a moment longer as I took the paper from Nyx and then dropped my eyes to read it.

Game on.

She'd look so pretty in a cage, don't you think?

My lip curled in disgust. "Bastard," I snarled.

"We need to find him," Graham snapped. "Vetticus is it? Why haven't you tracked him down yet? First the photos and now this? He's getting bolder—"

"Again with the demands," I growled. "I don't need to do anything. This is much deeper than just a few photos and a spray paint job. Do not assume you know what's going on."

"Then tell me," Graham demanded, taking a step towards me. "We're all involved now, North. I've helped you with the warehouses...I've listened to a plan I don't understand. I need to know who Vetticus is. I can't protect her if I don't know what I'm supposed to be protecting her from!"

I turned to Nyx. "Stay here with her. Get a crew in to clean this up—" My phone rang and I saw it was Atlas.

"Is she okay?" He asked as soon as I picked up.

"As okay as can be expected," I said shortly.

"Good. Listen, Tex hasn't reported in and no one can get a hold of him."

I cursed and turned to Nyx again.

"His tracker is offline," Atlas went on. "I told the men to no longer go anywhere alone."

"Activate the sleepers in his supply lines," I said. "I want his river cut down to a damn stream by tomorrow."

"Copy that."

I hung up with Atlas and addressed Nyx. "He took Tex."

"Fuck," Nyx cursed, running a hand through his hair, a grim look on his face. "I know, I know—" he said when I fixed him with a look. "We knew this would happen—"

"What?" Graham interrupted incredulously. "What do you mean you knew this would happen?"

I finally rounded on him, fed up with his interruptions and distractions.

"I have been planning this revenge for over a decade and nothing—" My voice raised as my passion and anger raged. "—nothing will stop me taking down everything Vetticus has ever touched. He took everything from me—from Nyx and Atlas too—and countless others that are no longer with us. They all deserve vengeance and I will give it to them by any means possible. This is not some quick spur of the moment operation. I have spent years planning and putting pieces into play. Everyone knows the risks. You will follow orders, or you will stay the fuck out of my way."

Graham's face was downright murderous, his jaw so tightly clenched I was surprised I couldn't hear his teeth grinding together. He stepped closer to me and shoved a finger at my chest.

"I really hope you know what you're doing, North, because take a good look around you—" he threw open his arms. "You have a hugely successful global enterprise, loyal men who would follow you literally to the grave, and a woman who loves you," he turned away as his passion overcame him then turned back. "She fucking loves you, T. And I just really hope all of this is still here when you finish burning the world down. Is revenge really more important than the people who love you?"

"My revenge *is* for the people who love me," I said quietly.

Graham shook his head, his anger tinged with sadness. "They just want you, Theron. They don't want you to give them retribution—they just want your heart and that requires you to still be alive to give it."

"I'm afraid it's not that simple."

"It fucking can be," he said.

I hoped he of all people would understand. But I also knew I was wrong for leaving him in the dark. He'd helped with a few jobs but he didn't know everything. It wasn't fair. I knew this. And yet I couldn't bring myself to tell the whole story yet—especially to Kaelin. It was too much...too emotional at a time where I couldn't afford to focus on that.

I looked down at my phone and dialed Demetrius.

"Atlas is going to activate the sleepers in the supply lines," I said when he answered.

"I'll call my contacts," Demetrius said. "By the end of the day he won't have any suppliers left."

I got off the phone with Demetrius and headed towards my Aston. There was nothing I could do about Kaelin and Graham at the moment—but it didn't stop me from the twisted feeling in my gut and the strong suspicion I was making too many wrong decisions.

17

NYX

As soon as North started arguing with Graham, I went back inside the house. That was not my business and even though I agreed with Graham, North was not going to listen to anyone in regards to this and I had to respect that. I walked inside and found Kaelin trying to scrub the spray paint off her french doors.

"I have someone coming to do that," I said.

"I need to do something," she said, dropping the brush back into the soapy water.

"Understandable," I said. "Do you have another one of those?"

We scrubbed in silence for a few minutes but from the scrunched up look on her face and the furious strokes of the brush; I knew I was in for a barrage of questions.

"Why is he such an asshole?" She muttered.

I laughed out loud. "He is—but he means well."

"Why won't he tell me what's going on?" She threw down the brush.

"North is a complicated man," I put my brush down as well and pointed her to a barstool. "I'll make some coffee—I take it you're not going to be sleeping anytime soon." She gave me a small smile and sat down while I moved around the kitchen.

"How come you know the way around my kitchen so well?" She asked suspiciously.

"Do you really want to know?" I asked, winking at her.

She frowned but didn't answer. She was quiet the entire time the coffee was brewing and when I put a spoonful of brown sugar into her coffee; she sighed as though she was resigning herself to something. I slid the mug across the counter to her.

"Sometimes I feel like I know you and Atlas better than I know Theron and I'm not even intimate with you guys," she said.

"We can change that," I winked. "All you have to do is say the word, baby girl."

She blinked and then laughed, taking a sip of her coffee. I watched some of the tension bleed away from her face.

"Not going to lie, I have thought about it." Her cheeks tinted an adorable pink as she buried her face in her mug again and warmth spread through me at the thought of her fantasizing about Atlas and I.

"We've thought about it too," I chuckled. "Regardless of that though, when you belong to North, you also belong to Atlas and I."

"You guys are all close," she stated.

I nodded. "Circumstance brought us together but now I can't imagine my life without either of them."

"He still is such a mystery to me," she said in frustration.

"Like I said, he's a complicated man," I shrugged. "But I will tell you this: he is the best leader I've ever had the honor of following."

"But that doesn't tell me who he is," she sighed.

"Sure it does—a good leader is dependable, adaptable, takes care of his people and is ruthless in the pursuit of their goals."

"That sounds almost—honorable? I thought you guys killed people for a living?"

"A good leader doesn't have to be a good person," I chuckled. "And I want to be clear, we are not heroes even though we can be selfless for each other at times."

"You'll burn the world, but only for the people you love?"

"Exactly—fuck everyone else."

"I guess I just have to settle for that?" She looked down into her mug of coffee, frowning in thought.

"Is it settling?"

"I just don't like secrets..."

"He's just trying to keep you safe."

Kaelin looked up at me, and her eyebrows raised. "That's keeping me safe?" She gestured behind us at the french doors. "And I really hate what that implies—keeping me safe—from what? And why can't I be included in helping to keep myself safe? I'd like to think I wouldn't be that much of a liability."

"I think it has more to do with the fact he didn't anticipate having you be a factor in his life right now," Nyx said carefully. "I don't think—no I know—he doesn't know what to do with the feelings he has for you at a time when all of his energy needs to be directed elsewhere."

"I don't want to make things harder for him," she grumbled. "But I also don't want to sit here and wait for shit to go down. It makes me feel like a possession of his."

"Is that so bad?" I teased.

She hit me playfully on the arm but I could see the past lingering in her eyes.

"It just—scares me a little I guess because I was a possession to Cooper..." she said. "Not that it's the same at all—I don't know...I'm not making sense," she finished lamely.

"I get it," I said.

And I did. I understood exactly what she was feeling.

We'd been possessions to Vetticus. His toys he liked to play with—in all ways. We had been his obsession and it was not something I wanted to repeat.

I didn't know what was going on in North's head, honestly, that would be scary—but I did know I'd never seen him look at anyone the way he looks at Kaelin. It was like looking at a break in the storm that usually raged in his eyes. Anyone who could make him come out of the shadows, at least for a little bit, was important.

"How about I make us some pasta," I said.

Kaelin's eyebrows shot up. "You can cook?"

"Why is everyone always so surprised by that?" I grumbled.

Kaelin giggled. "I just usually only see you holding a gun, not a wooden spoon."

"Well, let me show you one of my many skills then." I dug around in the fridge.

"You have more?"

I turned towards her, my arms full of supplies and gave her a cheeky grin.

"Baby, you'll have to ask Daddy North for permission to see the other ones." Kaelin burst out laughing. I winked and vowed to spend the rest of the night pulling more of those from her.

18

THERON

Over the past two days, I didn't see or hear from Kaelin or Graham. They were always on the back of my mind but I was buried under a mountain of other things—the big one being putting everything in place to draw Vetticus all the way out of the shadows. He'd started to take my men—I'd just gotten a text that Sakari and Knox were missing now. As much as I hated it, that meant the plan was working. I was almost to Kaelin's house when a call from Nyx came through the car.

"He blew up the fucking building!" Nyx shouted as soon as I picked up. "He blew up *NorTac*, North. Half of the building is gone apparently!"

"Fuck," I slammed my fist on the steering wheel.

Luckily it was later in the evening so most of the people had gone home from work. The building would have been mostly empty, which was Vetticus' point—it was a proverbial warning shot across the bow to get me to sit up and listen.

He was done with my games and I was done too.

"What do you want to do?" Nyx asked.

"I'm pulling into Kaelin's driveway now," I said.

"Fuck, really? Did she text you?"

I didn't answer, and Nyx sighed. "This should go over well. See you in a minute then."

I pulled up to Kaelin's house a moment later and Nyx met me at the door.

"*Atrox* is a sinking ship. It's time to move on Albatron," I said without preamble. "Call King in Italy—get a tail going."

Albatron was the shadow man behind *Atrox*. I'd only come across him once and the experience had put him right up on the top of the hit list with Vetticus. Since then we hadn't found much on him but I got the gist he was powerful and had his hand in a lot more than just *Atrox*. He was rumored to often be at the games and I was banking on that being true.

King was the leader of our Italian team who helped lead our European sector of *NorTac*. West had located Albatron in Rome and I needed King's team ready to keep tabs on him.

Kaelin appeared around the corner. "What are you doing here?"

"I wanted to talk to you," I said.

"Are you ready to tell me what's going on? I'm getting texts that there was an explosion at the *NorTac* buildings."

"It's getting taken care of—"

Her eyes flashed. "Is that your answer for everything?"

"I think you should come stay at Alpha One for a while," I said.

"No. Not until you tell me what's going on. I'm not going to just be locked in a house like one of your possessions—"

"It's to keep you safe—"

"Fuck being safe, Theron!" She shouted. "I don't even know what that means anymore! Maybe I can help! You know what I do for a living—"

"I know who you are but so do a lot of other dangerous people."

"I thought you'd give me more credit than that after everything," she said, her voice shaking. "I can take care of myself."

"But you shouldn't have to!" I said, my own temper rising. "This is my problem. I never expected you to come into my life—"

"Oh, so you regret meeting me? Do you regret buying me? Do you wish I was a fucking sex slave you could just lock up somewhere because sometimes that's how I think you still fucking see me!"

I took a step towards her. "I don't regret meeting you—"

"Then tell me what the fuck is going on!"

"Enough!" I shouted. "I want you to listen very carefully—I do not regret meeting you and I certainly don't regret buying you. That was the best money I ever spent—I don't see you as a sex slave, I had respect for you even when I thought you were only that. You dug under my skin with your tenacity and fire, and the strength you possess is staggering. You make me feel things I have no idea what to do with because I've been so wrapped up in my own shit for the last decade that I have no clue what I'm going to do once it's over or if there will even be anything left—"

"North," Nyx said from behind me.

"I didn't expect to have to deal with you and Graham—"

"North," Nyx said again.

"What?" I whirled on him angrily.

"Lachlan was just shot—" I heard Kaelin gasp. "—they're rushing him to the house now, Doc's on his way there."

"Fuck!" I roared.

I turned back to Kaelin but there was a grim look on her face and she crossed her arms over her chest. She'd closed me out again.

"You should go," she said. "Sounds like you have a lot going on."

I growled in frustration and with one last look at her; I stalked towards the door.

"Nyx, leave Viktor and Kon here—come with me." I hesitated at the door and turned back to see her lower lip tremble even as anger sparked in her eyes. She had to watch me leave, again.

"I meant what I said. I care about you and would never be able to forgive myself if something happened to you."

Her lips pressed into a thin line and I wished I could say something to erase the hurt in her eyes.

"I don't know if that's enough," she whispered, then turned and disappeared deeper into her house.

19

ATLAS

We'd been going non-stop the last few days, and I was starting to feel the fatigue. Then this morning, I'd received a text from Lachlan letting me know Knox and Sakari hadn't checked in, so it was assumed they'd been taken too. It was to be expected but it still sucked. I was headed back to Alpha One, looking forward to a quick beer and maybe some time with Nyx if I could get him away from Kaelin duty, when my phone rang.

"There was an explosion at *NorTac*!" Lachlan yelled over the phone.

I could hear his bike in the background as he raced down the road.

"What?"

"Sounds like it's pretty bad," Lachlan continued. "Luckily it was mostly empty. I'm headed there—" I heard a screech of tires and then the line went dead.

"Lachlan?" Dread coiled in my stomach. "Lach! Damnit."

I whipped the car around, pulling up the tracking app on my phone and getting the location of Lachlan's tracking device. He was on one of the back roads headed into the office from Alpha One. I wasn't far.

I rounded the bend and came full speed on his location only to drive straight into gunfire. I drifted the car into the middle of the road in between Lachlan and his motorcycle that was laying in a ditch. He was behind it trying to take out an SUV with three men shooting at him. I pulled my gun and jumped from the car as Lachlan scrambled up the bank.

"Ammo?" He panted.

I tossed him a clip, and we popped up, peppering their car with bullets. I took out one man and motioned for Lach to flank the other two with me. As we rounded the car, the two men decided they'd had enough and put their SUV into drive, peeled away on smoking tires. The road curved quickly and they were gone.

I turned to Lachlan who stumbled, clutching his stomach. He was bleeding. I hurried to his side and he grimaced as I threw his arm over my shoulder.

"This is why I hate when you and Nyx ride those fucking bikes," I growled, dragging him to the SUV and depositing him into the passenger seat. He huffed a laugh as pain lined his features.

"Just adds to the thrill," Lachlan joked.

He was bleeding pretty heavily as I sped towards Alpha One, already on the phone with Doc who would meet us at the house. Then I dialed Nyx.

"Nyx—Lach was shot. We're headed back to the house—"

"How bad?"

"I'm still alive," Lachlan groaned. "My bike isn't though."

"Fuck, really?" Nyx cursed.

"Seriously?" I snapped. "It's a fucking bike! Lach is bleeding all over my car and you two are worried about a fucking bike?"

"Sorry Nyx," Lachlan said breathlessly. "He's probably going to take yours away now."

"Like hell he will," Nyx exclaimed. "Did you hear about the explosion? North is here now—"

"Yeah, that's where we were headed. I'll drop Lach off and then head over there."

Lachlan slumped over in the seat as he passed out.

"Fuck, Nyx, he passed out—" My hand reached across the console, pressing over his wound as his own hand slipped. "I have to go."

I hung up with Nyx, frantically trying to drive and apply pressure to Lachlan's stomach. I screamed through the gates and slammed to a stop at the front door of Alpha One. Luckily Doc was getting out of his car and rushed up to the passenger side. Together we got Lachlan out of the car and into the house.

Once I made sure he was situated with Doc in the infirmary, I headed back out to my car. I needed to get to *NorTac* to assess the damage and field law enforcement. I knew there was nothing I could do at home—he was in the best hands with Doc.

I sped back through the streets of the city, settling into the chaos of the moment. We knew shit would get crazy and part of me was reveling in it, knowing this was the beginning of the end. The other part was scared as hell something would happen to the people I loved. The last decade those bonds had only strengthened until I really didn't know what I would do without them.

I hoped I didn't have to find out.

I saw the lights and the yellow tape before I saw the building. Several blocks outside of the blast radius were cordoned off so I parked and got out. When I approached the tape, I nodded to the cop.

"I'm with NorTac. I need to speak with whoever is in charge."

I flashed my employee card. The cop looked me up and down then lifted the tape, nodding at me to follow him. The closer I got to the building, the more it was swarming with activity. The cop was saying something to someone but I was staring at the building—or what was left of it. One entire side was gone, smoking and still crumbling as it settled. The rest of it had collapsed down and I could see they were worried about it falling over into other buildings or the street as it was listing precariously. Overall, the damage was extensive. Message received.

"You're with Northern Tactical?"

I turned to the cop. One that looked like they were more in charge than the last one.

"Yeah," I nodded.

"We're still securing the area," he said. "Any idea why you'd be targeted?"

I shook my head, turning to look back at the wreckage.

"No, I don't," I lied.

Thank god the arsenal we kept underground wasn't completely under the office but stretched out another block. We'd sneak in once things cooled off and move everything. Otherwise, the rest was a loss we were willing to take.

I handed the cop my business card.

"I'm available to answer any questions," I continued.

My mind drifted back to when I'd stood on this same sidewalk, looking at the brand new building North had just bought. Nyx and I had looked up at the tall skyscraper, watching them finish putting 'NorTac' on the top and feeling like we were starting something big.

And we had. Now it was crumbling down in front of me.

Only, that's not what it represented to me.

The cop excused himself and I suppressed a smirk. While it had been a cool building, we weren't attached to it. It was all a means to an end and this end just meant an even better beginning.

20

THERON

I stormed through the front doors of the house that now felt more empty than it had in years. Nyx was on my heels as we made our way to the small wing of the house directly off the front door that served as our infirmary. The wonderful doctor we contracted with, Doc, as we affectionately called him, met us in the hallway.

"He's fine," Doc said to my unvoiced question. "Or he will be. The bullet nicked his liver, and he has a broken rib." Relief coursed through me, and I saw Nyx's shoulders sag as the tension left him.

"You can see him tomorrow, right now I've sedated him so his body can heal," Doc continued. "I'll stay a few more hours to make sure he remains stable."

"Thanks, Doc," I said, shaking his hand.

Nyx's phone rang as I turned and headed down the hall towards West's wing of the house. I'd known this was going to be rough before it got better. If I'd wanted easy and simple, I would have just spent the last ten years tracking him down and taking him out with an unsuspecting .50 cal from a distance. But of course, I'd wanted to make him suffer, knowing I'd have to endure the pain as well.

I found West sitting at his computer, code running across a screen in front of him as he sat back and watched it. The news was playing on low on another monitor, showing the destruction of the *NorTac* building. Sure enough, the bomb had taken out ten floors on the south side of the building and it was currently on fire.

"Turn that fucking shit off," I growled.

"He's giving us a fight, that's for sure." West removed the news feed and glanced up at me.

"Any luck finding the guys?" I asked.

"No, Vetticus turned their trackers off or cut them out—I'm not sure but they're dark. I'm still looking though. Is Lach okay?"

I nodded. "Atlas dropped him off here and then went back to run interference with law enforcement."

"If you need me in the field—"

"No, our strength lies in everything you're doing right now. We don't know where Vetticus is and that's the last piece of this entire puzzle. What's the status on Albatron?"

Nyx came in and handed both of us a beer.

"I talked to Theo earlier and King's team is trailing him. They'll keep us apprised."

"Good—" My phone rang.

"He's made contact," Demetrius said when I answered.

"You know what to do," I replied.

"Are you sure you want to do it this way?"

"I'll see you on the other side, my friend," I said.

Demetrius sighed. "I hope you know what you're doing."

21

GRAHAM

After storming away from Kaelin's house, I'd needed some space as much as the rest of us. I'd tried reaching out to Kaelin, but she said unless I was ready to talk to her about what was going on, I shouldn't bother. So here I was, pulling up to Alpha One after texting Nyx. I'd only been here one other time and the impressive compound still left me in awe.

I pushed open the front door and was greeted by Atlas.

"Ah, both dogs home in the doghouse," he winked and then laughed as I scowled at him. "Come on, Nyx told me you were coming—let's go shoot some shit—that always makes me feel better."

We headed downstairs to the gun range.

"How is she?" I asked as I loaded a few clips.

"Nyx said she's still pretty pissed off," Atlas said. "And hurt."

"Can't you tell her what's going on?"

Atlas finished loading an entire clip before he spoke again. "Don't get me wrong, I think she should know, but I support North. This is something we've been planning for over a decade—you and Kaelin weren't something we anticipated having to contend with."

I loaded another clip.

"Even though we went through the same trauma as he did, it's still not really my story to tell. We want this just as much as he does. Like he's said before, we will do whatever we need to do in order to succeed in this."

"Even at the cost of family?"

"The world will be a better place without Vetticus and *Atrox* in it and if that means we have to sacrifice ourselves to get our revenge and retribution for our families and the ones we've lost along the way—then yes. At the cost of everything—our morality, our love, even our lives—I know it doesn't make sense—"

"No, that's the problem," I sighed. "It does make sense. My brother was taken and I hunted down every single person responsible—then at the end of it all, I tried to take my own life because that's the road of destruction I wrought. I just never expected to be on the other side of things."

Atlas nodded, and we continued to load and prep a few guns.

"North wants to tell you," Atlas said, breaking the silence. "Including you lately means he trusts you and wants you to be a part of it all. The story is just daunting—I mean, there's a lot that went down and it's exhausting to tell it all. Most of us have been around since it all began and he hasn't had to fill anyone in for a long time. It's not an excuse, but I think it's something that's stopping him. He takes on a lot to protect us."

"Which is just so at odds with who I thought he was," I sent a target out into the range and turned back to Atlas. "He fucking bought and raped Kaelin for fuck's sake. And up until recently, that's the kind of man I thought he was."

"Oh, he still takes what he wants," Atlas chuckled. "But the Warren wasn't what it looked like, I can tell you that much. There are other things going on besides the Vetticus thing—" he shook his head. "But all of that is very much not my place to disclose."

I wondered what horrors caused a man to willingly put himself into that type of situation but I had enough questions about North and I didn't feel like adding more so I pushed it away for now.

Atlas sent his own target out then turned to me. "North is a complicated man who does things based on his own moral code. He's arrogant, ruthless, violent and by all accounts a sociopath—but, he is a relentless and dedicated leader, loyal and protective to the ones he's claimed as his own, and he's saved my life so many times, even if I didn't need this as much as him, I'd still be by his side."

I nodded. "That's what I'm starting to see. And I admire him for that. I just wished he'd be more forthcoming."

"He will, in his own time," Atlas said.

22

KAELIN

I was still so angry at Theron and Graham that I'd told them I needed a few days. I didn't understand why they couldn't just tell me what was going on. Theron was right when he said I didn't want to think about it—but that was when it was just harmless death threats. I only meant I didn't want to think about the 'what ifs.' This was definitely beyond that now and I wanted to know what caliber threat we were dealing with.

Obviously, this was some long standing vendetta between Theron and one of his enemies—I gathered that much—but I also was hurt that he hadn't asked me for help. I was the CTO of a fucking military company for god's sake. I know Theron had power and money and plenty of resources, but I always imagined the three of us tackling any enemy together—not me being locked away like some sex slave.

I guess I still harbored some insecurities about the Warren. Sometimes I wondered if he really wanted to be with me or if he still believed I was his property. I liked to think that wasn't the case, but now I wasn't so sure.

Theron had now left me twice without telling me what was going on and each time hurt worse. It didn't help that each time he seemed on the verge of trying to put into words how he really felt about me but fell short each time.

I wasn't about to help him figure it out.

We were adults and if we couldn't express how we felt about each other, I didn't want that kind of relationship. I was down for unconventional, but communication was universal and I needed at least that. So far, we were falling drastically short in that department.

I sat at my desk in my office. It was nearly ten o'clock at night and the other offices were dark. Maeve had gone home hours ago and I just couldn't bring myself to drive home. Nyx had been great the last few days but I missed my house not being overrun by Theron's men. Not to mention, now I didn't feel safe in my home again, a feeling I hadn't felt in some time.

I sighed, I really should get going, I wasn't going to sleep here, that would be silly. I tapped my phone, debating on whether I should call the guys and end my silent treatment. Maybe I would just call and hear their voice—that was harmless right? I dialed Graham.

"Hey, beautiful," he said. His deep voice washed over me, making me smile. I heard gunfire in the background.

"Hi," I said. "Are you at the range?"

"Yeah, at Alpha One," he said. "Still at work?"

Of course he knew where I was. "Yeah, just leaving actually."

I gathered my things and headed for the elevators.

"How's Lachlan?" I asked as the elevator descended.

"He's doing well, except for the fact he's refusing to rest," Graham said with a chuckle. "But Doc says th—" The phone went dead.

"Graham?"

I looked at the screen. The call had dropped.

I tried calling him again as the elevator passed the tenth floor but the call wouldn't go through. With a ding, the elevator opened into the lobby and I walked out, still messing with my phone. I tried to send a text, but the message went through green and said undelivered.

I'd just rounded the corner of the elevator hallway when the night lights abruptly cut off, casting the entire lobby into darkness. If it wasn't for the massive two-story wall of windows facing the front street, I wouldn't have been able to see anything. As it was, the street lights provided a bit of light. I got an uncomfortable feeling as I passed the vacant front desk. I picked up my pace only to stumble to a stop. A shadow moved near the doors leading to the garage. I took a step back.

The shadow moved again, and then a man in all black was running towards me. Fear clutched me as I turned and raced towards the stairs leading up to the second floor atrium.

I risked a glance behind me and wished I hadn't. He was too close.

I reached the landing before the second set of stairs and a weight slammed into me, sending us both to the ground. Panic overwhelmed me and for a moment every single defense move I'd ever been taught left my head. His hand came around to cover my mouth and I realized I was screaming,

Then it was like a calm stole over me and everything Theron and Graham drilled into me came rushing back. I got out of his hold, slamming my knee into his groin. Gaining my feet, I raced the rest of the way up the stairs.

The second floor was mostly tables and chairs in front of a small cafe and multiple lounge areas with a water feature and greenery. I threw down a potted tree into the man's path, causing him to stumble as I raced across the space, throwing chairs as I crossed into the cafe area. He reached me and grabbed me from behind, pulling me to him with a growl.

"I was warned you'd be a spicy one," the man panted.

I stomped on his foot and elbowed him in the face. He let me go.

I ran into the kitchen, bent on finding a weapon but he was right on my heels and we crashed into the prep area and into a massive shelf of pots and pans. The sound was deafening as everything fell around us. I scrambled across the floor and a hand curled around my ankle, dragging me backwards. I clawed at the slick floor, looking for anything I could use. I saw the knives had been spilled across the tile, mixed with the pots and pans. I grabbed one, just as he flipped me onto my back.

"You're lucky Vetticus said not to kill you because you're really testing me, bitch."

In answer, I sat up and brought the knife down. He was quick and deflected it so that instead of his neck, it bit into his shoulder. He cried out but didn't let go of my calf, instead, his jaw clenched and he yanked me towards him hard with a growl. His hand closed around my neck while the other yanked the knife out. He replaced his hand on my neck with the blade, pressing down until I hardly dared breathe for fear of it digging into my skin.

"Be sure to share with Kraven what happened here," he sneered. "Compliments of Vetticus."

My breath was painful gasps as his other hand fumbled with my jeans. I fought him with my hands and kicked out at him. He slapped me so hard my ears rang and I whimpered as the knife bit into my skin under my jaw.

Our combined strained breathing was the only sound as he finally unbuttoned my pants. I struggled again and just as he was about to hit me for a second time, there was a gunshot and blood exploded over me. The man's body knelt suspended in place for a moment before it toppled forward on top of me. I shrieked and scrambled out from under it, twisting to see who'd shot him. A pair of familiar grey eyes the intensity of a raging storm met mine as Theron stepped into view.

My exhale of relief turned into a sob as I got to my knees, taking deep breaths to calm the panic before I could even think about getting to my feet. He grabbed my arm, helping me stand, and I clutched at him, burying my face in his chest. He dug his fingers into my hair and held me against his beating heart that felt as erratic as mine.

"How did you—? Did Graham—?" I couldn't finish any of my sentences as I pulled my face away enough to look up at him.

"Graham called me when your call dropped," he said. "Are there others?"

I shook my head.

"Graham's coming." He must have had a comms unit in because a moment later Graham rounded the corner of the kitchen, his own gun out and ready.

"Wyatt is dead," he said to Theron.

"Who?" I asked.

"I had a man on overwatch—sniper across the street—" he said when he saw my confusion. Theron gently pushed me towards Graham and he held me just as tightly.

"Fuck, beautiful. Thank god you called me," he said.

I was rapidly collecting myself and with the drop in adrenaline came my anger at the situation. I pushed away from Graham and held out my hands, closing my eyes briefly to grab onto the thoughts raging through my head.

I opened my eyes and looked directly at Theron. "Who is Vetticus?"

He was good at hiding his surprise, except I knew him so intimately I saw his jaw clench and annoyance briefly crossed his features.

"An old enemy," he said.

"Well, that man told me this was a message from him," I said and watched Theron's eyes grow black with intensity. "He used your name 'Kraven,'" I added. Graham and Theron exchanged a look and my eyes narrowed. "Okay, I need to know what's going on and I need to know right fucking now."

"It's complicated," Theron said.

"It's complicated?" I echoed. "It's complicated? That's all you have to say? After someone broke into my house and now nearly raped me? It's fucking complicated?" My voice had slowly risen until I was definitely yelling the last few words, my chest heaving in fury.

My jaw dropped when Theron had the balls to take out his phone and make a call. I looked over at Graham, who ran a hand over his face like he was just as frustrated.

"Nyx," Theron said. "I need a clean up crew at Phox. Vetticus sent someone to rough her up—she's not hurt—Wyatt is dead—yeah." He hung up and gestured towards the door.

"Let's go," he said.

"Are you fucking kidding me?"

"I'm not having this conversation here!" Theron snapped, part of his control slipping.

My mouth pressed into a thin line but I knew he was right and stormed my way past him out into the atrium. No one spoke as we made our way down to the garage. The men kept their guns out, on alert for any additional threats but we made it to the cars without issue.

"Get in," Theron said, gesturing to his Aston Martin. When I didn't move his jaw clenched. "That wasn't a request."

I looked over at Graham but he holstered his weapon and nodded to the Aston. Big help he was. *Traitor.*

"Meet you back at Alpha One," Theron said to Graham.

Graham held the door open for me as I sank into the passenger seat.

"I'm not staying at Alpha One," I said petulantly.

His knuckles were white from how hard he was gripping the steering wheel but he didn't speak. The next few minutes as the lull of the car began to smooth my anger, I became hyper aware of the fact I was covered in blood. My red stained fingers dug into my thighs to keep them from shaking and a wave of claustrophobia assaulted me.

My chest constricted and I was suddenly gasping in gulps of air, trying not to make it obvious I was having an anxiety attack. Except Theron was way too observant for his own good and the car whipped over to the side of the road. His hand snake its way around the back of my neck.

"Look at me," he said firmly.

I turned my head but focused on his other hand resting on the middle console, refusing to meet his eyes.

"Breathe, darlin'," he murmured.

A rogue tear slipped down my cheek as I took multiple shaky breaths and finally could inhale fully. Theron's hand retreated, but not before he wiped the tear away and pulled the car back out onto the road. I looked out the window, not wanting to see the blood on me or look at him.

We drove the rest of the way in silence and when we pulled up to Alpha One, I shoved open the door before the car was even fully stopped. Graham arrived and stepped out of his car just as Nyx came down the steps with Atlas on his heels. Theron approached me, taking me by the arms to try and stop me from going inside. I jerked out of his grasp but he tried to grab me again.

"Kaelin—"

Before I could think through my actions, I slapped him across the face. Hard.

Theron froze and I watched him try to get his face under control. No one dared move. I heaved in breath after breath as I fought for control and steeled myself as I waited for the retaliation I was sure to receive from him.

Except it never came.

I expected him to grab me. Shove me into the car at my back.

Drag me into the house.

Something.

Instead he did...*nothing*. And for some reason that was so much worse.

He looked at me, nodded once, then turned and disappeared into the house.

23

GRAHAM

You could have heard a pin drop when Kaelin slapped North as we all waited for the retaliation. Except it never came. Instead I watched him disappear into the house. Nyx immediately followed him while Atlas came down the steps and put his arm around Kaelin, talking to her quietly as he led her into the house.

"Graham can take you to get cleaned up," Atlas said, looking at me over her head. I pulled her against me and this time she let me lead her upstairs to the room I'd been staying in. I helped her out of her clothes as the shower water heated.

"I shouldn't have slapped him," she said finally.

I kept my smile hidden as I helped her pull down her jeans.

"I think he'll survive," I said dryly.

"But—I did it in front of Nyx and Atlas...and you," she insisted. "That's so disrespectful. I just couldn't take it anymore. I'm so tired of his bullshit."

"I'm sure they've done their fair share of punching each other."

I gently pushed her under the spray and leaned against the entrance to the shower. She watched the water run red for a minute before she grabbed soap and scrubbed the rest away.

Kaelin finished showering in silence. She didn't have any clothes here so I gave her one of my oversized t-shirts that swamped her but also did things to me that weren't appropriate at the moment.

"I'm finding out what's going on," she said finally.

The look on her face when she turned to me was one I'd seen a few times when we were surviving together. A strong resolve to get what she wanted and fuck everything else.

"Yeah," I nodded. "It's time. Whether he likes it or not, we need to know."

"So you'll support me now?"

"Princess, I've always supported you," I said, wrapping my arms around her. "I only know bits and pieces, not enough of the full picture to tell you anything. I'm sorry you think I'm keeping things from you. It isn't my story to tell anyway—but at this point, it's escalated to include us."

Kaelin nodded. The silence was broken by her stomach growling and I chuckled.

"Let's get you something to eat," I said, nodding towards the door.

We made it down to the kitchen and she hopped up on a barstool while I rummaged around the kitchen. Anytime I turned to look at her, she was chewing on her bottom lip, staring off into space with a crease between her brows.

"I'll be right back," she said abruptly.

I didn't protest but watched her leave the kitchen. I knew better than to think she was just going to the bathroom.

She was looking for trouble.

But maybe it was time she found some.

24

THERON

I heard Kaelin's voice from down the hall. "I'm sorry—"

I found her in West's room. One glance inside and I saw several of his monitors had *Atrox* information displayed and Kaelin had just jumped up from West's chair wearing nothing but an oversized t-shirt.

"North, I'm sorry—I stepped away for a minute—" West insisted.

I held up my hand to stop him. Kaelin went from looking sheepish at being caught by West to fuming mad as she rounded on me.

"What the fuck is all of that?" She demanded, throwing her hand back at the monitors. "What is *Atrox*? And why the fuck are there invoices from *Phox* here?"

I didn't answer for a long moment. Maybe it was her slapping me that solidified it, although we'd talk about that later—but it was time to stop running. It was time to tell her.

The commotion had drawn Graham. I could feel his presence lingering in the doorway. *Good.* It was time to pull them all out of the shadows and show them the real hell.

"Show her," I said to West.

He'd been trying to slowly slink out of the room but froze at my command before moving over and taking the seat Kaelin had vacated. He pulled up a few invoices and *Atrox* business information with a photo of Vetticus.

"*Atrox Gaming Inc.* is an underground company that kidnaps individuals with military and law enforcement background and forces them to play in live action capture the flag games with live ammo—"

"What—like a video game?"

"Yes—Vetticus is a recruiter. Teams are owned and sponsored by rich men and the games are broadcasted for people to bet on the outcome of the players. Me, Nyx and Atlas were on one of Vetticus' personal *Atrox* teams. He held us captive for nearly three years."

I'd stunned her to silence.

She was staring at me, lips parted and eyes wide with shock as she took in everything I said. After a moment, she shook her head.

"What does *Phox* have to do with this?" But her eyes went to one of the invoices and I saw her face fall in the glow of the screens. "Oh shit..."

"Military drones. We have invoices going back years. There's something else too."

I hesitated. This was the part I had the most trepidation around.

"What's the other thing then? Tell me, Theron. It's time," she demanded.

"Show her the other thing," I said to West.

West hesitated. "Are you sure?"

"Do it."

He clicked a few buttons and another photograph filled the screen.

Kaelin leaned forward to get a better look.

"Oh my god..." She turned to me, eyes wide.

I heard Graham make a sound behind me as he pieced it together at the same time. The resemblance was all in the eyes. The person I thought was dead—only to discover a few years ago that she was in fact very much alive.

"Her name is Emersyn," I said. "Emersyn North. She's my daughter."

"I-I don't understand," Kaelin said breathlessly.

"I know," I said. "But you will."

It was time to go back to the beginning.

16 YEARS AGO

Vengeance and retribution require a long time; it is the rule.

C DICKENS

25

THERON

"Do you believe in God?" Cole asked.

His feet were kicking back and forth above the water where we sat on the dock. I had no idea what was going on in his little ten-year-old brain to provoke such a question.

"I'm not sure," I said honestly. "Why?"

"Tommy says God is in charge," he said. "Does that mean even you and mom have to listen to him?"

I smiled. "I'm not sure if I trust someone I can't prove is real."

"Tommy said that's called faith," Cole said sagely, his blue eyes turned up to look at me.

"What do you think?" I asked him.

Cole was quiet as he looked back out over the lake. "It's kind of fun to think about someone creating all of this." He gestured to the serene lake in front of us and then back behind him, encompassing the woods and our family cabin situated up a small slope. It was beautiful and peaceful.

"Maybe this is what heaven is like," he said.

"Maybe."

"I don't like thinking we just disappear once we die," Cole said.

"Why are you thinking about dying?"

He shrugged his small shoulders. "Tommy said if I don't believe in God, I won't go to heaven."

"Tommy says a lot of things, doesn't he?" I grumbled.

"Well, his dad is a pastor," Cole said. His grin made his dimples pop.

"I think religion is a great comfort to people who are looking for that sort of accountability and structure in their lives." I put my arm around him and pulled him into my side. "But you can believe whatever you want, son. That doesn't make you any less of a good person."

Cole seemed satisfied with the conversation and nestled into my side

more. I squeezed him to me and kissed the top of his head. I reveled in
these small moments with him. I'd been deployed during much of the twins'
younger years and now spent every moment I could catching up on all the
time I missed.

Movement in the water caught my eye.

"I think you have a fish!" I said.

Cole stood up and grabbed his pole, excitement lighting up his face as he
reeled in the line.

"It's heavy!" He said.

I came and stood next to him, ready to lend a hand if he needed it.

"Easy does it—pull the pole back and then reel the slack in," I instructed.

I saw the flash of silver scales as the fish thrashed against the surface and
then it was in the air as Cole reeled it up onto the dock.

"I caught a fish!" He exclaimed, jumping up and down.

I laughed and grabbed it, carefully taking out the hook.

"And a nice sized one too."

I handed it to him by the mouth and showed him how to hold it.

"Hold that up," I said. "And let me take your picture."

"Emy is gonna freak!" Cole giggled as the fish whipped its tail, splashing
water on him. I pulled out my phone and framed the picture.

"It's nearly as big as your head," I grinned. "Do you want to release it or eat
it?" Cole seemed to consider it seriously before crouching down at the edge
of the dock and gently dropping the fish back into the water. He stood up as
he watched it splash away and I put my arm around his shoulders.

"I don't want to take him away from his home," Cole said.

"Fair enough," I turned us towards the cabin. "Let's go see what the girls
are making for dinner."

"I hope it's not fish!" Cole laughed and ran up the hill towards the house
calling for his twin sister. "Em! Wait till you see the fish I caught!"

26

THERON

I walked into the kitchen and came up behind Whitney. I wrapped my arms around her and breathed her in. She smelled like wood smoke mixed with her vanilla perfume. I looked over her shoulder at the pot she was stirring.

"What are you making?" I asked.

"Spaghetti."

Whit turned her head and looked at me before pressing her lips to mine. My hand slipped up into her hair and the kiss deepened as I touched my tongue to hers, tasting the wine she was drinking as she made dinner. My other hand slowly slid down her stomach to the top of her jeans, my fingers teasing the edge before slipping beneath. Just as I was about to touch her clit, I heard a rustling and two voices spoke in unison behind us.

"Ewwww!"

I yanked my hand back, and we turned around to see the twins staring at us from the other side of the kitchen counter. Luckily our bodies had blocked my explorations from looking like anything but innocent hugging, but I still narrowed my eyes at them.

"Nothing wrong with your mother and I loving on each other," I said.

"Yeah, but kissing is gross," Emy said, pushing her riot of blond hair out of her face in order to stick out her tongue. I kissed Whit once more on the side of her head as she smiled and went back to stirring the sauce, then I turned towards the kids and smirked.

"Oh really?" I stalked towards them. "Gross huh?"

"Yup!" Cole said. "Full of cooties!"

I lunged for them and they both screamed and scattered, running for the living room. I chased after them, deciding to go after Emy first. She ran around the couch, laughing hysterically. Cole threw a pillow at me before I launched myself over the couch and grabbed Emy as she ran past me.

"Got ya!" I pulled her in and kissed her excessively all over her face while she shrieked and laughed.

"No! Cooties! Ewww!"

Cole came up behind me, and a pillow hit my back.

"Let her go!" He said around his laughter.

I turned and grabbed him with my other arm, pulling them both in and planting kisses anywhere I could as they squirmed and laughed so hard they became breathless. I laughed as I let them go and we all collapsed onto the couch.

"Dad, show Emy my fish!" Cole said. Emy crawled up on my lap and nestled against my chest while I pulled up the picture on my phone.

"It's huge!" She giggled.

"I told you!" Cole said, looking proud.

"Can I catch one?" Emy asked, lifting her head to look at me.

I nodded. "Sure, tomorrow morning you can give it a go."

"I bet mine will be bigger," Emy teased.

"Nah uh," Cole said.

I fixed Emy with a look, warning her against retaliating and she smirked at me but closed her mouth. She put her arms around my neck.

"Daddy, can you read *Little Red Riding Hood* tonight?"

"Again?" Cole whined. "Can't we read something else?"

Emy frowned and stuck out her bottom lip in a pout that could have melted even the strongest of authoritarians and I chuckled.

"Pleeeeease," Emy pleaded. "Can you tell the version where the girl scares away the wolf?"

"That's not even how it goes," Cole complained.

"I *know*," Emy said, scowling at Cole before turning back to me and fixing a brilliant smile on her face. The smile she always gave me when she wanted something. I couldn't ever say no. "I like when you make up different versions."

"Well, I like it when the wolf eats the grandma and the mountain man comes and rescues the girl," Cole said.

Emy rolled her eyes. "It's so boring though—everyone knows that story."

"That's the point," Cole argued. "It's a fairy tale."

"I can tell it both ways," I interrupted, ending the feud.

"Cole!" Whit called. "Come help me set the table."

Cole ran off and Emy settled back against my chest. My arms went around her as she snuggled into me. We sat in silence for a long time just looking out the window at the lake and listening to Cole tell Whit all about the fish he caught.

"I think I'd be too afraid to fight the wolf," she said.

"Really? Even if it was threatening Cole?"

She seemed to think about that seriously for a long moment.

"Maybe, but I'd still be scared."

"Sometimes we have to do things even when we're scared."

"Have you ever been scared?"

"Yes, many times," I said.

"Yeah right," Emy said. "Name one!"

I laughed. "When I proposed to your mother."

"What? No way!" She lifted her head to look at me.

"Yup," I said, grinning. "I was terrified she'd say no."

She giggled, and I tapped her nose. "Being brave opens up a lot of doors and takes you out of your comfort zone which is where all the magic happens."

"I guess," Emy said. "But that doesn't sound very scary."

"Well, regardless, whatever it is—only by moving through fear can we lead a courageous life. Fear shouldn't ever stop us from living, loving or protecting those around us."

"Dinner is ready!" Whit called from the kitchen.

"Dinner!" Cole echoed after her.

I chuckled and extracted myself from Emy as I got to my feet.

"Let's go eat."

A few hours later, I passed Whit in the hall as she came out of the kids' bedroom.

"Meet me on the porch?" She asked.

I pulled her to me and kissed her. "Can't wait, gorgeous."

I walked into the room she'd just left and walked over to the bed Cole was in. I kissed him on the forehead as I pulled the covers up under his chin.

"Night, bud," I said.

"Night, Dad," he answered, his eyes already heavy with sleep.

I walked over to the other bed and kissed Emy's nose. She wrinkled her face in protest but couldn't help the giggle that escaped.

"Night, Em," I said.

I headed for the door and turned off the light.

"Love you," Emy said.

"I love you too."

"I love you more," Cole chimed in.

"Impossible," I said with a smile, before softly shutting the door.

I walked out onto the back porch and found Whit sitting on the steps looking out over the moonlit lake. I sat down behind her so she was sitting between my legs and wrapped my arms around her.

"Cole asked me about God today," I said dryly.

Whit chuckled. "Yeah, he's been hanging out with Tommy at school lately." She leaned back against me. "Tommy has been being bullied, apparently."

I smiled against her hair. "I don't know where he gets his kindness from."

She laughed. "I have no idea. But I think it's sweet."

"He's a good kid." Pride swelled in me at the thought of how kind and thoughtful Cole was. "So is Emy."

"Emersyn is chaos reincarnate," Whit said dryly. "But we know where she gets *that* from." It was my turn to laugh, and I nuzzled into her neck, nipping her ear.

"I don't know—I seem to recall there being countless summer nights you ran wild around town." She turned her head and met my gaze, her eyes reflecting the moonlight.

"It was all to catch your attention," she said mischievously.

"You have it, baby," I whispered. "You've always had it." I brought my lips to hers and kissed her before pulling back.

"Come on—"

We got to our feet, and I took her hand, pulling her towards the dock. At the edge I yanked her back into me and she laughed breathlessly, running a hand down my face and looking at me with a reverence that made my heart ache. I didn't know if there was a God, but when she looked at me like that, I had to believe there was something divine.

We undressed each other in the moonlight, and for a moment I stood soaking in her raw beauty. She looked like a goddess of the night. All shadows and curves with hints of silver when the moon hit her dark hair.

"Stunning," I murmured.

I grabbed her hand, and without hesitating pulled her off the dock with me into the water. We surfaced, and she immediately was in my arms, legs wrapped around my waist as I kept us afloat. Her lips found mine, and we breathed each other in as though our shared breath was the only thing keeping us alive. Maybe it was. As we clung to each other, I wondered how in the world a man like me could ever be blessed with a life like this.

27

THERON

The next morning I went out on a little rowboat. Emy sat across from me, determined to catch a fish of her own. I'd allowed the boat to drift around a little curve of the bank and sat and readied her line for her.

"Alright, let's see if you can catch one bigger than Cole's," I said and winked at her. She smirked at me, an almost comical expression on her young face. It made her eyes scrunch up, and I bit back a laugh.

"I can do that—I always beat him."

"You two are competitive for sure," I said dryly, handing her the pole.

"Well, I *am* older," she insisted, lifting her nose in the air as she cast the line out.

"You're twins," I said flatly. "You're the same age."

"Yeah, but mom said I came out first!" She said proudly.

I chuckled, letting her have it. I watched her as she settled back to wait for her fish to bite. I had no idea where she got her bright blond hair from. Whit showed me pictures of when she was younger and her hair had been a dark blond so she said Emersyn's hair would probably darken with age like hers had, but right now it was as bright as a wheat field at sunset.

She might have Whit's hair, but she had my eyes. Blue eyes, nearly gray, stared out over the world with the wonder and curiosity of a child. I sighed, thinking about all the men I'd have to beat off of her when she was older. She was going to be a beautiful handful. Emy's line bobbed and her eyes lit up excitedly.

"I got one!"

"Bring it in easy," I said, leaning forward with the net ready.

She bit her lip in concentration, brow furrowed as she brought the line in, the thrashing fish sending up splashes the closer it got. By the time it was flopping on the bottom of the boat, Emy's face was flushed with victory, already gloating.

"It's so much bigger," she said smugly as she watched me pull out the hook.

"Well, pick it up, let's document it."

I showed her where to pick it up, and she lifted it as I pulled out my phone. She smirked for the camera and I took the picture, smiling down at it afterwards. As much as she tried to be smug, the look on her face in the picture was one of pure childish joy for beating her brother.

"I want to bring it home," she said.

"Okay, if we do that, you have to kill it and we'll have it for dinner." She looked at me then back down at the fish for a long moment, watching it gasp for air as its struggles diminished the longer it was out of the water.

"How do I kill it?" She asked. I pulled my knife from my belt and laid it against the fish.

"Cut here." I flipped the knife and handed it to her. "Careful, it's sharp."

"I *know*, dad," she whined.

I didn't know if it was the right thing to do, handing a knife to a ten-year-old. The blade looked comically large in her smaller hand. But I'd learned how to hunt at an early age and if my kids wanted to learn, I was more than eager to teach them.

Emy laid the knife on the fish, grasping the body as well as she could with her other hand. The fish thrashed again, and she almost lost her grip. I made my hands lay flat against my thighs, worry washing over me at the thought of the knife slipping and cutting her. But she adjusted and put her weight into it, then dug the blade into the fish. When it was dead, she looked up with pride.

"Good job," I said, reaching out for the knife. I could see she wanted to try and hand it back the way I'd done, but I grabbed her wrist before she could handle the blade. "Do you want to try and catch another?"

"No, let's go home and show Cole!"

We docked the boat on the shore and Emy picked up her fish. I slung my arm around her small shoulders and kissed her hair.

"You did good," I said. "I'll have to show you how to—"

The crunch of gravel caught my attention, cutting off my words. Two black SUVs pulled up around the front of the house. Five men with assault rifles climbed out the first one. Followed by six in the second. They hadn't seen us yet. Without a second thought, I pulled Emy behind a tree and knelt down in front of her.

"Who are they?" Emy asked apprehensively.

I had no idea, but it didn't look good.

I took her by the shoulders and met her gaze. "I want you to run into those woods and hide. Do not come out until I come find you, understand?"

"What about mom and Cole?"

"I'll get them." I looked back at the house. One man appeared around the corner of the wrap-around porch, sweeping the backyard. I pulled out my knife and wrapped her hands around it.

"If anyone but me comes after you—aim here—" I pointed to a few areas on me. "—or here." Her lip quivered as she stared at the knife in her hand. I pulled her chin up so she had to meet my eyes.

"Got it?" I tried to keep my voice level and calm but I could tell I was scaring her. "Emy, do you understand?"

Her eyes widened and filled with tears but she nodded quickly. I grabbed her head and pulled her in, kissing her fiercely on the forehead before pulling back and meeting her eyes. I didn't want to leave her like this—unprotected—and my heart lodged in my throat.

"Can you be brave for me?" A nod. "That's my girl. I love you. Now—go!"

I turned her and lightly shoved her towards the trees. She took a few steps and turned back.

"Go!" I barked, and she took off.

My heart lurched again, but I shoved aside my fears and let my military training surface as I drew my .45 and stepped out from behind the trees. I was yards from the porch when the man turned. I put a bullet in his head and took the stairs in one leap to grab his AR and some extra ammo. I checked the gun quickly before moving towards the back door.

I didn't stop to wonder who these men were. Their gear was generic and gave away nothing regarding what organization they were working for. The weapons were military grade, but that didn't mean anything. They could be contractors, hired hit men—I didn't know. The only thing on my mind was getting Whit and Cole out safely.

I carefully opened the back door and edged inside. I cleared the living room and heard hushed voices from the kitchen. Edging around the corner, I carefully revealed the kitchen, keeping out of sight. There were two men standing on the other side of the island. I stepped out and pulled the trigger.

I dropped both men before I had to lunge for the cover of the island as the gunfire drew a man in from the family room. He walked in spraying bullets. I stayed low and watched his reflection in the oven before I leaned out and fired, hitting him in the leg. He went down, and I quickly stepped out to finish him.

Heading for the doorway of the family room, a man rushed in with no regard for his corners. I grabbed his gun before he could fire point blank. I slammed my elbow into his face just as arms wrapped around me. I backed hard into the wall, heard a grunt, and quickly turned my gun to fire into his stomach. His grip loosened enough for me to lunge forward and tackle the other one into the family room.

I lost my gun in the scuffle and dodged to the side as he came at me with a knife. I met his attack with a sharp hit to his neck that sent him crashing backwards into the coffee table. I lunged for the gun at the same time as the other man and once I grabbed it; I twisted onto my back and shot him in the face. He fell forward onto me.

I shoved him off and heard movement upstairs as the floorboards creaked. Fear clawed its way through my composure again as I made my way up the stairs, clearing the hallway and each room along it. I held my breath as I nudged open the kid's room but it was empty.

I saw the master bedroom door cracked and headed towards it, already knowing I wasn't going to like what I found.

I pushed open the door.

28

THERON

D addy!"

Whit and Cole were huddled together on the floor near the window, gripping each other tightly while a man trained an AR on them. Just the sight of a gun being pointed at my little boy had my blood running hot. Cole's eyes were fearful as they met mine and Whit had a cut above her eye along with a bloody lip.

Rage ignited in me as I took a step forward only to feel the barrel of a gun get pressed into my temple from a man standing just inside the door.

"Drop the gun."

This came from a man seated in the armchair across the room. He was not much older than me, maybe mid to late thirties with a hawk-like face and thin build. He was all harsh edges and long limbs with slicked back black hair and sleeves rolled up his forearms revealing a tattoo on his left arm that looked like a logo or a brand I didn't recognize. He was the only one not wearing tactical gear and carried himself like the one in charge.

"Drop the gun," he said again as we stared at each other.

I hesitated, but I knew I wouldn't be able to do anything without risking Whit and Cole so I slowly lowered the gun to the ground and it was kicked out of my reach.

"Have a seat," the man in the chair said, gesturing to the bench at the foot of the bed. I slowly made my way over to it and perched on the edge. The man's features twisted into a cruel smile.

"I expected some excitement from you," he said, looking me over. "You didn't disappoint."

"What do you want?" I growled.

The man smiled. "You military men are all the same. At the end of the day you feed off of violence."

"I'm retired," I said.

"Ah, but it never really leaves you—the bloodlust," he said. "I'm assuming you dispatched my team downstairs. I bet it felt good to kill them."

I didn't say anything and he chuckled. "It always amazes me how you all think you can commit all the atrocities of war and then come home and do this—" he gestured around the house and encompassed Whit. "—playing house, thinking you can live a normal life." He looked back at me. "You get bored, don't you?"

"You don't know anything about me."

"Actually I do," he said. "I've read your file. It's a provocative read."

"My file?"

He stood up and walked over to Whit and Cole. I went to rise but the masked man pushed me backwards with his AR shoved against my chest.

"You have quite the resume." He ran his Glock down Whit's cheek, brushing her hair behind her ear with the barrel. She cringed and leaned away. "Had all the makings of a career soldier—except for her."

"Don't fucking touch her," I snarled. I went to stand again, but the man pressed the gun against Whit's temple and I stilled. She whimpered, eyes wide looking at me fearfully.

"Who are you?" I demanded. He turned back to me and Whit clutched Cole tightly as silent tears trailed down his cheeks.

"I go by Vetticus," he answered. "I'm a recruiter, trainer, sponsor...I wear many hats."

"A recruiter for what?"

"*Atrox Gaming*," he said.

"Never heard of it."

"That's intentional," he smirked. "One of those invitation only things."

"If this is an invitation, I'm declining," I said.

"Unfortunately, it doesn't work that way," he said. "If *Atrox* wants you for the games, there's not much you can do about it."

"Games?"

Vetticus chuckled. "I save the best for the teams I sponsor of course. Perks of the job and all that. We'll see if you make the cut. I have a feeling you'll be a crowd favorite."

"Let her go," I said. "I'll go with you—just let her go."

Vetticus' eyes sharpened, and an amused look crossed his face.

"You are not in control," he said. "You'll learn that the hard way I'm afraid."

"Dad—" Cole whimpered.

Vetticus' head whipped towards him and he reached down and pulled him out of Whit's arms.

"No! No!" Whit struggled to hold on to Cole but the man behind her grabbed her and dragged her backwards. She thrashed against him until he slapped her and she fell back against the wall. I surged to my feet, only to get the butt of the rifle across my face. I fell to one knee, wiping blood out of my eyes and glared over at Vetticus who now held Cole in front of him.

"Cole, look at me," I hissed. "It's okay, bud—"

I didn't know what else to say but the minute his eyes met mine, it seemed to take the edge off the fear and he wiped the tears off his face. Vetticus crouched down behind Cole and my attention jumped to him.

"He can't help you, kid," Vetticus sneered, cruel amusement glittered in his eyes. Cole was still looking at me and seemed to draw strength from my anger because he scowled and then to my surprise, he snapped his foot back and kicked Vetticus between the legs. His grip on Cole loosened enough for him to slip out and run to me. I didn't hesitate and pulled my knife from my boot as I knocked the gun trained on me aside and slammed the blade into the man's thigh. He collapsed, giving Cole a clear path out the door.

"Cole, run!"

I saw Cole take off down the hall and launched myself at Vetticus. We crashed into the wall, plaster cracking around us as I got my arms around his neck. He punched me and we careened into the nightstand, toppling the lamp. I landed a solid blow to his head, and he dropped, dazed and unsteady. I heard a cry, but it was from the man holding Whit. She'd grabbed between his legs and sent him to his knees. I pulled her to her feet, and we sprinted out the door.

"Where's Emy?" She asked once we were in the hallway.

"I sent her into the woods."

We made it down the stairs, and I dragged Whit around the corner and straight into the man I'd stabbed who left to hunt Cole. I attacked him and wrestled the gun away as Whit scrambled down the hall towards the kitchen. I disarmed the man quickly and smashed the gun back into his face. He stumbled back, and I whirled towards him.

I was about to pull the trigger when I heard a gunshot behind me. I turned and watched Whit stumble backwards into the kitchen island. She looked down at her stomach and clutched it as she turned to me slowly, shock in her wide eyes.

"No," I breathed.

I reached her just as she fell and guided her to the ground. I grabbed a nearby hand towel and pushed it under her hands.

"Here—it's okay—it's okay baby, I got you."

She sobbed and clutched at my shirt. "Theron—"

"Don't talk, it's okay, you're okay—" My hand left a bloody smear on her cheek. She whimpered, and a sob escaped as pain lined her face before her eyes slowly dropped closed.

"No...no! Whit!" She slipped out of my arms as I frantically tried to wake her. "Whitney!" I called her name as I patted her face repeatedly. Her eyes fluttered, and she moaned.

"You're gonna be fine! Please...Whit, hold on—" Fear clutched me and my vision blurred as I felt my heart seize in my chest at the thought of losing her. Shadows loomed over us, and then I was being dragged away from her.

"No!" I fought viciously to get back to her.

"Enough!" Vetticus roared.

"Daddy!" I froze.

Another set of hands joined the first and dragged me to the edge of the family room where Vetticus once again had Cole in his clutches.

"Touching. It really is. But I'm tired of this game. I have a better one in store for you," he said. "It's time to go."

The world slowed and I watched in horror as Vetticus brought the knife in his hand up to Cole's neck. Panic gripped every fiber of my soul. I was lunging for him, fighting with everything I had. The knife moved across Cole's neck.

"NO!" I roared. "No! Cole!"

All I saw was blood.

"I'm going to kill you!" I screamed.

Cole. My boy. So much blood.

Chaos took over.

Everyone was moving and screaming at once.

Pressure slammed into my head and the ground rushed up to meet me as I watched Cole fall. The coppery scent of blood assaulted me as a knee drove into the back of my neck, holding my head down as my son's blood pooled across the wood towards me.

I scrambled in it, my hands clawing the floor as I attempted to get to him. Unhinged sounds came from me as my body shook with grief and rage and the overwhelming urge to take him into my arms.

His little hand reached out and I just barely grasped the tips of his fingers as I watched the life drain from his eyes, still open wide in surprise.

No. No. No. Please god, no.

He couldn't be dead.

But as vacant eyes stared back at me, I had to face the horrifying truth. Bile rose in my throat as the growing pool of his blood touched my cheek. I was sobbing now, with no idea what words were coming out of my mouth.

Someone was screaming. It might have been me.

My ears were ringing and I heard a cry of distress as I was hauled to my feet. I fought savagely, my attention shifting to Whit still laying on the kitchen floor. Her eyes were open in horror, tears pouring down her face. She stretched out a bloody hand towards me, her mouth forming my name and then I was being dragged outside towards one of the SUVs.

Panic set in and I fought viciously to get back into the house. The sting of a needle bit into my neck and everything grew hazy. Sounds receded and before the world went dark I smelled gasoline and realized this couldn't be heaven—I wasn't blessed like I thought—this was hell and I was finally being called home.

29

THERON

Awareness swept through me slowly. I thought the pain would come with it, but there was only a deep numbness as though the pain was so deep and vast I simply couldn't wrap my consciousness around it. I was naked, restrained with my arms above my head, only able to support myself on the balls of my feet. My hands were already numb, but I felt something trickle down my arms and looked up to see blood running from my wrists rubbed raw by the metal.

The room I was in was large, empty and dark except for a skylight high above me casting me in a bright spotlight. I was incredibly thirsty, my throat so dry I couldn't swallow around my swollen tongue. Whatever they'd drugged me with had left me with a hangover but that was nothing compared to the agony that assaulted me as soon as the memories crashed through me.

Nothing could numb me from that grief. I choked on my breath as it was ripped from my lungs, the pain so visceral and raw, it had me sobbing again.

My family—*gone*. Not just gone. *Dead*.

All because of me.

I wanted to die—but I didn't have the means to do it. I looked up again, wondering if I could make the chains cut deep enough into my wrists to allow me to bleed out. I sagged harder against them, if nothing else to welcome the pain because it was no less than I deserved.

What kind of man was I? I couldn't save my family.

The twins. Whitney. Everything I loved—gone.

I hoped whoever came through that door would kill me. I wondered if I begged, if they'd do it for me. But I already knew if these people wanted me dead, I'd already be dead. My breath was a ragged sound in my chest as I hung there reliving the nightmare on replay. My silent sobs made the chains rattle and echo through the black abyss surrounding me.

I don't know how long I hung there, floating in and out of consciousness, before I rose to the surface of awareness and realized someone stood before me.

"Ah, you're awake." Vetticus stepped fully into the light and fury unlike anything I'd ever felt before overwhelmed me. I strained against the chains, using the pain to fuel me. A rough growl escaped, the only sound my parched throat would allow. My feet slipped in blood and I went still, my energy quickly spent. He approached and ran his hand along my jaw, a light in his eyes.

"Your anger is like a drug to me," he said. He gripped my chin tightly and yanked my head closer. "The hate bleeding off you is intoxicating."

My entire body was vibrating with the need to get my hands on him and the inability to do so was enough to push my mind to the edge of insanity. Vetticus chuckled darkly as he watched my struggles.

"You're nothing but a wild animal," he said. "It is so easy to reduce men like you down to your base instincts."

He released me and patted my cheek harshly.

"What do you want?" I rasped.

"To mold you into the perfect player one."

He signaled to someone, and the chains loosened enough that I fell to my knees, barely having the strength to catch myself before I face planted into the concrete. The chains hissed along the ground as I dragged myself through the blood, trying to get to Vetticus. He watched my progress with amusement, which only drove my fury higher.

I gathered all my anger, pulled as much strength as I had left, and whipped the chain out at Vetticus. It curled around his ankles and I yanked, falling backwards as I brought him with me to the ground. He recovered quickly and landed on top of me with the chain pressed hard against my neck. He put his weight into it as he leaned over me and my struggles weakened. He brought his face close to mine and sneered, a wild light in his eyes as he drank in all of my pain.

"I'll enjoy finding your breaking point," he purred.

Blackness crowded my vision and the pressure on my neck receded as his hand caressed my face in a strangely intimate gesture. There was a prick in my neck and the weight of him retreated off my chest. Warmth spread through my blood as two men lifted me under my arms and dragged me across the room. The drug made the room grow fuzzy, and the voices sounded hollow.

Pain erupted across my skin and their grip on my arms felt like a million knives. I struggled and gasped as every sensation was heightened and expressed in pain.

"Like it?" I heard Vetticus somewhere behind me. "It makes your touch receptors translate every sensation into pain."

The men dropped me to my knees and handcuffed my wrists in front of me to a length of chain attached to a ring in the ground. Vetticus appeared and his finger trailed a line of fire from my temple down my neck. I barely bit back the moan that threatened to escape as excruciating pain followed wherever his touch went. I tried to move out of the way but I swayed on my knees and my wrists hit the end of the short chain. His fingers closed around my throat and I hissed, trying to breathe through the assault on my senses. My eyes watered and sweat broke out over my body. Somewhere through the haze of fire I heard Vetticus laugh.

Releasing my neck, he patted my cheek. The resulting explosion in my head made the room spin, and I collapsed onto my side. The impact to the concrete, while not hard, felt like a car hit me. Vetticus grabbed my hair and hauled me to my knees. Even the sweat on my body hurt as it slid down my chest. My entire world was pain unlike anything I'd experienced before and soon, despite everything, I was cowering away from Vetticus' touch.

I curled into a ball and shook as his hands ran over my body, driving me further into the corners of my mind to escape.

The drug eventually wore off, and I slowly noticed the room come back into focus. I was on my side, my cheek plastered to the concrete and I shivered violently as the sweat on my body grew cold. I was thankfully alone and the only thing my mind could grasp onto was the act of breathing.

In and out. One breath after the other.

Survive.

Why I suddenly wanted to survive and not die, I wasn't sure. Revenge? Human nature? Maybe it was simply the fact breathing was something tangible to focus on because anytime I tried to grab onto a thought it left as quickly as it came. So I simply took one breath after another and let my eyes fall shut as the darkness dragged me under.

30

THERON

I woke up to water being splashed on me. I sputtered and choked on the onslaught but then frantically tried to gather what I could as it ran into my mouth. I welcomed anything to ease the intense thirst plaguing me. A man came over and released my wrists leaving me unrestrained but I didn't even have the strength to sit up. Vetticus walked over and stood with his hands shoved into his pockets, a smirk on his face.

"We're going to play a game," he said. "I'm going to give you an order. If you obey, you get rewarded, if you disobey, you get punished."

I stayed where I was on the ground; the anger towards him flared again, but it gave me less strength than last time and it was hard to hold on to. My body wanted rest and didn't want to entertain my frantic, volatile mind.

"Sit up," Vetticus said.

He stared at me for a long moment when I didn't move. A slow and cruel smile pulled at his lips and electricity shot through me. It originated from my spine and locked up my entire body in a painful rigor. When it stopped, the pain left immediately, replaced by a deep soreness. I glared up at Vetticus who pulled a device from his pocket.

"We put a chip between your shoulder blades," he said. "It has many uses—GPS, identity marker...but also delivers a nasty shock whenever I press this button. Now, I'll ask again—sit up."

Before I could think about it too hard, I struggled to my knees.

"Crawl to me," Vetticus said.

I looked at him through narrowed eyes. There was an evil hunger there as his mouth curled into a smirk. He made a show of it as he lifted the device and hovered his finger over the button.

I didn't move. He pressed the button, and I collapsed again.

"Crawl to me," Vetticus repeated.

I rolled onto my stomach and laboriously got to my knees again. I stared at him, my stubborn nature refused to give him the satisfaction of my submission. He shook his head in amusement and shocked me again. It seemed to go on longer this time.

It stopped, and I groaned as I pulled myself once more to my knees, only to topple sideways as the room spun. I caught myself on my forearm and waited until the room grew solid once more.

"Pride has no place here," Vetticus said. "Crawl to me."

Again, I refused. Again, he shocked me.

This time when it stopped, I fell forward with my face pressed against the concrete. The tears poured down my cheeks as my eyes watered. Every muscle was sore, and I turned my head and rested my forehead against the ground. I pulled one laborious breath after another into my aching lungs. My body screamed at me to stop this, to just submit, but my mind broke down every reason not to. He could not win.

"Crawl. To. Me," he demanded.

I sucked in breath after breath and refused to lift my head. The chains shivered against the concrete as my body shook from shock and fatigue but still the small voice in my mind refused to obey him.

When the shock came again, I passed out before it ended.

I don't know how long I was out for. When awareness slowly came back to me, I was alone and they hadn't restrained me again, which told me they didn't think I was a threat. I didn't blame them. I was barely coherent. I rolled onto my back and that effort alone caused me to break out in a sweat.

My mind tripped over itself as I struggled to form any kind of thought about my situation. I would not win like this. My body would give out before my mind ever did and if I had any hope of taking out my rage on this man, I needed to be able to at least stand on my own. At the moment, I wasn't even sure I could get to my knees.

I closed my eyes and took one deep breath after another drifting in and out of consciousness. I hated to admit it but Vetticus was right—pride didn't have any place here. As much as it physically made me ill to think about—I needed to play his game. I needed to focus on survival. Time didn't exist anymore, just the amount of breaths I took as I willed my body to stay with me.

I would survive because only then could I get my vengeance.

I would do it for Cole. I would do it for Whit.

I would do it for Emy, because a small part of me hoped she'd escaped. I couldn't think about that too hard though because it brought me too much pain and guilt.

Was she still in the forest? Terrified?

Even worse, what if Vetticus had found her?

Regardless, I would play his game until it was time to play mine. I would get my revenge in this life, or I'd die trying, but I'd give myself every advantage possible and that meant leaving my ego behind—for now.

He didn't know how much of a monster I could be.

Vetticus returned, and I watched his shiny brown shoes cross the room until they were in front of my face. He crouched down, sucking on his teeth as he looked me over.

"Like a wild animal who doesn't know when he's beaten," he sneered. "You'll want the reward I have for you today but first you need to do as you're told."

There was a pause. "Crawl to me." I lifted my head and met his eyes.

"Crawl to me," he said again, the challenge written all over his face.

I pushed myself to my knees as I thought of a million ways I wanted to make him scream. Then I dragged myself forward a foot, as I thought about all the ways I wanted to kill him. Driven by gruesome thoughts of Vetticus' death by my hands, I crawled another few feet, slowly pulling myself across the ground until I collapsed on his boots, spent and seeing stars as they exploded across my vision.

Vetticus crouched down and yanked my head up. I scrambled to get my hands under me, breathing hard through my nose, teeth bared as our eyes clashed. He brought a cup to my lips, and I tasted water as he poured it roughly into my mouth. I choked, water cascading down my chin as I struggled to swallow. He shoved my head away.

"On your knees," Vetticus commanded.

I pushed myself onto my knees, slouched over, barely able to hold my head up as Vetticus grabbed my chin. My eyes took a moment to focus on him and when they did, anger surged through me only this time I held my temper in check.

"Good boy," Vetticus crooned. "You know what comes next," he said.

A prick in my neck was the only warning before I was thrown back into the world of agony as he used the serum on me again. He drove my body past every pain threshold I had and my mind sank deeper into the safety of the darkness where thoughts of revenge festered and grew. With every painful touch and barked command, I found strength in my resolve to survive long enough to dedicate whatever was left of me to his complete annihilation.

31

THERON

*D*ays, weeks, months...

I wasn't sure how much time had passed but when my mind finally emerged from the darkness I'd escaped to, I realized I wasn't in the warehouse anymore. Smooth slabs of stone were cool under my cheek and I heard the buzz of voices that sharpened by the second. I lifted my head and found a face staring at me through the bars a few inches from me.

"Hey, sleepyhead," the man grinned.

"Don't traumatize the newbie, Nyx. You remember how that felt—"

"Yeah, I had your ugly mug staring at me not saying anything—way more creepy."

I rolled onto my back and saw an electric lantern high above me emitting a warm glow into the cell. I turned my head to the man, who leaned tattooed arms against the bars as he looked down at me. He ran his hand through black hair long on top, buzzed at the sides and flashed me that lopsided grin again.

"Welcome back to the living, my friend," he said. "I'm Nyx—that ray of sunshine is Atlas." He nodded to the cell on my other side and I turned my head to see a man with a brooding frown and dark blond hair tied up in a bun sitting on a cot.

I used the bars near Nyx to haul myself to my feet. The cell was clean, with a cot, blanket and pillow along the far wall and a toilet with a sink half partitioned in one corner. Sweatpants, a t-shirt and a sweatshirt sat folded on the end of the cot. I looked down and realized I was still naked and half stumbled over to the clothes to pull on the sweatpants.

I leaned heavily on the sink and turned on the water, drinking deeply from the faucet. I splashed some on my face and closed my eyes as I let the cool liquid restore some of my faculties. The effort was enough to exhaust me and I looked over at Nyx as I sat down on the cot.

"What is this place?"

Nyx shrugged. "Hell—or something similar. Probably purgatory."

"So far this place is like prison," Atlas said, glaring at Nyx. "We get to go out for a few hours every day and the only thing to do is workout."

"Don't worry, they'll bring food soon," Nyx said.

"That's his favorite time of day," Atlas said dryly.

"This may be like a prison, but the food definitely isn't," Nyx said. He looked me over again. "So, what's your name?"

"North. Theron North."

"What branch were you in?" Atlas asked. At the curious look on my face he went on. "Everyone here is military or law enforcement. We were both SEALs."

I nodded. "So was I. How long have you two been here?"

Nyx shrugged. "Probably about a month." He looked to Atlas for confirmation and the man nodded.

"Hard to tell. He's slowly been filling the cells."

There was a commotion down the hall, and Nyx grinned. "Dinner time!"

Atlas rolled his eyes. Two guards made their way down the row of cells as they distributed trays of food through a slot at the bottom of the bars. Two water bottles accompanied the food. I walked over and picked up the tray; the smells made my mouth water immediately. There were two grilled chicken breasts slathered in BBQ sauce, mashed potatoes and a pile of steamed broccoli.

"See what I mean?" Nyx took his tray over to his cot. "Food is top-notch."

"That probably just means they're fattening us up for something," Atlas grumbled.

I took a few bites and couldn't help but close my eyes as the rich taste overwhelmed me. I couldn't remember the last time I'd eaten. I ate most of the dinner but couldn't finish all of it after being starved, although I did down a full water bottle before I stashed the second under my cot for later. Nyx and Atlas bantered back and forth but simply the act of eating exhausted me and as soon as I couldn't eat anymore, I lay back and fell asleep almost immediately.

That night the nightmares came.

So much blood.

My hands were covered in it as I reached for Cole and then Whit's bloody hand as it extended towards me, my name a silent plea on her lips. I jolted awake, frantic to get Cole's blood off my hands. I twisted them in the blanket, wiping them over and over again on the fabric even knowing the blood was only in my mind. My skin was clammy with sweat as tears ran down my face. I stared up into the darkness and focused on my breath as I attempted to calm down. I'd failed my family, and I wasn't sure I could ever forgive myself for that.

I don't know how long I let myself drift into my memories of them, but it physically hurt and I knew if I was going to survive in here, I needed to put the memories away. It was time to compartmentalize like I was good at. I needed to be ruthless and calculating. If I was going to be thrown into the pits of hell, I needed to be every bit the demon birthed from these shadows in order to survive and find a way out.

Only then could I plan my revenge.

Only then could I hope for any chance at retribution.

My memories wouldn't save me and the guilt had the potential to drown me. It was all better if I just left it alone and focused on what was in front of me because they weren't alive. There was nothing waiting for me outside of these walls.

I closed my eyes and willed my mind to empty, shoving the memories of my former self deep into the shadowed corners. Maybe one day it would be safe enough to pull them back out.

32

NYX

Rise and shine, it's workout time," I called out just for the satisfaction of watching Atlas roll his eyes. I watched the newbie, North, slowly pull himself out of bed and throw on a t-shirt. I remembered that feeling vividly, and I didn't envy him. Coming out of Vetticus' initiation session was brutal. Dead gray eyes swept the cell. Right away I recognized North as one of those men you encountered in the military sometimes—cold, detached—with a quiet authority that demanded obedience. Violent by nature but not recklessly so.

If I'd learned anything during my time as a SEAL, it was the quiet ones who were the most dangerous and lethal. They were always the first to charge into the fray, not to be self-sacrificing, but because combat was in their blood and it was just what they did.

I looked over at Atlas who was retying his hair up in a bun, looking like a viking in all his bronzed, sculpted glory. I wasn't one to usually admire a man but there was no denying Atlas was beautiful. I shook my head and turned to the door again—I was not just checking out a dude. It didn't help that I felt like I'd known him for years instead of just a few weeks. There was a magnetic quality about his quiet demeanor. He was almost too perfect, and I didn't like it.

I wanted to see him messy, undone—*fuuck*.

I needed to get laid. Not having sex for a few weeks was doing terrible things to me. I ran a hand over my face and pushed all of that away as the doors of our cells opened. There were about forty of us that made our way down the hallway towards the two sets of double doors leading outside. I hated being caged and sometimes the confines of the cell messed with my mind and made me feel like everything was closing in on me. All of that went away as soon as I stepped outside. I took a deep breath of fresh air, letting the sun hit my face.

Atlas and North followed behind me and I turned to see North squint violently as he tried to adjust to the sun he probably hadn't seen in weeks. I watched the men head off to different sections of the yard as they divide into their usual cliques. The back area was a full track with grass in the middle where one group headed to start a game of football. The next section held two basketball courts and the part closest to us was a full gym set up under some mesh awnings. There was every kind of workout machine you could want. The entire thing was enclosed by high fences wrapped with barbed wire and towers guarded by snipers.

"Come on, let's get a run in first," Atlas said.

We walked to the track and stretched a bit before we took off, setting a slow pace initially so North could at least go a lap with us. He was still weak, but I knew that wouldn't last long. Atlas and I picked up our pace after the first lap, leaving him to acclimate on his own.

"Nice guy," I commented once he was out of earshot.

"You mean unhinged," Atlas scoffed. "I can see it already."

"Aren't we all?"

"Not like him. You know what I'm talking about."

"Yeah, I do. Might be helpful to have one of those in here though," I said. "Someone not afraid to mess up their pretty face." I grabbed Atlas' head and shoved him playfully then took off at a quick sprint.

"Fucker," he barked a laugh and ran to catch up to me.

We ran two miles and stopped when we made it back around to North. He tensed when I slung an arm around his shoulders but didn't object.

"We're gonna go work out, you coming?" After exhausting ourselves with a circuit of weights, we walked back up to the grass to stretch and sat around looking out over the yard.

"Where do you think we are?" North asked. Atlas shrugged and squinted out past the fence at the vast stretch of forest and mountains.

"Could be anywhere honestly."

"Yeah, no one knows. Everyone was knocked out when they were brought here. For all we know they could have put us on a plane and we could be halfway across the world," I added.

My thoughts darkened for a moment as I thought back to the night they'd taken me. My baby sister had been visiting me, although at twenty-six she was far from a baby, I still called her that affectionately. We were close, and she would come see me occasionally or as I liked to say, come check up on me. When I'd gotten out of the military, I'd been in a dark place. Two attempts at taking my life later, she'd started calling me every day and visiting frequently. Together we'd pulled me out of that space and I had her to thank for my renewed outlook on life.

That is until they came and brutally murdered her in front of me. My face must have betrayed my thoughts as I stared off into space because Atlas snapped his fingers in front of my eyes and I blinked to refocus.

"Hey—don't go there," he said.

I scrubbed a hand over my face and shoved the thoughts away. He was right—I couldn't go down that dark path. Not here, where the depression was liable to send me instantly spiraling.

"*Atrox Gaming,*" North muttered. We looked at him curiously. "That's what he said to me," he went on. "That's who's behind this, apparently."

"What do you think the games are?" I asked, welcoming the distraction.

"It has to be tactical—we're all either military or cops," Atlas said.

"Fuck—like live action COD?" I shook my head. "Why does part of me really not hate that idea?"

Being in the military, I'd gone on plenty of missions, and they weren't always fun with bullets flying at you and people you cared about getting blown up. But then there were the times the darkness would take over. The adrenaline kick—the sickness in my mind that thrived on violence. When my humanity would shut off and something from the shadows would take over. The monster inside me that craved the blood on my hands. The part of me that reveled in the high of living in the gray, dealing out death like the Reaper himself.

That is after all, how I'd gotten my call sign—*Reaper.*

For all the lives I'd collected.

"He said he saves the best for his team," North said.

I laughed. "I mean, this sounds like some real life gladiator shit."

"That's why he has to traffick people. No one would volunteer," Atlas said.

It was a sobering thought. I didn't know what this all meant but now that my sister was gone, the monster inside me didn't have anything stopping him and he needed retribution—paid in blood—for what was done to my baby sis. I would play Vetticus' games, but only until I could get my hands around his neck and show him who I really was: *The Reaper come to claim his soul.*

33

ATLAS

TWO MONTHS CAPTIVE

A ll I'm saying is I'm an ass man," Nyx said, flashing me a brilliant smile so at odds with his appearance. He was the definition of shadows, with his black hair long on top, short on the sides and dark eyes a color in between black and brown.

He had tattoos covering his chest, back and arms all the way down to where they spilled over his hands and fingers. I could see tan lines where rings usually adorned him and sometimes I'd see him try to play with them, as though it was a habit he hadn't yet lost even though the rings weren't there anymore.

Despite his generally positive demeanor, there were times I'd see his mind drift and shadows would take over, filling his eyes and spilling over where it was almost physical in the way his entire personality darkened. He was a brooding, sarcastic and dark humored playboy with a look that could tear you to pieces or melt you into a puddle—sometimes I wondered if they were one and the same. I was drawn to him in a way I couldn't explain and despite only knowing him for a few months; it felt like I'd known him for years. Now North was here and in a few short weeks, the three of us had become inseparable.

I racked the bar of the bench press and sat up. "I like to have a pillow," I said, sticking out my hands and acting like I was going to rest my head on a woman's chest. "What about you, T?"

I stood up, and North took my place. He laid back on the bench and positioned his hands on the bar.

"I like a woman with a good personality," he deadpanned before beginning his set.

Nyx and I burst into laughter. North had slowly been warming up to

Nyx and I the last few weeks. Like I'd said to Nyx in those first few days of meeting him, he was one of those men who thrived in the military because of how much of a sociopath he was. His eyes held the haunted look of someone who'd lost his humanity a long time ago, if he'd ever had it at all.

I'd held on to mine for as long as I could. I was still trying to hold on to the scraps of it if I was being honest. I couldn't bear the thought of letting it go for fear of what I would become. Vetticus had shredded it further when he'd taken me from the safety of my civilian life and torn my loved ones away. He'd killed both of my partners in front of me—my wife first, then my husband. They'd been my anchors to my humanity. The ones who'd shown me the true meaning of love made even more potent by being in a polyamorous relationship. Now there was only darkness left where their light had been and everyday I sunk deeper into its depths where all I thought about was revenge.

North finished his set and sat up, breaking through my morbid thoughts.

"Have you guys even lost your virginity yet? What are you like teenagers still?" He said. We weren't much younger than him, mid to late thirties, but he enjoyed making fun of us for it.

"Ha ha old man," Nyx said. "Very funny. I lost my virginity to an Italian beauty the first year I was deployed abroad."

"Are you bragging, Nyx?" I joked.

Nyx held up his hands with a grin. "I'm just saying—Europeans know how to do it better in my experience. At least I wasn't the cliche like Atlas over here—"

"Fuck off," I laughed.

"What do you mean?" North asked, starting another set.

"I lost my virginity at eighteen to a girl I knew in high school a few weeks before I went in—"

"Where?" Nyx prompted.

"The back of my truck," I added.

"Like a typical Cali boy," Nyx chuckled.

I had to look away from his teasing eyes. I didn't want to admit it but I was quickly developing a crush on this shadowed contradiction of a man. I would never say anything, not here, in this place where vulnerability and affection didn't have any business showing its face. But the stirring in my gut was there whenever he turned that cheeky grin on me. I'd started looking for ways to bring it out and I'd been relentlessly telling myself to stop to no avail, especially since he seemed to portray himself as straight.

Nyx looked over at North. "What about you, T?"

He sat up again and leaned his forearms on his thighs. "Same as Atlas actually—high school sweetheart before I went in. But I did it the proper way—in her bed while her parents were asleep."

Nyx barked a laugh, and I shared a smirk with North before I saw his face grow cold. Turning to see what he was looking at, I saw trouble in the form of three men making their way towards us. I recognized the one in the middle. Yuri was a swarthy, stocky, bullish man with a perpetual frown that pulled his features into an ugly countenance.

"Clear off if you're just going to bullshit on the equipment," he said.

"I've got one more set, then it's yours," North said easily.

"Nah, I think you're done now."

"Fuck off, Yuri," Nyx said. "It's not like we don't have enough time."

"I wasn't talking to you, asshole." Yuri's eyes never left North's, and I sighed. I knew a pissing match when I saw one. Unfortunately for him, North was not one to suffer insecure fools. Sure enough, he dismissed Yuri by laying back and starting his final set.

Yuri's jaw ticked in anger as he stepped forward. Nyx and I went to block his way and he lashed out at Nyx and attempted to punch him in the face. Nyx easily dodged it and grabbed Yuri's shirt as he pulled back his own fist to retaliate.

North sat up abruptly. "Stop," he demanded.

The authority in his tone was unmistakable and Nyx immediately paused, his eyes black pits and his humor gone as he glared at Yuri. Yuri smirked at him as though he'd won something and knocked Nyx's hand off his shirt, smoothing down the fabric as he did. North stood up but one look at his face and I wanted to take a step back myself. His gray eyes were iced over and had the look of a predator luring in his prey. Yuri didn't see it, or chose not to, I wasn't sure, but he continued forward, obviously gloating.

Before he could reach the bench, North attacked with a quick punch to his jaw. Yuri staggered into the weight rack and North twisted his arm behind his back then slammed the man's neck into the bench press bar. Yuri choked and flailed but North simply applied more pressure, calm and collected. Yuri stilled, chest heaving as he gasped for air.

"I said I have one more set," North growled. "But now, it looks like I have two."

A chill rushed through me at his words, his presence filled the space with a dangerous undercurrent of violence. Yuri's two counterparts stepped forward like they were going to help him, but I blocked their way with Nyx at my side. Yuri jerked in North's grip again.

"Don't fucking test me," North snarled close to his ear before he yanked him up and threw him towards his men. Yuri stumbled, his eyes wild as they hatefully bounced between the three of us. He swiped at his bloody lip and pointed at North.

"Watch your back," he snarled. He spat on the ground at our feet and stalked off. We watched him go and after a moment, North resumed his position on the bench and started another set as though nothing had happened. Nyx shook his head and leaned against the weight rack.

"Boredom gets to people," he said. "I want to punch someone too but I'm not about to do it over some gym equipment." North grunted as he sat up and regarded Nyx thoughtfully.

"I'm surprised you didn't clock him."

Nyx shrugged. "You gave an order." A half smile pulled at North's lips.

"You are the ranking officer," I said dryly.

Nyx stretched his neck from side to side and cracked his knuckles. "My time will come." He gave North a long look. "Plus, I had a feeling you needed to punch someone more than I did."

He wasn't wrong, North had a tension about him I was familiar with and knew would boil over, eventually. It was only a matter of time. A man like him was in control until he wasn't and then god forbid someone get in his way. Regardless, I definitely had grown fond of the guy. He had his moments where I'd see the darkness and intensity lift and for a moment he'd be present.

Would we all be like that in the end? Weighed down by our past with no hope of escape except through violence and vengeance. I hoped not, but looking at North, I knew a monster when I saw one and he didn't try to hide his like the rest of us.

I'd been a phantom in the field, a sniper sent to be invisible—there to deal out death and then disappear like it never happened. My call sign reflected that—*Phantom*. I wondered if that was what I would become once all of this was over—*a ghost*—nothing more than an apparition of shadows and regret that would eventually just...*disappear*.

34

THERON

THREE MONTHS CAPTIVE

I knew that wasn't the last issue we'd have with Yuri and a few weeks later things came to a head in the showers. Atlas and Nyx were drying off across the room and I was still in the shower area about to step out when everything happened in seconds.

Yuri appeared around the corner of the shower stall and shoved me into the wall, landing a solid punch to my jaw. His two men attempted to grab my arms, but I'd been waiting for this moment ever since I threatened him—and I was ready. Murderous thoughts were running through my head and for the last few weeks, I'd been itching to hurt someone. The nightmares were especially bad lately and with them came the desire to let out all of my pent up rage against Vetticus. It had to go somewhere.

I ripped one man's arm nearly clean out of its socket, rewarded by a sharp cry of distress before I kneed him in the face. Yuri wrapped his arm around my neck. I shoved him back against the wall with my body and used Yuri as leverage to kick out at the second man after he landed a punch to my stomach.

I hardly felt the hits, and I quickly lost my control. I slammed Yuri backwards against the wall again and elbowed him in the side before launching myself forward and dislodging him over my shoulder. I straddled him and landed blow after blow to his face as the shower water rained down on us. My fury was unstoppable—it was no longer Yuri underneath me but Vetticus.

I heard a crunch and saw red as blood sprayed over me. The body underneath me went limp, but I was past stopping. I was past the point where I was in control. The rage, the adrenaline, the absolute rush of release was intoxicating. I vaguely heard yelling and hands tried to grab me. I lashed out at them and they receded until an arm snaked around my neck and bodily pulled me away.

"North—North, it's over, man." Nyx was in my ear, his arm tight around my neck as my chest heaved for air. As my vision cleared, I saw the destruction before me. Yuri was a bleeding mess on the tile. His blood ran in rivers down the drain as the shower continued raining down. Atlas was crouched over him, his fingers on what was left of his neck, his face unrecognizable.

"Dead—" Atlas said rather unnecessarily. He looked over at me with an unreadable expression on his face.

I tapped Nyx's arm. "I'm fine."

He hesitated briefly before letting me go and just as I gained my feet; the guards stormed in and shoved me against the tile wall, dragging my wrists behind my back and cuffing them. The shower room went silent as the men lingered near the walls. I was pushed to the center of the room and knocked to my knees. Vetticus walked through the door smoking a cigar. He stopped in front of me and took in the scene, his eyes trailing over Yuri's body before they landed on mine.

"Killed a man already," his eyes trailed over my naked body. "With your bare hands no less."

I glared at him. "Come a little closer, I'll show you how I did it."

"You'd enjoy that," he said dryly. He took a puff of the cigar and exhaled, purposely sending it down into my face.

"There is a time and place for killing people around here and unfortunately in the showers is not one of them," he continued.

He stepped to my shoulder and pressed the lit end of his cigar into my collarbone. The moment it touched my skin, I turned and rotated my legs out, catching him behind the knees and sending him to the ground. I rolled and landed a kick to his jaw before the guards were on top of me, pinning me face down onto the cold tile. I watched Vetticus get to his feet as the guards hauled me back to my knees. He swiped at the blood on his lip from where he'd scraped it across the floor.

"You just never learn," he growled through clenched teeth.

I saw the glint of brass knuckles before they connected with my face. I breathed in the pain, the adrenaline still potent in my blood and lifted my face to sneer at him. His hair was out of place and there was passionate anger in his eyes. He hit me again, and I tasted blood. The next hit had me seeing red, my ears ringing as I slumped down onto the tile supporting myself on an elbow. Vetticus stopped and waited for me to look up at him. He was panting, teeth bared in contempt. I spit blood at his feet, enjoying every second of seeing him out of control.

His eyes took on an evil glint then. "Do you know how much I enjoyed your wife's screams while I watched my men rape her?"

I froze, and my eyes narrowed. Rage, hot and overwhelming, flooded me violently. He grabbed my hair and jerked my head up towards him as I growled low in my throat.

"Pussy isn't really my thing," he said, raking his eyes over me hungrily. "But blood certainly is. She looked stunning, covered in blood and my men's come—right before I burned the whole house down around her."

I tried to get to my feet to attack him, how and with what, I didn't have a clue, but he shoved me away and when I straightened, he hit me hard in the jaw, sending me back to the ground.

"And you know what else?" He rasped out. "I found your secret—the one you tried to hide in the woods. To your credit, she put up a fight. For a child, it was pretty impressive. Was that your knife she was carrying?"

My blood ran cold then hot, and I got back to my knees.

No. No. Not my little girl.

I nearly choked on my despair as it battled with my inability to take a breath through the agony constricting my heart. I'd wanted to continue to think she'd been able to get away—to survive.

"If you touched her—" I growled.

"I showed her how to properly handle a knife. I don't think she'll forget the lesson."

"Fuck you! I'm going to kill you!" I raged.

Vetticus saw the moment my emotions completely overwhelmed me and he smirked, delivering the final blow.

"They were twins right?"

My control snapped, and with a snarl I lunged to my feet and head butted Vetticus hard enough for his head to snap back and blood to gush from his nose. I pushed forward to come at him again, but he recovered and slammed his fist into my face, sending me into the arms of two guards who sent me crashing back to my knees. Vetticus stepped up and grabbed my hair again, forcing my head back painfully in order to look up at him. I jerked in the guards arms but they held me firm as Vetticus ran his finger across my split lip, smearing the blood.

"Your family is gone. You have nothing. I. Own. You," he snarled, his face so close to mine I could see the fire burning there. "You will bleed when I say you can bleed. You will kill when I say you can kill." He drew a knife from his belt and held it against my neck. "And you will die, when I say you can die."

"Do it," I snarled, pressing forward.

For a moment I thought he might, the glitter in his black eyes took on a sinister hunger. But then he smiled and dragged the knife down my neck, cutting into my skin enough to draw blood but not enough to do any damage. I welcomed the burn of it.

"Tempting—but no, not yet," he said, his composure slowly sliding back into place. "And quite frankly, you don't deserve it. You deserve to live with your failure—unable to save your family—pitiful."

I nearly choked on my fury and pushed forward so we were nearly eye to eye as he hovered over me.

"You're right," I growled viciously. "I deserve to suffer—and I will suffer... every day until the day I get to drive that knife into your fucking heart."

"Through vengeance there will be peace," Vetticus purred, his eyes flashing with something dark and evil. "I will look forward to that day—if only to prove to you your hell is eternal, with or without me in it."

He shoved me away from him and walked out of the showers. The guards yelled for everyone to get back to their cells and yanked me to my feet, personally escorting me back. Once in my cell, they uncuffed my wrists and the door locked behind them. I could feel Atlas and Nyx watching me as I pulled on sweatpants and paced the room like a caged animal, unable to sit still. I went over to the sink, throwing water on my face with shaking hands and watched the water run red as I tried to calm myself down.

I punched the wall above the sink.

Once. Twice.

A third time—until my knuckles bled—trying to find a place for all the anger to go.

"North," Nyx barked, breaking the spell.

My fist landed against the stone one more time before it stayed there as I leaned heavily over the sink, my emotions erratic. My skin was tight across my bones, as though my soul needed to rip myself apart to get relief from the overwhelming assault of memories and feeling of helplessness. I turned the water off and slid down the wall, drawing my knees up and resting my head in my hands.

Some time later, I heard Nyx settle next to the bars.

"Do you want to talk about them?" he asked.

I thought about it. All the good and happy times were on the tip of my tongue—eager to be spilled—but I couldn't.

"Not here," I rasped. "Not in this place."

I stayed like that for the next few hours. Nyx and Atlas talked across me but didn't intervene. My thoughts were dark, tortured and erratic. They went from wanting to kill myself, to wanting to kill everyone else, to all the minute details of how I would torture Vetticus if—*when*—I got my hands on him. Once I'd exhausted all of that, my thoughts grew more clear and as the adrenaline bled away, I knew what I needed to be in order to survive here.

Powerful under the guise of being powerless.

I would survive so I could tear Vetticus apart piece by bloody fucking piece.

35

THERON

SIX MONTHS CAPTIVE

Not that I believed in god, but if there was someone watching out for me, he'd given me an unexpected gift in Nyx and Atlas. Despite only knowing them for a few months, these guys somehow felt like long-time friends. They cut through the darkness in my soul. They were both polar opposites of each other in the strangest ways. Nyx was all reckless shadows he kept tame with dark humor and Atlas, while ever the brooding Viking, still managed to keep us grounded in the present with compassion and reason.

"Six months," Nyx said.

He shook his head as he stood at the bars of the cell, looking across mine as Atlas made another mark on the wall where he'd tried to keep a tally. Six long months that ran together with the monotony of routine. We'd thrown ourselves into our workouts and I'd added grappling and hand to hand instruction on top of the weight training and endurance. We'd spent the last few months honing our bodies into lethal machines, each of us at our peak performance. I'd never been in this kind of shape in my life, even while I was in the military. This was a whole different level of perfection.

I'd crafted a body made to kill.

Despite becoming obsessed with our regiment, the boredom was slowly taking its toll. Atlas frowned at his tally marks and finally shook his head.

"It's probably not exact, but close," Atlas shrugged. "I was taken around the end of March."

We all fell quiet, lost in dark thoughts. I hadn't heard their stories yet, but it wasn't my place to ask since I wasn't forthcoming with mine. When Nyx had asked, I'd refused, not wanting to bring my most cherished memories into this place. The closer I got to them though, the more I wanted them to know—even if it was only so that they'd realize why I was going to do whatever possible to make sure Vetticus suffered for taking them from me.

"My sister's birthday would be any day now," Nyx said quietly.

I turned to look at him but he was fixated on the tally marks on the wall.

"She would have been twenty-seven," he continued. "She was all I had left, and he took her from me."

"He'll pay for what he took from us," Atlas said. He came and stood at the bars, gripping them firmly, his green eyes dark with conviction. "We've all lost people at his hands. That won't go unpunished."

"How are we going to get out of here?" Nyx whispered, bringing his hand up to his mouth discreetly. He didn't have to look at the cameras in our cells, we were all very aware of their presence.

"The tracker is going to be the hard part," I said. "We have no means to remove it."

"Something will come to us," Atlas said. "We just have to be patient."

"I'm not good at being patient," Nyx grumbled.

"Good thing you have us then," Atlas said and flashed him a quick smile.

Nyx's face softened slightly and his gaze held Atlas' for just a moment longer than necessary before he dropped it as though realizing he was staring. Atlas looked smug about something but it quickly disappeared. I wondered about them. Sometimes their banter could almost be confused with flirting although nothing blatant. I was just getting to know them well enough to see it. I don't think Nyx realized it but Atlas certainly did.

While I didn't feel that way about either of them, it made us that much closer to each other to the point where I was beginning to feel protective over them. They teased me that I was older and even though it wasn't by much, the role of protector was quickly enveloping me. I had a fondness for them, but sometimes I wondered if I was capable of affection or if it was simply a matter of them belonging to me.

"Do you think the game has started yet?" Nyx suddenly asked. Atlas cocked his head at him in a silent question. "Do you think people are watching us already?"

His gaze finally jumped to the surveillance camera up in the corner of my cell. Each cell had an identical one, and I had no doubts Vetticus liked to watch the feeds. Atlas flipped it off aggressively.

"If so, I hope they are as bored as I am," he grumbled. "If his plan is to bore us to madness, he's doing a very good job."

"You eager to go out and get shot?" I asked dryly.

"We don't even know if that's really what the games are," Atlas answered. "He was very—"

A loud bell sounded throughout the cells. It was the same one used to notify us of when we were about to go outside except it wasn't time for that. It was nearly the time when the lights would go out for the night. I got to my feet and walked to the front of the cell, looking down the hall. Murmurs and questions rose in the air from the men in the other cells and I exchanged glances with Nyx.

Atlas sighed and gave Nyx a look of exasperation. "Looks like we're about to find out."

My cell door clicked loudly as it unlocked, followed by Nyx and Atlas'. Several more clicked open but as I stepped out into the hall, I realized it was only seven of us. Guards appeared at the end of the hall, motioning us with their guns to follow them.

Instead of heading outside, they cuffed our hands behind our backs, cut off our shirts and led us down a set of stairs into a large basement under the cells. Vetticus watched us file in and the guards put us on our knees in a row facing a smoldering fire pit. Once we were all situated, he spoke.

"You are all property of *Atrox Gaming*, a company that specializes in live action, capture the flag style military missions. You are the lucky seven that I've chosen for my A team and I will be making it official today. Your time has finally come to play in the games. Tomorrow you'll enter the arena."

He stepped to the fire and pulled out a burning iron from the coals.

"These men are your teammates. There will be three to four other squads of seven in the game—they are your opponents."

Vetticus came over to the first man in line and two of his men came up and held him still. He pushed the brand into the man's chest below his collarbone. Besides the hiss of his breath as the pain overwhelmed him, he didn't move or make a sound. Vetticus removed the brand and went back to the fire.

"Your objective is to capture the target and bring it back to your safe zone, or DZ, before the time expires—or be the last team standing." He grabbed another brand and repeated the action with the next man in line.

"The games are televised to select individuals who can place bets on you, your team and other factors associated with the games. Each map is different—the bullets are real—if you die, I replace you. Winners get rewarded—losers get punished."

Vetticus let his eyes settle on me when he said the last part and I suppressed a shiver at the look that passed across his face. He didn't say what the punishment was, but based on the sadistic shit he'd demonstrated already, I didn't want to find out.

"The games will occur every few months to allow for adequate recovery time should any injuries occur."

I tensed when he got to Nyx, watching out of the corner of my eye as the brand was pushed against his skin. Next was Atlas. Sweat glistened on his chest and he was glaring murderously at Vetticus but he didn't make a sound. Then it was my turn.

Vetticus' eyes turned sharp and his mouth twisted cruelly. He pressed the brand into my skin and the pain was nearly all-consuming. I fought through it and when he pulled it away, sweat was rolling down my body. He grabbed my chin roughly and leaned close to me although he spoke loudly to address all of us.

"You are nothing but a soldier—a player one—a pawn," he growled. "And you are going to make me a lot of money."

Vetticus stared into my eyes as I glared back at him, feeling nothing but a hatred that burned as painfully as the "V" he'd just branded into my chest. He patted my cheek harshly and walked back over to the fire, carelessly tossing the iron back into the flames he turned to us again.

"Each of you may choose your call sign for the games."

Vetticus pointed to each of us and we went down the line giving him a name. *Vyper. Colt. Dutch. Preacher. Reaper. Phantom.* I thought about using my old call sign but when it was my turn, that's not the name that came out.

"Kraven," I said.

Kraven the Hunter—a Spiderman antihero. He was a big game hunter who hunted people for sport and was known for calling Spiderman "the most dangerous game."

My heart hurt at the thought of why that name had popped into my head. Cole had loved Spiderman. We'd read all the comics, even though Whit didn't like me to because they were surprisingly violent and dark. It had become a cherished secret between Cole and I.

I pushed the memory of Cole away. Until Vetticus was cold and dead six feet under, Kraven would be synonymous with determination and unyielding strength fed by a lust for vengeance achieved by any means possible, even at the sake of my own morality.

"Bring me a victory. I'll accept nothing less," Vetticus said. His voice cut through my thoughts and brought me back from my mind running wild with plans of his demise. "Good luck."

He gave us one final look before leaving the room. I looked over at Atlas and Nyx, then down at the V on my chest, bright and inflamed.

Game on.

36

NYX

Well, that had been quite the pep talk. The brand hurt like a bitch but I tried to ignore it as we were led out the door and back up the stairs. We remained cuffed but instead of going back to our cells, we were directed to a different door that led out to a waiting cargo van. We got into the back and the door shut behind us, throwing us into blackness.

We drove for several hours. I tried to follow the twists and turns but it became too much after the first hour. By the third hour, the road turned into a relatively well kept dirt road. We slowed down, going at a moderate albeit bumpy speed. No one spoke. There wasn't anything to say. We were cuffed. We had those damn trackers in us and we had no clue where we were or where we were going. Trying to plan anything would have been suicide and I think we all realized it.

When the van finally stopped, the doors opened and cold air blew through the back sending a shiver through my body. I was one of the last to hop down and what I saw took my breath away as efficiently as the cold air against my bare chest. We were somewhere in heavily forested mountains.

Off in the distance sat a tall, modern mansion. Most of it consisted of floor to ceiling windows across all three stories. Where it wasn't windows, it was dark metal and black concrete. Modern and sinister, it sat on its perch overlooking a vast forest as far as the eye could see. Isolation at its finest.

Turning to my left, I saw another building, and this was where we went. Equally modern and aesthetically pleasing, it was a one story structure built of stone, metal and glass. We passed through the front doors and through two additional checkpoints until the doors opened up to a large room with seven cots along the far wall. The floor was gray concrete with several rugs and there was even a sitting area in one corner. The vaulted ceilings rose above us and one entire wall was glass that looked out over a covered gym area and a sloping lawn beyond that.

The far edge of the yard held a dirt trail that ran in a circle around a pond. The entire yard was once more surrounded by high barbed wire fencing. Looking at the other side of the room, there was an open doorway where I glimpsed a full bathroom with a massive double head shower, toilet and two sinks set into a wide vanity. I whistled low as I took it all in.

"Fancy," I muttered.

It was almost...cozy. That is of course if I ignored the surveillance cameras dotting the corners of the room and the fact the door had bars on it. The cuffs were removed, and the guards locked us in. One of them stood at the grate in the door and addressed us.

"You are now one of Vetticus' personal Atrox teams and if you survive the games, you will return here after each one. The door to the yard will automatically unlock from noon to five every day. Meals will be delivered at 8am, noon and 5pm. Change into the new clothes and put the discarded ones in the bin there." He gestured to a flap in the wall near the door.

Once he was gone, we chose beds. North chose one on the far side, closest to the glass doors, I went next to him with Atlas next to me. Each bed had two sets of clothes folded neatly. I picked up the sweatpants and sweatshirt which were now a dark shade of forest green instead of gray.

"Another white t-shirt. Fashion at its finest," I said. I pulled it over my head, followed by the sweatshirt then went and stood at the glass doors. The sun had long since set, but the yard was lit up with high-powered floodlights, revealing every corner and blade of grass in stark contrast.

"I hope we don't have to sleep with those on."

"Are you done complaining?" Atlas asked. "Jesus—this isn't a five star resort."

"Are we sure? Maybe we're being Punk'd. Ashton!" I turned and called into the room, peering up at the closest camera. "Mm, doesn't look like it." I flipped off the camera instead.

"So how are we going to play this?" I turned to see who had spoken.

Vyper. He was the definition of a jarhead. Close shaved head, nearly bald, with eyes that had seen some shit. His only tattoo was of a snake wrapped around his arm and ended with the snake's head open and striking on his chest. He had several vicious looking scars running across his abs.

"How about some introductions first?" North said. I couldn't tell what he was thinking as he studied Vyper and the others, but that was nothing new.

"I go by Vyper in the field. I'm a Marine."

I already didn't like him. The man beside him spoke up next. He was blond and didn't look a day over eighteen—a child—with a pouty set to his mouth. He was unassuming. A face I'd forget in a crowd.

"Names Colt. I'm a Marine too."

"Now that looks like a complainer," I murmured to Atlas under my breath. His lips twitched as he tried to hold back his amusement.

"Dutch. Marine—I'm a sniper." Short brown hair, kind brown eyes—he reminded me of a puppy that had been kicked too many times and now resorted to biting the hand that tried to show affection. Quiet, calculating—but lost. *Aren't we all?*

"Preacher. SWAT—law enforcement for ten years."

Intelligent blue eyes swept the group and landed on North, giving him a once over. He knew who was really in charge. I could tell he was used to leading—giving orders, not taking them. There was a no nonsense way about him. He didn't have any visible ink on his bare chest, but an ugly scar ran across his neck in a way that made it very apparent someone had tried to slit his throat. He oozed cop energy. North nodded to him and then all eyes were on me.

"Reaper. SEAL," I said. "All around—I'll do whatever."

"Phantom. SEAL," Atlas said. "I'm also a sniper."

Everyone looked at North. "Kraven. SEAL."

"Alright then," Vyper said. "Anyone object to me taking point?"

No one objected but one look at Vyper and I already knew what kind of person he was and it wasn't someone I wanted leading me into a war zone. I exchanged discrete looks with Atlas and North and saw we were on the same page. North sat down on his bed and I sat on mine facing him. Atlas joined me at the foot and I leaned in.

"Him as team lead? Really?"

North's jaw ticked but otherwise he remained emotionless.

"Let's feel out the first game and see what we're really getting ourselves into. Then we can formulate a better plan."

"Maybe the arena is where we can find a way to escape," Atlas said. "They're handing us live weapons."

Before North could answer, Vyper spoke up again. "Alright, let's talk strategy and then try to get a few hours of sleep. We don't really know what we're getting into but we should all be on the same page when we get out there."

I sighed. It was going to be a long night.

37

THERON

The next morning we were fed breakfast and then cuffed and put into the back of the enclosed van. I estimated the drive to be about an hour along windy, bumpy dirt and gravel roads. When we finally arrived at our destination, the van opened into a room with seven sets of full tactical gear. Everything from helmets to boots. We were uncuffed, and a message came on over a speaker.

"When these doors open, you'll be released into the arena. The objective is to bring the target back to your safe zone which is right outside these doors."

I stripped and started putting on the gear as the others followed suit.

"Along the wall outside, there are comms units to communicate with each other and a map of the arena. There are three other teams of seven you'll be going against. It's kill or be killed. A final reminder—if any of you get any rebellious ideas, the tracker we've placed in you will detonate. There are cameras recording visual and audio everywhere. Good luck."

When I was done, I turned to Nyx and tightened his vest, making sure everything was in place, then did the same to Atlas.

"I don't care what this fucker does—we stick together out there, got it?" I said, my voice low to be heard by only them.

"Copy that, boss," Nyx said. Atlas nodded.

"Just another day, boys," Vyper said eagerly as the doors opened.

We stepped out into the sunlight, and the doors closed ominously behind us. I walked over and grabbed a comms unit. I stuck it in my ear as I surveyed the map crudely scrawled on the wall.

"Comms check," Vyper said.

The map was a classic city grid but when I turned to look at the actual arena; it looked like a war zone. The buildings were crumbling ruins, many of them looking like they'd been blown up with their entire fronts gaping letting us see the inside. Others were missing windows and doors or were simply a mess of concrete in the streets. The roads were pocked with craters from explosions and there were even a few burned and gutted vehicles. It looked like a war-torn city—eerie and desolate.

"Looks like we have a sixty-minute countdown," Vyper said.

I looked over my shoulder at the other side of the door where a red digital clock was set at sixty. A buzzer sounded and Vyper had us move out as the clock began the countdown.

"Phantom, Kraven, Reaper—rear guard. You three—on me," Vyper said.

We spread out into a formation and quickly made our way down a street in front of us. In the first building we found a few .45s and a handful of grenades but no ammo. We cleared the next few buildings and by the time we were approaching the center of the map, we'd found enough to outfit each of us with a firearm. The only problem was ammo.

"We should split up," Vyper said. "Kraven, take your team and finish clearing this street. Holler if you find an ammo dump."

"Copy," I said.

I gestured to Nyx and Atlas and we took off down the street. I took the lead because I had the only gun with ammo so far—a .45 pistol with a single clip. Nyx also had a .45 and Atlas had an AR but both were empty. I was cautious going into the next building. It was another crumbled ruin with the entire south corner gone revealing a gutted concrete three story. On the second floor Atlas found a loaded sniper rifle, and we found a case of .45 ammo. As we loaded up, I looked around and saw a camera in the room. It wasn't the first I'd seen. Nearly every spot on the map so far looked covered by a camera. They were watching, and they were listening through our comms.

"Let's move out," I said.

We crept down the street quickly and stopped at a burned up van. I poked my head inside and instantly went on comms.

"Vyper—ammo dump."

"Copy. Gather what you can and finish clearing your section. There's a large crossroads east of you. Meet us in the general store."

"Any sign of the target?"

"Negative."

We loaded up on as much ammo as we could carry before continuing on. I could tell Nyx was itching to talk but like Atlas and I, he kept glancing at the cameras and frowning.

We were almost at the crossroads when I heard AR clatter and motioned them both to hold. I moved to the corner and looked down the next street. I heard the gunfire again but there was nothing in sight so I motioned Nyx and Atlas up to me. We advanced another block and came to the edge of the crossroads. I saw Vyper and the men flanking the entrance to one road alongside a gutted convenience store. I was about to motion for us to make our way across when Atlas laid a hand on my shoulder.

"Sniper—bell tower," he said.

"Of course," I muttered.

"It wouldn't be a game without a camper," Nyx chuckled.

"How much do we want to bet the target is in that church?" I said.

Vyper barked out a laugh over comms. "Poetic of him. Phantom, go camp your ass in that building next to you—"

"Not alone," I stated flatly.

"We're not in a video game, Kraven."

"Exactly. I'm not having him go up alone to get picked off."

"Stop arguing and let's make a move," Colt snapped.

"He's right, we can't stay here," Dutch said.

Atlas dropped his sights. "He's occupied with something on the other side of the church. We need to move now."

"On me," I said and jogged out into the courtyard, sliding behind a wrecked trolley. Once Atlas and Nyx joined me, I advanced again until we were one building away from the church entrance. I saw Vyper get into position in the alley near the church just as the concrete near my head exploded.

"Fuck," I hissed, ducking back around the corner.

I watched Vyper and the others run towards the church entrance leaving us to draw the fire.

"Bastard," Nyx cursed.

"Can you take out the sniper?" I asked Atlas.

He looked around and then up at the building we were leaning up against.

"Yeah, give me a sec." He climbed through a blown out window and a minute later he came back on comms. "We've got company. There's an entire team coming up the road to the left of the church. I have a clear shot of the sniper."

"Send it," I said.

A moment later I heard a rifle shot ring out.

"Sniper down," Atlas reported.

Two more shots followed. "Took out two of the team before they disappeared into the church."

"Come down." I looked around the corner and heard an explosion rock the church followed by gunfire.

"What the fuck?" Vyper exclaimed over comms. "Taking heavy fire—target is—target is in a cage! It's a woman!"

"Repeat that?" Nyx asked.

"A fucking cage, Reaper—get your asses in here! We need ammo and backup!"

We bolted for the front of the church and charged through into chaos. The pews were destroyed or shoved against the walls leaving the massive middle area open and exposed. At the altar, as though put there as a sacrifice, was a large cage with a woman huddled naked, locked inside. Vyper, Preacher and Dutch were on one side of the altar behind a column exchanging fire with another five men across the way. There wasn't any sign of Colt.

We immediately dove for cover as one of the enemy soldiers opened fire. Nyx and I scrambled backwards as the stones exploded at our feet. Atlas had gone the other way and was making a run for the stairs leading up into the gallery.

I grabbed Nyx and hauled him to his feet just as three smoke grenades went off sending the entire space into a thick haze. I used the wall as a guide, feeling Nyx's hand on my shoulder, as I made my way towards the altar. I saw a muzzle flash and nearly walked straight into the barrel of a gun. I knocked it away and went to the ground on top of the man, a mixture of instinct and training kicking in. I landed on him and got in a few solid punches before a sharp knock to my head gave him the advantage and we rolled across the church floor.

I was temporarily breathless as my back slammed into a broken pew. The second cost me and the man took advantage by landing a few punches to my face before his hands found my neck. My hands scrambled to both sides, searching for anything to use as a weapon. My fingers closed around a piece of wood and I brought it up, striking it against the side of his face. I scrambled to my knees, yanking a knife from his belt as he toppled over and followed him down to the ground. I plunged the knife into his neck, jerking it sideways so hard the bones of his spine scraped across the blade.

I heard chatter over comms. "Vyper, open the cage!"

I looked up to see the smoke had thinned, revealing Nyx on his back with a gun in his face. I yanked the knife out of the man beneath me and threw it across the space. It impaled the man in the arm and the shot aimed at Nyx's face went wide. I launched myself at the man a moment later, taking him down and fighting for the gun as we rolled. I gained control and with a snarl, shoved the gun under his chin and pulled the trigger. His head exploded, coating me in more blood. I quickly ran a hand over my face to clear my vision and nearly shot Nyx as he came up with an AR in hand.

Another man ran towards us out of the diminishing haze. Nyx and I both raised our guns but before he'd even made it another step a rifle shot rang out and he dropped. I looked up at the same time as Nyx who saluted the gallery.

"Thanks," I said.

"No problem, boss," Atlas answered over comms. "I have two targets pinned in the back room. Vyper is at the cage."

I rushed with Nyx over to the cage.

"Move!" I demanded. "Why the fuck haven't you opened it yet?"

I shoved Vyper out of the way, ignoring his protests. Raising my gun I shot the lock and threw open the door. The woman was huddled in the back, her wrists handcuffed in front of her. There was a blindfold over her eyes and duct tape over her mouth. I grabbed her arm and dragged her out, throwing her over my shoulder.

"Let's go!" I barked. "Atlas—any movement out front?"

"Negative."

I was already moving towards the front doors. The woman was struggling in my arms, making it difficult to carry her.

"Vyper, Preacher—rear guard—"

"Since when are you giving orders, Kraven?" Vyper demanded, jogging to catch up. I rounded on him so fast he nearly ran into me.

"Since this has become an utter shit show," I snarled.

"Fuck you! I did what I had to do! I'm not taking orders from you!"

"We don't have time for this!" Preacher demanded, gun pointed towards the back door that had inched open as we stood arguing. I drew my .45 and pointed it at Vyper.

"Decide. Now. Or I'll consider you a liability," I panted.

Vyper's eyes narrowed and his lips thinned as he glared at me.

"Copy," he said through gritted teeth. I threw a look at Nyx who nodded. I didn't trust this man with a gun at my back.

"Preach—Dutch, up with me," I snapped.

They pushed open the doors and checked the area before motioning us out. Atlas joined us and we took off across the courtyard at a run. The woman was screaming against the duct tape and pounding on my back. She wasn't strong enough to do any damage, but it was difficult to run, hold a gun and carry her. We reached the other side of the square at a dead sprint and spread out along the sides of the road leading deeper into the buildings.

I threw the woman down at my feet and tore off her blindfold, then ripped off the duct tape. I crouched down in front of her and grabbed her by the neck, dragging her close.

"I will knock you out if you continue to resist me," I said in a deadly tone.

Her wide blue eyes were filled with tears but she nodded quickly. She was covered in dirt and Vetticus had painted a giant crosshair in red paint on her chest. I bared my teeth at it in disgust before I looked both ways down the street. Vyper had his gun trained towards the church.

"Movement at the front door."

"Let's move!" I tossed the woman back over my shoulder and motioned for Dutch and Atlas to push forward again. We made it a block before Atlas signaled for us to hold at the corner of a four-way city block.

"Four incoming from the north road—" Atlas reported.

"Three from south—"

"Fuck—" Preacher said. "The two from the church, plus a third coming up behind."

I looked around at where we were. We couldn't risk getting pinned down.

"Atlas, Dutch—grenades north and south on my go—" I watched them pull two grenades each and pull the pins. "Go!"

They threw the explosives, and we took off across the street. I heard the explosions nearly simultaneously, and then the gunfire tore into the ground and buildings as we sprinted across the street. I felt something bite into my leg and stumbled, the weight of the woman nearly taking us both to the ground. We reached the other side and Preacher and Vyper were busy pinning the enemy advancing behind us as we pushed forward.

Suddenly, we were taking fire from ahead of us.

"Here! Cover!" I shouted, directing us into a nearby building. There was no getting around it, we were surrounded. "Back exit?"

"Yeah, there's one that leads into an alley," Nyx said, coming out from sweeping the back room.

"Let's move," I said.

Nyx and Dutch led the way through the back door and we all spilled out into the alley. Vyper and Atlas covered our backs as we pushed deeper into the shadows between the buildings, climbing over rubble and stumbling over loose footing. My limp was becoming worse and then Nyx was there.

"Let me take the girl," he said.

He didn't wait for my answer as he grabbed her from me. I didn't protest, simply took his AR he pressed into my hands and we were off again. We were almost to the other side of the alley when two men rounded the corner nearly on top of us and shot Dutch point blank in the face.

All hell broke loose. A grenade rocked the ground around us, sending Nyx and the girl into a nearby wall. At the other end of the alley, Preacher was exchanging blows with one man, Atlas with the other. Instinct had long since taken over and I laid cover fire behind us, pinning the advancing teams at the far entrance of the alley. I didn't like how trapped and exposed we were in this bottleneck. I saw Vyper out of the corner of my eye grab the woman.

"Only one of us needs to get the target across the line," he said before he disappeared.

I didn't have time to curse his name six ways till fucking Sunday for ditching us. As soon as the other team ducked away to reload, I ran over and helped Nyx to his feet. He was dazed and had a nasty gash on his shoulder but otherwise seemed okay.

Atlas and Preacher had dispatched both of the men quickly but Preacher had a limp now and one of Atlas' eyes appeared nearly swollen shut. To top it all off, we were dangerously short on ammo and not nearly as close to the DZ as I'd like.

"On me," I commanded.

Atlas took the lead with Preacher behind me while I supported Nyx who after a few steps shrugged off my help. We jogged through a neighboring building, encountering no resistance. We were a block from the DZ when I heard gunfire.

Two teams were after Vyper as he tried to make a run for it—it was a straight shot to our DZ, but I watched him get a few yards from safety and a bullet hit him in the thigh, sending him to the ground. The woman was thrown to the side as he fell. She scrambled away, terror in her eyes as bullets flew by her.

I watched the opposition reach her and grab her as she screamed and struggled. I was already on the move, Atlas cleared two men out of my way and then I was on the soldier. I ripped the woman away from him and shoved her towards Preacher. My fist connected with his jaw and then my gun was at his head and I pulled the trigger.

I watched Nyx slit a man's throat and shove him to the side at the same time Preacher dragged the woman into our zone ending the game. The buzzer sounded immediately and the sound of drones filled the air. In seconds, military grade drones were hovering above us, replaying the same message over and over on a loop.

"Game over. Return to your bases."

"Fuck that!" A man on the other team said angrily. He made to step over the boundary line and a drone immediately shot him in the head.

Silence descended on the group and I watched the other men make the smart decision and run off back towards their own safe zone. Ignoring the drones, I stalked over to Vyper who was clutching his thigh, chest heaving as he tried to catch his breath.

"What the fuck, Vyper?" I demanded.

"What's wrong, Kraven?" He sneered. "Not happy you weren't the one to win it for us?"

"No, I'm pissed because that was a fucking disaster out there," I yelled. "We're lucky we only lost Colt and Dutch!"

"Oh, we didn't lose Colt," Preacher said. "Vyper left him behind."

Vyper glared at Preacher then looked back at me and shrugged.

"He was a liability," he said casually.

"You're the liability, Vyper," I said. "I don't trust you."

"Too bad—this isn't the real world, Kraven," Vyper said. "This is a fucking game. I'm not losing because some pretentious fuck is used to giving orders—"

"You're right," I nodded. I pulled my gun and pointed it at him. "This isn't the real world."

"Whoa—Kraven," Preacher protested and took a step towards me but I watched Nyx casually step in his path.

"Do you want this man at your back, Preach?" Nyx asked.

Preacher's lips pulled tight, realizing he was outnumbered.

"Come on, Kraven," Vyper said. "It's just a game—"

"I'm not dying here because you can't execute," I hissed. "You left a man behind. You hesitated at the cage. You left your fucking team—we won't get through this if we don't work together."

Vyper rushed me and knocked the gun away. He hit my injured calf and I went down with him on top of me. I struck the side of his face with my gun, the force knocked him sideways and I got to my feet. I kicked him in the chest, sending him backwards in the dust.

"Fuck you, Kraven!" He spat at me.

I stepped towards him, raised the gun, and pulled the trigger.

No one spoke as his body went slack, and I heard the drones fly away. I can only imagine the show we'd just put on for whoever was on the other end of that feed. I tossed the gun away and stripped my vest off, a wave of claustrophobia rushing over me. When the double doors opened, I walked through them without looking back.

The drive back to Vetticus' estate was quiet. The woman wasn't with us when we loaded into the van, so it was just Preacher, Nyx and Atlas with me. My entire body hurt and my leg was throbbing. The others weren't in much better shape, we'd definitely be feeling it in the morning. Once we arrived back at the estate, we stepped out of the van into a familiar forest scene, the estate ever watchful on its perch among the mist shrouded trees.

The guards directed us inside where our first stop was a large infirmary with a full hospital set up. There were several operating tables, hospital beds and all manner of instruments needed to triage and treat most injuries. Three stone faced nurses stood ready to receive us with the guards watching our every move, ARs ready as they stood watch over the exit.

The all male staff tended to every cut and bruise on my body, dosed me with painkillers and gave me an IV of fluids all while handcuffed. It was efficient and thorough. I was less injured than the others so I was first to return to our quarters down the hall. Once the guard removed the cuffs and left me alone, I immediately went and turned on the shower.

I stayed under the spray, letting the scalding water wash away my sins. I expected to feel something...remorse maybe, regret, especially for having to kill Vyper...but all I felt was empty as my mind replayed the entire game.

Nyx and Atlas had impressed me.

Nyx was ruthless and aggressive. He was always thinking ahead, and he anticipated his teammates moves, and acted accordingly. I felt like I'd been working jobs with him for years. He never hesitated, never questioned and didn't fall apart under pressure, instead he seemed to expand into it. He took risks but only if he knew he could do it without endangering his teammates.

Atlas on the other hand was the definition of a soldier. He obeyed orders and executed with precision. He moved off of Nyx and I, observing us before making his own move to support and defend. He was lethal with his rifle—a dead shot every time—one of the best snipers I'd ever encountered and his accuracy wasn't isolated to just his sniping. I'd seen him shoot a man in the eye, then take out the second one the same way all within less than two seconds.

Now that I'd seen them in action, I knew we could build a good team around the three of us. But the others had to buy in too or there'd be no cohesive action and that would just result in all of us getting killed. The longer you worked with a team, the closer you became and the better you knew each man intimately and could work off of that instinctively. I knew the three of us would be dangerous, but I was worried about having more teammates like Vyper. Someone who saw this as simply winning or losing. It wasn't that black and white. But for now, all I could control were the three of us and that was a good enough place to start

38

NYX

Well, that was...interesting."

"That's one way to describe it," Atlas muttered.

We were stitched up, showered, and now I was exhausted. I threw myself into an armchair and swiped a bottle of water, draining it in one go. North was sitting in sweatpants, reclined on the couch with his arms across the back. Atlas sat next to him, looking over the food that had been waiting for us when we got back. He didn't seem to have any qualms about eating after what we'd just done whereas I needed a minute to decompress before I even thought about consuming anything other than water. Preacher was staring out the windows, arms folded across his bare chest. I could see his scowl reflected in the glass.

"Preach, come sit down or something, you're making me nervous," I said.

He was still wound so tightly and something about him was on edge. I didn't like it. He turned and walked over but his scowl didn't leave his face. He looked at the food then fixed on North.

"That was a fucking disaster," he snapped. "What the hell were you thinking killing Vyper?"

Ah. There's the problem.

North looked up at him calmly. "He was a liability. That man would have cost us the game or more importantly our lives."

"So you're just going to off anyone you deem a liability? If they're not good enough for you, what, you're just going to put a bullet in them?"

"Preach, come on," I said. "You were with him the most. You can't tell me you trusted him..." Preacher didn't even look at me, still glaring fiercely at North who didn't break eye contact.

"Yeah, I know but that's not the point. There needs to be some sort of structure or we'll descend into chaos and we'll just all be killing whoever we want, whenever we want."

"That's a very cop thing to say," I chuckled, and he shot me a glare.

"Don't bring that into it," he snapped. "I think I handled myself just fine out there with all you jarheads."

"That's a marine—"

"I don't fucking care," he hissed.

"Is that what you're worried about?" North asked. "That I'll kill you?"

"You're welcome to try," Preacher growled. "Many have."

North looked amused but shook his head. "I would agree with you—from what I saw you handled yourself out there—"

"So what, I have nothing to worry about?" That seemed to make him angrier, and he scoffed and looked away.

"We're not going to just go around killing teammates," Atlas grumbled.

"You can't guarantee that," Preacher said. "Your friend here is unpredictable—that's just as bad as Vyper in my opinion."

Atlas and I were right in our assessment of him in the beginning—North was a force in the field—a true team guy. An absolute lethal soldier who anticipated, planned and executed with ruthlessness and precision. I didn't see him as unpredictable—in fact, he was the opposite. Unlike his usual closed off self, I found I could clearly read him in the field and work off of him so we were in sync—a flow state I craved during missions because of the way I could perfectly combine my instincts with orders so I could operate at my personal peak performance. Like a good leader, North quickly learned my personal idiosyncrasies and made them work for him. He did the same thing with Atlas, working us quickly into a well-oiled machine.

"Sit down, Preacher," North said.

Preacher hesitated, but I watched North's eyes sharpen, I knew a test when I saw one. When he still didn't move, North's jaw ticked, but he didn't blink. Instead, I saw Preacher try to match him but North's entire energy radiated fuck with me and find out. Finally, with a low growl in his throat, Preacher sank into the other armchair. North leaned forward and rested his arms on his thighs as he looked at Preacher.

"I want you to understand something," he said. "Men like Vyper are the first ones to get themselves killed in the field. I'd love to interview his teammates and I bet you they'd have similar experiences with him like we had today. But that's not why I killed him—I killed Vyper because all he cared about was winning the game. All I care about is getting myself and my team—" He stressed my team and gestured to Atlas and I. "—home alive. He only cared about himself and getting the glory of being the one to win it. I don't want that kind of man at my back. It's not about skill—we can deal with someone who doesn't know everything or doesn't execute perfectly. I can't deal with selfish bastards who have no regard for the man standing next to him."

He leaned back and crossed his ankle over his knee.

"Good teams—the teams that really excel and get everyone out alive—they assimilate, they work to capitalize on the individual to achieve cohesiveness. They work off everyone's strengths and fill in the weaknesses. Vyper was not capable of doing that."

As North was talking, Preacher was slowly losing his scowl. He couldn't deny North had a point and while the cop in Preacher probably would always despise taking the rules into our own hands, he was logical and could see the appeal, and the necessity, of what North spoke about.

"I can't promise I won't kill someone like that again," he said dryly. "But I can promise that I will do everything in my power to get myself and the people around me out alive. Because, Preacher, this is all a means to an end. I want to survive so I can get out of here and make Vetticus regret ever even knowing my name. Is it a game? Sure. But survival is more important and when it comes to that, we play by our rules."

Preacher was silent, regarding North with less of a scowl and more like he was trying to decide something. After a breath, he nodded once and sat back in the chair.

"Alright," he said begrudgingly. "My trust has to be earned and I can't say after today I'm there yet..."

"I expect nothing less," North said.

A commotion near the door had all our heads turning in that direction as a guard entered dragging the woman from the game behind him. She was now clean and instead of red paint she was wearing a red bra and panty set. She looked young and in shock but her eyes were glassy, making me think she might also be drugged.

"Reward for winning today," the guard said before dropping the girl in the middle of the room.

No one spoke. We all stared at the girl who was kneeling on the rug and trembling. I sighed and ran a hand over my face.

"This is fucked up," I muttered as I stood up. "What's your name, sweetheart?" I watched her eyes jump to me and trail warily over my naked chest as though I was going to jump her at any second.

"Lana," she murmured just loud enough to be heard.

She pushed a brown curl off her face and wrapped her arms around herself, goosebumps breaking out over her skin. I walked over to my bed and picked up my sweatshirt and handed it to her. She looked up at me, the fear so potent I could feel it coming off her in waves, but she slowly took the sweatshirt from me and put it on.

"What does he expect us to do with her?" Preacher demanded.

"I'm your—you know—reward," she said quietly.

"You mean—does he expect us to fuck you?" Preacher asked incredulously. Lana nodded, her lip trembling as she looked up at me again.

"Jesus—" I muttered. I ran a hand through my hair and looked over my shoulder at the others.

"The winning team gets me for the night," she murmured.

39

ATLAS

I scowled at the implications of Vetticus dropping our prize off for the night. I knew I wasn't going to touch her and based on the looks on Nyx and North's faces; they weren't either. I stood up and walked over to my bed, sitting on the edge facing Nyx. I watched North get up and head to his bed too.

"I'm not going to touch you," he said. "Can't speak for the others though."

He laid down on his bed and closed his eyes, throwing an arm over his face and effectively shut everything out. He'd been everything I knew he'd be today during the job. Fearless, bold and lethal—like he'd told Preacher, he took our strengths and used them to his advantage instead of trying to mold us into what he wanted. A true leader and I was happy to follow him. I'd already grown to like him and trust him but after today, those feelings had grown tenfold. There was no going back—we were bonded by blood now and the way we all worked together had been a beautifully dangerous thing to behold.

"I'm not going to do anything either," Nyx said. He leaned his head back against the wall behind him and looked over at me.

"Don't look at me like that," I said. "I'm not touching her."

My heart ached at the thought of everything Vetticus had taken. I missed my partners terribly and thought about them every day. Nyx must have seen the despair in my eyes because he swung his legs over the edge of the bed and faced me fully.

"Where'd you learn to shoot like that," he asked.

I knew he was trying to distract me and I let him. I rubbed the back of my neck and threw him a small smile.

"My dad was a big game bow hunter and sharpshooter competitor. I've been handling guns since I could walk. I started competing when I was a kid and throughout my teenage years before I enlisted."

"It shows," Nyx said, looking impressed which filled me with a warmth I wasn't expecting at his praise. "That's where you get your speed from then."

I nodded. "Comes in handy out there."

"If Vyper hadn't made it such a disaster, I would have almost considered today—fun," Nyx said, a smirk pulled at his lips as he regarded me with those dark eyes where his shadows liked to dance.

"Seriously? You enjoy getting shot at?" That came from Preacher who'd been listening from his place in the armchair.

Nyx turned to him and shrugged. "Sometimes the only way to feel alive is by looking death right in the face."

Preacher blinked at him and shook his head. "I can see why you're called Reaper," he grumbled, but a ghost of a smile flickered across his face before he looked away.

Nyx chuckled. "Something like that," he said easily.

"How did you get the name?" I asked.

Nyx shrugged. "Ah, it's not a good story but the cliff notes version is I had the highest kill count on my team and I would usually wear a skeleton face covering when I was just hanging around. One day, the guys were telling a story about a specific job—details aren't necessary but basically the Grim Reaper was referenced. From then on, I was either Grim or Reaper. You know how those things go—sometimes things just stick."

That made sense. After seeing him in the field, the way he flirted with death was both exhilarating and nerve-wracking. He wasn't quite reckless; he cared about his team too much for that, but he definitely pushed the line hard. The name fit him.

Preacher grabbed a sandwich and walked over to the girl who'd walked over to the glass doors and was looking out at the landscape as it slowly descended into late afternoon. He handed it to her with a soft smile.

"We're not going to touch you," he said. "The last three beds are open if you want one."

I watched him walk past us to his bed where he lay down and closed his eyes. I looked back at Nyx and he raised his eyebrows at me. I got the message—Preacher was a strange one but not unlikable. He was just a cop who'd found himself in with a bunch of soldiers who barely had morals. He seemed to live his life by a code of some sort and even though he hadn't hesitated to jump in and kill people, I could tell it didn't come naturally to him like it did the three of us. Still, he'd survived Vyper and the game, so I was interested to see how he'd fall in with us.

The next morning, a commotion woke us up.

Several guards swarmed into the room followed by Vetticus. I was instantly awake, watching him as he crossed the room to the bed Lana was in. He grabbed her by the hair and dragged her into the middle of the room. I saw the gun in his hand and jumped out of bed at the same time as the others, but the guards pointed their weapons at us and we all froze.

"I see my reward was not appreciated," Vetticus said, his gaze sweeping the room. The fear was back in Lana's eyes as she knelt at Vetticus' side, his fist in her hair. She whimpered as she grasped his wrist with both hands.

Without warning, Vetticus pressed the gun to her head and pulled the trigger. The gunshot was deafening in the enclosed space and I watched in horror as Lana fell dead onto the rug, blood quickly seeping across the fabric staining it crimson.

"This is what happens when you don't take advantage of your target after a win," he nudged the body with his foot. "I have no use for her."

Vetticus turned and exited as quickly as he'd entered. Two guards dragged the body behind them as they left, leaving us to stare at the puddle of blood in the middle of the floor.

"What the fuck," I muttered.

"He's insane," Preacher exclaimed.

"It's all about control," North said quietly.

Nyx and I exchanged a look before he sank back down on his bed.

"Didn't know he cared about us like that," he said crassly but the joke was weak, even for him.

It was a good reminder of just how unhinged of a person we were dealing with. It was just one more thing we had to do in order to survive this long enough to get out.

40

THERON

A week went by and Nyx, Atlas and I settled back into our routine.
Now that I knew what to expect, I wanted to add in strategy meetings to discuss the best ways to navigate the maps and what to do in worst-case scenarios so we'd all be on the same page if shit went down. Today was our first one, and I'd chosen a spot out in the middle of the lawn, far away from the cameras and any listening ears.

"So what do we know?" I asked.

"The target is a human being," Nyx said dryly.

"Yes, which makes her a variable. She's only fixed until a team gets to her. Having a target with a mind of their own could get complicated," I said. "What else?"

"We start out unarmed," Preacher said. "Ammo is pretty scarce."

I nodded. Preacher had slowly been coming around. At first he was doing his own thing and only talked to Nyx and sometimes Atlas, but yesterday he'd stopped by the weight rack as I was finishing my set.

He watched me as I sat up.

"How's the leg?" He asked.

"It was just a ricochet luckily," I said. "Didn't even need stitches."

There was a slightly awkward silence, and I looked up at him, then nodded my head towards the lawn. "We're about to do some hand to hand—you're welcome to join."

Today, he'd joined us in our workout routine and now he was sitting next to Nyx, chewing on a blade of grass and contributing to the conversation.

"Yeah—ammo seems to be random. It's either in a cache or randomly loaded into some guns but not others. It's paramount we spend the first part of the game outfitting ourselves and finding enough ammo to go into the offensive and then sustain us on the defensive," I said.

"We have sixty minutes," Atlas said. "And the drones are very serious about boundaries and rules."

I thought back on how the soldier had crossed the boundary and the drone shot him down. It was definitely a deterrent not to get out of line or do anything shady after the buzzer ended the game.

"The tactical gear was a surprise," Preacher said.

"Yeah, I was half expecting he'd make us go in this," Nyx chuckled, plucking the sweatshirt off his chest.

"I wonder if the map is going to be different each time," Atlas said.

"Knowing Vetticus, I bet it will be," I said. "He wouldn't want us to get comfortable."

"Makes planning difficult," Preacher said.

"There are cameras everywhere," Atlas said. "And they listen to us through our comms units I'd imagine."

"That's going to add another layer to escaping," Nyx said.

"We'll have to get the trackers out quickly," Preacher added.

"When are we going to try it?" Atlas asked.

"I think we need to be careful," I said. "When we make a move, we need to execute it flawlessly or Vetticus will tighten things up and make it even harder. Right now I don't think we have enough information to guarantee success."

Surprisingly, it was Preacher who agreed first. "I agree. We need more information. I don't want to 'try'—I want to make sure we don't have to attempt it a second time."

"After the next game we'll have another discussion about logistics with that," I said. "How are we going to account for new team members?"

"I think as long as we're the core four, they follow our lead or they can go off on a suicide mission for all I care," Nyx said. "Let them dig their own grave." He looked at me pointedly and winked.

I looked around the group. Atlas nodded and Preacher shrugged.

"That's a variable for sure," Preacher added. "But I think if they want to go rogue, we just do our own thing. A four-man team can still get the job done."

"Then North doesn't have to shoot anyone," Atlas said dryly.

"Exactly!" Nyx exclaimed.

I shook my head in amusement. "Alright, what could we have tightened up last game?"

"Jesus," Nyx said. "Everything?"

"At least you weren't stuck with Vyper," Preacher said with a shake of his head. "I didn't disagree with you on the fact that he was a liability. He didn't check his corners, hoarded ammo and left Colt behind without even a see you later."

"Yeah, exactly why we're letting the feisty ones get themselves killed from now on," Nyx said. "I think we fell apart in the church."

"Everyone was kind of doing their own thing," Preacher agreed. "I think I spent more time yelling at Vyper to open the damn cage than actually communicating with anyone else."

"I agree with that," I said. "Tactics kind of went out the window and we had no communication with each other at all."

Preacher looked around at us. "Despite that you guys looked like you'd been working together for a long time."

"Aw, thanks Preach," Nyx grinned.

Atlas shook his head. "Well, it does have a lot to do with what North was talking about earlier about leadership."

Everyone looked over at me. "I agree—but a leader has his work cutout for him if there's no skills to work with in the first place and luckily, there is no shortage of that here."

"Okay, okay—" Nyx gushed. "Enough with the sappy compliments."

We moved on to other topics, but my mind wandered back to the thoughts of escape. If we could hone our skills, build the team out and bide our time—we could find a weakness in Vetticus' games and capitalize on it. We just had to be patient.

41

THERON

EIGHT MONTHS CAPTIVE

We stood in front of the double doors again. We'd gone through the same song and dance as before—cuffed, loaded into a van and driven to an unknown destination using mostly roads far too bumpy to be paved. It made me question where exactly we were to warrant having enough space to house so many intricate maps.

When we arrived at our destination, we unloaded into the staging room where we put on our gear. I was adjusting Preacher's vest when the doors opened and three men walked in. A red head with a cocky smile took us in.

"It's play time boys!"

I looked over at Nyx who ducked his head to hide a smile and Atlas just looked at them with annoyance. Preacher didn't even spare them a glance and instead turned towards the doors.

"What's your name, soldier?" I asked him.

"Billy. This is Vince and Dash."

I nodded. "I'm Kraven. That's Preacher, Phantom and Reaper. This your first game?"

"Yes, sir," Dash said.

"I have two rules; follow orders or fuck off and if you go rogue, you're on your own. We work as a team, we survive as a team and if we really execute well together, we win."

"Have you won yet?" Vince asked. I went to stand in front of the door by Preacher as the announcement looped.

"Yeah boys," Nyx answered for me. "You're on the winning team now."

The double doors opened, and I stepped out into the bright sunlight to an entirely different scene than the first map. A wide field of grass up to my thighs stretched off into the distance where I could see an old rail yard with a dilapidated train sitting on a track. There was a water tower off to the right, another one on the left and a handful of relatively intact buildings sitting in between them. The small space in front of us was mowed short and just like before there were comms units and a map on the building wall next to the doors.

"Fuck," Atlas cursed. "We're going to be sitting ducks coming back."

"We'll just have to kill everyone then," Billy said.

"Easy Rambo," Nyx said. "You're no good to us dead."

"There isn't a reward for heroics here," I said.

"What's the move, boss?" Atlas said, looking at me.

"Why is he in charge?" Billy asked.

"Because he's proven he's not a fuckup," Nyx snapped. "You barely look ready to have your training wheels come off."

Billy opened his mouth to fire off a retort, but I held up my hand.

"I told you before, you go rogue, you're on your own. The target is a woman in a cage, the objective is to bring her back here. You, Dash and Vince sweep that eastern section of the rail yard. We'll meet at the middle crossroad here," I said pointing at the map.

"The target is a woman?" Dash asked.

"That's what I said."

"Be sure to load up on as much ammo and fire power as you can," Preacher said. He shoved a comms unit into Billy's chest.

"Copy that," Billy said with a smirk.

The buzzer went off and Billy motioned for Dash and Vince to follow him. They took off towards the eastern section of the rail yard. Preacher watched them jog off.

"It's like Vyper all over again," he said with a sigh.

I agreed with him but I didn't care. If someone wanted to be reckless and treat this like a real video game, they could do as they damn well pleased but I didn't want anything to do with it.

"Let's roll out." I motioned for the men to follow and we took off at a jog across the field. The first cargo car we came to had two .45s, and some grenades. We swept through the two next to it and found an ammo cache.

"Sucks to be the kids," Nyx chuckled.

I shoved a clip into the gun before loading up on ammo. Preacher carried the other .45. In the next car we found a sniper rifle for Atlas.

"You know someone is going to camp on those water towers," he said almost wistfully as he checked and loaded the rifle.

"Well then, we know where to aim," I said as I looked out of the railcar to plan our next move.

"Billy, status report," I said.

"Found firearms, working on ammo now," Billy said over comms.

"Copy that."

We were at the edge of a cluster of buildings. They stretched a few blocks deep before they gave way to another sloping field that led down to a farmhouse. I studied the building for a long moment.

"Damn it," I muttered. Nyx followed my gaze and shook his head.

"What?" Preacher asked.

"They're thinking Vetticus probably put the target in the farmhouse," Atlas explained, taking a peek himself. He lifted his rifle up so he could look through the sights.

"Well, I'd like something heavier than a .45 if we're going to take a barn that's exposed like that," Preacher grouched.

"I agree," I said. I looked back at the buildings near us.

"Let's sweep a few of these buildings," I said. "See what we can find. Preacher, Nyx—those two," I pointed out the two buildings. "Atlas with me."

I ran across the dirt road, and Atlas and I methodically cleared two buildings. We found an AR, a few more grenades, a knife and another .45, then quickly met the others back at the railcar to assess our haul.

"Vetticus sure has a thing for .45s," Preacher muttered. "Not that I'm complaining—"

On top of what Atlas and I found, Preacher had come up with another .45 and a handful of smoke grenades. Nyx found another sniper rifle. We checked the firearms and loaded them then moved onto the next building. We hit pay dirt there and by the time we were ready to move on, we were all armed with an AR, two .45s and an assortment of grenades. In addition to all of that Atlas had his sniper rifle and the one Nyx found.

"Feel better, Preach?" Nyx asked with a grin.

He chuckled. "Fuck yeah."

"Billy, what's your status?" I asked over comms.

Silence. "Billy, come in."

I exchanged looks with the men. "Dash—Vince, come in."

Nyx shook his head. "Fuckin' kids man."

"That was fast," Preacher muttered.

I gave up trying to reach them and went and stood near the window, looking carefully out at the barn on the bottom of a gently sloping hill.

"You know if we're wrong, we just lost this game," Preacher said.

"Isn't that where you'd put her?" I asked him.

Preacher frowned but didn't reply. Beyond the barn were a few railcars and the water tower sat like a silent sentry nearby. Atlas had his rifle up.

"Already a camper up there," he said. "He's busy looking at something slightly east of us though."

"What about the barn?" I asked.

"All quiet."

"Do you think that vehicle works?" Nyx asked. I looked down at where he was looking and saw an old wartime jeep sitting near the barn. It looked less decrepit than everything else around it.

"Could be worth a look," I said. "Alright, we're going to follow that dry river bed to that bridge, then Atlas—I want you to take out the sniper. Nyx watch our six—Preacher with me." AR clatter rang out somewhere deeper in the cluster of buildings behind us, lending us a sense of urgency to get moving.

"Go!" We dropped into the river bed and followed it at a quick pace to a cobblestone bridge about eight feet above our heads. Atlas quickly set up in a corner on his stomach, setting his sights on the water tower. Nyx was on the other side, watching the buildings we'd just come from.

"Fire when ready, Atlas."

"Incoming," Nyx said. "Team of six at the buildings—sniper setting up second-floor window."

"Preacher, see if you can get that jeep working. Nyx, stay here and cover Atlas—take out that other sniper. I'm going for the target."

"Copy."

Atlas fired. "Sniper down."

"Go!" Preacher and I took off across the small open area, weaving until we hit a low stone wall and vaulted over it.

"Laying cover fire," Nyx said.

The gunfire started up and Preacher and I took off again. I left Preacher at the jeep and ran around the side of the barn. I peeked through one of the loose slats and sure enough, there was the cage in the center of the straw covered ground. I saw a team entering from the back doors. They spread out, three took stances facing the front doors while two flanked the leader who headed for the cage. I tossed a smoke bomb through the open window above me and ran towards the back. I edged inside and quickly took out the first man I came upon.

"Gettin' a little hot out here," Nyx said. I could hear the gunfire over his comms and then a grenade went off.

"Get down here," I whispered. A man rounded the hay bale, and I grabbed his wrist, quickly shot him in the face and crept through the smoke to another hiding spot.

"Jeep might work," Preacher said. "Everything looks good, electrical works, want me to start it up?"

"Not yet—" A body collided with me and I went down.

We rolled through the hay across the floor as the smoke dissipated. My AR tangled under me and the man's gun slammed into my face as he gained the upper hand. Through the blood, I shoved my body up and rolled, grabbing for his gun. He pulled the trigger and my ears rang as the bullet just missed my head. I ejected the clip and slammed his elbow in the wrong direction making him grunt in pain and loosen his hold on the gun. I pressed it to his head and pulled the trigger, killing him with the remaining bullet.

The smoke was nearly all the way gone, and I saw Nyx and Preacher join the fight near the door. I rushed up to the cage. Inside was a naked woman like before, except this one had somehow removed her cuffs and was working on picking the lock with a piece of metal. She saw me approach and tried to speed up her efforts.

"Back up," I barked. I raised my gun to the lock. After hesitating briefly she did as I asked and I shot the lock off. "Are you going to walk nicely out of here or do I have to carry you?" I asked.

She pushed dark red hair out of her face and glared at me. "I'll walk."

"Target acquired!" I called. "Preacher—"

"On it!" He called, running out to the jeep.

"Get to the jeep!" I shouted.

I felt more than saw movement behind me and shoved the woman at Nyx just in time to turn around and dodge a knife to my neck. I used the man's momentum to send him into a wood post, stunning him. I turned towards the doors again just in time to see the woman push Nyx away from her, putting him into enemy fire. I watched a bullet hit his neck, and he went down.

"Atlas—get her to the jeep!" I barked. I reached Nyx who had a hand on his neck and a wild look in his eyes.

"Is it bad?" He asked.

"Can't be if you're still here," I panted.

I yanked him to his feet and together we ran out the front doors. I threw him into the front of the jeep and replaced my hand on his neck with his own just as the engine turned over.

"Let's go! Let's go!" Atlas shouted.

He was shooting at the advancing team who was sprinting towards us. A grenade landed near the jeep just as Preacher kicked up a cloud of dirt as he peeled out of the barnyard. I joined Atlas in the back, laying cover fire as Preacher sped down a dirt track towards the open field.

A bullet hit the car frame near my head. Atlas was busy taking out the team pursuing us so I grabbed the other sniper rifle and braced myself against the crossbars. The ground was bumpy, uneven and Preacher was now driving erratically to avoid getting picked off. Bullets were flying everywhere from both the sniper and the enemy.

I looked through the sights but I knew it would be nearly impossible to land a good shot. I lined up as best I could and pulled the trigger. The shot went high, hitting the tower above the sniper's head. It caused him to duck down along the edge, giving us a few precious seconds. I heard a pop, and the jeep lurched and listed to the side.

"The tire was hit!" Preacher shouted. "We're a hundred yards out!"

The jeep limped further before it smashed into a shallow ditch and threw us all forward. Nyx hit the dashboard, I slammed into the crossbars and Atlas was thrown across my legs.

"Go! Go! Go!" I shouted.

Preacher dragged the woman from the jeep and took off through the field. Nyx fell out of the jeep onto the ground, his hand still pressed firmly to the bleeding wound at his neck. I risked a quick look and was relieved to see it wasn't gushing. At least that meant it probably hadn't hit anything vital.

Nyx and Atlas lay cover fire for Preacher as I set the rifle on the hood and found the sniper again. A few rounds peppered the vehicle, and I cursed and ducked down, just barely taking cover. I popped up again and put the sniper in my crosshairs. I felt Atlas at my back and heard his rifle fire as he covered me from the advancing team on the ground.

"Fifty yards," Preacher called out on comms as he counted down the yards to the drop zone. I took a deep breath, steadied my finger on the trigger and trusted Atlas not to get my head blown off. I released my breath, pulled the trigger and with a jerk the sniper went still.

"I'm out," Nyx said, ducking back down and tossing his gun aside.

"Twenty!" Preacher yelled.

I turned my sights on the advancing team only to have Atlas yank me down to avoid a string of bullets. He leaned out, spraying his AR at them.

"Ten!"

The buzzer sounded, and I heard the drones as they advanced on the teams to ensure compliance. I moved over to Nyx and tore a strip off my shirt, wrapping it around his neck.

"Fuck man—" He panted. "That was a close one."

He met my eyes, and I saw the adrenaline had overtaken him, the shadows had completely consumed his eyes. Covered in dirt and blood with violence dictating your every move and having just executed a successful mission—no adrenaline rush could ever hit as hard as this.

I yanked out my comms unit and tossed it at the jeep. I looked at Atlas who did the same and then Nyx followed suit. We both hoisted Nyx up, but he swatted us away.

"It's my neck, not my legs," he griped. We walked back towards the DZ through the tall grass and a hum of a drone followed us. I looked up to see it hovering. Without warning, I pulled the .45 I still had on me and shot it down just to piss off Vetticus, then continued walking. We came up on the DZ to find Preacher crouched in the grass catching his breath. I walked up and shook his hand.

"Great job, Preach," I said.

The tension around his eyes lifted slightly. "Thanks." He gripped my hand tightly. "Boss," he added with a curt nod. I returned the nod and turned towards the doors as they opened.

"Where's the girl?" I asked.

"They took her already," Preacher said.

"No sign of Billy and the other two?" Nyx asked.

Preacher shook his head.

42

NYX

We were back in our quarters—stitched up, showered and picking at the food left for us. The doors opened and the woman from the games was delivered. As soon as the guards left, North advanced on her angrily. She retreated quickly at the intensity in his eyes until she couldn't go any further. He grabbed her jaw and shoved her hard against the brick wall.

"You almost got Nyx killed out there," he snarled.

"Fuck you—" she hissed. "I don't care what happens to yo—" He shoved her head back against the wall again with a growl.

"T—" I said.

"Do you know what happened to the last target we won?" North demanded, ignoring me. The girl's eyes watered at the intensity of his grip but she didn't speak.

"We didn't take advantage of her so Vetticus came in and shot her in the head." Fear flickered across her face.

"What?" She gasped.

"I've half a mind to let him do the same with you," he said angrily.

"No—" She protested.

North pushed away from her and turned to me, his eyes drifting down to my neck that had fresh stitches and a new bandage. It was just a deep flesh wound that had bled a lot and while it would probably scar, it wouldn't have any lasting problems. It was close and I'll never forget the way the world slowed down and the frantic look on North's face when he saw me go down.

"She almost got you killed out there," he said to me. "I'll leave the decision up to you."

"No—please—I'm sorry—" She took a step towards us.

North turned back to her. "You should be begging Nyx to spare you. Maybe apologize to him first."

She came over and knelt in front of me, clutching at my sweatpants and looking up at me with tears clinging to her lashes.

"I'm sorry—so sorry—" she said in a shaky voice.

I studied her for a moment and contemplated killing her. She'd been a liability out there and we were already putting ourselves in enough danger. But, I was alive. I threaded my hand through her hair, softly at first then tightened my grip, making her wince. I yanked her head back, so she had to lean awkwardly forward to look at me. I leaned down close.

"If you fuck us over again, I won't stop North from having you killed. Understood?" I said darkly. "Or maybe I'll just do it myself."

"Y-yes," she said in a breathy tone.

I straightened and plucked at her bra strap. "Take off your clothes," I demanded. She quickly obeyed and once she was naked, I pushed down my sweatpants just enough to free my cock. I couldn't deny the adrenaline of fighting made me fucking horny. I stroked my length a few times, getting myself all the way hard while she watched with apprehension.

"Have at it then," I said. I kept a firm grip on her head but allowed her to move closer and take me into her mouth.

Fuck yes. The feeling of her tongue sliding over my head before she took me into her mouth was heaven. My eyes shuttered as the pleasure cut through the adrenaline and my muscles tensed in an effort to hold back from ramming my dick down her throat.

Soon her shallow sucking wasn't enough. My other hand joined in holding her head and I set a brutal pace. Tears streamed down her face as she choked with each thrust down her throat. Her hands gripped my thighs, but she didn't protest or struggle and took everything I gave her. My lips curled into a snarl as I looked down at her with hooded eyes, taking out my aggression and pent up anger on her mouth.

"Fuck," I gasped.

Movement drew my gaze away from her and landed on Atlas who'd leaned back on the couch, a dark look in his eyes as he watched me. His eyes jumped up to land on mine. A hungry look and a mischievous smile tipped me over the edge and with another groan I shoved her head down, making her take all of me as I came down her throat, my eyes locked with Atlas before I threw my head back, relishing the feel of her swallowing around my head.

I let her go, and she sat back on her heels, gasping as she choked slightly, swallowing what she could. I looked down at her and ran my thumb over her bottom lip, swiping some of my come. I pushed my finger into her mouth and she dutifully sucked it off.

"Good girl," I murmured.

I pulled my pants up and collapsed onto my bed, leaning on my elbows. I looked over at Atlas and flashed him a rogue smile.

"I revise my earlier statement about being an ass guy—I might be a mouth guy." My gaze dropped involuntarily to the bulge in Atlas' sweatpants. Atlas chuckled and my eyes snapped up to him to see amusement dancing with desire.

"You can be an ass man too," he said.

There was no missing the underlying message there. I'd never been interested in a man before, and I wasn't sure if I was interested in men or just interested in Atlas. Our connection went beyond anything I'd ever experienced before and was a convoluted mess of friendship, the trust that came with serving with someone and whatever this was. All of it centered around the fact I felt like I'd known him for a lifetime.

"You're right," I said lightly. "Why choose?"

We held each other's gaze for another moment longer, both of us trying to decipher what the hell was going on. I had a feeling he knew more than I did. All I knew was that when my dick had been down her throat and my eyes had landed on his—for the briefest moment, I'd pictured him on his knees for me instead.

43

THERON

The woman got to her feet and took a few steps towards where I sat on the edge of my bed.

"Stop," I demanded, and she froze. "Crawl."

"What?"

"Crawl to me."

The room fell completely quiet. I didn't take my eyes off the woman but I could tell Nyx, Atlas and Preacher were watching. I saw defiance flash across her face and her lips thinned but she slowly dropped to her knees and lowered onto all fours. Glaring hatred filled eyes at me, she crawled across the ground until she was kneeling between my legs. Her eyes were on the ground and were quickly welling up with tears as the emotions of the day overwhelmed her.

"Good girl, Red." The nickname came quickly and slid easily off my tongue.

Her gaze went to mine, and I watched a tear slide down her cheek. I brushed it away with my thumb and rested my forearms on my thighs.

"Spread your knees." I kicked her thighs gently apart revealing her pussy. "Touch yourself."

Surprise crossed her face, but she didn't question me and I watched her bring two fingers to her pussy and slowly rub her clit.

"You're wet already," I said, smirking at her. "Someone doesn't hate this as much as your mind would like you to. Did you enjoy Nyx shoving his cock down your throat?" There was that anger again like I anticipated. Shame, then denial were always the first emotions.

She opened her mouth to flash back at me and I shoved two fingers between her lips, sliding them across her tongue and into her throat. Usually I wouldn't make that a rhetorical question but I wasn't in the mood for her brattiness. She gagged and saliva flooded her mouth, dripping down her chin and onto her heaving chest as her breathing picked up.

Her skin grew flushed as her fingers picked up the pace. My other hand fisted her hair, holding her head in place when she tried to move away from my fingers down her throat. She gagged again and her eyes watered. I brought my wet fingers between her legs and slid them inside her while she rubbed her clit. She moaned and closed her eyes, panting as I curled my fingers into her g-spot.

"Look at me," I demanded softly.

Red's eyes snapped to mine, and I watched the anger and defiance get pushed out by submission. She whimpered as she got closer to the edge and she grew wetter around my fingers, her pussy clenching as her hips pushed against my hand. She cursed and whined, panting as her release hovered just out of reach.

"Please—" she gasped. I growled my approval, not expecting she would ask my permission to come.

"Please, what?" I said.

"Please, may I come?" She was squirming against my fingers, panting and her skin flushed to a pretty pink all over her face and chest.

"Nyx forgave you, but don't think for a second I'll tolerate bullshit like today again. Understand?"

She nodded quickly. "Yes, sir."

"Good girl—ride my fingers, make yourself come."

She spread her knees wider as she leaned forward, grinding on my fingers. I stopped teasing her and let her find her rhythm and pressure until her eyes shuttered again.

"Eyes on me," I commanded. Her pleasure filled gaze clashed with mine. "Come for me," I said, my voice rough.

Her pussy squeezed around my fingers, and then she was coming with a soft cry. I stroked her through her orgasm, watching every gasp and twist of her features as she claimed every bit of the wave she was riding. When the tremors subsided, I withdrew my fingers from her pussy and shoved them back down her throat.

"Suck," I commanded.

She looked at me with eyes half shuttered, as she closed her mouth around my fingers and gently sucked her release off them. My cock was hard in my pants and I pulled her to her feet and walked her to the wall where I shoved her face first into the stone, holding her there.

I freed my cock and in one quick thrust, shoved inside her. We both groaned and her hands curled into fists near her head. I closed my eyes, not wanting to look at her. I fucked her hard, one hand in her hair, the other digging into her hip. She tightened around me and I couldn't deny how good it felt to have my cock buried in pussy again.

Her whimpers and soft sounds pulled me higher, and my release blazed up my spine. My movements grew rapid and my breath shallow as I felt my come fill her. I took a few deep breaths before pushing away and pulling my pants up. I didn't bother seeing who she went to next but went straight into the bathroom. I turned the sink on and let the water run, pressing my palms flat against the countertop and meeting my gaze in the mirror.

I hadn't had sex since Whit and the act made me think of nothing but her as much as I tried to push her from my mind. I couldn't help but recall her soft curves, the sounds she made, the look in her eyes when I made her come...but mostly, the adoration and love for all my dark corners that she effortlessly accepted.

It'd been almost a year now since Vetticus ruined my life, yet it felt like only days. I wondered if the ache would ever go away. I wondered if missing them would ever hurt less than it did right now. But mostly, I wondered if I'd ever be able to move on.

Red was nothing but a warm hole to fill because Vetticus demanded it of us. I should have felt something about having to fuck her—regret, sadness at Whit's memory maybe—but I didn't feel anything. Not a damn thing except the emptiness that seemed to plague me.

What would I be after this? A shell of who I was before?

I wasn't sure I even knew who I was before this.

Violence was in my blood—for as long as I could remember. Even growing up, an abusive father, narcissist mother, I'd learned to look after myself and manipulate the world into working for me. Until I'd met Whit and became a father myself. Emersyn and Cole were like a light to the darkness wrapped around my soul. When I was with them, I left the shadows behind. But now, the shadows were free again, the darkness nearly suffocating in its hunger for revenge. There was no pushing it back and I was convinced by the end of this, there wasn't going to be any light strong enough to drive it back.

I finished up in the bathroom and walked back out. Nyx and Atlas were passed out in their beds and Preacher was still indulging in Red. He had her bent over the edge of the couch, a hand around her throat as he drove into her. I fell into bed and threw my sweatshirt over my eyes, listening to the sounds of sex and wondering what fucked up thing Vetticus would come up with next.

The next morning they came and took Red away. She didn't look back as the door shut behind her. I turned and saw Nyx struggling with the bandage at his neck. I walked into the bathroom and slapped his hand away.

"Thanks," he grumbled. I peeled it away and frowned. Any further left and he wouldn't be standing here. The anger surged all over again and I caught Nyx staring at me in the mirror.

"I didn't expect you to make her come last night," Nyx said.

"It was hot wasn't it?" I grumbled.

Nyx chuckled. "Yeah—but you didn't have to."

"I know," I said, not offering anything more. His eyes were drilling holes in my face as I wrapped the dressing around his neck, careful not to make it too tight.

"I guess I don't understand what the problem is," I said dryly.

"You were ready to kill her minutes before that."

"Sometimes you have to manipulate the body before the mind will follow. She probably won't do what she did out in the field again. I figured a different kind of death would be more effective."

Nyx chuckled and shook his head. "That oddly makes sense."

I finished tying off the bandage.

"We didn't even ask what her name was," Nyx said.

"Does it matter?"

Nyx tilted his head in agreement and brought his hand up to his neck.

"That was the closest call I've ever had."

"Did it change anything?" I asked. He looked more thoughtful than afraid as he grinned at me in the mirror and shook his head.

"I wondered...if I'm the Reaper, then who's coming for me?"

"The devil himself probably," I mused, returning the grin even though on the inside I wasn't smiling. I hated how close I was getting to these men, including Preacher. It only made my obligation to them more profound. They were my responsibility, and I hated it. I hated it because when they died, I'd be alone again. Nyx may be the Reaper but the devil followed me everywhere I went, and it was only a matter of time until he claimed everyone around me.

One day, it would be each of them.

44

ATLAS

TWELVE MONTHS CAPTIVE

This game was a disaster.

"Atlas!" I turned at the sound of North barking my name.

"Find that fucking sniper!"

We were currently pinned down behind a run down barn. The ground sloped away in front of us and ended in a rapidly moving river. The bank soon rose to steep cliffs and in the distance was a massive bridge where we could see the target's cage sitting in the middle. We had to cross the open area and somehow make it over to the bridge without getting shot by the team across the river. There was little cover—only a few sparse trees and one low running stone wall I was very hesitant to trust with my life.

We'd already lost one of the new kids. I couldn't even remember his name but we'd run into another team in the rundown country town behind us and they'd shot him point blank.

"Nyx, cover," North ordered.

I pulled back and with Nyx following, went into the building next to the barn. It was a blown out ruin of a two story building but there were still stairs to the second floor and I ran up them, mindful of the gaps. I lay down in the debris from the blasted out wall and looked through the sights of my rifle. I scanned the far bank of the river. That side sloped gently like ours and was almost a mirror image with buildings high on the bank. The sniper pinning us was in one of them. I heard the impact of bullets below me as we were hit again and I saw a flash of glass reflected in the sun.

Got ya.

Adjusting my sights, I zeroed in on him. He was hiding in a similar rundown building, but I was slightly above him giving me the advantage. I took a breath and on the exhale pulled the trigger.

I watched his body go slack through my sights.

"Clear," I reported.

"Copy," North said. "You and you—get to that next building, we'll lay cover fire. Nyx wait here and watch Atlas' back. Atlas make sure no one else decides to camp on us. Preacher with me."

I heard North, Preacher and Nyx lay cover fire as the two new kids raced off to the next building, then covered North and Preacher as they ran to join them. I took out another soldier and scanned for more. I wished I had eyes on the bridge but my angle was wrong.

"No longer have eyes on the enemy. They're moving towards the bridge."

"Copy," North said. "Atlas—you and Nyx see if you can find a hide with a view of the bridge."

"Copy."

I made my way back down to Nyx and together we rushed to where the others were situated behind a rock wall. This was the last building closest to the bridge. Nyx and I bypassed the team and headed up into a nearby building. It was a little farther away, but it had a better view of the bridge. I settled on my stomach and looked through the sights towards the bridge.

"Target confirmed," I said. "Middle of the bridge."

Whoever got to the target would be exposed for an uncomfortable amount of time. The bridge was nearly a half mile long and the drop off the side was dizzying before it plunged into the rapids.

"It looks like she's handcuffed to the bars this time," I said.

"Rocky, Finn—head towards the bridge, stay low."

They took off, and I quickly took out a soldier hiding behind some bushes near the edge of the bridge on the other side who was taking aim at them. Then I heard gunfire on our side of the river.

"Fuck—Nyx—"

"On it—" I heard fighting and close combat.

"Damn it, Preacher's hit," North said.

I looked out over the landscape again, cursing under my breath. Rocky and Finn were pinned down behind that ridiculous rock wall. I was about to take out another sniper when pain erupted through my shoulder and I recoiled at the impact. I slipped and fell down a few stairs as I scrambled away for cover, then Nyx was there.

"I got ya," he said. "Atlas was hit." He threw my arm around his shoulder and half carried, half dragged me out of the building and into the neighboring one where he put me down beside Preacher.

"Pull back!" North demanded.

"Leave them!" Rocky snapped over comms. "It's right there! We can do it!"

"Negative. Pull back," North answered.

"Fuck that—I'm going—Finn?"

"I'm game, let's roll," Finn replied.

North lifted his head above the wall just enough to watch the fools race off towards the bridge. They'd been nothing but trouble this entire game. Putting themselves and us in questionable situations. North growled in frustration before kneeling next to me. He pulled off my tactical gear and ripped my shirt off.

"They're right, you should go, T!" I said, trying to push him away from me. "The four of you can still—" The pain made me dizzy, cutting off my words, and I was sweating profusely even though it wasn't hot. But I didn't want us to lose because of me. We were so close and this would be our first loss.

"You're lucky this was a ricochet and not a full .50 cal," North grumbled, ignoring me as he quickly did a field dressing on the wound and manhandled me into a sitting position.

"I'm serious," I said, wincing at the movement.

"It's not worth it," Nyx answered, gun trained on the street.

"I'm not losing you over some stupid game," North snarled.

Preacher was leaning heavily against the wall, blood running down his side. He looked deathly pale. North had tied half his shirt around the wound but his breathing was labored, his face creased in pain.

"Back to the DZ," North said, lifting me to my feet and slinging my arm over his shoulder.

"Come on, Preach," Nyx said, doing the same for him.

"Looks like it's the four of us again," I said as we piled into the van at the end of the game. We'd been yards from the safe zone when the buzzer had gone off signaling the end of the game. The kids hadn't returned.

"If they'd stop giving us children, we might actually be able to hold our numbers," Nyx muttered.

"At this point, I'll take anyone who doesn't treat this like they'll respawn somewhere," Preacher said weakly. "I know I'm not a soldier, but I wouldn't want those kids at my back during a raid."

"I think we can make you an honorary one at this point," Nyx said dryly.

Preacher gave him a weak smile. "Oh good, I get to be a jarhead now—"

"I told you, that's a marine," Nyx said in mock exasperation.

"Same thing."

"Oh, he did not just say that," Nyx said, looking over at me and then North. I laughed but quickly stopped when it jostled my shoulder.

"He's messing with you," I said.

Preacher just looked smug or tried to, before he grimaced and shifted to try and alleviate the pain. I leaned my head back against the van wall, trying to shut off the discomfort. It may have been a ricochet, but it was deep in my shoulder sending an ache through my entire arm. I was lucky the sniper was a shit shot. That and the fact I'd settled behind a thick wall of concrete and steel. Close calls weren't new to me, I'd had my fair share when I was deployed and my fucked up brain just didn't know how to take an attempt on my life seriously.

All I wanted was to get out there again and do better.

We got back to the estate, and they filed us through the infirmary again. They didn't believe in true pain management apparently because they barely numbed my shoulder before digging into the hole left by the bullet fragment. I lay on the table cursing and sweating and tried not to give into the urge to murder every single person poking at me. Preacher wasn't fairing much better next to me. He was viciously cursing and calling the nurses every horrible name known to man. It would have been funny if I wasn't being subjected to the same thing.

Finally, they were done and after dosing us with pain pills, sent us back to our quarters. Preacher limped along next to me, looking pale and murderous. My arm was throbbing and all I wanted to do was lay down and sleep. I didn't want to think about the fact we didn't win. The girl wouldn't be coming and instead we were going to find out what the punishment was for losing.

Nyx was pacing in front of the door when we entered. His concerned gaze swept over me before he saw I was still in one piece and he relaxed, giving me an easy smile.

"Miss me?" I joked. Before he could answer, two of the guards followed in behind us and flanked Nyx.

"Hands," one of them said.

"What? Why?" North barked.

In answer they grabbed Nyx and shoved him against the wall, cuffing his wrists behind his back while the other held us at gunpoint.

"Where are you taking him?" I demanded.

North's features hardened, and he took a step towards the doors.

"What's going on?" He demanded again.

But they didn't answer and instead, all we could do was watch Nyx get dragged out the door and the ominous click of the lock behind them.

"Where do you think they took him?" Preacher asked.

"Is this what happens when we lose?" I asked. "Someone gets taken?"

No one answered me.

An hour passed and still Nyx hadn't come back. Preacher had dozed off, exhausted and in pain but I couldn't sleep and instead resumed the pacing Nyx had abandoned, walking back and forth in front of the door.

"Atlas, sit down," North snapped. "You're not doing anyone any favors if you pass out."

I gritted my teeth in irritation but sat down in an armchair, fixing my attention on the door and trying not to let the fear and apprehension overwhelm me. Nyx still hadn't returned when the lights went off in the cell, casting the room into darkness. The only light was the glow of a lantern down the hall and soft moonlight coming in from the windows.

Despite trying to stay awake, I realized I'd dozed off when a few hours later, movement in the hall startled me awake and then guards were dropping an unresponsive Nyx inside the cell. I jumped to my feet, glancing at North as we both hurried over and knelt next to him. He was naked and in the moonlight I saw bruises all over his body. I hauled him half into my lap, trying to rouse him as North checked his pulse.

"What the fuck," I muttered. "Nyx—" I patted his cheek gently.

"Is he drugged?" North asked.

"He must be—hey—Nyx—wake up—"

Nyx moaned and his eyes fluttered open only for him to jolt in my arms and lash out, his eyes wild.

"Hey—you're okay—" North said.

Nyx drew in great heaving breaths when he realized where he was. He rolled onto his side between North and I, resting his head in his hands as he supported himself on his elbows. His body was shaking from the comedown of the drug he'd been on and whatever the fuck Vetticus had subjected him to. I put a hand on his shoulder and he flinched.

"What did they do to him?" Preacher asked.

He tossed a sweatshirt and pants to us.

"Nyx, put these on," North said.

He let us help him with the sweatshirt but once we got him to his feet; he yanked the sweatpants from my hands and shoved them on himself. When I reached out a hand to steady him, he stumbled back a step.

"Don't—don't touch me—" he said, his voice hoarse.

He headed over to his bed and North and I trailed after him. When he climbed under the covers; we stood nearby looking down at his indistinct shape with concern. After a moment, I heard North growl softly in frustration before stepping over to his own bed. I did the same, and it wasn't until we all settled on the verge of sleep that I heard Nyx speak through the darkness.

"We can't lose again."

45

🔥 🔥 🔥

THERON

The next morning, Nyx didn't get out of bed. Breakfast came and Atlas tried to get him to eat something but he shook his head and turned his back on him. When it was time to go out to the yard, he refused again and simply lay there staring at nothing. The three of us went without him, trying to get through a workout without taking our anger out on each other.

"We need to find out what they did to him," Atlas growled as we walked around the track. It was almost time to go back in and we'd all nearly killed ourselves trying to expel all the excess frustration and energy. Atlas had busted his stitches and Preacher looked pale again but anytime one of them tried to sit still, they only jumped back up a moment later. I knew the feeling—idleness made for busy thoughts and no one wanted to be in their heads right now.

"Yeah—whatever it was, it was bad," Preacher said. "Do you think it really has to do with losing?"

I shrugged. "It must because this is the first game we've lost."

We walked in silence for a full lap. We'd made a lot of mistakes this last game. None of us liked to lose and now we'd just been shown how high the stakes really were.

"He was covered in bruises," Atlas growled. His jaw was clenched so hard I could hear his teeth grinding together. The look on his face was murderous.

"He was tortured then," Preacher said with disgust. "Every man has a breaking point. Vetticus finally found his."

When we got back, Nyx was sitting on the edge of his bed with his head in his hands. He looked up when we entered and his eyes were sunken and bruised. Atlas handed him a water bottle and Nyx's hands had a tremor to them as he took it. He nodded his thanks but refused to look him in the eye. In fact, he avoided direct eye contact with all of us, something he'd never done before.

I stood near the glass doors and watched him, debating how to handle him. Something terrible had obviously happened and now he'd retreated into himself. I couldn't afford to have someone like that out in the field. If we were deployed, he would have been pulled from duty immediately. I needed sharp and focused minds. The other part of me was foaming at the mouth to tear Vetticus apart for reducing Nyx to this.

He was mine to protect, and I'd failed.

The atmosphere of the room was awkward and tense. I could tell Atlas and Preacher didn't know what to do either. I watched them try to go about their normal routines, but so much of our day involved Nyx's banter and sick sense of humor that it all felt wrong.

Dinner was delivered, and we all sat down in the sitting area to eat together like we did every day. Nyx hadn't moved from his position on his bed and was now staring at a point on the ground.

"Fuck this," I muttered.

Atlas straightened at my tone and Preacher paused with a piece of broccoli halfway to his mouth. I could feel their eyes on me as I walked over and stood in front of Nyx. I waited until he looked up at me. He didn't meet my eyes but focused on a point over my shoulder.

"Look at me," I commanded.

Nyx sat up straighter and while his mouth thinned, his eyes slowly slid to mine. They were haunted—the darkness in them muted, like he'd lost a part of himself and didn't know what to do without it. His hands were balled into fists so tight his knuckles were white and I could practically hear his heartbeat pick up as the anxiety of meeting my gaze took over.

"You don't have to talk about what happened—"

Nyx tried to look away.

"No—look at me, damn it," I demanded harshly.

His gaze snapped to mine, but I saw the anger there and I nodded once.

"Yes, get angry," I said fiercely. "Whatever he did to you—" I spoke deliberately and made sure he was holding my gaze "Don't let him win." I said each word hard and slow. "He wants to break you. He can and he will. But just know, whatever happened, I don't think any less of you for what you had to endure to survive. None of us do."

I put my hand on Nyx's shoulder and watched him visibly flinch. He felt like a tight wire about to break.

"*Fuck. Him*," I said as I leaned closer. "That goes for all of you," I pitched my voice so the others could hear while still looking at Nyx. "Whatever happens in this place, we endure it, we survive it. We don't hide—got it?"

The others murmured their replies but Nyx still hadn't spoken. I saw the anger in his eyes. It was better than nothing. I'd rather he be angry with me than withdrawn and numb.

"That's an order, soldier," I said dangerously.

"Yes, sir," Nyx answered.

I walked away then, letting him compose himself. It was his choice now. He would either come out of this with anger as fuel, or he would collapse in on himself and we'd lose him.

I really hoped that wasn't the case.

46

NYX

The shame clung to me and I couldn't shake the oppressiveness. I hated feeling like I should have fought back even though he'd made it impossible. Vetticus had restrained me, drugged me and subjected me to psychological and sexual abuse. Now, I couldn't look anyone in the eye and I wanted to both scream and murder someone with my bare hands. I was currently attacking the punching bag in the gym while the rest of the guys worked out nearby. I was shirtless, drenched in sweat but furiously trying to get rid of the rage inside me. My shoulders were aching, and I was gasping for breath when I finally stopped.

We only had about thirty minutes left to be outside so I took off across the lawn to the dirt track that circled the pond. I did sprints until I couldn't anymore and collapsed on the soft grass, staring up at the sky.

I heard the steps of someone and turned to see Atlas lower himself down near me. He stretched his legs out and leaned back on his hands as he followed my gaze up to the sky. It was a gloomy day and my sweat was quickly growing cold on my skin. Atlas tossed me my t-shirt, and I put it on with a grateful nod of my head. He passed me a water bottle next and watched me take a sip. I felt awkward in my body after last night. I'd hoped working out would bring me back but apparently it was going to take time.

I'd always prided myself in being resilient, tough and unbreakable under pressure. Vetticus had stripped all of that away in hours with a drug and his fucked up personal sexual vendetta. The fucked up part was, he'd manipulated my body but he broke my mind. For a moment I'd lost my anchor to reality and myself, and he'd capitalized on it. I was embarrassed and filled with shame that I couldn't endure it. I was afraid Atlas would ask me about what happened but when he finally spoke it wasn't what I expected.

"I think our escape plan is going to have to center on finding the perfect map," he said.

"What do you mean?"

"Well, a map like this last one wouldn't be a good choice. It's too open and exposed. A map like the first one—the torn up city—that would be easier, less exposed."

I nodded. "Makes sense. We have a little problem though."

"The trackers, yeah."

"I mean, we have access to knives during the games so it'll just be a matter of getting them out quickly. It'll all have to be timed perfectly."

I forced myself to meet his eyes—I'd promised North I wouldn't hide.

"How's your shoulder?" I asked him.

"Hurts like a bitch," he grumbled. "I could really use some pain killers—or a shot of whiskey at least."

"Oh god, alcohol," I moaned. "I'd kill for a stiff drink right now."

"I bet there's some in that house," Atlas said, looking off at the massive mansion ominously watching over us from its perch on the hill. I frowned, knowing there was.

"That's where they took me," I said quietly. I don't know why I said it because I didn't want him to pry and ask questions, but instead of speaking, his gaze hardened as he looked at the house. I didn't know what he was thinking, but he finally held up his hands as though he was holding a rocket launcher and made a sound effect like he was firing.

"One day," he said. "I'm going be holding an actual rocket launcher aimed at that building." He sighed and stood up, taking a moment to dust himself off before he held out his hand to me. I hesitated.

"I don't want to talk about it," I blurted out. "And I don't want anyone's pity." Atlas' eyes narrowed. He shook his head and gave me a small smile.

"No one pities you, Nyx," he said dryly. "We just want you to be okay. If you want to forget—we'll forget—if you want to talk about it—I'm here to listen—if you want to plan all the ways we're going to brutally murder Vetticus when we get out of here, then by all means, please give me all the graphic details. But pity you?" He shoved his hand forward again. "It's just not what we do." I grabbed his forearm and climbed to my feet but when I tried to extract my arm, he pulled me closer. I froze.

"We're in this together," he said, but it almost sounded like a question.

The memory of watching him touch himself as I came down Red's throat jumped into my head but I quickly shied away from it. After what Vetticus did, was I allowed to think about Atlas that way? Or was that now a product of Vetticus' abuse? Did I want another man touching me sexually after everything I'd just endured? I pushed it all from my mind. Those were questions for another day—one day.

Instead, I nodded and gave him a small but grateful smile.

"Yeah, we're in this together."

47

ATLAS

A few days later, I woke up abruptly and lay in the darkness wondering why. Then I heard sounds coming from the bathroom and saw Nyx's bed was empty. I walked over and stood in the doorway watching as he punched the tiled wall, methodically, his knuckles already bleeding. I reached out a hand and touched his shoulder. He rounded on me, his hand going to my throat and he pushed me hard up against the wall with a snarl.

"Don't fucking touch me," he hissed.

My hands stayed by my sides even though the impact jarred my shoulder something terrible. My jaw tightened at the jolt of pain and his eyes immediately dipped to the bandaged wound. He cursed and instantly let me go. He turned and ran both hands through his hair, making it stand up on end. I hated seeing him like this, leaning heavily over the sink with both hands flat on the tile and his head bowed between his shoulders. He was usually the one with all the quips, the dark humor and the shadows in his eyes that just begged to come out and wreak havoc. I hated to see him hurting and knowing there wasn't anything I could do to help.

"Nyx," I said.

He looked at me in the mirror. The moon's weak beams filtered through the skylight above us, flashing briefly in the blackness of his eyes.

"Talk to me, Nyx," I whispered. He bared his teeth in annoyance and shook his head as he looked away.

"Fuck off. I said I don't want to talk about it."

"I know but—how can I help you?"

He rounded on me again but didn't lash out this time.

"You can't help me—it's all up here," Nyx hissed, pointing to his head. "That fucker dug himself under my skin and I can't—I can't get him out. I'm too weak—"

"You're not fucking weak," I snarled, taking a step towards him as my own anger flared. "I see you, I know you and I would never use that word anywhere close to you."

He shook his head again as though I didn't understand. "I can deal with pain, Atlas," Nyx said. "But he—he drugged me and then touched me. He broke through every wall, associating touch and pleasure with something so vile I can't even bear to think about it now!"

My blood ran cold then hot as fury flooded me so fiercely I couldn't breathe. Thinking something like that had happened and actually hearing it from Nyx's mouth were two very different things.

"You know, I think I even could have handled the abuse if it had just been purely sexual," Nyx rasped, his voice heavy with annoyance and pain. "But he used that pain drug on me again and he talked the entire time. He knew things—things about my past, about people I loved, and he used it all against me." He leaned back heavily against the counter and dug his hands into his hair.

"We're his obsession," Nyx said flatly. "He gets off on everything. All of it. Watching us—controlling us." I bared my teeth and took another step towards him, horrified by his words but also pissed the fuck off.

"No, he is not in control," I growled.

"But he is, Atlas." Nyx looked up at me and I saw something that scared me more than anything he'd just said.

I saw defeat.

I grabbed him by his shirt and shoved him hard against the counter.

"You do not give in to him," I said viciously.

"You weren't there," he snapped. "You don't know what it was like."

He shoved at my chest but I didn't budge.

"Unfortunately, I know all too well what you just went through." My voice was ice even as my blood boiled with my own repressed memories of trauma I hadn't unpacked in years. "When I was ten, a family member raped me—repeatedly—using psychological manipulation by threatening my family."

Nyx went still.

"I'm not telling you for any other reason than to help you hold this. North was right; Vetticus will break us, I know its coming, but he will regret every touch, every word and every fucking bit of what he's put us through when all of this is said and done."

Both of our chests were heaving with emotion and I realized through my anger, I still had a death grip on the front of his shirt. I released him and took a step back.

"I'm sorry that happened to you," Nyx said.

"And I'm sorry too, Nyx. But don't you dare pity me—I didn't once pity you during all this so don't you fucking dare turn it on me now."

"Never," he whispered.

We stared at each other for a long moment and then I took a hold of his hand and examined his bruised and bleeding knuckles.

"Did it help?" I asked.

"No," Nyx said in a tone that was finally close to his usual dry humor.

I looked up and flashed him a quick smirk.

"You know what will?" I grabbed a paper towel and ran the water. I dabbed gently against the cuts before looking back up into that black abyss I was in danger of getting lost in. "Winning. Planning our escape. And getting the fuck out of here." I took his other hand and put it over the paper towel before I turned to head back to bed.

"Atlas," Nyx said. I looked over my shoulder. "Thank you."

One step brought me back in front of him and I bravely brought my hand up, gripping the back of his neck.

"You matter—to us, to me—we can do this."

He nodded, and I breathed a sigh of relief when I saw the defeated look was nowhere to be found. Instead, the deadly look of resolve was back, and I knew he was eventually going to be okay.

"Together right?" He said quietly. His hand rose to match mine and his fingers curled around the back of my neck sending something hot and visceral flashing through my blood.

"You better fucking believe it."

We pressed our foreheads together, the closest we'd ever been. I longed to step over the line and explore this feeling rising up through our friendship and connection, but not here, not now. Not in this place where our demons were fighting for control, threatening to consume our humanity.

I gave him one last look before heading back to bed. As I lay down and closed my eyes, I wondered if we'd be able to stay sane through this—to stay human. If we did manage to escape, would there even be anything left to save?

48

THERON

SIXTEEN MONTHS CAPTIVE

The weeks turned into months and Nyx slowly came back to us. A week before the next game, he'd pulled me aside and told me what Vetticus had done to him. By the time he was done, he had to physically grab me to stop me from attacking the guards who had just dropped off dinner. I had every intention of storming that god forsaken mansion and beating Vetticus to death.

"Hey, whoa, T—stop," he'd said. "I told you all this because you told me not to hide. I know how dangerous someone who isn't all mentally there is out in the field and I refuse to be the liability because my mind isn't clear."

I'd grabbed him by the shoulder and watched his shadows rise to meet mine. "I am going to get us out of this and then we will spend however long it takes getting our revenge." The sneer on Nyx's lips and the dangerous glint in his eyes made my words all the more potent.

"I like the sound of that, boss."

Now, I stood staring at the double doors about to step foot into another game and the stakes were higher than ever. I could feel Nyx's nervous energy vibrating next to me but when I looked over at him, he was focused. The doors opened, and we stepped out into the awaiting arena. I immediately went to stare at the map on the wall. Atlas passed me a comms unit while I studied the crude drawing.

"This is going to be a close quarters game," I said.

Nearly the entire map was a low-lying forest area with a few platforms concealed in trees. There was a large stream that ran diagonally through the map and a cluster of buildings scattered here and there. A road wound through the trees with no visible destination.

"What's the play?" One of the newbies asked.

I'd stopped trying to remember their names. Two of them looked young, but the other was eyeing me critically. He was older than me, maybe in his forties, bald, with a gruesome scar cutting through his eye and across the side of his mouth, drawing it down into a perpetual frown.

"First priority is always fire power and ammo," I said. "You three take up the rear guard. Target will most likely be in one of these platforms. No heroics—we work together—we all get back alive."

The two young soldiers nodded but I could see the fire in their eyes for adventure and blood and knew we probably wouldn't be coming back with them in tow. The other one I wasn't sure about. He looked like he'd seen some shit and possibly had potential to not be an idiot.

I led the way quickly through the forest and we picked up a few .45s, a sniper rifle and an AR. Once we'd finally outfitted everyone with firepower, we'd made it deep into the map and were coming up on the first platform. When it came into view, I had the team spread out and drop behind cover.

"You and you—" I said, pointing to the kids. "Up top." They eagerly jumped up and hurried to the ladder built into the trunk of the tree.

"Ammo cache," one reported over comms.

"Load up," I said.

They returned to the ground, and we distributed the ammo then continued on. When we got to the second tree house, the kids went up again.

"There's a cage, but it's empty," one of them said. I motioned for the group to hold and climbed up into the perch. I walked over to the cage and noticed a set of bloody handcuffs, a piece of duct tape and a blindfold sitting nearby.

"Did someone take her already?"

I'd already briefed them about how the target was a woman. Apparently, Vetticus found it amusing not to tell anyone what we were hunting for. Shock value for the viewers no doubt.

"No—the lock is picked, not shot." I pulled a strand of red hair sitting on the cage door. The target was Red again from the looks of it. I looked around the ground and saw a few drops of blood leading back to the door.

"Come on," I said. I dropped to the ground and looked around the base.

"Our target is on foot this time," I said.

"She escaped?" Preacher asked.

"Appears so."

"She went that way," the scarred man said.

"What's your name?" I asked.

"Kane."

"Are you a tracker?"

"Something like that," he said.

He wasn't paying attention to me but looking through the foliage at the trail Red had left.

Before anyone else could comment, he walked off. "This way."

Preacher looked at me but I motioned for us to follow Kane and we headed after him. We formed up around him and headed deeper into the map. A few minutes later we heard the first sounds of gunfire but it didn't sound close. We crossed the stream, and it took Kane a moment to find where the trail picked up again. The woman had followed the water for a bit. We saw a building through the trees and Kane paused and motioned for us to hold.

"You three check out the building. We'll do a perimeter sweep," I said. "Meet back here."

Once they ran off, Preacher looked at me. "Do you think she's in there?"

"No—she got free herself, knew to follow the stream to hide her trail—she's too smart to use the buildings as cover. She knows that's where the teams will think she is being caged."

I led the men through the trees to sweep wide around the building. We spread out a few yards apart, looking for any signs of her. I saw a flash of red hair then bullets tore into the trees near us, making us dive for cover. I strained to see the shooters and instead saw Red make a run for it away from the building and back towards the stream. I jumped up and sprinted to cut her off.

We both heard the voices and dropped for cover. I saw a small team of three walking through the trees straight towards Red's hiding place. I pulled a grenade and threw it in the opposite direction. When it went off, Red shot off, but I reached out an arm and snagged her as she ran by, wrapping a hand around her mouth to cut off her yelp of surprise.

"Quiet—" I demanded in her ear, pulling her hard against me as I shoved my back into a tree.

She went limp in my arms when she heard the voices of the enemy walking nearby. As soon as they were out of earshot, I let go of her mouth. She whirled around, fire in her eyes but it dimmed slightly when she saw it was me. I pulled Red into a crouch with me and looked around at the trees before looking her over.

"Target acquired," I said, keeping a firm grip on her upper arm. "About a hundred yards from the structure—near the stream—"

"Following the stream was a good call," I said to her. "But next time, make sure your wrists aren't dripping blood everywhere."

She held up her wrists and cursed quietly.

"Why'd you escape the cage?"

"I'm not going back to Kai's group," she said bitterly. "I can't risk them finding me first."

"T—coming up on your location," Nyx said.

"Hey, Red," Nyx said, as soon as they appeared through the trees. Kane and the two kids had rejoined us and were eyeing the naked woman with varying degrees of interest and surprise.

"You know her?" Kane asked.

"She's been the target in the last couple games," Nyx said. "Gave me this to remember her by." He pointed to the healed wound on his neck. Her mouth thinned, but she didn't say anything.

"Alright, it looks like we're going to be heading into the action..." I sent Kane and the kid up front. I gave Red to Preacher, and Nyx, Atlas and I took up the rear. We were spread out when all of a sudden one of the kids went down with a cry that was abruptly cut off as he disappeared from view. Nyx and Atlas approached the edge of the pit.

"Looks like an old hunting pit—or Vetticus decided to add in some surprises," Preacher said.

Nyx peered over the edge. "He's gone."

Kane was careful of where he led us after that. We'd only gone a few more yards when I glimpsed movement through the trees.

"Contact—" Kane shouted.

A grenade exploded nearby, cutting him off and sending us all diving for cover. I dove against a tree and braced for the attack I knew was next. The first two men reached us. Nyx and I took them out quickly. I dodged away to avoid getting shot in the head from his partner behind him. I slammed the man into a nearby tree where I hit his hand repeatedly until he dropped his pistol.

He pushed me off, only to come at me with a knife in his hand. I knocked away his quick attack, sacrificing a hit to my ribs to avoid the blade. We clashed again and fire blazed across my chest as he slashed at me before I could block.

Another hit and the knife dug into my side.

With a grunt of pain, I went down on one knee. He yanked the knife out and came at me again, hoping to finish me but I lunged up with a growl and tackled him into the bushes. We crashed through the underbrush and rolled down a slope. He was on top of me as we plunged into the creek.

We'd both lost our guns at this point. All I had was a knife in my boot that I couldn't reach. He punched me in the face and I inhaled water before I hit him several times. I shoved him off me and scrambled to my knees in the shallows. We both saw the gun on the bank at the same time and lunged for it. I grabbed his leg and yanked him back into the water. He came up with a rock and tried to take my knee out with it as I passed him. I slipped avoiding it and he went for the gun again.

He came up with it, turned and pulled the trigger.

There were only feet between us and I couldn't stop in time. The gunshot was deafening and made my ears ring. The only thing that saved me from certain death was at the last second I twisted away, and the bullet cut deeply into my bicep as it grazed me. My momentum took us back into the water as I collided with him.

I heard the gun go off again near my head as we fell.

We thrashed in the water, each attempting to gain the upper hand. He dug his fingers into my side and I folded to my knees where he quickly shoved me onto my back and leveled the gun at my face. There was no way I could move in time and everything slowed as I watched him squeeze the trigger.

The gun clicked. *Empty.*

I didn't have time to breathe a sigh of relief. He growled a curse and clubbed me across the face with the gun before tossing it away and shoved my head under the water, holding me there with his hands around my neck. I struggled in an attempt to get him off but my hips were wedged between two larger rocks and I couldn't get purchase with him sitting on my chest.

My hands closed around a rock and I slashed it across his face, which eased his grip enough for me to break the surface for air. He recovered and shoved me down again. Black started to crowd my vision, and I inhaled a bit of water, making me sputter.

I wasn't going to go out like this though—on my back in this fucking hellhole. I reached down, fumbling for the knife I'd seen in the man's boot sheath. Just when I thought I was going to black out, my fingers closed around the hilt. I yanked it out and blindly stabbed up into his chest under his ribs. I knew I'd missed his heart, so I pulled it out and stabbed him again. He pulled away, and I exploded to the surface.

I didn't bother with trying to catch my breath. Wheezing and sputtering water, I watched the man crawl towards the shore, blood tinting the water red. I lunged for him, shoving his face into the mud. I straddled his back, grabbed the knife I had in my boot and jammed it with excessive force into the back of his neck.

His body went limp under me and I retched up water. Each cough and gasp of breath was a stab to my chest. I heard static in my ear and yanked out my comms, realizing it was useless now.

I climbed off the body and knelt in the sand on the bank, taking deep breaths to steady my adrenaline and to get my brain to think straight again. My hand went to my side where blood was pouring from the knife wound. My vest was restricting. I tore it off, tossing it aside so I could breathe easier. My shirt was next, and I looked down at the stab wound.

It seemed deep, and I quickly ripped my shirt and did a quick bandage to slow the bleeding. I used the rest to awkwardly wrap my arm, gripping the fabric in my teeth to tighten the knot.

Shirtless and in only a pair of standard camo pants and boots, I headed up the bank, pausing carefully at the top. The gunfire was off further in the trees and there wasn't any movement around me so I stood up and did a quick recon of the area. Bodies littered the ground, most of them were the enemy but I came upon the other kid on our team, a bullet through his neck.

I knelt next to him and gently extracted his comms unit and weapons. There were only a few rounds left in the current clip and after looking around the area, I only found one full clip leaving me frustratingly low on ammo. None of the handguns left at the scene had any rounds left in them so I didn't bother. I shoved my knife back in my boot and put the comms unit in my ear.

Chatter instantly assaulted me from my team and I stumbled to my feet with a growl of pain as I clutched my side. I wiped the rest of the water from my face and took off carefully through the trees.

49

NYX

We'd lost North somewhere back near the creek and I couldn't see Kane, Preacher or Red nearby.

"North—" I called over comms. "North come in."

No answer.

Two men appeared out of the trees, too close for guns and I lunged for one while Atlas went after the other. The man landed a solid hit to my jaw sending me stumbling back against a tree and I barely dodged a bullet as he fired nearly point blank. He fired again and the earth near my head exploded.

I have no idea what kind of luck was on my side to avoid a death shot—twice—but I wasn't complaining. The devil obviously wasn't ready to see me yet, and I was just fine delivering others to him in my place.

I whipped onto my back and fired, hitting the man in the face. I heard another gun go off and looked over to see Atlas get the upper hand only for a third man to appear out of the trees behind him and level a gun at his head.

Atlas slammed a knife into the man under him. I lunged to my knees and fired over his shoulder just as his eyes rose to meet mine, a feral look in them. He looked over his shoulder as he heard the man fall and I climbed to my feet and ran over. I offered him a hand up.

"Nice shot," he panted.

I pulled him up and grabbed his neck, frowning as I ran my thumb over what looked like a ricochet bullet that grazed his neck and disappeared just under his ear. My adrenaline was going too heavy to feel any real emotions, but I bared my teeth at the sight.

"I think that was meant for you," he said with a smirk.

I met his gaze and his eyes darkened. I realized we were very close to each other and the sight of him covered in blood was sending heat through me at an alarming speed.

"Wanted to match me?" I asked, my voice coming out gruffer than

I anticipated. He flashed me a quick grin, stark white against the blood splattering his face.

"Where are the others?"

I let go of him and took a step back as I ran a hand over my face and looked off through the trees. I shook my head. I didn't know.

"North—come in—North," I said over comms. Nothing.

"Nyx—" It was Preacher, but he wasn't speaking over comms.

"Fuck," I hissed. Preacher was stumbling to his feet several yards through the trees, his head and face covered in blood. A lot of blood. I jogged over and Atlas followed.

"What happened, where are you hit?" I demanded.

"Fucker hit me with a rock," Preacher said. "A few times." He had blood running down his face. Atlas gingerly touched the back of his head.

"You're going to have a nasty headache later," he said. "But I think you'll live. It's just bleeding a lot."

"Where's North? Kane?" Preacher asked.

"Can't reach them on comms," I said. "Where's Red?"

"She ran off—two of them went after her but so did Kane."

"Kane—" I said over comms. "Kane, come in."

"Where are you fuckers?" Kane's voice crackled in my ear. "I'm about half a mile east from where the grenade went off. Managed to kill one of the fucks that took the girl but the other now has her held up as a hostage."

"Copy that. On our way," I said.

I holstered my pistol and picked up my discarded AR, checking it over before motioning for Atlas and Preacher to fall in behind me.

We crept up on Kane's position and saw he was in a standoff between one of the opposing teams in a small clearing. Both men had guns pointed at each other. Kane was half hidden behind a tree and the other man was holding Red in front of him. Before we were noticed, I motioned for Atlas to flank him.

"We're in position," I whispered to Kane over comms. "Hold."

"Copy," he muttered.

"Just shoot him!" Red shouted to Kane.

"Shut up, bitch," the man said, tightening his hold around her neck.

"Fuck you, Dogtail, I'm not going back to Kai," she said.

"Keep him talking," I whispered to Kane.

"What kind of a name is Dogtail?" Kane called out.

"Your mom gave it to me," Dogtail called back.

"Your mom didn't have time to give me a nickname," Kane said. "She was too busy choking on my dick." I had to hide a smile and Preacher let out a breath that sounded very much like a laugh.

"Jesus," I muttered under my breath. "We really trading mom jokes right now?"

"I'm in position," Atlas called in.

"Finally—put us out of this misery," I said.

A moment later the crack of a rifle rang out, and Dogtail dropped, dragging Red with him. Red scrambled up and raced across the clearing to Kane who wrapped an arm around her, gun still outstretched. Preacher and I joined them and Atlas appeared at a jog through the trees.

"Let's go," she said urgently. "He said Kai was on his way."

"Kai?" I asked.

"He's the leader of one of the other teams," she said.

There was genuine fear shining in her usually detached cold eyes. I nodded and signaled for us to move out. I took point with Red behind me while Atlas and Kane watched the rear guard.

We were almost to the lookout where we'd found the cage when we heard gunfire and Kane went down with a curse and grabbed his leg. A group of soldiers came out of the trees. Kane lunged for Red and pulled her towards cover as I dodged bullets. I collided with one and we slammed against a tree. I used his gun to shoot his friend coming up behind me, then used my own to shoot him point blank. The body fell, and I followed it. I slammed the butt of my gun into his face for good measure.

Then again, because it felt good.

The rage bubbled up, unstoppable and suddenly the man under me wasn't a nameless soldier but Vetticus. I continued to beat him with the gun. Everything disappeared except his face, leering at me. I was out of control and in that moment I lost who I was completely. It should have scared me but it didn't. There was only white hot rage that overflowed and spilled out of control around me.

I couldn't stop. I didn't want to stop. The release was intoxicating.

Warm blood dripped down my arms and sank into the ground under me, churning to mud with every movement. Then my gun was torn from my grip and hands grabbed my face. I was pulled roughly forward and Atlas swam into view, followed by his voice yelling at me. Reality rushed back to me so fast I got lightheaded.

My vision focused and his eyes, hard as steel, pulled me back to myself.

"Nyx!" He was shouting at me. "It's not him! It's not him!"

I blinked and when he saw he had me; he released my face and sat back on his heels. I looked down between us to see a body that was barely a body anymore. I staggered to my feet and turned to see the rest of the group watching me with varying degrees of emotions on their faces.

Kane was looking at me with amusement. Red looked terrified. Preacher gave me a quick glance of resigned annoyance before he went back to scanning the trees, watching our backs while I had my little breakdown. Atlas handed my gun back to me and I saw his gaze quickly sweep over me with a look that I could have sworn looked equal parts concern and hunger before he turned and motioned for us to move out. The clarity I had now was potent and for the first time in weeks, I knew I'd moved past the worst of the trauma.

Violence begets violence.

In this world, in this life, it was the only thing holding me together.

50

THERON

The moment I put the comms unit in, I heard gunfire.

"Atlas—take out that sniper," I heard Nyx say over comms. "Kane—right flank."

"Nyx—location?" I called.

"Fuck, boss—good to hear your voice, I was about to send Preach back for you—we're fifty yards east of the target perch. A team has us pinned down with a sniper and AR in the roost."

"Copy."

Instead of heading east, I headed toward the enemy team to catch them from behind. I saw them spread out along the edge of the treeline near the perch with the sniper and AR trained on my men pinning them down in a depression between some fallen trees. I settled down on my stomach, forcing aside the surge of pain it caused and brought the AR I'd found up to look through the sights. Between the AR and the handgun, I only had a few bullets—I hoped it would be enough.

"I'm in position behind the enemy, at your two—" I muttered into comms.

"Do you have a better bead on the sniper?" Atlas asked.

I adjusted to take in the perch.

"I can take out the gun," I said, although my target was the man's hand on the trigger. It was the only thing visible sticking out of the doorway.

"On my go," Nyx said. I steadied myself and readied for the shot.

"Fire when ready," Nyx said.

I breathed out and pulled the trigger. I watched the bullet slam into the gun right above the man's trigger finger. I didn't wait but trained my gun on the nearest enemy on the ground and took him out.

"Go!" I called as the enemy hurried to regroup. I had time to take out one more before bullets bit into the ground around my hiding spot. I jumped up and ran through the trees, hearing bark explode as I passed. A ricochet whistled past my ear.

"Atlas—get the target across the line!" Nyx shouted over comms.

Minutes later the buzzer sounded, and I collapsed heavily against a tree, gasping in air and clutching my side. I ripped the comms unit out and headed back towards the DZ.

Nyx looked relieved when I came limping out of the treeline.

"Fuck! Where have you been?" He took in my disheveled state—wet, bloody and covered in mud. "You went for a swim? Seriously, T—leaving us to fight the war—bad form—" His words got cut off as I punched him in the shoulder, my eyes scanning him for injuries.

"I'm fine—" he said. "Atlas took a ricochet but nothing deep. Kane got shot in the leg but he's good. Preach might have a concussion but he looks worse than it is—"

He wasn't wrong. Blood covered Preacher's entire head, but he bared bloody teeth at me in a grin and gave me a thumbs up.

Nyx looked back at me. "You look like you were waterboarded."

"Little waterlogged, yeah," I said, trying to breathe around the stabbing pain in my side.

The doors opened and I stumbled as I took a step towards them. The ground lurched under me as a wave of dizziness assaulted me. Nyx was at my side in an instant, throwing my arm around his shoulder. I stumbled my way through the double doors. The last thing I remember was Nyx trying to speak to me as he carefully lowered me onto the ground and then the darkness took me away.

I woke up in the infirmary. The stab wound had nicked my lung and ended up being a little more serious than I'd first thought. I had a broken rib, and the bullet wound on my arm had gone all the way down to the muscle. There were also copious amounts of cuts, scratches and bruises. By the time I returned to our quarters, Nyx was beside himself with worry. It looked like he'd been pacing in front of the door again and when the guards brought me back; he watched me limp in with relief.

"You look...like death," he said.

"Gee, thanks," I muttered.

They'd given me painkillers, but I felt like one big walking bruise. I carefully walked over to my bed and pulled on sweatpants before sinking down against the pillows.

"Do you want food? Water?" Nyx asked.

I shook my head, hiding a smile as he hovered. They'd given me fluids, and I didn't feel like my stomach could handle food yet. He sat down on the edge of his bed and leaned on his forearms. He was watching Kane who seemed to be inspecting every inch of the space.

"He's been doing that since we got back," Nyx muttered.

"How long have you been here, Kane?" I called.

"Year and some change I think," he said. He ran his hand over the back of the couch. "Pretty nice digs. Definitely a step up from the cells."

"Yeah well, welcome to Vetticus' personal Atrox team," Atlas said dryly. "Only the best for his little toy soldiers."

"How long have you all been playing?" He asked.

"What's it been?" I looked around at the guys. "Over a year now, probably. This is our fourth game," I answered.

"Are the maps different every time?"

Atlas nodded. "The only thing that's been consistent is the target. It's been the same woman. When she gets dropped off here—"

"Whoa, wait, what?" His eyebrows shot up. "She stays here?"

"Just for the night."

"And yes, it's exactly what you're thinking," Preacher added dryly. "To the victor goes the spoils and all that."

As if that was the signal, the door opened, and the guards dropped off Red. She wore the same outfit as before—a red bra and panty set. She looked around and glared moodily at us.

"Ah, always a ray of sunshine," Nyx said sarcastically. "I would think you'd be happy to be with us again after how scared you looked at the prospect of going back to—what was his name? Kai?"

Her glare softened, and a wariness flickered across her face.

"Tell me about this other group," I said. "Who's Kai?"

"Kai is the leader of Vetticus' other team," she said quietly. Nyx walked over to her and pushed her hair off her face. She barely held back a flinch. His knuckles brushed across an old bruise on her neck. It was mostly faded but still carried a slightly yellow tone.

"Is that where this artwork came from?" He asked.

"He's a sadist," she said, her voice trembling.

"Sounds charming," Nyx said. "Nice work on your cage earlier."

"Maybe Kai was killed this round," Preacher said.

She shook her head. "I doubt it. He's going to be pissed now," she added. "You killed his second."

"That fucker Dogtail?" Kane asked.

"Yeah, he was pretty pissed about the loss at the rail yard," Red went on. "He talked about teaming up with the other teams to take you down."

Nyx and I exchanged a look, and I shook my head.

"We'll deal with that later," I said. "Did she behave this time, Nyx?" I asked without looking away from Red.

"She did," he walked around behind her and his hand slid around her neck, pulling her back against him. His other hand ran along her hip and settled on her stomach.

"Undress her," I ordered.

51

NYX

My hands ran up her arms and slid the straps of her bra down slowly before flicking the clasp open. It slipped to the ground. I couldn't resist palming one of her breasts and rolled her nipple between my fingers until it was hard and she arched into my touch. My other hand came up, and I did the same to the other one. I heard her give a sigh of pleasure and her body pressed harder against mine.

My hands traveled down her sides and when they got to her hips, I snagged her panties and continued, dragging them down her legs. I knelt behind her as she stepped out of them and nipped her butt hard enough that she jumped and a strangled sound escaped her lips.

"What did he do?" North asked, amused.

"He—he bit me," she said a little breathlessly.

"Atlas," North said. "Take her mouth."

Something jumped in my gut as I watched Atlas walk over. He'd taken out his cock and was stroking himself. I couldn't tear my eyes away as my hands dug into Red's hips from my position kneeling behind her. It felt like I was kneeling for Atlas and when my eyes moved to his, his lips turned up in a wicked smirk that had my cock jumping in my sweatpants. Atlas continued to stroke himself but he wasn't looking at Red, he was looking at me. I somehow tore my eyes away from him and nudged Red's legs apart.

"Open up, love," I murmured.

She widened her stance, and I ran my thumbs up the inside of her thighs and grazed her pussy. Pulling her apart, I licked one long stroke from clit to ass. Red shuddered and nearly lost her balance. Atlas grabbed her hair and bent her over to take him into her mouth. I watched her lips wrap around him as I ran my tongue along her pussy. My fingers found her clit, and she moaned around Atlas' cock. My eyes locked with Atlas, knowing everything I did to Red was impacting his pleasure.

It was a head rush I didn't want to come down from.

"Ride his face, baby," Atlas gasped as he stared hard at me, lips parted.

Red pressed her hips against my face, moaning around Atlas' cock as he shoved into her throat over and over again. I sucked her clit and lightly scraped it through my teeth, making her cry out around his cock and stagger forward. Atlas' groaned as the motion made him sink further into her mouth. He thrust deeply and held his cock there, his firm grip in her hair stopped her from pulling back.

"Fuck, Nyx," he gasped. "Whatever you did, do it again."

I couldn't tear my eyes away from him. I bit her clit again, and she squealed. The most delicious moan escaped Atlas' and his eyes shuttered. A grin pulled at my lips—I was painfully hard now.

"Fuck her, Nyx," North said.

His demanding voice swept over me and I suddenly wanted him to command us both—I wanted to see just what he would make Atlas and I do. If it wasn't for Vetticus watching—which I knew he most assuredly was—I had no doubts North would have pushed the boundaries. It's who he was. And part of me wasn't sure I would've done anything to stop him.

I stood up, my hard cock straining against my sweatpants. I pulled them down and ran my hands up and down my length slowly, watching as Atlas' gaze dipped to watch. His jaw flexed and his eyes were molten pits of forest shadows just begging me to explore their depths.

I grabbed Red's hips and buried myself in her pussy in one solid thrust. The movement sent Red forward into Atlas and they both groaned. Atlas' gaze jumped to mine and each thrust of my cock into Red had pleasure playing across his face as he gritted his teeth against the sensations rolling over him.

"She likes sucking your cock," I panted. "Every time you hit her throat she clenches around me."

"Nyx." My name was a breathless plea on his lips and it made me even more turned on. My gaze raked down his body and I watched his abs flex and wished I could run my tongue over every indent—I wondered what he tasted like. His hands gripped Red's hair, and I imagined them gripping my cock. I bet his hands would be just the right amount of rough. My eyes went back to his, and a slow smile pulled at my lips. I slapped Red on the ass which jolted her into Atlas.

Atlas groaned. "Fuck," he breathed.

So quietly I was sure no one but me and maybe Red could hear, he fixed me with a look of pure dark desire and said; "Come with me."

"Jesus," I gasped. I gritted my teeth as those words alone nearly sent me spiraling. A few more thrust and we were both panting. I reached around and fingered Red's clit, causing her to clench around me and moan around Atlas' cock. She came a moment later, crying out as her orgasm rushed through her.

I saw the moment Atlas was about to break and it was my name again on his lips that sent me over the edge with him. My release hit me hard and fast—dark and reckless and brimming with the unknown of what we'd just unleashed together.

52

THERON

I couldn't tear my eyes away from the tension that erupted between Nyx and Atlas. In another setting, I absolutely would have pushed the line just to see what I could get them to do to each other. I wasn't interested in joining, but I sure as hell liked to watch and orchestrate the pleasure between them.

But not here.

Not here where Vetticus could capitalize on their connection and use it against them. Not here, where our pleasure was only a facade, another way for him to control us.

Nyx pulled out of Red and helped her stand up. Atlas pushed her hair out of her face with a small smile. She looked up at the two of them with a glazed look of pleasure and a little bit of awe in her eyes.

"That was really hot," she said breathlessly. Nyx flashed her a quick grin and winked.

"Go to Preacher," I told her.

Preacher had his arm thrown over the back of the couch where he had watched the entire thing. He was already hard and stroked his cock slowly.

"You three put on quite a show," he said as Red approached him. He pulled her onto his lap and with his hands on her hips, brought her down on top of him. He groaned softly as he slid inside her, not seeming to care that Nyx's come filled her.

"They got you nice and wet for me." He dipped two fingers into her pussy and brought them back to her ass, swirling her and Nyx together.

"Ever been taken there, sweetheart?" He asked.

She nodded. "A few times—I—I didn't like it," she said quietly, her forehead creased in concern.

"I'll be gentle," he said although his eyes held a dark sinful look as he rubbed his fingers between her ass cheeks and pushed them forward. She whined softly in protest. "Just relax, I'll make it feel good."

She leaned forward into his chest, hands gripping the back of the couch near his head in a death grip. Nervous energy was etched all over her face but it slowly gave way to pleasure as she moved up and down on Preacher's cock. Preacher buried his two fingers all the way in her ass and slowly moved them in and out in time with her riding his cock. Red started panting and grinding her hips against him, speeding her movements up as she chased her pleasure. I had a perfect view of Red's ass and I watched Preacher slide his fingers out and gather some of her wetness then he pushed three fingers in. She stopped and squirmed on his lap.

"No—" she gasped. "It's too much."

"Keep going," Preacher said firmly.

His free hand found her clit, and after a few strokes she moved her hips again. Her breathing became erratic, and she made whimpering noises that made Kane curse softly under his breath from where he sat nearby in an armchair.

"You going to come for me?" Preacher murmured. He looked up at her flushed face as his fingers stretched her ass. A gasp escaped her lips, and she nodded. "I need your words."

"Yes, please—I'm going to come," she whined. He teased her clit and a moment later, she shattered on his lap, gasping and crying out as the waves of pleasure crashed over her. She coated Preacher's cock with her come and her movements slowed as she hummed in satisfaction. But Preacher wasn't done. He lifted her off of him and stood up.

"Hands and knees on the couch. Facing them," he demanded.

She obeyed, briefly meeting my eyes with a nervous look. She knew what was coming as Preacher positioned himself behind her. I couldn't see what he was doing but from the look on Red's face, he was slowly working his way into her ass. She hissed and tried to move away.

"Push back, beautiful—relax for me."

He pushed forward more, and she whimpered but didn't protest.

"Fuck, you're so tight."

He gave a solid thrust that made her curse and whimper but his hand came around and played with her clit and as soon as she relaxed, he pushed forward and his hips sat against her ass.

"Such a needy ass, gripping me so tight," he panted.

He moved slowly at first to let her adjust.

"Your pussy likes it too," he rumbled. He must have his fingers inside her because her lips parted and her eyes shut and a look of rapture crossed her face. "There we go."

He picked up the pace and he brought both hands to grip her hips, driving into her hard enough to provide us all with a view of her breasts bouncing. Red gripped the arm of the couch in a death grip but it was pleasure that was overwhelming her now and soft moans escaped her until she couldn't take it and pressed her face into the cushion.

Preacher looked down and pulled her ass apart to watch as he drove in and out of her. He growled in pleasure and a few thrusts later his hips stuttered and he threw his head back as he came. He slowed his movements and looked back down, admiring the way his cock looked as he dragged his come in and out of her ass.

"Beautiful," he muttered. He gave her a quick spank as he withdrew for the final time. He grabbed her hair and pulled her up to look at him. She looked dazed, and he ran his knuckles over her cheek.

"Such a good girl for me," he said. "I told you I could make it feel good."

Her face transformed into glowing pleasure as she basked in his praise. She got off the couch, and took a few steps towards me but I shook my head and nodded at Kane.

"Show the newcomer what victory feels like," I said.

Kane didn't waste any time. He'd apparently watched as much foreplay as he could stand because he grabbed her and forced her to her knees. He pressed his cock against her lips. He was rough and Red quickly had tears and spit running down her face. He held his cock down her throat until she choked and scrambled for air, then he pulled back just enough to let her gasp in a breath before doing it again. Her eyes fluttered, and she almost passed out but he somehow took her right to the edge without her going over. It didn't take long after that and after a few more thrusts; he pulled out and came all over her face. She took it without complaint and when he was done. He smeared his come from her cheek to her mouth.

"Clean it up," he rasped. She sucked his fingers clean, and he repeated the process until his come was gone from her face.

"I think I enjoy winning," he said loudly to the room.

Red looked exhausted as she made her way over to me, and to be honest I wasn't really in the mood. My entire body hurt—pretty much everything except my dick. I growled as she climbed onto my lap, wincing as she brushed my side.

"Easy, beautiful."

 She rocked her hips, rubbing her wet pussy along my cock.

"I'm glad you won," she whispered.

I sighed and leaned my head back.

"Losing is bad for our health it would seem," I said quietly.

"Mine too," she whispered.

"You're going to have to get me hard again," I said to her. She nodded and slid down my body until her tongue swept over my length from base to tip. She took me between her lips and I closed my eyes, sinking into the pleasure. It didn't take long, and I grabbed her hair and pulled her up to me again.

I ran my hands up her thighs and lifted her hips. She grabbed my cock and eased her way onto me until she was sitting with me fully inside her. I ran my hands up her back and into her hair. My hand gripped hard and yanked her forward, bringing my lips near her ear.

"Did you like getting your pussy and ass filled by my men, Red?"

She looked through her lashes at me.

"Yes, sir." She leaned forward, and I let her, dropping my hand from her hair. She dragged her lips along my neck and nipped my ear. "Let me take care of you now."

My approval rumbled in my chest as I closed my eyes and turned my mind off to everything but the pleasure she was eliciting.

At first it was weird having Kane with us. After so long of it just being the four of us, I had to get used to there being someone else on our team. He didn't quite fit in with us but we included him as best we could. Nyx thought he was amusing. Atlas was always staring at him trying to get a true read on him and Preacher was just annoyed.

But despite his quirks, Kane was just a man who'd seen too much and somewhere along the way, his mental state had decayed into who he was today. Erratic, unpredictable, but skilled in combat, tracking and sharpshooting. He hadn't put any of us in danger in the field and he'd followed orders. As long as he continued doing that, I didn't give a shit how weird he was.

A few weeks after the last game, Nyx and I were walking around the dirt track. Atlas was lounging in the grass nearby, Preacher was working out and Kane was standing in the middle of the lawn looking out into the forest.

"What do you think he's doing?" Nyx muttered. "He's been doing that for almost thirty minutes now."

"He's a strange one," I admitted. "But he took care of business out there and he made it back so I guess I can't really fault him for a few strange behaviors."

"Yeah, we'll see how long he lasts," Nyx said. "What are we going to do about Kai's team? I don't like the idea of him turning the other teams against us."

"I don't see how the other teams would want that," I mused. "There still can only be one winner...why would they let Kai win?"

"That's true," Nyx shrugged. "Have you thought any more about the escape plan?"

"I think we need to make a move soon," I said. "I don't want to wait until morale drops to a point where we can't execute at the highest level. I'm afraid Vetticus is just going to chip away at us until we're so far gone there's nothing left to save."

"I've had that thought too," Nyx said quietly. He opened his mouth to say something but stopped.

"Spit it out, Nyx," I said.

"What happens if we lose again?"

"You're not getting taken," I said flatly.

"You can't know that—"

"Yes. I can," I turned to him and stopped him with a hand on his arm. "Because he's going to take me instead."

"What? No—T," Nyx protested. "I—I can handle it—" I held up my hand to stop him.

"I'm not doing this because I think you can't handle it—"

"I mean, I kind of lost it for a minute," Nyx interrupted. "I'd understand if you thought that way."

I stepped closer to him, my jaw clenched in anger. "It means you're still human. I want you to keep that part of yourself for as long as you can," I said fervently. "I see your shadows, I see who you become out there, we're all a little fucked up like that—but you also still have a heart in there, Nyx. It's black, and it's a little beat up," I gave him a smile. "But it still works."

"And yours doesn't?"

"I don't know," I said honestly. "But it can only be me. I don't want Atlas going either, because I fear what will happen if he's subjected to that trauma again."

"He told you?"

I nodded. "After you told me what happened to you, he shared his story with me. It can only be me."

"But—"

"I'm not backing down on this, Nyx," I said firmly.

"But what happens if you break?" He asked. "We need you, T."

"No, it has to be me because I'm already broken," I said. I hesitated to tell him everything. I'd said I wasn't going to talk about my family in this place, but I needed him to understand. "His men shot and raped my wife—and then slit my son's throat—in front of me."

Nyx was silent.

"He was referencing my daughter that time in the showers with Yuri," I continued. "I'd sent her into the woods to hide. But apparently he got to her too."

Nyx pressed his lips together and instead of offering pity or an apology— he knew me better than that—he settled his gaze on the mansion.

"He has a lot to atone for," he said coldly.

"He does. So let me deal with him."

I was being honest; I didn't think Nyx was weak. I thought he was stronger than all of us for actually allowing himself to feel and work through what happened instead of shoving it aside. I firmly believed the only reason he was able to come back to us for the next game was because he sat with his feelings and talked to Atlas and eventually me. I couldn't do that. I didn't talk.

I boxed it up and shoved it into a corner and operated in the gray because I didn't want to feel anything—good or bad.

Did my heart work?

At one point I'd thought I knew what love was but the longer I was here and the longer I sank into my plans for revenge, the more it seemed to get farther and farther out of reach. Maybe, in a selfish way, I wanted Nyx and Atlas to keep their humanity so they could be my anchor, otherwise I was afraid one day I'd wake up and discover there was nothing left of me.

Not even the broken pieces.

"How'd you get your name, Preacher?" Kane asked.

We were inside for the night and Preacher was laying on the couch lost in thought. "You don't ever say anything religious or nothin'," Kane continued.

Nyx hid a smile at Kane's blunt and personal question. Kane had a habit of not filtering his thoughts. He'd asked Atlas why he wore his hair in a bun when it was more practical to just shave it all off. Atlas had looked at Kane's bald head and raised his eyebrows before shaking his head and walking off, refusing to humor him.

"I'm not religious anymore," Preacher said. Kane just looked confused. Preacher sighed and sat up.

"I used to pray before every job. Made a point to include any of the team who wanted in on it. It was just a ritual I had going on." Preacher saw all of us invested in his answer. He tilted his chin up and ran his fingers along the scar on his throat.

"Problem is—I didn't see God when I was close to death," he looked at Kane. "I saw the devil."

"Why'd you choose that name here then? You could have been anything," Kane said.

Preacher shrugged. "It was my old call sign."

He paused for a moment before continuing. "I don't want to forget who I am in here. God has forsaken me—but I can't abandon myself. We have to compartmentalize, but at what point do we lose ourselves and become what Vetticus wants us to become?" He shook his head sadly. "I may have killed and done some terrible shit—and I may even go to hell for it—but I'll be damned if I lose myself enough to forget everything he took from me."

Silence fell as we all digested what he'd said. Then Kane ruined it. "So how'd you get the scar?"

Preacher looked at him in resigned amusement and shook his head.

"A serial cop killer broke into my house," he said. "Came up behind me and—" he ran his fingers across his scar again.

"Jesus," Nyx muttered.

"They say when you get close to the end you see lights and tunnels—angels—that sort of shit—" He shook his head. "I saw nothing but fire, and shadows that looked an awful lot like demons." He rubbed his neck like he could still feel his life blood bleeding out over his hands.

"I woke up in the hospital. I guess the guy had dragged me into the nearby wetlands and left me to die. It's a miracle anyone even found me. According to the medics, I died on the way to the hospital—was out for over five minutes. I couldn't talk for months afterwards but I'm alive. Haven't prayed since."

"You don't think it was God who gave you that miracle?" Kane asked.

"I don't know what to believe anymore," Preacher said. "But I do know, when I was on the verge of death and when I died, there wasn't anyone welcoming me home, just dragging me further into hell. My faith felt real foolish after that. Why would I continue to pray to someone who's just going to abandon me in the end?"

"You don't believe in forgiveness?"

"God supposedly loves sinners, right? Yet the true villains go to hell. What's the difference between me and someone who's evil? We're both doing it consciously, so should I still ask for forgiveness? How can I ask for forgiveness when I know I'll have to sin again tomorrow? And sure, maybe you could argue that I don't enjoy it or whatever like a truly evil person—but maybe I'm just lying to myself about that too." He shook his head. "Anyway, now that I know I'm most likely not going to heaven, I just don't see the point."

Kane fell silent with the rest of us while we all thought about what Preacher said.

"How'd you get your scar, Kane?" Preacher asked.

Kane relaxed back on the couch.

"I was captured while on a job," he said. "Tortured for information."

"Where did you serve?" Nyx asked.

Kane yawned and stretched out on his bed. "I was GGK."

My eyebrows shot up, and Nyx whistled low in appreciation. From the look on everyone's faces, Kane was making a lot more sense to them. GGK was an elite commando unit of the Malaysian Army. They faced some of the toughest training out of any unit in the world.

"They of course didn't get anything from me but they did ruin my good looks," he joked.

"I've seen a video where you guys do live firing target practice with each other," Atlas said.

"Have to trust the man standin' next to you," he said easily. "Or in this case, across from you. I will say, your balls shrivel up real quick when you have to put that paddle between your legs for the first time though, but you get used to it."

Atlas chuckled and shook his head with a look on his face as though all his questions had just been answered.

"I commend you guys for that," he said. "The US would never."

"Eh, you guys are capable though," Kane said, waving his hand. "You especially." He pointed to Atlas.

"Talk about performing under pressure," Nyx remarked.

Before anyone else could respond, the lights turned off, plunging us into darkness and signaling the unspoken agreement of it being time to call it a night. I settled back and now that the mystery of Kane was solved, my mind traveled back to what Preacher had talked about.

What made us different from evil men? Evil was knowing you were doing something bad or hurting others and doing it anyway. Wasn't that what we all did day after day?

The belief of the devil implied the existence of God because like the paradox of life, there is no good without evil. There is no light without the darkness.

There is no life without death.

Maybe that was our purpose—to be the dark that allowed the light. To be the evil, so there could exist the good. To go to hell, so that others could go to heaven.

It was all too philosophical and as I drifted off to sleep; I agreed with Preacher—I didn't know what to believe anymore and I wondered if that made me smart, or nothing more than a damn fool.

53

THERON

TWENTY MONTHS CAPTIVE

We'd been put on a cargo plane and flown—somewhere—to get to this map. I could hear the ocean on the other side of the doors. When we stepped out into the sunlight, the smell of brine and seaweed hit me in the face as the clammy sea breeze tore through us. But I wasn't looking inland—my gaze was out to sea, where a massive carrier was anchored a few hundred yards out. Vetticus had added shipping containers to the deck to break up the vast area where planes would usually sit.

"Well, shit," Nyx muttered.

I jammed my comms unit into my ear and scanned the shoreline. There was a motorized inflatable boat beached just above the tide. The buzzer went off, and I knew we needed to get on that ship. We all took off and worked quickly to push the boat into the water. Nyx took the tiller and we jetted off through the breakers.

As soon as our feet hit the deck, Nyx turned to me. "Welcome home I guess?"

It had been years since I'd been on a ship. My work as a SEAL had taken me inland, but this was still familiar. We saw another team climb over the other railing and one of the men stopped and watched us. His eyes landed on me and he pointed his fingers like he was firing a gun.

"If I had to guess, that must be Kai," Nyx said dryly.

None of us had weapons yet, so with a last smirk from Kai, we took off our separate ways. Nyx led us into the bowels of the ship where we found weapons and ammo fairly quickly. Then we had to decide where to look for Red first.

"Let's split up," I said. With such close quarters it made little sense to run seven deep. I sent the two new kids plus Kane to search the engine room.

Nyx and Atlas would search the crew quarters and cargo hold and Preacher and I headed towards the pilothouse.

Preacher and I worked our way up top again and slowly swept the boat. I hated clearing ships because of the tight corners and narrow hallways. It was the perfect place for ambushes and I made sure the knife I found was easily accessible.

I signaled for Preacher to hold as we came up on a few shipping containers. I heard footsteps around the corner, then they paused. I looked at Preacher, giving him another hand signal and then we attacked. There were three of them. I quickly took out the one closest to me, knocking away the other one's AR while Preacher took out the third. They didn't get off a single round.

We weren't the only team headed to the pilothouse and as we made our way down the hallway leading in; we hit a team of four already inside. I quickly motioned for Preacher to go one way and I took the other, dodging as bullets bit into the metal next to me. I returned fire, but they ducked out of sight.

Suddenly, a knife came low around a corner and bit into my thigh. I went down with a curse, only to stumble to my feet as he pulled my handgun from my belt and aimed it at me. I yanked the man's arm forward, ejecting the clip and removing the slide, effectively disabling the firearm. I brought my elbow up and slammed it down on his arm, sending the man to his knees as he tried to avoid a broken arm.

The second man fired, but I pulled the other one in front of me so he killed his teammate. I shoved the body at the gunman. When he went down, I tackled him and repeatedly rammed his head into a metal pipe.

Over and over and over again—I lost myself in the blood lust as his head fell apart in my hands. Blood coated my vision, turning the world red. A hand on my shoulder had me whirling around with the man's sidearm.

"Fuck," I gasped a curse as Preacher batted the gun away and I sagged against the wall, still half straddling the destroyed body beneath me. Preacher glanced at the body quickly then looked at something across the room and stepped over me.

My chest was heaving as I inhaled breath after breath that smelled of blood and gore. I tried to grab onto some semblance of my humanity but the blood lust was screaming through me, setting every atom in my being alight. Preacher picked up the radio and tried it, only to throw it viciously against the dash in frustration.

"It's never that easy," I panted, climbing to my feet.

I grimaced and grabbed onto the center console with a hand slippery with blood up to my elbows. I was covered in it.

"Worth a try," he shrugged. Preacher looked at the knife still in my leg, sucking on his teeth. He nodded towards it.

"Usually I'd say to leave it in but—"

"Yeah, I know—"

I tore a strip off my t-shirt, seeing a towel nearby I grabbed that too. I put the fabric in my mouth so I had it ready and wrapped my hand around the hilt. Preacher watched the door while I took a few quick breaths and counted to myself before yanking the knife straight up. I growled in pain, my hands shaking slightly as I wadded the towel up against the wound and used the strip of t-shirt to tie it in place. I picked up my AR and lashed out with a vicious kick to the body next to me with a growl of frustration. Asshole.

I nodded to Preacher. "Let's move out."

I limped my way after him as he led the way out of the pilothouse.

54

ATLAS

A grenade rolled down the hallway towards us. Without a second thought I launched myself at Nyx. We collided and crashed through one of the cabin doors as the grenade went off. We rolled across the floor and I ended up on top of Nyx as debris rained down. My ears rang.

Nyx moved over me, gloved hands holding my face as he shouted. His voice sounded far away as the ringing in my ears continued. He was frantically looking me over for injuries. I looked over his shoulder to see a figure darken the door and grabbed my hand gun, shooting him down. Sound roared back to me and I struggled to my feet.

"Let's go," I panted, grabbing for Nyx as my equilibrium returned.

"You good?" Nyx asked.

I nodded. We needed to get out of this death trap of a hallway. Bullets whipped through the doorway and Nyx and I broke apart, quickly finding cover on either side of the entrance. Nyx pulled a grenade from his vest and looked at me, miming a count before he pulled the pin and threw it out into the hallway. We heard shouts before the explosion and quickly followed it out clearing what was left of the small team of four. Then we left the cabins behind.

"Target acquired," Kane's voice came over comms. "She was restrained in the engine room. Making our way up top now."

"Copy that," North said. "Report in."

"Atlas and I just left the crew quarters, headed up," I said.

"Meet us where we left the boat," North answered.

"Copy," I replied.

Chaos greeted us as soon as we came up on the top deck. Teams were engaged all across the ship and up on the level above us. I saw North make a move with Preacher towards the ladder leading down to the boat. Kane and Red appeared next while the two new recruits laid down cover fire. I was surprised they were still alive. At the last second, I saw the glint of glass and threw myself back against the nearby shipping container.

"We're pinned by a sniper," I said over comms.

Nyx motioned for me and we headed the other direction until we reached another crossroads in the stack. He pied the corner and we continued down a narrow gap until we reached the edge of the ship's railing. Looking down the line, I could see North hanging off the rail, helping Red down the ladder while Kane and the kids laid down cover fire a few yards away behind a stack of crates.

"North—take the target and go," Kane shouted.

"We can swim it," Nyx confirmed over comms. "Go, North!"

"Copy that," North said.

I could tell he wasn't happy but getting all of us off the ship in one go wasn't looking good unless we could take out the sniper. Nyx crept down the ship's edge but as soon as he got to the open area we'd have to cross, I saw the sniper again.

"Get down, Kane!" I shouted at the same time I yanked Nyx back. Kane listened and ducked just as a shot buried itself in the wood where his head had been. He looked at me and gave me a thumbs up before he popped up and resumed cover fire.

"He's buried in some metal scaffolding, I can't get to him," I grumbled as I risked another look at the sniper hide. I heard the kick of the boat motor as North tried to get it to catch. Another attempt and it still wouldn't take.

"We'll cover you," Kane said over comms. "Get in the water."

Nyx and I quickly stripped down to only necessary clothing, packed our pockets with ammo and clutching the AR to our chests.

"In the water in three," I reported.

I heard the engine of the boat catch and it roared to life. Nyx winked at me with a grin before launching himself off the side. I followed right after. The wind ripped past me and my feet hit the water. It was nothing I hadn't done a million times—if anything I was as comfortable in the water as I was on land. I surfaced and pushed my gun across my back, then looked around for Nyx. He popped up and we headed to shore.

55

THERON

It couldn't be helped. I didn't enjoy leaving the team on the boat but I knew we'd be exposed if we didn't have someone covering us on deck. I also knew everyone on the team could swim their way back without any issues so when the engine finally caught, I whipped it towards shore with Preacher on the bow and Red huddled in the middle. Halfway there, gunfire ripped into the water near us and I glanced over to see another inflatable with five men headed our way.

"Preacher!" I shouted, but he'd seen them and was already opening fire. He took one man out before the craft banked hard and slid into the side of ours. Preacher launched himself into the other boat. I followed, tackling another into the water. We thrashed in the surf, churning up the foam and wake until the pull of the breakers grabbed us. It threw me and the man into the shallows where I was first to regain my feet.

I pulled my gun and shot him.

Static assaulted my ears. I yanked my comms out and threw it aside, in the same breath cursing Vetticus for not making the comms units waterproof. I looked down the shoreline and saw Red sprinting towards our safe zone except Kai had just made land close by and was in between her and the DZ. She slid to a stop and started backtracking.

We all sprinted towards each other. My leg was screaming at me as I urged myself faster. Red rushed by me. I collided with Kai at full speed. We hit the ground with so much velocity we rolled all the way into a dune above the tide, throwing sand everywhere.

The impact threw us apart and knocked the air from my lungs. I looked over to see him gasping in the sand in a similar position. We scrambled to our feet, both having lost our weapons in the initial impact, we had nothing but our fists as we rushed each other. It was messy, unrefined and physical. We were both so lost in the fight, it was a primal urge driving us back to the basest of our instincts and training.

"Fuck you, Kraven," Kai hissed. "I'm not losing again."

"Tired of being Vetticus' favorite?" I taunted.

He rushed me again with a growl. Again and again we clashed, each landing hits that had us both coming away bloody. I landed on top of him. He dug his hand into my knife wound and landed a solid blow to my jaw. Pain erupted across my entire body. My vision dimmed and he was able to shove me away. I lay scrambling in the sand as I watched him take off towards Red. I managed to get to my hands and knees but an attempt at getting to my feet had me falling back down. I cursed as I watched Kai grab his gun and then he was on Red.

Looking down shore, I saw Nyx and Atlas jogging out of the surf. My second attempt at getting to my feet succeeded, and I took off towards them. Nyx was ahead of Atlas and I watched in horror as Kai, using Red as a shield, raised his gun towards Nyx.

He pulled the trigger and the gunshot rang out across the beach.

I watched Nyx fall.

Red was screaming as Atlas aimed for Kai. By some fluke, Kai stumbled as Atlas pulled the trigger and the bullet hit him in the shoulder instead of the neck. Kai aimed his gun at Atlas and I choked on a breath as he pulled the trigger.

Empty.

Kai tossed the weapon away and dragged Red down the beach. Atlas aimed his sights at Kai but his gun must have been empty too because he tossed it away and gave up on Kai in favor of Nyx. He fell to his knees next to him.

I made it to them just as Atlas was ripping Nyx's shirt down his chest revealing the bullet hole. I collapsed on my knees on Nyx's other side.

"No, no, no—Nyx!" I patted his cheek, my breathing frantic. I checked his pulse, it was low and slow and his breathing was shallow.

Then it fucking stopped. I cursed repeatedly and started compressions.

"You don't get to die," I panted. "Don't you dare fucking die on me!"

I gave mouth to mouth and went back to compressions, terrified I was going to lose him.

"Come on, Nyx—" I gasped.

More air. More compressions.

More air. More compressions.

More air—

Nyx gasped for breath, sputtering. He grimaced and blinked rapidly before looking at me.

"Jesus, North—you want to kiss me you just have to ask."

"Fuck you—" I croaked weakly.

I fell back on my heels into the sand, exhausted and drained. Relief coursed through me so fast I closed my eyes as the world spun. Atlas took over, applying pressure to the gunshot wound as Nyx sat up with a groan.

"Don't fucking scare us like that!" Atlas demanded.

The buzzer interrupted any reply as it blared out over the landscape, mocking our defeat. Nyx looked over at me, a new fear shining in his eyes.

"We lost," he said. "Fuck! You should have just left me and gone after Red!"

"Fuck off," Atlas snapped. "He had two men waiting for him down the beach and we're out of ammo."

I didn't have the breath to argue with Nyx. Movement up the beach caught my eye and I looked up to see Preacher supporting Kane as they limped towards us. Kane was bleeding heavily from what looked like several gunshot wounds. I heard coughing, and we all turned towards the ocean to see the two kids coming out of the surf. Kane and Preacher reached us as Atlas and I helped Nyx to his feet, supporting him between us.

"Looks like you three had some fun," Kane rasped. "And look! The kids made it back!"

I didn't even care to know what we all looked like as we shuffled our way back to the safe zone. The sour taste of our loss permeated the air and the dread of what awaited us back at the mansion loomed ahead as the mouth of the doors swallowed us up and took us back to hell.

56

THERON

Kane and Nyx took the most time in the infirmary. Kane had multiple gunshot wounds, several life threatening and once Nyx was deposited back with us, we were informed Kane would need to be kept sedated overnight to finish repairs.

The guards stood at the door. "Vetticus is requesting one of you. You choose or we make the choice for you." I didn't think it was possible for Nyx to grow paler, but he did as I stepped forward.

"T—" he protested, but I held up a hand.

"We talked about this," I said.

Without another word the guards cuffed me and escorted me out of our building and across the large expanse of land towards the estate. We entered through the front doors and walked down a dimly lit hallway.

The guards led me into a sitting room and into a corner where they stretched each arm out and chained it to either wall. The guards cut my clothing from me, leaving me naked, then left the room to reveal Vetticus sitting in a high-back chair, ankle crossed over knee, with a glass of whiskey dangling from his hand.

"Ah, this is unexpected. I didn't take you for a sacrificial lamb, Kraven," he said easily. "Little selfless of you don't you think?"

I didn't reply.

"Your team had quite the game today," he went on. "I thought you guys had it for a minute there."

Vetticus swirled his glass and threw back the rest of it. He stood up and walked over to stand in front of me.

"All of you have grown very close, haven't you..." He shoved his hands into his pockets. "When that happens I get a little—antsy. Of course you remember what happened last time you showed me a similar weakness."

He chuckled. "Of course, I doubt you'd forget something like that."

I glared at him but kept my mouth shut.

"Although, maybe this isn't about feelings or being selfless." He studied me and tilted his head slightly. "Maybe this is about ownership. You think those men are yours, not mine, and that you'd rather do the suffering than have me destroy your possessions. It's more of a control thing."

He seemed satisfied with that assessment and leaned closer with a smile. "We're really not that different—you and I."

"I know," I said. That seemed to surprise him.

He straightened and cocked one eyebrow. "Most people would deny it."

"I know what I am," I growled.

"And what are you?" He purred.

"A monster," I said. "But unlike me, you think you can make people like you through control. Or I should say your perceived power."

Vetticus scoffed. "There's nothing perceived about my power."

"Maybe."

"And why can't my power influence my popularity?" He smirked. "Changing someone's perception to obtain redemption—it's all about manipulation, baby."

I laughed, a harsh bitter sound. "Redemption? You deal in fear and someone who fears you will never give you their true self. We are purveyors of death, you and I...birthed from destruction. We break people. There is no rise out of the darkness—no redemption for people like us."

I knew what I was—a broken man who viewed people as possessions because it was safer than actual affection. And I now saw Vetticus for what he was—a lonely man who thought he could buy love with power.

"You say we break people?" Vetticus repeated quietly.

His hand ran down my face. I refused to flinch as his touch traveled across my jaw and his thumb pressed against my lower lip.

"Do you think because you're broken, you're unbreakable?" He murmured.

He dragged his thumb across my lip and his hand dropped and drifted over my cock. I gritted my teeth and watched as the fire of desire flared in his eyes.

"Do what you brought me here to do, but just know, one day, you will feel the consequences of the monster you helped create. You don't know the darkness you've awoken in me." I leaned in closer. "I will kill you. But not before I show you the true meaning of what it is to break."

Vetticus tightened his grip on my cock, stroking the length. I wasn't hard, but he did it again and I knew he was going to force me down that road.

"Game on" he said gruffly. He ran his thumb over the head of my cock. "We'll just have to see who breaks first." He pulled a syringe from his pocket and jabbed me in the neck. He ran his nose along my jaw to whisper in my ear.

"Either way, you're mine now."

The room spun as the guards dropped me back into the cell.

I saw shapes rush me and heard Atlas and Nyx murmuring. Hands grabbed me but they felt foreign and unwanted. Vetticus tried his best to prove he could break me and a small voice in my head said he'd come close—too damn close.

He'd drugged me with a drug that made me nearly immobile but heightened every touch and sensation. Taking a scalpel, he'd painted small strokes all over my body, edging me with his hand at the same time until I was burning up, consumed by pain and unwanted arousal. But it wasn't the pain or pleasure he was pulling from me that almost broke me, it was how he spoke of my family during the entire thing until I wanted to rage at him to shut the fuck up.

My body did what it needed to do and when he made me come, I felt nothing but the empty feeling of being used. The psychological torture on the other hand was what had caused tears to stream down my face and my hands to ball into fists in fury and despair.

"Theron—" Nyx was shoving a sweatshirt over my head.

As the room came into focus, I saw Nyx's face solidify in front of me.

"Help me up—" My voice was rough.

They helped me over to the bed and I shoved sweatpants on then sat down and put my head in my hands, willing the room to stop spinning. My head was pounding and my mind was mentally exhausted from the torment Vetticus had inflicted.

I'd said I was unbreakable—but maybe I was wrong. I caught a glimpse of Nyx's face as he went to walk away and I grabbed his wrist.

"Don't you dare feel guilty," I growled at him, looking up at his haunted face. "Make no mistake—there is nothing I won't do to survive this," I said fiercely, my composure cracking. "He can try to break me—fuck, he might even succeed at some point—but his greatest regret will be keeping me alive, because when I get out of here, I'm going to take it all down."

57

NYX

The next day, we were all hurting. My chest was killing me and when it was time to go outside, we all stiffly went out and sat on the lawn. The two new guys kept to themselves, I'd finally learned their names—Vance and Ridley. Kane said they'd held their own and weren't a bunch of careless bitches—his exact words. They were currently walking the track in the distance. I turned to see Atlas watching me.

"I'm fine—" I sighed.

"You died," Atlas hissed, and I saw some emotion flicker in his eyes before it disappeared into the anger that took over.

"North brought me back to life with his kiss, I'm fine, seriously," I joked.

Atlas shook his head and with a growl stood up and abruptly stormed off.

"What's with him?" I asked. I watched Atlas walk away and turned and saw North giving me a level look like he knew exactly what was going on. I didn't even know what was going on.

"He was really upset yesterday," North said.

"Yeah? Well, I don't really enjoy his close calls either," I grumbled.

Preacher chuckled, seeming to catch on to something I still wasn't sure I was understanding. Was Atlas concerned as a friend or something else? What did that even mean?

"Fuck both of you," I grumbled. Shame from my time with Vetticus rose, and I stood up, needing to move. I walked off in the opposite direction of Atlas and threw myself down under the only tree that was inside the fenced area. I pulled up grass and shredded it between my fingers as I let myself carefully think about Atlas.

He was handsome, no denying that even objectively. Did I feel more? I couldn't forget the energy we'd shared a few times, most recently with Red between us, but there were also times during the games where the blood lust danced with something else just as feral and wild.

Whatever this was—if it even was anything—needed to be pushed down for now. I trusted Atlas with my life and that's where it would stay. I couldn't afford to be weak here and that included catching feelings for my best friend.

Some time later, I saw North approach, and he gingerly lowered himself down next to me, leaning against the trunk of the tree. He tipped his head back and closed his eyes, not saying anything for a long moment.

"Do you want to talk about it?" He asked.

I sighed. "There's nothing to talk about."

North was quiet for a beat. "I think we should try to escape soon."

"You have a plan?"

"We take out the cameras during the game, cut out the trackers—run far away."

"That's it? You make it sound easy."

I heard him smile. "Simple, not easy. I don't even know where in the world we are, do you?"

I shook my head. "Not a clue."

Despite what he'd said last night, I still felt guilty for having him take the fall for the loss. I wanted to say something, but I didn't know how to word it without him getting pissed off.

"Do you want to talk about it?" I asked, turning the question on him.

He fixed me with a look. "There's nothing to talk about."

"Touche," I chuckled. "It looks like for once we have a full team going into the next game."

"That will be a welcome change," North agreed. "Tomorrow we'll start preparing. We'll be able to fully strategize now."

"Here's a question: do you want to try and escape with a full crew? Or does it matter?" I asked.

"Might be easier with a full crew," he said thoughtfully. "But it also depends on the map. Let's get the group together. It's time to make a plan."

A few minutes later we were all sitting on the lawn together, and North addressed the group.

"I want to talk about an escape plan so that when the correct map comes along, we can execute and go. The objectives are to take out the cameras, remove the trackers and run with as much weaponry as possible."

"All we need is a decent head start," Atlas said.

I looked over at him but he wouldn't meet my gaze. I wondered at how he was taking things so personally, like it was my fault I almost died. But I knew that wasn't the reason he was upset. He'd realized he'd gotten attached and was probably angry with himself for allowing it to go that far. I didn't blame him for that—I felt the same way. I hated how much I didn't want to lose him.

"We're definitely going to need the right map for this," Preacher said.

North nodded. "If it's an open concept like the rail yard, it won't work because the drones will see us from a greater distance. The ideal map would be a cityscape or the forest would have worked too."

We talked for the next hour about different strategies and the pros and cons of different scenarios. There was no getting around the fact that Vetticus was going to know where on the map's perimeter we escaped because of the cameras—if we took them out, he'd know. If we left them live, he'd see. But as long as we could get a head start, we could probably make it out.

"We really only need the cameras down to hide us removing our trackers," Kane said. "If we time it, we can knock out the cameras and take out the trackers before the first drones get to us."

North nodded. "Then keep the trackers live, showing us still in the building and run."

"That could work," I shrugged. "It would give us a bit of a head start."

"We have no idea if he has any perimeter measures in place," Vance said.

North nodded. "It's a risk, sure, but we'll bring as much firepower as we can and take it as it comes."

"Sounds like a plan," Kane said. "What are we calling this op?"

"It should be something kind of mundane so when we call it out, Vetticus won't have any idea we're initiating," Ridley offered.

"Operation Give 'Em Hell," Kane said.

"That works," North nodded. "We'll wait for the right map to come along and then it's go time at my signal."

After that, the discussion turned to strategy and planning the next few weeks on how we wanted to prepare for the next game. At five o'clock, we headed inside for dinner. I pulled Atlas aside while everyone else headed through the glass doors.

"I'm sorry for making a joke earlier," I said. "Honestly, if I don't joke about it, sometimes it gets a little heavy."

Atlas nodded. "I'm sorry too—I'm just tired, Nyx," he sighed. "We've been here for over a year now. Did you know that? By the time the next game comes around, it'll just about be two."

"I know, I feel better now," I said, alluding to the plan. Now that we were closer to the cameras, I didn't want to openly talk about it. "Don't you?"

Atlas shrugged, and I frowned, not liking the slump to his shoulders and the sad, faraway look in his eyes.

"I don't know," he said. "I don't know how much more of this I can do."

He flashed me a quick, sad smile and walked inside. I followed, but I wasn't hungry anymore. I was only getting through all of this because of the men at my side—North and Atlas kept me sane in here. They kept me focused and lifted my spirits. I didn't like seeing Atlas look so defeated. I knew what that feeling was like in here and it was deadly. I just hoped we'd be able to make a move soon, or I didn't know if we'd last long enough to escape unscathed.

58

THERON

The following week, we'd just finished working out and were starting a strategy meeting when the guards came into the yard—something they never did.

"Kraven, Vetticus wants to see you."

"Why?"

"Fuck if I know, hands behind your back."

I looked at Nyx and Atlas, both looked ready to protest, but I barely shook my head and while they didn't look happy about it, they both refrained from acting. I did as the guards said and after they cuffed me, the concerned looks of the men followed me as I was escorted out of our building towards the mansion.

Instead of leading me into the same room as before, I was escorted into a dining room where a large table dominated the center of the room. The guards put me in a chair and cuffed my wrists in front of me, attaching the middle to a ring in the table.

"Good evening!" Vetticus said cheerfully as he swept into the room. He was followed by a group of kitchen staff carrying dishes that wafted amazing smells throughout the room. They set everything down on the table and Vetticus shooed them away and regarded me with a smug look on his face.

"Hungry?" He asked.

I didn't answer.

He came and perched on the edge of the table next to me.

"I was thinking about our conversation from last week," he said. "All the other men are so...dull. They just curse and call me names and then plead with me not to fuck them."

He reached across the table and grabbed a bottle of wine that he poured into a glass, speaking as he did.

"It made me realize that you and I have something...special. I'm not supposed to have favorites but, well, here you are." He held the glass within reach.

"Wine?"

I looked at the glass and then away and he chuckled.

"Ah, I see," he took a sip from it. "If I wanted to poison you, it wouldn't be through wine." He stood up and grabbed my hair, pulling my head back. "Open your mouth."

I refused, glaring up at him, my hands twitched on the table where they lay cuffed. He smirked and took another sip of wine then leaned over me, letting some of the liquid fall from his mouth onto mine. My breathing picked up as I tried to keep my anger in check, as the wine spilled over my chin and down my bare chest.

"Do you want to see what happens when you don't play nice?" His eyes jumped over to a monitor on the wall and it flickered on. I saw Nyx, Atlas and Preacher all tied to chairs, naked and blindfolded. "I pulled your favorite three—I figured you wouldn't care too much for the others but these are the ones you seem to be the most *possessive* of."

Fuck. I cursed silently, my jaw clenched tightly in rage. Vetticus turned my head towards the screen more and I watched someone push the button for Nyx's tracker. Electricity shot through his body. There wasn't any sound, but I saw Atlas and Preacher struggle, their mouths open as they yelled at whoever else was in the room.

"Stop," I growled.

"Are you going to play nice? Look, you're the one who wanted my attention and now you have it."

I couldn't tear my eyes from the screen, my breathing growing erratic. The shocks finally subsided and Nyx slumped forward in the chair as much as his bonds would allow. Vetticus dragged my chin back to his.

"I won't touch your team as long as you do what I say," he said. His gaze dipped to my mouth, still sticky with wine. He ran his tongue from my chin up my jaw, cleaning up any lingering drops of liquid. "Do we have a deal?"

I didn't reply quickly enough because he sighed and made a motion with his other hand. My eyes jumped back to the screen to see a man approach Atlas with a knife. He dug it into his chest and I watched a line of blood appear as he dragged it across his skin. Atlas took it with gritted teeth until the man dug his fingers into the cut, coated his hand in blood and smeared it on Atlas' cock.

He went rigid, his chest heaving as the man roughly handled him. I struggled against Vetticus' grip, the cuffs clashing against the ring holding me to the table.

His hand dug into my scalp. "I've half a mind to watch Reaper lick the blood off Phantom's cock but I think they'd enjoy that too much. Don't you?"

He pulled my head to his again. "Do we have a deal?"

I took deep breaths through my nose in an attempt to control myself, feeling like at any moment I could detonate. My gaze flickered over to the screen again to see the man still abusing Atlas. He was yelling something and then his head snapped forward and he head butted the guard who quickly punched him in retaliation. The guard returned and trailed his hand through Atlas' blood again, drawing a path down his stomach.

I looked back at Vetticus.

"Yes," I ground out, nearly choking as I forced the word out.

The moment I spoke, the man retreated from Atlas and my eyes shuttered in relief which seemed to amuse Vetticus. He released my head and took another sip of wine. I sank back against the chair, getting as far from him as the wood allowed.

"They can hear us in there, but I think I'm going to let them watch too."

My eyes jumped to the screen to see the men's blindfolds get removed. Atlas and Nyx took two seconds to check in with each other before their eyes were on the screen where they must see me. Their mouths moved as they shouted something.

Vetticus chuckled. "How cute—they're saying don't listen to me. Don't worry about them. What is a man to do when you all want to be self-sacrificing? Except Preacher—he's a quiet one isn't he?" Vetticus studied the screen.

"I had a feeling he was going to be a favorite with the sponsors," Vetticus said conversationally. "He and his wife were incredible. She was military so breaking them was a journey, let me tell you. At the end, before I cut her throat in front of him, she turned and simply said, 'I love you. I know you'll give him hell.'" Vetticus shook his head, awe in his eyes. "It was a shame I couldn't bring her along too, but alas, I had orders."

I watched Preacher's face and could tell he was hearing every word Vetticus was saying. His hands were in fists and his chest was heaving with hatred. I tore my eyes away from the screen to Vetticus who was watching me carefully, swirling his glass of wine.

He dipped his thumb in the red wine and ran it along my bottom lip before sliding his hand around my neck and pulling me forward. His lips hovered over mine and I went to jerk back but he chuckled darkly.

"Remember what happens if you fight me," he murmured, his breath coasting over my face. I froze, and he closed the distance, pressing his lips to mine. I didn't kiss him back as his lips moved to suck the wine from my bottom lip, biting on it gently then harder. I hissed as he broke the skin. A low rumble escaped him as he pulled back, his eyes half closed in pleasure and his lips stained red with blood and wine.

A knife appeared in his hand. He traced it across my collarbone before digging it into my skin. I growled low in the back of my throat. He slowly dragged the knife across my chest as he watched my every move, his eyes never leaving mine. He was careful not to mess up his brand, but let the knife trail a path under it. The blood tickled as it ran down my stomach and sunk into the waistband of my sweats. Vetticus pulled the knife back and took another sip of wine, then he slowly dumped the glass over my chest. The alcohol burned as it ran across my skin.

I didn't make a sound except to breathe heavily through my nose. I refused to give him anything. If he wanted to play, I'd let him play. As long as he didn't touch my men, he could do whatever he wanted to me.

If I broke, I knew I could come back from it. There wasn't a corner of my dark mind that scared me or a part of my humanity I wouldn't give up to survive this.

His lips were parted and I could see the lust and desire shining in his eyes as he watched wine and blood run freely over my body. His hand trailed down and rested on my cock still covered by my pants.

"You got so hard for me last time," he rasped. His hand moved over me again before he took his knife and cut through the sweatpants to free me. I gritted my teeth in displeasure when his hand found bare skin. His face was so close to mine I could feel his breath again. I fixed my eyes at a point between my hands and tried to ignore him.

"How would Whitney touch you?" He asked.

I couldn't help it, hearing her name on his lips sent me over the edge. I lunged forward and slammed my head into his. He cursed and reeled back, blood running from his nose. He backhanded me across the face but his breathing was erratic and I could see the bulge in his pants from where he was hard, turned on by the violence.

"You can think of her if it helps," he sneered. "Although I'm probably not as gentle as she was."

"Don't," I snarled. "Say. Her name." I was nearly breathless with rage as he approached again. This time he knelt next to me and brought the knife to the

V branded into my chest.

"Do you like pain with pleasure?" He asked. His hand stroked me as he teased the knife along the V, not cutting into the skin but scraping it along the scar tissue. I looked straight ahead, refusing to react again.

"The next violent thing you do, I will punish your men," he said, then his mouth was on my dick and his knife dug into the V at the same time. I slammed my head back against the chair at the assault of the conflicting sensations. Nausea swept over me so thick I nearly gagged as he dragged the knife down one side of the V, sucking the head of my cock as he did.

He did it again, cutting the other side as he took me into his mouth. When he was done with the V, he moved to my thigh, cutting deeply into me in time with his mouth. After five cuts, I still wasn't hard, and he sat back on his heels.

"This should help," he purred. He pulled a needle from his pocket and jammed it into my thigh. "It's my own personal cocktail. Different from last time. This one you'll feel everything heightened, and it will make you rise to me, but you'll still be able to move."

Whatever he'd injected worked quickly, flowing like fire under my skin and setting every nerve ending ablaze. The cuts on my skin began to burn and as he took me into his mouth again, I could feel sweat break out on my body as pleasure overwhelmed me. I was breathing heavily and my hands shook from how hard I was digging them into the table.

I tried to will my mind somewhere else, but he dug his fingers into the cuts on my thigh and dragged his teeth along my cock. A groan escaped my lips, and I gritted my teeth in anger, my head falling back against the wood again in frustration.

"Your wife was beautiful," Vetticus said, replacing his mouth with his hand. I was getting harder by the minute as the drug raced through my system. My mind grew foggy, and it was hard to grasp onto thoughts. Vetticus' voice sounded hollow as he continued to speak about my wife. What she must have felt like, the sounds she made when his men raped her. How despite everything they made her come. I fought back when he said that but his hand went around my neck, cutting off my air as his hand continued to work me. Even though I mentally tried to fight it, I could feel him bringing me to the edge. Vetticus stood up when I was seconds away from breaking.

Before I could register what was happening, he took the knife and slammed it into my hand. The blade impaled it onto the tabletop. He released my cock and I made a sound of distress, collapsing forward, chest heaving at the sudden assault.

He edged me closer with pleasure and pain, bringing me close to the point of release but never throwing me over. He pulled out his own cock, stroking himself with his hands covered in my blood. Perched on the edge of the table, his breath picking up as he stroked himself. Through the pain, I could tell by his breathing he was close. With a groan, he wrapped his hand around the knife and as he yanked it out, he came all over my chest to the sound of my pained groan. I collapsed back in the chair, writhing in distress.

I must have blacked out because when the nightmare swam back into view, Vetticus was stroking my cock using my blood and his come. I tried to move, but he grabbed my hair and dragged me towards him.

I looked past him to the monitor the men had been on but the chairs were thankfully empty now. He yanked my face to him as I shifted, trying to escape my release quickly blazing a trail through me. This time he didn't stop and as I came, he pushed down on my hurt hand, making my body explode in a painful climax of anguish and agony.

"Yes, come for me, Kraven," he purred as I fell forward.

My sweat slicked forehead landed on his thigh and I didn't have the energy to lift it. The room spun, so I closed my eyes, my body shaking as the sweat grew cold on my skin. His hand caressed my hair, and I tried to hold myself together.

"You bleed so prettily for me," he murmured, petting my head again in a long, smooth stroke. "Sleep now, I'll take care of you."

I didn't want to pass out, but my eyes wouldn't open and he continued to pet me as I sank into the blissful oblivion of unconsciousness, pushing everything that had just happened away. I'd make him pay one day. For now, I'd survived another day, and that was enough.

I told myself nothing that happened to me here meant anything—it was all a means to an end. Fuel for the fire that would one day wreak havoc on the world and burn down everything in its path until all that was left was Vetticus and then I'd burn him too.

But not before I fulfilled my promise—to show him what it really meant to break.

59

THERON

TWENTY FOUR MONTHS CAPTIVE

I was kneeling in Vetticus' dining room again. The guards had come for me shortly after dinner. The door opened behind me and the sound of Vetticus' footsteps across the wood floor announced his arrival. I stared straight ahead, eyes anchored on a point across the room and fists tightly clenched in the cuffs that held them. Not for the first time, I wished I was free. Anywhere but in this nightmare I'd found myself in. Vetticus came around in front of me and dropped a pair of camo pants and combat boots on the floor.

"Put these on. We have somewhere to be."

I didn't speak but did as he asked. Once dressed, he led the way out the door, his guards escorting me behind him. As we walked through the house, I realized it was a lot larger than what could be observed from outside and the structure actually extended far back into the mountain itself. We finally came to a set of large oak double doors and Vetticus pushed them open revealing a large ballroom. In fact, it was huge.

The ceilings towered high above me, disappearing into the shadowed dome. The polished floor was black and so were the pillars and stone walls. Despite it being nearly empty, it was obvious Vetticus was hosting a gathering. The household staff scurried around the massive space, setting out food and drinks.

Vetticus led us across the expanse of the room to where pedestals lined the far wall. They were just large enough for a man to stand on comfortably and several feet off the ground to provide height. Spotlights shone down on each one. Vetticus shoved me towards the middle one—I counted seven.

"That one is yours."

I stood facing the room and Vetticus pulled a chain from behind the stand, locking it around my ankle. It didn't allow for any movement besides a few inches either way. Stepping back, he looked up at me, gave me a smirk and headed back across the room leaving me alone on my perch.

I'm not sure how long I stood there, but slowly people began to filter in. A few more men were placed on the pedestals around me and I realized this was a showcase of sorts. A time for the other sponsors to show off their top players. Statistics were projected on the wall behind the other players and I turned my head to see a similar set up behind me. It showed my name—Kraven—and a list of notable stats. The number of kills I had to date. How many games I'd played and the number of my victories vs my losses.

Looking at the other men, I only recognized one: Kai

He stood on the pedestal to my right. We were far enough away to make talking impossible but I caught his eye and he subtly flipped me off, letting me know exactly how he felt about seeing me. All of us were shirtless and I noticed we all had different brands to signify the team we belonged to. Except for Kai and myself who both had V's. It made me wonder why Vetticus was allowed two teams.

As more people filed into the ballroom, the atmosphere became more lively with music and chatter filtering through the air. People would come up and observe us, making me feel like an animal put on display. The longer the night went on, the more aggravated I became. The whole thing was bullshit. Showy, pretentious bullshit.

A group of men came to stand in front of me, studying me over the rim of their drinks. They held themselves with importance and seemed to draw attention from people in the room. One of them, a man with blond hair and a sour twist to his mouth tilted his head as he studied me.

"This is the one who killed O'Connor in the forest, isn't it?" He asked.

"Yeah—I heard Albatron was not happy," another snickered. "That was his top player."

Before they could continue with the gossip, Vetticus sauntered over to the group. The men straightened up and the atmosphere changed, tension charging the air.

"Gentlemen," Vetticus purred. "Admiring my top player?"

"He's certainly impressive," the blond said. "I heard he's caught Albatron's eye." Irritation flickered briefly across Vetticus' face but he smirked and shrugged.

"He's welcome to look all he wants," Vetticus said. He directed the men down the line with flourish of his hand.

"Have you made your bets for tonight?" He asked.

I didn't hear the men reply as they drifted away out of earshot. I wondered who Albatron was. The owner of Atrox? Another sponsor? Maybe—definitely someone of high status within the company. I filed the name away.

Vetticus obviously had a lot of privileges and was respected, and slightly feared, by most people here. For the next hour I periodically caught sight of him moving about the room talking and mingling. He was in his element.

An hour or two passed and people were beginning to make their way through an archway off in the corner of the ballroom. When nearly everyone had disappeared, guards came and one by one unchained us and led us through a different door.

The room they took us to was vastly different from the ballroom. It was dimly lit, dank and smelled like mildew and copper. I heard a sizable crowd cheer from down a hallway. The guards escorted man after man down the hallway and they wouldn't return. Soon it was only Kai and I sitting on a bench.

"Sounds like some fight club shit," he said.

When I didn't reply he looked over at me. "We'll see what you're made of without your little friends around."

I still didn't say anything. I had no desire to be the entertainment but it didn't look like I had a choice.

I stepped out into a sunken dirt arena with Kai on my heels. Eight foot tall walls surrounded us and above that was chain link fencing where the crowd sat looking down into the ring. The dirt beneath my feet was already muddy with blood. The guards unchained our wrists and stepped out.

The crowd went wild and turned into a roaring mass of noise I couldn't decipher. I stayed where I was, watching as Kai began to circle me until he disappeared behind me out of sight. My attention turned to the stands. I found Vetticus almost directly in front of me and locked eyes with him.

Now I understood what he meant when he asked if the men had placed their bets. Kai made another circle around me and was at my back again. I felt the moment he made his move and he landed a punch to my kidneys before kicking my legs out from under me.

I let him. I fell to my knees in the dirt, my stare still fixed on Vetticus.

Kai circled back around in front of me and darted in to land a punch to my jaw. My head whipped to the side. I slowly returned my gaze to Vetticus. The crowd was still loud but the tension was heavy—I could feel their confusion sitting in the air above me. I was supposed to be the top player and I wasn't doing anything.

Kai rushed in, delivering another hit to my face. This one sent me down onto one arm and blood assaulted my mouth as he split my lip. I straightened and looked at Vetticus. I let the pain stoke the fire of contempt inside me. I spit out blood onto the dirt in front of me and bared my teeth in a bloody grin.

Fury transformed his features and I couldn't wipe the sneer from my face. Kai continued to attack, although he also seemed frustrated by my lack of participation and his advances became vicious and calculated. Kai came in close and hit me hard enough to send me to the ground. He crouched down, pulling my head up to look at him.

"What are you doing?" He growled through clenched teeth. I refused to answer him and struggled to my knees.

He hit me again.

I fell onto my hands and watched the blood drip from my mouth.

"Fight back," Kai hissed.

The crowd was nearly silent now and when I looked up at Vetticus, I saw murder in his eyes. Once I was back on my knees, Kai delivered a blow to my stomach, kicked me hard in the side and landed a wicked punch to the side of my face. I fell into the dirt, dazed. As I was dragging my body upright Kai grabbed me by the neck and leaned in close.

"You know what he's going to do, right?" He murmured. "He's going to take it out on your team."

"Since when—are you—a team player?" I panted.

His lips thinned into a grim line. "It's a game, Kraven. It's a game, and you're losing."

I bared bloody teeth at him. "Do you want to know—what happened—to the last person who—said that to me?"

Kai threw me away and I collapsed into the dirt again. I spit out more blood and looked up at Vetticus. He was standing against the fence now, gripping the metal links.

Kai was right. But I needed to prove a point. Even when he'd taken everything—even when he thought he was in control—it was a tenuous power because I was not broken. I did not fear him. I was not a pet to be caged.

My fingers curled in the dirt as I sensed Kai behind me.

I'd proven my point. It was time to prove another.

I turned and flung dirt into Kai's face.

He was completely caught off guard and I was on my feet in seconds. The crowd gasped and instantly the volume escalated as I advanced on Kai quickly and methodically. I attacked and dragged his arm behind him before delivering a brutal hit to his elbow, instantly breaking his arm. His cry was lost in the crowd's thirst for blood. He collapsed and I kicked him the rest of the way down.

My heel pressed into his neck, cutting off his air and for the last time, I lifted my gaze to Vetticus. I didn't think it was possible, but he looked even more angry than before. I barked out a laugh and crouched down on top of Kai, putting even more pressure on his airway. He struggled, clawing at my leg, but he only had one arm, the other lay useless at his side, clutching at dirt.

"You're right Kai, this is a game—" I hissed. "—*my game*—and I don't plan on losing." I jerked my entire body down, putting all my weight into my heel and Kai's body went limp, the light faded quickly from his eyes as I crushed his airway.

As soon as I stepped away, the crowd became deafening. I looked up but Vetticus was gone. I'd pay for this later. I'd pay for making him look like a fool. He would not tolerate his toy playing him in front of these people. Not to mention also killing his other top player.

Was it a reckless thing to do? Absolutely. But for right now, victory was sweet. I laughed again and my shoulders shook with it. I couldn't stop. Even when the guards came and cuffed me, my laugh followed me back through the ballroom, back through the house...it echoed off the mountains as they led me all the way back to the cell.

The guards uncuffed my wrists and the door clicked shut at my back. My men all looked at me as I continued to chuckle. I had to look a mess— cut up, bloody and covered in sand. Not to mention deranged because I was practically leering at them.

Nyx blinked. "Do I want to know?"

I shook my head and walked off towards the bathroom.

"Someone told me this was all just a game."

Preacher scoffed and shook his head. Atlas ran a hand over his face in exasperation and Nyx barked out a laugh.

I passed a confused Ridley. "What am I missing?"

"He killed the last man who said that to him," Preacher said.

I turned on the water and the spray blocked out any further conversation. I didn't bother waiting for it to heat up but stepped into the cold, letting it shock my system.

I was playing the game—*my game.*

But this was also a game of survival—and there were no rules.

60

THERON

It was no surprise that Vetticus was in a bad mood when I was delivered to him a few days later. He was sprawled out in an armchair dangling a glass of whiskey in the air with a scowl on his face. He waved his hand at the guards escorting me and they pushed me into the matching chair across from him before going to stand on either side of the door.

Vetticus looked at me, resting his chin on his palm. I sat rigid in the chair, staring at him coldly like I always did. He threw back the rest of his whiskey and set the glass carefully on the table next to him.

"Do you think I'm stupid?" He asked.

When I didn't answer, he reached into his pocket and pushed the button for my tracker. The shock tore through my body. It was quick but left me slumped in the chair. Breathing heavily, I sat up, my cold stare now deadly.

"That wasn't rhetorical," he said dryly.

"No," I lied.

"Well, that's good. The other night I could have sworn you were thinking it." He pulled the device from his pocket, twisting it around in his hand while he watched me.

"I know you're planning to escape," he said bluntly. He studied me for a reaction and when I didn't give him one, he went on. "Don't worry, I can't hear what you're saying when you have your little pow wows but you're at full strength for a game for the first time and I don't know why but I have this strange feeling you're close to making a move."

I wasn't surprised he'd come to that conclusion. It's not like it would be a surprise to have people held captive plan an escape. Now, we'd have to be even more careful. He stood up and walked over to the table, selecting a few pistachios and cracking them loudly.

"You can imagine how upset it makes me when I think about losing you."

Vetticus tilted his head at me, looking annoyed.

"I've been giving you too much rope. Taking out my other top player was—foolish. I really can't afford to lose you now."

There was more silence as he stood watching me and eating the nuts slowly until they were gone. He dusted his hands on his pants.

"Do you even know where we are?" He asked. "Do you have any idea?"

I turned my head to look at him. "Does it matter?"

He chuckled. "No, I suppose it doesn't. You're going to try it regardless. Every time you take out a camera, I wonder to myself if this is it—if this is when I'm going to have to kill you." He walked over and ran his hand across my face. I leaned away from him in disgust, looking anywhere but up at him.

"I hope it doesn't come to that. You know how to keep me on my toes and it surprisingly is something I love about you," he murmured. "I'm actually looking forward to hunting you down though. Our reunion will be extra sweet." He leaned closer and his grip tightened on my jaw, turning my head towards him and forcing me to meet his eyes.

"And just so you know. When I catch you—and I will—I'm going to take great pleasure in torturing Phantom and Reaper in front of you and then killing them slowly." Vetticus moved away before I could do something reckless and he slouched down in his chair again.

"I'll have fun making Preacher scream," he went on as though casually discussing the weather. "I'll have to build the team up again," he shrugged. "But it'll be worth it."

Vetticus nodded to the men near the door and they came over and pulled me to my feet. Without a word, Vetticus left the room and the guards followed with me in tow. We walked through the house until we'd descended into the basement and I was shoved through a steel door. My entire team was kneeling in the center of the room with their hands cuffed behind their backs.

"I want to make things very clear to you, Kraven," Vetticus said. "When you decide to act a fool...when you decide to pull at allll that rope—" He walked around behind my men, his hand running over Nyx's hair. "It's not you who I'm going to punish."

Vetticus came back around in front and pulled his gun from his belt.

"I thought I already made that very clear, but I guess you need a stronger reminder." He raised the gun and pulled the trigger.

Ridley fell backwards, a bullet straight through his eye.

Nyx cursed quietly under his breath while the others' breathing picked up. Vetticus jerked his head and his guards descended on Kane. Three of them beat him brutally for several long minutes until Vetticus held his hand up. They immediately stopped and stepped away, leaving Kane a bleeding mess on the ground. He struggled to his knees, his chest heaving and his eyes blazing with hatred. He spit blood savagely onto the ground in front of him.

The guards moved to Atlas next. They yanked him to his feet and dragged him over to a barrel. At Vetticus' signal, they pushed his head down under the surface. At first Atlas didn't struggle but inevitably his oxygen ran out and he thrashed in the guards' grip.

"Stop—let him go!" Nyx had to be restrained. "Fuck you!"

They finally pulled Atlas' head up, allowing him to grab a stuttering breath before pushing him back down. I tried to get to my feet but Vetticus turned towards me and whipped his gun across my face, sending me back to my knees.

"Stop," I demanded.

Vetticus nodded to the guards holding Atlas but it wasn't for them to stop. They let him come up for a breath and as he coughed and gulped in air, they shoved him back down. He started struggling almost immediately. I was grinding my teeth to dust at this point. Nyx was being restrained while Preacher, Kane and Vance looked on helplessly.

"Who do you belong to?" Vetticus asked, sauntering in front of me.

I didn't answer right away and he smirked wickedly. "I won't let him up until you say it."

I looked over at Atlas.

"You," I snapped. Vetticus held up his hand to his ear.

"North!" Nyx shouted frantically.

"I belong to you," I growled.

Vetticus motioned and the men released Atlas. He yanked his head up and gasped in air as he fell to his knees, He coughed up water and leaned against the barrel as he fought to catch his breath.

"Phantom," Vetticus said. "Who do you belong to?"

Atlas glared up at him, his chest rising and falling rapidly as his hair hung in dripping strands on his cheeks.

"You," he panted hoarsely.

"Good boy," Vetticus grinned.

He pointed to me. "Take him back upstairs, I'm not done with him yet."

Vetticus followed after us and turned at the door. "Beat them all then take them back. But keep in mind we have a game in a few weeks."

The following few weeks leading up to the next game were dark and miserable. It became routine for Vetticus to bring me in to spend time with him every few days. Nyx, Atlas and Preacher were pulled in occasionally to ensure I complied. Vetticus would force them to watch some of it—a reminder of his control. Sometimes it was Kane and Vance but he knew who I was more closely possessive of and used it whenever he felt I needed an extra reminder of who I belonged to.

A few weeks into it, Nyx pulled me aside, a worried look in his eyes along with a little guilt.

"North, don't worry about us," he insisted. "We can take some of this from you—"

"Fuck off, Nyx," I growled. "I said I'd handle it."

"I know but this—this is..." He couldn't finish the thought, just looked at me as though he was worried. They all did. I'd catch Atlas looking at me when he thought I wasn't paying attention and even Preacher approached me.

"Hey boss, fight back," he said.

I continued beating the shit out of the bag I was punching, caring little for the throbbing in my hand that still hadn't healed all the way from when Vetticus impaled me on the table.

"Fight back," he pressed. "Please."

The plea caught me off guard and I stopped and looked at him.

"Not going to happen, Preach," I said firmly. "Besides, it wouldn't matter in the end. He has...feelings for me." I ground out the last part and went back to taking my aggression out on the bag. "You're just collateral damage at this point. There's no point in you guys getting hurt too when he's just going to turn around and still do what he wants to me. Fighting back doesn't help, it only makes things worse for everyone."

"Yeah but—"

"Preacher, leave it alone," I snapped.

Now, I could see Atlas staring at me from across the lawn and knew he was going to come to me next. I'd just finished a run around the path and was fighting to catch my breath. I'd been pushing myself hard lately—mostly to get out of my head. It was my only escape these days. Sure enough, Atlas came over and ran a hand through his hair, retying his bun.

"I know why you're doing this," he said.

I opened my mouth to feed him the normal fuck off speech but that was not what I'd been expecting him to say so I shut my mouth and waited for him to go on.

"You're doing this because you think you deserve the punishment," he continued. "And look, I get it. I feel like I deserve to rot in the deepest pits of hell for how badly I failed my family but you don't deserve this. No one does."

"He chose me, Atlas," I said. "And I do deserve every second of this punishment."

"I know he chose you. He has some fucked up crush on you and I know fighting will only make it worse for all of us, so I'm not going to tell you anything else but this: when you need us, when all of this becomes too much, we'll be here. I don't care if it's tomorrow or years from now."

He put both hands on my shoulders and looked me in the eye. "If you won't let us stand by you now and suffer with you, let us be there when you can't go on anymore."

I cleared my throat at the emotions shifting just beneath the surface. He was right. I was doing this because I deserved the pain and felt it was my punishment for my failures. I didn't know when it would become too much but I nodded and grabbed onto his arm, gripping him hard.

"Thank you."

He gave a curt nod and dropped his hands.

"You told us not to hide, T. I'm holding you to that same directive."

61

ATLAS

THIRTY THREE MONTHS CAPTIVE

Usually I could turn off the outside world when I was on a mission, but today, every time I looked through my scope, all I saw were apparitions of Vetticus in all the targets I landed on. I knew what Nyx meant; he was under my skin, trying to consume every part of me.

The map was another huge spread out environmental, so the hope of putting the escape plan into place was dashed the minute we stepped outside the doors. North had told us Vetticus knew we'd try to escape. He hadn't seemed phased when he mentioned it—I guess it's pretty obvious that people being held prisoner would think about those kinds of plans but it still didn't make me feel good to know he was expecting us to make an attempt every time we shot out a camera.

North was having us do that more frequently now to throw him off. We'd throw a whole grid into darkness and then pop back into visibility as soon as we heard the drones coming. It was in part to practice, to see what his response time was, but also we did it just to piss him off.

"Atlas, sniper on the roof, second building in," North barked. "Vance and Casper—go with Kane to clear that building ahead."

Somehow we'd managed to keep a team of seven for the last two games. We'd won the last one with minimal injuries and a successful execution. If we thought that was going to stop Vetticus from having his fun with North, we were wrong. He'd decided North was his and continued to pull him in every few days.

I didn't know how North was managing. I was barely keeping it together, and I didn't know how much longer I could do this. We were all sinking deeper into our heads, even Kane, who until recently hadn't seemed phased by much. But lately even he'd been moody.

I found the sniper and dialed in, then pulled the trigger.

Miss. *Fuck.*

I gritted my teeth, adjusted and the second shot took him out.

"Sniper down," I growled.

"Copy, meet up with Nyx. Preacher, with me," North ordered.

I made my way quickly down from the hide I'd been in and found Nyx guarding the alley between buildings. I tapped him on the shoulder and we carefully made our way towards the edge of the small cluster of buildings. We turned a corner and Preacher and North were waiting for us. I looked out over the view and saw a massive ruin sitting in the middle of a field. The only cover besides the ruin itself was the forest far to the east and the buildings we were currently taking cover in. I saw a team already booking it across the field far to our right.

"Ammo cache," Kane's voice came over comms. "Headed your way."

"Copy that," North answered, not taking his eyes off the ruin. Kane arrived soon after and we distributed the ammo amongst us while North quickly laid out the plan and signaled for us to go. We raced across the field, keeping our eyes peeled for the enemy. There was no sign of the third team.

We hit the ruin and spread out, methodically sweeping it. It was so large; we didn't encounter the other team until we hit the middle where a large courtyard sat and in the middle was Red's cage. She'd shut down over the last few months and was sitting dejectedly behind the bars, staring listlessly off into the distance. She no longer had the fire like she had in the beginning and there were no more escape attempts from her. She was always in her cage. The last two wins she'd told us Kai had turned even more violent and when she wasn't being used as a target in the games, she was available to the guards.

We were all just so tired.

Bullets bit into the stone around us and we ducked back down before returning fire.

"Kane, Vance, Casper—go right," North said. "Atlas, Preacher—left flank."

I let Preacher take point, and we made our way around the left side of the ruins. The rumble of thunder cut through the occasional round of gunfire and the first few drops of rain tapped down around us, quickly turning into a steady rainstorm. The landscape grew dim as the clouds thickened and the wind picked up, masking our footsteps. Preacher threw up his hand, halting us and I crouched down, a hand on his shoulder.

He gestured a few hand signs, indicating he saw a muzzle behind some rubble. I nodded, and we adjusted our path in order to hold the element of surprise. Preacher took out the nearest one, and I brought down the second, then we advanced down a narrow gap between columns.

"Two down," Preacher whispered over comms.

"Copy," North responded.

We came around behind the other team. They must have only sent those two out to scout because the remaining five were spread out along the ruin, firing across the courtyard at random. We saw Kane appear as he closed the loop on the right flank and Preacher signaled to him to move on his mark. A quick nod and he relayed the info to Casper and Vance.

We took out two immediately before the others dove for cover among the copious amount of stone and fallen pillars. I glimpsed North and Nyx make a move on the cage as soon as we engaged and then I had to dive behind a pillar to avoid a spray of bullets.

"Fuck, Vance down," Preacher called over comms.

The rain was coming down harder now, making a mist rise around us. I moved around the pillar and joined up with Kane who was engaged with two of them. He'd tossed aside his empty AR and was grappling through the mud with one. The other stumbled to his feet and rounded on me. He somehow dodged the shot I aimed at his chest and slammed into me. We went down and the viciousness of his attack drove me backwards against a massive piece of granite. He pulled back long enough to point his .45 at my face and pull the trigger.

Click. Empty.

He cursed at the same time I gasped in relief and finished sweeping my AR up. I pulled the trigger and dropped him.

"Target acquired, let's go!" North shouted.

I met up with Preacher and Kane and we took off across the field at the same time we saw North, Nyx and Red make a run for it. A gunshot rang out and Kane dropped next to me.

"Fuck! Third team is waiting in the buildings!" Preacher shouted.

We scrambled to lift Kane who was bleeding from his stomach. Another shot and we lurched down again as Preacher was hit in the leg.

"Go, you fools," Kane snarled, shoving me off him, which saved me from a kill shot as a bullet bit into the ground where I'd been standing. "Go!" He barked at me. "Give me that."

He pointed at my sniper rifle and I tossed it to him. The rain was pelting around us now, thundering into the ground as he laid prone in the tall grass. Casper dropped next. He was dead before he hit the ground, a bullet through his eye. Dread settled in my gut, we were dealing with a dead shot.

"Kane's down," I said over comms.

I pulled Preacher along with me as best we could, trying to take a route I knew would make it difficult for the sniper. But he'd turned his attention to North and Nyx. I heard a shot come from behind us.

"Sniper down, go!" Kane said weakly over comms.

"We'll come back for him," Preacher panted as we made it to the buildings. I didn't know if he was saying it for my benefit or his.

North appeared at a crossroads with Nyx dragging Red behind him. North's side was bleeding from where a bullet grazed him and Nyx was favoring his shoulder, but they were both alive which is all I cared about at the moment.

Preacher shoved me off of him, insisting he could walk just as a grenade exploded nearby, sending us all to the ground. Smoke, mist and rain made visibility shit and as my ears rang, I heard shouting and gunfire. I staggered to my knees and used a wall to pull myself to my feet. A man came through the mist—I fired, dropping him.

Preacher was pulling me with him and as the world rushed back to me, the noise was deafening. Nearly a full team had converged on our location.

The next few minutes were a wild blur of survival, training and instincts as we fought through the village. The four of us were a seamless machine, having now worked these missions with each other for over two years we could anticipate each other's reactions.

It's the only reason we made it nearly all the way to our DZ before a man rounded a corner so fast, he nearly took out North. Somehow, North's reaction time was fast enough, and he dodged sideways at the last second. Sometimes I was convinced that man wasn't human, and this was one of those moments because as he twisted, he came around and used his AR to shove his attacker against the wall. I didn't have time to see more because I saw Nyx get flanked by two men and rushed to his side. He was grappling with one of them when we saw Red get dragged away.

"Go!" Nyx shouted at me. "I've got this! Go!"

I took off after Red. The pursuit seemed to surprise the man dragging her away because I was nearly on him before he noticed, the rain must have masked my footsteps. He shoved her away, sending her hard into the hood of a burned out car. It looked like everyone was nearly out of ammo because we both tossed our guns away and collided with fists.

I had the upper hand until the wet stones underneath me caused me to slip and a blow to my head sent me down hard. When the world stopped spinning, the man and Red were gone. I cursed and scrambled to my feet, looking around through the pounding rain, trying to determine which direction they'd gone. I found a .45 with a few bullets in the clip, chose a direction and jogged down the street.

I'd almost made it back to where we were ambushed when the buzzer sounded. My knees weakened and I knew in my gut we'd lost. I leaned against the wall, wiping water from my face and trying to pull myself together as despair tore through me so intensely I lost my breath. I'd never gotten anxiety before, but it was the only way I could describe what I was feeling. My chest tightened and I couldn't take a full breath as I rested my forehead against the wall and fought to compose myself.

I'd lost this one. I should have held on to Red.

"Did we win?" Kane's voice, now a weak whisper, came over comms. I pushed away from the wall.

"No," North said. "We're coming for you, sit tight."

"No," Kane sighed. "This is it for me."

"Fuck off," Nyx snapped and relief surged through me hearing his voice. "They can patch you up—"

"I'm done, man," Kane rasped. I picked up my pace at the tone of his voice, heading back where we'd left him in the field.

"It's been an honor, gentlemen," Kane continued, his voice nearly unintelligible over the raging storm. "It's a beautiful day to die, this storm—it reminds me of that poem. How's it go?"

"Kane—hold on," North demanded.

"*Though wise men at their end know dark is right*," Kane quoted. "'*Because their words had forked no lightning*—'"

As though the world was listening, the sky erupted, lightning crackling across the sky. "—*they do not go gentle into that good night.*"

"Kane!" Preacher pleaded, the tone of his voice tearing through me.

"'*Grave men, near death, who see with blinding sight*," Kane continued, ignoring us. "'*Blind eyes could blaze like meteors—Rage, rage against the dying of the light.*'"

There was a pause.

"'*Rage against the dying of the light...*'" he muttered. "Give 'em hell for me."

A gunshot cracked through our comms units.

I pulled up short, my chest constricting and I was surprised when I choked on tears suddenly mingling with the rain running down my face. I don't know how long I stood there, listening to the silence in my ear. But it was North's voice that got me moving again, this time back towards our DZ.

"'Bless me now with your fierce tears, I pray.'" His voice was rough. "'Do not go gentle into that good night—'" the emotion surged through his tone as he breathlessly finished, fierce and angry. "'Rage, rage against the dying of the light.'"

"Rest easy, brother," Nyx said.

I don't know how I made it back to the DZ. My thoughts were dark, twisted and matched the storm raging around me.

Bless me now with your fierce tears…

Bits and pieces of the poem cut through my thoughts and I couldn't stop the devastation that slid painfully through me like a blade piercing my heart. I stumbled across the line of the DZ where the others stood but I didn't see them.

All I saw was the end. I was done.

Do not go gentle into that good night.

The .45 still dangled from my hand and as I dropped to my knees, I brought it to my head.

Rage, rage against the dying of the light.

62

THERON

Atlas dropped to his knees. The devastation and hopelessness on his face was so complete I was already moving towards him as he slowly raised the gun to his head. I watched as the barrel drew even with his temple and his finger gripped the trigger. His eyes landed on me with an apology and the empty look of a man at the end of his rope.

I wouldn't reach him in time.

Then Nyx was there. He tackled him to the ground and they rolled through the mud as Nyx fought to gain control of the weapon. He finally pinned Atlas, straddling him as rain pummeled the ground around them. He yanked the gun away from him, quickly unloaded it and threw it out of his reach. Nyx climbed off of him and Atlas staggered to his feet. He turned and came at Nyx, throwing a punch that landed on his jaw. Nyx's head snapped to the side.

"Do it!" Nyx hissed, taking a step forward, glaring at Atlas with fire in his eyes. Atlas hit him twice more and Nyx went down on his knees in the mud.

Blood ran from his lip and his eyes were wild as they looked up at Atlas. He bared his teeth in a bloody grin.

"That's it—take it out on me!" He slammed his fists against his chest, trying to provoke Atlas who was pacing in front of him like a wounded animal. Atlas' chest was heaving, fists clenched at his sides. His hair had come unbound and stuck wildly to his face and neck. They were both covered in mud.

Atlas hit Nyx again. Preacher stepped forward as though to intervene but I put a hand on his shoulder to stop him.

"Don't," I said quietly.

They both needed this. Nyx stretched his arms out wide in surrender and Atlas hit him again, sending Nyx backwards into the mud. Atlas fell on top of him, punching him again and again until he realized what he was doing and staggered off him with an appalled look on his face. He went to storm away but Nyx rolled to his knees, supporting himself with an arm as he surged to his feet.

"Don't walk away from me!" Nyx demanded hoarsely.

Atlas' shoulders heaved as he stopped with his back to Nyx, fists clenched tightly at his sides. Nyx got the rest of the way to his feet.

"You think you can just leave us?" Nyx fumed. "Leave me?"

Atlas whirled around and took a few steps towards Nyx.

"Don't you get it?" Atlas scoffed. He threw up his hands. "There is no getting out of this fucking place! I'm done!"

"So what, you're giving up?" Blood ran down Nyx's face from several cuts and the look on his face was deadly. "I didn't take you for a fucking coward!"

Atlas took another step towards Nyx, his jaw clenched and rage flashed through his eyes in tandem to the lightning going off around us.

"You're a lot of things, Atlas," Nyx continued. "But a coward isn't one of them."

Atlas shook his head and went to turn again but Nyx snarled and stepped forward. His hand lashed out and grabbed Atlas by the shirt.

"I said don't fucking walk away from me," he growled. "Don't let him win goddamn it!"

Atlas whirled on him, his fist flying towards his face but Nyx let his rage get the best of him. He grabbed Atlas, and sent him to his knees. Nyx grabbed a fistful of Atlas' shirt and yanked him forward as he brought his face close to his, a snarl on his lips and fury in his eyes.

"I am not dying here," Nyx said fiercely as he blinked the rain away. He jerked Atlas forward harshly again. "Do you hear me? We'll get out of this—together—that's what you said right?"

"I was wrong—"

"*Fuck you*—" Nyx snapped as he emphasized each word.

"That's enough!" I said, stepping forward finally. "Let him go, Nyx."

They glared at each other, each of them trying to calm their surging emotions. Nyx shoved Atlas away.

"So your word means nothing then?" Nyx snapped.

The tension was heavy as the air crackled with electricity. Atlas didn't speak, the look of blank despair back on his face. Nyx bared his teeth in disappointment and this time it was he who turned away. I saw the anguish and rage on his face as he headed towards the doors leading inside. We were fracturing and I couldn't do a damn thing about it.

63

NYX

I was a mess when we got back to the estate. I was furious but only because when I saw Atlas raise the gun to his head, I was terrified I was going to lose him. I knew what it felt like to want to end all of this but being on the other side, watching someone come so close, someone I cared about—it made me want to hit him until he came to his senses. Instead, I'd let him hit me hoping to make him feel something other than the numbness that drove someone to the edge.

I didn't even bother stopping by the infirmary. I went into the bathroom and cleaned myself up, wanting to feel every cut and bruise because it meant I was still alive. I'd tweaked my shoulder during a fight, it wasn't serious, but I relished that pain as well. I pulled off my shirt and dabbed at the cut across my jaw from where Atlas' hook had caught me.

"I'm sorry," Atlas said from the doorway.

"It's fine, it's just a few cuts and—"

"No, not for that," Atlas interrupted.

He held my gaze in the mirror. I sighed and shook my head, looking away.

"Is that why you were angry at me? Before?" I asked, referencing the time when I'd nearly died on the beach.

"Yes, that's why I was angry at you, asshole," he grumbled.

I nodded and continued dabbing at the cut. He watched me in the mirror and finally I sighed.

"I don't know what I'd do if I lost you or North—Preach too, but you and North are—important to me," I said. "I wouldn't see the point in going on if you two weren't around."

"I know, and I'm sorry for scaring you," Atlas said. "That moment with Kane fucked me up, Nyx."

"He went out on his terms," I said. "He was in control in the end and I think that was important to him. We're all struggling right now."

Atlas nodded and ran a hand through his still damp hair that was starting to curl around his face. I watched his hand in the mirror, wishing it was my fingers brushing the hair behind his ear.

"I'm worried about North," Atlas admitted, trying to change the subject. "He said he's fine but there's only so much a man can take—obviously."

"He won't accept help," I muttered.

"I know, I didn't even bother trying. I told him we'd be here when he finally reached his limit. That was all I could think of to say."

"So you'll be here then?" There was an edge to my voice. "Or are you going to try and leave us again?"

Atlas chewed on his bottom lip and I wanted so badly to tug it from between his teeth and put it between my own. When he didn't answer, I turned and stepped towards the door, frustration making those thoughts leave as quickly as they came. His hand on my chest stopped me. When he still didn't speak, my jaw clenched.

"I need your words, Atlas," I ground out.

"I'm not going anywhere," he said finally.

I stared at him for a long moment and nodded. I waited for him to move his hand so I could leave but he didn't. Instead, I watched his gaze sweep across my chest and tattoos, landing on the one that if someone ever bothered to stare long enough, it always caught their eye. It dominated one side of my chest and swept down to my side. Heat flooded me at his attention and his eyes darkened. They flickered up to me briefly before going back down to follow the design along my body.

"I never noticed that one before," he said quietly, his brow furrowed.

I huffed a laugh. "Well, I do have a lot. Sometimes they all blend together."

"A wolf and a raven."

The wolf was running down my chest, twisting back in near my abs with his mouth open towards a raven that was in flight as though his path would cut across my body and the two would circle each other. His fingers twitched on my chest as though he wanted to trace the ink. His touch made my chest tighten and the urge to touch him back was incredibly strong.

"Why did you get that?" Atlas asked.

"I have a feeling you know, my viking—" I'd been meaning to add *friend* to the end of that sentence but for some reason my voice stalled in my throat, leaving it sounding an awful lot like an endearment. A slow smile curled his lips as he tilted his head and studied me intently.

"Wolves and ravens symbolize many things in Norse mythology."

"Success in an upcoming battle being one of them," I said. "A lot of good it's done—"

"You're still alive aren't you?" Atlas said, his eyes sharpening.

"That's fair," I admitted. I ran a hand over where my raven was, since his was on my wolf. It was one of my favorite tattoos although I was speaking truthfully when I said I had a lot. Sometimes when people looked, they only saw the ink as a whole, not the individual art. Atlas seemed to remember he had his hand on my chest because he blinked rapidly as though coming out of a trance and his fingers curled ever so slightly like he wanted to keep them there. He reluctantly dropped his hand.

"Thank you for stopping me today," he said quietly.

"Anytime you need me as a punching bag, you just let me know," I winked at him. "Especially since you're not sorry for giving me these." I waved a hand over my face. He gave a breathless laugh and looked at me sheepishly.

"Alright, I'm sorry for messing with your pretty face," he said.

"Aw, you think I'm pretty?" I teased.

He fixed me with another one of his smoldering looks before he turned towards the sink.

"I'd use a few other words before pretty," he said gruffly and just like that our playful banter shifted to heated undertones. "Especially when you're still covered in blood from a fight." He met my eyes in the mirror and we stared at each other for a moment that went on just a little too long.

"Fuck," I muttered. I ran a hand through my hair, breaking the moment. "You say things like that—"

"I shouldn't," Atlas interrupted. "Not here at least."

We stared at each other again, so many things going unsaid between us.

Finally, I nodded. "I'm glad you didn't leave us, Atlas," I said.

"Me too."

With a last smile, I left him alone in the bathroom, still feeling every inch of where he'd touched me and feeling like we'd only added more question marks to whatever the fuck was going on between us. All I knew for sure was that walking away from him in that bathroom only made me feel more empty and unsatisfied and I didn't have any idea what that meant.

64

THERON

The van pulled up to the estate after the game. The men were escorted into the infirmary and I was taken directly to Vetticus who was sitting at his dining table eating dinner. I was naked and bloody, covered in mud and freezing cold from the storm. They kept my hands cuffed behind me and kicked me down to my knees.

Vetticus stood up, wiping his mouth and letting his gaze rove over my body. He grabbed my chin, leaned down and pressed his lips to mine. I was still wound up tightly from the game and jerked away from him, only for him to bite my lower lip hard enough to draw blood. I hissed at him but he just chuckled and slid his tongue along my mouth, slowly licking away the pain. He pulled away with a hooded expression in his eyes and patted me roughly on the cheek.

"Pity about Kane," he said. "I have one of the best trauma surgeons on call, we could have given it a good go at saving his life."

I didn't say anything, my anger already simmering just beneath the surface as I fought to keep myself in control.

"And then Phantom," Vetticus shook his head. "That one would have hurt, I'm sure. Good thing Reaper was able to stop him."

He looked at me as he said it. "They're close, aren't they?"

I know Nyx and Atlas had been being careful about exploring whatever sort of underlying feelings they felt for each other, not wanting Vetticus to use it against them. But Vetticus watched us excessively and for someone who knew us intimately, it wouldn't be hard to tell there were deeper feelings there than just friendship.

"I should explore that," Vetticus mused.

I could tell he was trying to get a rise out of me or some kind of confirmation he was right. I stared straight ahead, refusing to meet his eyes. This was how these visits normally went anyway. He would bait me then abuse me and when he was done, and I was nearing unconsciousness, he'd tell me he loved me. That was more recent. Even more recent was him trying to get me to say it back to him. He knelt behind me and ran his hands up my thighs to my cock and started stroking me.

"I like when you're still dirty from the field," he said, his breath tickling my ear. He shoved two fingers into my mouth, fish hooking my cheek and dragging my head back against his shoulder. I could feel the bulge already in his pants. "Covered in blood because of me."

He removed his fingers and trailed them between my ass before pushing them inside me. I ground my teeth as he stretched me and stroked me at the same time. I wasn't getting hard but his breathing picked up as he grew more aroused and his hands became rougher.

Releasing my cock, he grabbed my wrists and pulled up, forcing me to bend forward as the pain jolted through my shoulders. I heard his zipper and the sound of him spitting. It landed on my ass and with that as lube, he shoved inside me. He pushed me all the way forward onto the ground and drove inside me, gasping in pleasure.

"You're going to bleed for me now too," he panted.

I blocked it out and went somewhere else after that. Shoving the pain, humiliation and anger aside and instead thought about everything I was going to do to him when I got free. He meant to degrade me, take away my power and tarnish the person I knew myself to be.

Rape was control—rape was power. Vetticus used it as a way to psychologically torture me but also because he truly thought he could get me to love him.

But I wasn't normal. I was just as fucked up as he was. Except he didn't know how to manipulate the body with the intent of the mind catching up and I had every intention of not giving this demeaning experience any power.

Vetticus pushed my arms up further, the pain cutting through my thoughts as he used the leverage to push my face into the wood and drive into me in hard strokes. Then a burning sensation flashed across my back, once—twice— as he ran a knife across my skin. I struggled, trying to pull away, but it only made him hum in pleasure and redouble his efforts. He set the knife against my skin and slowly dug it in, making all my mental walls fall apart as he made another agonizingly slow cut across my back. I heard the knife clatter to the floor and then his fingers were scrubbing across the cuts.

"You were made for me," he gasped.

His hips stuttered as he got close to the edge.

"Made for me—fuck—I love you..." he panted. I broke out in a sweat and my own breathing was erratic as I tried to push the throbbing pain in my body out of my mind.

"Say it back," he ground out.

I was silent.

"Say it back," he demanded again.

Silence.

The room was almost eerily quiet except for the sound of his movements.

Finally, he couldn't hold out any longer and spilled inside me, groaning out another declaration of love for me. He pulled out but didn't let me sit up.

"Say it back," he panted. I heard the hiss of his knife across the ground and he lay it against my back in warning.

"Fucking say it!" He shouted.

But I would die before I ever said those words.

He leaned down over my body.

"Next time I'll fuck you with the knife and then my dick until you tell me what I want to hear," he threatened.

When he finally stepped away, I collapsed onto my side and curled in on myself, feeling my sweat drip onto the floor as I pressed my face into the cool hardwood. Relief that he was done surged through me and I couldn't stop shaking as shock set in. Blackness thankfully came for me and I sank into unconsciousness.

When I woke up, warm water was spilling down on me as I lay on the floor of a shower. Vetticus' hands were traveling over my body, surprisingly gentle as they washed my cuts, my ass, even the scratches and minor injuries from the game. My entire body hurt and I tried to move away from him but I was so weak and in so much pain, I didn't get far. I felt the bite of a needle on my neck and the familiar warmth of the drug swept through my blood. He used his mouth on me and although I tried everything I could think of, the drug hardened my dick for him.

The drug heightened all sensations to an almost painful degree. His mouth was uncomfortable, too stimulating, and I groaned and whimpered whenever he scraped his teeth across my length. My eyes were shut with exhaustion and when his mouth left me, I couldn't open them to see what he was doing.

His hands gripped my cock and excruciating pain made me thrash on the tile. I turned my head and was sick. The ground was heaving under me.

"A little something to remember me by," Vetticus said. His thumb brushed over the head of my cock and the pain made me heave again but there was nothing to empty. "I'm going to pierce you again and then you're going to fuck me."

I tried to shake my head but I couldn't even do that. The pain came again, and the drug made every nerve ending light up until I couldn't handle it and passed out.

When I came to, there was a weight on my hips and I couldn't move. Vetticus was on top of me riding my dick. I was in so much pain at this point, I turned my head and threw up again. A soft sob escaped me and I completely broke. Finally giving in to the breakdown, I was thankful when the darkness came to take me away.

There was no easing awake. The next time awareness hit, I surged up and was violently sick, this time off the side of my bed in our cell. I hung off the side of the bed, one hand gripping the frame as I gasped in breath after breath.

"Easy, here's some water," Nyx said.

When the world stopped spinning, I sat up, wincing hard as pain rolled through my body. I accepted the water as I carefully swung my legs over the side and took a long drink. I lowered the water bottle to see all three men hovering, worry lining their faces.

"It was bad this time, wasn't it?" Atlas stated.

I must have looked as shitty as I felt. I was going to deny it, but I simply looked at him and nodded. A murderous look took over Nyx's face, but it still warred with the guilt I saw every time I came back from my time with Vetticus.

"He wants me to tell him I love him," I said quietly. I hadn't been planning on telling them anything of what went on but that seemed important. "I think it's just going to get worse. He's—he's getting more violent."

"Okay, that's it—you're done," Nyx snapped. "I'm done with you taking this like you're the only one deserving of this torture."

"Nyx—"

"No, god dammit, he's going to kill him!" Nyx growled, rounding on Atlas who'd spoken. "You seriously are okay with him being subjected to this over and over again?"

"Nyx is right," Preacher said. "This has gone on long enough."

"It's fine—"

"It's far from fucking fine," Nyx fumed. "We saw what he did to you."

"This isn't a matter of redirecting his attention." I hissed. "If I refuse, or make things difficult, he's just going to bring you guys in and torture you or even kill you in front of me. Then he's still going to do whatever he wants to me."

Nyx surged to his feet, digging his hands into his hair. "This is bullshit."

"I know, but there's no point in you three getting hurt if it's not going to help," I insisted.

I was exhausted as despair settled heavily on my shoulders, dragging my body down with the pain. It was getting to be too much. We were falling apart—our compartments where we'd carefully placed everything were cracking under the strain. The ruin and destruction when they broke would be catastrophic and most likely deadly. I went to stand up and nearly passed out again as a wave of dizziness swept over me.

Nyx jolted like he wanted to help me but I held out my hand to stop him. He gritted his teeth but didn't say anything.

"I need some air," I said, looking pointedly at Nyx. I wanted to talk to them about our escape plan but didn't want to do it inside where Vetticus could eavesdrop.

"Alright," he grumbled. "Atlas help me bring some of the breakfast out."

It took me an embarrassing amount of time to make it to the middle of the lawn but I unabashedly sank onto a pillow the guys had brought out and carefully ate the cold breakfast they'd saved for me.

"It needs to be the next game," Preacher said flatly. "I don't care if it's a wasteland and we have to take out an entire swarm of drones."

"I agree," Nyx said immediately.

They all looked at me. I knew they were right. Vetticus was only getting more and more unpredictable and violent. He'd stop at nothing to make sure I was his and I was tired of it. I was tired with the constant threat on our lives.

I was just fucking tired.

We were losing ourselves. After Atlas' breakdown and this last torture session with Vetticus—reaching my own breaking point; I knew if we didn't go soon, there'd be nothing left to save.

I looked around at these three men I'd become so close with. We'd bled together, suffered together and I would never forgive myself if I dragged our agony out long enough to get one of them killed.

It was time to put an end to this.

"Next game then."

65

THERON

This was it.

We stood at the door about to start what would hopefully be our last game. It was two months after the incident that tipped us over the edge. Over the past weeks, we solidified the plan, discussed different strategies and refined our previous operation to only include the four of us. We'd decided as a team that we'd send the three new teammates away because they were too much of a variable to risk including them. The doors swung open and the most beautiful sight I'd ever seen greeted me.

A city.

There were no wide open spaces in sight on the map, just a grid of war-torn buildings, similar to the first map we'd played on. Dense forest surrounded the entire thing and as we walked out into the gloomy overcast day, we exchanged looks of relief and resolve.

This just might work.

I went about my normal routine of shoving a comms unit in my ear and studying the map. Then I turned to the three newcomers. I hadn't even bothered to remember their names. The buzzer announcing the start of the game sounded, and I gestured off to one part of the grid.

"You three—sweep these sectors. Find as much ammo and firepower as you can. We'll meet up in this courtyard."

They nodded and trotted off.

"Give 'em hell, boys!" Nyx shouted after them.

"Hoo-rah," Atlas said at my shoulder, acknowledging the code for our escape plan, even though we'd already decided this was the game regardless of the map, it still felt right to say it.

For Kane.

We went the opposite direction of the kids and methodically swept the first few buildings like we usually did. As soon as I found a .45 and ammo, I started taking out cameras. After about fifteen minutes of clearing buildings, we'd amassed an arsenal of two guns each and a comfortable amount of ammo. The only thing we hadn't come across was ironically a knife, which was pivotal to our plan.

It wasn't until we'd made it to the far side of the map, that during a building sweep, I found one embedded in a scrap of wood wall. I took out the cameras and we went to the next building. I could see the forest on my left, the shadows heavy under the treeline with mountains stretching as far as I could see. I didn't even care. We'd figure it out.

In the next building, I did my normal hand signal to sweep the building, but added the signal to take out the cameras. We shot them out and tore out our comms units, stomping them into the ground.

"Nyx," I barked.

He turned his back to me, dropping his vest to his elbows. I cut quickly into his shirt, and after feeling for the bump where the tracker was, I dug the knife into his skin. He didn't flinch, his adrenaline already shielding him from the worst. I dug the tracker out and put it on a slab of concrete at my side.

Atlas was next, and he did the same thing, then Preacher, then Nyx took care of mine. In under a minute, we had our trackers lined up on the concrete slab, all live and still transmitting.

"Go!" I growled.

We sprinted out the door and took off full speed towards the forest. It was a good hundred yards and my blood was pounding in my ears, listening hard for the hum of the drones. We hit the treeline and didn't stop, plunging into the forest. The footing was thankfully easy, with the trees spaced a foot or two apart with soft pine needles underfoot. I led the line, keeping my eyes peeled for any traps or cameras Vetticus may have placed.

We'd been running for about ten minutes when we finally heard the hum of a drone slowly gaining on us. These were military drones so they were equipped with heat seeking technology, night vision and all the other bells and whistles that made them deadly.

"Atlas," I barked.

"Three drones incoming," Atlas called.

We kept running, and I heard his rifle, three shots in quick succession.

"Drones down!" He called.

I looked over my shoulder to make sure he was following before we continued on through the trees. We crashed through a stream, up the bank and continued running on the other side. I was thankful for how fit we were and how much stamina we all had because I wanted us to run for as long as possible. I wanted to put as much distance as we could between us and the map.

An hour later, I slowed us to a walk to catch our breath.

"Kraven!" A voice rang out through the trees and we immediately took a knee covering each other.

"There," I muttered. "Off my two."

A lone drone hovered in the canopy, broadcasting Vetticus' voice.

"I knew you'd do this to me," he growled. "I commend you for getting this far, however, this is where it ends. I'm giving you one chance to surrender. None of you will be harmed—" I pulled my trigger before he could finish speaking and we were up and moving before the drone even hit the ground.

A few minutes later, more drones descended on us from above where they'd been hovering out of sight and sound. Bullets cut into the ground around us and we dove for cover. I scrambled behind a tree, bringing my rifle up as soon as my back hit the trunk. I took out two before bullets bit into the bark and one zipped around the tree to get to me. I took it out and turned to help the others. Afterwards we regrouped. Nyx had a graze on his arm but Preacher had taken a bullet in his shoulder.

"I'm fine," he ground out and motioned for us to keep going.

I pushed us into a jog again. For the next few hours we fought off swarms of drones but by the time the afternoon crept towards evening, we hadn't seen any for a concerning amount of time and we were nearing exhaustion. To make things worse, I'd started hearing the telltale whisper of rushing water somewhere in front of us that would mask any sound of the drones approaching. I could smell damp earth and hear the pounding of a waterfall when I heard Atlas shout.

"Down!" We dove for the ground as another cluster of drones shot at us. I landed in some bushes and twisted on my back, shooting one down before I scrambled to my feet and took cover behind a small rock outcropping. I leaned out and saw one whip by me and bank as it headed towards Nyx.

We both fired and hit it, sending it crashing into a tree.

"Clear!" Nyx called.

"Preacher is hit!" Atlas called.

I came out to see Atlas supporting Preacher as he clutched at his leg which was bleeding heavily from a bullet wound on the inside of his thigh. I tore off my vest and shirt, shredding it into a bandage. I quickly ripped his pants and wrapped it to try and stop the bleeding.

"Can you make it to the water?" I looked up at him to see his face tight with pain but he nodded curtly.

"Fuck—incoming!" Nyx said. We barely avoided a barrage of bullets.

"Let's go!" I got us moving and within minutes we came to a raging river with white water frothing over rocks as it headed south. Upstream, there was a pounding waterfall with mist curling from its base.

"Get in the water!" I had to shout to be heard. I shoved Nyx towards the water and helped Atlas with Preacher. Once they were all in up to their waists, I turned and shot down the two drones as they flew at me through the trees. Then I turned and launched myself into the current.

Night had fallen by the time I hauled myself up onto the bank, only to hear the click of a gun. I looked up, straight into the eyes of one of Vetticus' men.

"Round them up," he said.

My head dropped in frustration as they manhandled us out of the water. A short walk through the trees we came to a waiting SUV on a barely discernible dirt track.

The drive was a surprisingly short one and I was hauled out and forced onto my knees, a gun to my head with Nyx, Atlas and Preacher in a similar fashion next to me. We were in a clearing with a crude cabin, the rustic and decrepit feel offset by the two gleaming black SUVs sitting to one side. The headlights of one cast a spotlight on us as Vetticus appeared on the steps, casually cutting up an apple in his hands.

"Kraven, Kraven, Kraven." He tsked as he deliberately took each step down towards us. "Didn't I tell you? I knew you were going to do this to me," he chuckled but it held no humor.

Vetticus stepped up to me and I heard him eat another apple slice, then toss the core away. He wagged the knife towards me.

"You've gotten the farthest anyone has yet, so there's something."

He grabbed me by the hair and pulled me into the center of the clearing, closer to the steps. I scrambled to keep from being dragged before he quickly threw me down into the dirt. I lunged for him but his brass knuckles connected with my jaw and I collapsed back down as the taste of copper exploded in my mouth.

"Now, now—none of that," he said as he grinned down at me. "Do you remember what I told you would happen when I caught you? Because again—I was right—I said I'd catch you and here you are. But do you remember what I said—what I promised you?" He looked positively gleeful as he leered, his eyes flickered with the headlights, radiating pure evil.

I didn't answer. But I remembered. Dread pooled in my gut and I turned my head when I heard a commotion behind me. Atlas was being dragged towards one of the cars by two men. His struggles were weak and they easily threw him face down over the hood, stretching his arms wide so he couldn't move. A third man sliced his shirt off him.

I growled in protest and went to get to my feet, but Vetticus pressed his gun to my head, forcing my attention to Atlas. The man who'd cut Atlas' shirt off now held a whip in his hand and despite the gun, I jerked again in Vetticus' grip.

"Remember Kraven, you only have yourself to blame for this," Vetticus protested. "And baby, I'm just getting started."

The whip came down on Atlas' back and I was forced to watch as lash after lash was doled out. Nyx cursed viciously at Vetticus and went to rise to his feet, but the man with the gun to his head pistol whipped him back down, beating him into submission until he lay there unmoving, panting and grimacing as he watched the man beat Atlas. Atlas took it well in the beginning, only muttering a soft curse after the tenth but then Vetticus stepped in.

"Give it to me," Vetticus said impatiently as he strode over and yanked the whip from the man's hands. "You're obviously not doing it hard enough."

Vetticus drew his arm back and the moment the whip connected with Atlas' back, red bloomed where it broke the skin. He lasted through four more of those before a soft cry escaped him. Five more and he was visibly shaking against the hood of the vehicle, fists clenched as his wrists were tightly held in place.

Each lash after that was violent and bloody. He looked like a sacrifice, framed by the headlights. Forced to give himself over to the devil standing behind him. Nyx was in obvious distress. He struggled to his knees and with a surge of speed leapt to his feet and landed a solid punch to Vetticus' jaw.

"You son of a bitch!" Nyx raged.

The guards grabbed him and beat him again, sending up a cloud of dust illuminated in the glow. Vetticus brushed his fingers over his jaw before cracking his neck to work out a kink.

"Well that will wake you up," he said. "Fine, if you really want to go next, I won't object." He waved his hand and the men released Atlas. He slid down into the dirt. Unable to hold himself up, he slouched against the bumper on his knees, head against the grill, barely conscious.

Vetticus' attention was on Nyx now. He looked like a hunter, assessing his prey as he stalked closer. He still had the knife in his hand and he tapped it thoughtfully against his pursed lips.

"Kraven," he turned to me. "What did I tell you I'd do to Reaper?"

My jaw clenched as my breathing picked up. The man pressed the barrel harder against my temple, reminding me of my place.

"That was not rhetorical," Vetticus said. He walked back over to me and his hand snapped out and grabbed my neck. His thumb brushed across my lips and he stuck it into his mouth, sucking off the blood he'd smeared it in. A soft moan escaped him and his eyes lit up with a fiery lust.

"What. Did. I. Say?" He rumbled.

My jaw clenched. "You'd torture them—in front of me," I growled.

Vetticus nodded and shoved me away. He motioned for two men who moved towards Nyx.

"No—" I barked.

Preacher shouted obscenities but he was in bad shape and wavered on his knees, looking pale even in the light from the cars. Nyx yanked and jerked in their grasp, but it did nothing to stop the men from dragging him to a tree stump near the cabin. They knocked him to his knees and while one man held him down, another stretched his hand out flat. My gut twisted savagely in dread.

There were only a few yards separating us and I didn't realize I'd tried to get to him until the butt of the gun slammed into the side of my face and sent me to my knees. The threat of the gun was no match for how strongly I needed to get to Nyx. Nyx was cursing violently, fear and anger warring in his eyes. Vetticus strolled over and crouched down opposite him.

"I always did enjoy you Reaper," he said cheerfully. "You made me laugh more than any of the others. It's a pity you have to take the fall for your friend here. I did warn him." He shrugged. "This little debacle can't go unpunished— no one is getting out of this unscathed, that's for sure."

Vetticus pressed his knife against the base of Nyx's pinky finger. Nyx's chest heaved as he tried to get his breathing under control. I was cursing, shouting at Vetticus to stop along with Nyx's protests and Preacher's growled threats. But Vetticus just chuckled and pressed his knife deeper until Nyx's eyes shuttered and the lines of pain etched themselves into the crease between his eyebrows.

"Here's the thing—you don't need your pinky to shoot or do anything really so I don't think you'll miss it," Vetticus reasoned. "It's more of the principle of the thing."

He put all his weight into the knife and Nyx cried out as Vetticus sliced through skin and bone. Nyx moaned as blood poured from his hand, his face pale and glistening with sweat as he leaned against the man holding him, eyes tightly shut.

"Patch him up so he doesn't bleed out." The men dragged him off the stump and wrapped his hand tightly while he sat trembling in the dirt at their feet. When they were done, he clutched his hand to his chest, slumped forward over it. I was vibrating with rage.

Vetticus wasn't done. "Kraven, what did I promise you about Preacher?"

I hissed in displeasure and rage, my heated glare tracking Vetticus' movements as he stepped towards Preacher. He spoke to me over his shoulder but when I didn't answer, he turned to me fully.

"I'll just remind you—I said I'd enjoy making him scream."

Preacher was restrained, his fight weak from the blood he'd already lost. Vetticus grabbed his hair and yanked his head into a beam of light. He put the blade against Preacher's cheek, his eyes lit up with a sick pleasure at our pain.

"And I will enjoy this," Vetticus breathed.

His knife dug into Preacher's eye and Vetticus' word rang true as Preacher's scream cut through my blood like ice, sending a shiver down my spine. His screams echoed in my ears long after Vetticus shoved him away. Preacher clutched at his face, sobbing and writhing on the ground. The desire to kill Vetticus was so overwhelming I nearly choked on it as I watched him look around at us, clearly satisfied with the night's festivities. Vetticus took a breath and looked at me, a deadly smirk pulling at his features. He pointed his bloody knife at me.

"Don't you dare think I've forgotten about you," he sneered. "I've got something extra special planned."

While Vetticus disappeared back in the house, I looked around as the dust settled. Nyx was clutching his hand to his chest as he leaned against the steps. Atlas was still slouched against the bumper and Preacher had gone limp where he lay at the edge of the light, probably passed out from shock.

The door of the cabin slammed and I turned.

"No...NO!"

It couldn't be. There was no way.

A cry escaped my lips and I was on my feet, disregarding everything, even the gun to my head. I made it a few feet before I was knocked to the ground but that didn't stop me. I went feral, kicking up so much dust it threw the clearing into a haze.

Nothing mattered anymore because Vetticus was dragging my daughter down the steps.

My daughter—who was very much alive.

66

NYX

*P*ain.

It was all consuming to a point where it was a state of mind now, encompassing my entire body. I could feel shock begin to set in as I clutched my hand to my chest, taking deep breaths. Seeing Atlas get whipped was like enduring the lashes myself, although I knew that didn't compare to the pain he was feeling. The fury I felt was unlike anything I'd experienced before. It was almost like its own entity inside me—hot, festering, wanting to be unleashed.

Now we both watched as Vetticus dragged a young girl down the steps of the cabin and North fell apart. It wasn't hard to put it all together—it had to be his daughter. He went crazy, launching himself towards her only to get knocked down and continue his struggles in the dirt. It was hard to watch as he was beaten back by three of the guards. It took all of them to hold him as he continued to fight, his chest heaving in sobs and angry curses.

Vetticus had the girl by her hair. It was probably once a beautiful blond but it was matted and dingy now. I caught a flash of gray eyes strikingly like North's before Vetticus shoved her to her knees a few yards away from North. North was panting, both arms restrained behind his back and another man holding him in a chokehold but it was like he couldn't give up. He jerked against the hold they had on him, his eyes locked onto the girl.

"Emersyn—" His voice broke.

She was crying. Her tears made dirty streaks of mud down her face.

"I knew you'd like this surprise," Vetticus said cruelly.

"I'll go back with you—I'll do—anything," North said hoarsely. "Let her go—"

Vetticus barked out a laugh. "Come on now, Kraven—you know me better than that!"

"If you've touched her," North snarled, a fire in his eyes unlike anything

I'd ever seen.

"What if I have?" Vetticus taunted. "You couldn't do a thing to stop me."

"What do you want?" North demanded, sounding on the edge of panic. I'd never heard this edge to his voice before or seen him this undone. It broke my heart.

"What do I want?" Vetticus repeated. "I want you to submit—you've played your games, you've had your fun thinking you're in control—but that's over now. You're mine."

He waved his free hand at the guards holding North. "Let him go."

They hesitated and Vetticus sneered at North. "You move from that spot before I command you and I'll slit her throat right here."

The men released North and he slumped on his knees, devastation twisting his face into grief and pain.

"See, Kraven, you haven't really learned who's in charge here," Vetticus said. "I thought you did—you definitely had me fooled in the beginning. But thanks to your little stunt at the dinner, it's all been made very clear to me."

Vetticus ran a hand down Emersyn's face and she flinched. An audible growl came from North and his hands were shaking where they sat in fists on his thighs.

"Don't fucking touch her," he snarled.

"Again, I think it's how you look at me—I should have shut it down early but I happened to like your fire. Now it's simply annoying me. I won't make that mistake again, that's for sure. So we're going to do this right now."

Vetticus drew his knife again and held it to Emersyn's cheek. North stiffened and glared hatefully at Vetticus, moving as though to get to his feet.

"Stay!" Vetticus barked and North froze. "Look around you, Kraven. Do you really want to test me? Your team is a mess—your daughter is next—you have nothing."

My gut twisted with nausea as I watched North's devastation. The hopelessness pulled his shoulders down to a point I'd never seen before. Even through all of Vetticus' abuse and all the fighting and killing, he'd never looked so lost. The fire dimmed and sputtered as his gaze remained locked on Emersyn and I knew he'd do whatever he needed to do to ensure her safety. I just wasn't sure it was going to be enough.

Vetticus shoved Emersyn to one of his men and approached North who's eyes jumped up to his and the glare returned. Vetticus smirked and stopped a few yards from North.

"Crawl to me, Kraven," he said.

North hesitated for barely a moment before he crawled to Vetticus through the dirt. When he reached him, he sat back on his heels and looked up at him hatefully.

"See, you still have that look," Vetticus said, waving his knife in the air. "So angry. You just don't get it. I can do whatever I want to you."

Lashing out, Vetticus slammed his fist into North's jaw, sending him crashing into the dirt. He struggled to get to his knees but Vetticus came and kicked him down, landing several kicks to his ribs and legs. When he stepped back, North tried to rise again.

"You don't know when to stay down," Vetticus scoffed. "Like a stupid animal who continues to bite the hand that feeds him."

Vetticus grabbed North's hair and shoved him face down into the dirt, kneeling near his face.

"How does it feel knowing you still can't save your daughter?" He jeered.

Emersyn was sobbing now, her small shoulders shaking. She looked barely a teenager—twelve or thirteen—but it was hard to tell with all the dirt and grime on her.

North submitted. I watched his body go limp and the defiance sputtered and died. Vetticus felt it too and stood up. He went back over to Emersyn and taking her by the arm, threw her towards North.

North didn't hesitate but launched himself towards her. They collided, scrambling into each other's arms, both shaking. My heart lodged in my throat and my cheeks were wet. This was torture in itself—brutal and cruel.

North was murmuring to Emersyn who'd buried her face in North's shoulder, her arms tightly wrapped around his neck. He was clutching her to him, frantically trying to hug her and make sure she was okay all at the same time.

Vetticus let it go on for a moment before he walked over and threw his knife in the dirt near North. The sound of a gun being drawn brought North's attention back to Vetticus. There wasn't rage and defiance in his eyes anymore. They were dark, vacant and despondent.

"Pick up the knife," Vetticus said.

When North didn't move, he grabbed Emersyn by the hair. She shrieked as he pulled her away from North who tried to keep a hold of her. Vetticus shoved her to her knees and pressed his gun to her head.

"Pick up the knife!" Vetticus barked again.

North picked up the knife, his hand visibly shaking.

"I knew hurting you wouldn't work—hurting your team might work for a bit but in the end, that didn't quite do the trick either. You need to really learn who's in charge," Vetticus said. "You are going to cut her...right here—" Vetticus drew a line from above Emersyn's eyebrow, down crossing her eye, down her cheek to her jaw, just missing the corner of her mouth. "—on the face—with that knife."

North's face warped into a look of horror, then violence. "No, no—don't look at me like that or I'll make you cut off her hand."

North trembled, his jaw clenching and unclenching in an effort to neutralize his features.

"What are you waiting for?" Vetticus said. "If you don't do it, I'll kill all your men before doing something even worse to your daughter...then I'll kill her too."

Vetticus shoved Emersyn back to North. He brushed her hair behind her ear, searching her face and trying to keep his emotions at bay. His eyes were full of tears that hadn't fallen yet as he fought to keep his composure. Vetticus stepped to the side, gun pressed against Emersyn's head.

"Do you need a countdown?" Vetticus mocked.

I couldn't breathe, muttering curses with what little breath I could manage. I felt so damn helpless. I couldn't save anyone. Atlas was in bad shape, Preacher was passed out from the pain of losing his eye and I still couldn't wrap my mind around the fact I was one less finger than before. My mind balked at the thought but focusing on reality was not any better.

67

THERON

I looked up at Vetticus.

"Please..." I whispered brokenly. I was so far gone, I didn't even care about the look of triumph that crossed his face or the smug lift of his lips.

"I love it when you beg," he chuckled.

My hand trembled. I didn't know what to do. For once I was lost.

My team lay broken and bleeding around me. My daughter was in danger by my own hand with a gun to her head and the only way I could save her was by hurting her.

"Three..." Vetticus' voice broke through my thoughts and panic gripped me as he started the countdown.

"No..." I protested. My hand curled around the back of Emersyn's neck, pulling us closer. "It's okay baby..." I murmured, my voice broken and far from reassuring. "I've got you."

I pushed her hair out of her face and gripped her face in both hands.

"Look at me," I demanded, trying to remain steady even as I was breaking down. "You're so brave—"

"Two..."

"Okay!" I cried out, eyes jumping frantically to Vetticus and back to Emersyn. Her big blue, gray eyes were wide as they met mine, tears running freely in streaks down her face.

"Just do it," she whimpered. "It's okay, dad...you have to..."

My heart shattered. Everything came crashing down.

"One!"

Her eyes slammed shut and I quickly put the blade above her eyebrow.

"I love you..." I said, my voice breaking.

I dug the blade into her skin and slid it down her face, careful to avoid her eye. I may as well have been cutting out my own heart. The pain hit her and instinctively she tried to pull away from my hand, but my grip tightened on her neck. My vision blurred as tears fell and a sob caught in my throat as I continued down her cheek.

She was crying loudly now, her hands gripping my forearm as she gasped in breath after breath. She looked on the verge of a panic attack. I quickly finished the cut at her jaw and the knife dropped from my shaking hands even though I wanted to turn it on myself. Nausea rolled in my stomach and I quickly pulled Emersyn into me as she sobbed into my shoulder. I was shaking, trying to murmur words to her but they came out as sobbing gasps.

The embrace didn't last long before she was ripped from my arms. Vetticus tossed her away and I lunged for her only for Vetticus to shove the gun at my head. Emersyn started screaming and thrashing, trying to get back to me but Vetticus' men grabbed her. Her fight didn't last long.

"She's in good hands, I promise you that," Vetticus said. "Consider her my insurance policy that you won't do anything stupid again. Next time, it will be something worse you have to take from her."

I slumped on my knees, my shoulders shaking.

"That's better—" he smirked after studying my face. I had no energy left to fight. I was numb. The knife still lay in the dirt, covered in Emersyn's blood.

I wanted to die. I *was nothing.*

I was a horrible person—a fucked up father—I realized I was crying when I felt wetness drop onto the backs of my hands that sat clutching the fabric of my pants. I swayed on my knees. Vetticus gripped my jaw and pulled my head up to meet my gaze. If not for his grip on me, I would have fallen.

"Now...who do you belong to?" He purred.

I blinked. "You," I breathed.

Vetticus patted my cheek roughly. "Good boy."

The sound of another vehicle approaching along the dirt road drew everyone's attention. Even Vetticus cocked his head and straightened, watching the SUV approach. Men got out, equipped with assault rifles and stood around the car while one of them opened the back passenger door.

A man stepped out, fixing his suit before looking around at the chaos surrounding him with calm appraisal. He was a large man with a tan complexion and short styled black hair without a strand out of place.

"Albatron," Vetticus said, his tone surprised. He immediately dropped to his knees in the dirt and bowed his head. "Wh-what are you doing here?"

So this was the man behind the curtain. The one I'd heard them speak about during the party. His jaw ticked with obvious displeasure at being questioned as he stepped into the beam of the headlights.

"I was told you were having issues with some of your investments," Albatron said. "Is this true?"

His voice was a silky caress, yet the edge was sharp enough to cut glass. I saw Vetticus visibly shiver at the accusation. Albatron's perceptive gaze slowly scanned the clearing, lingering on me, my men and finally Emersyn. His head tilted curiously before his gaze swept back to Vetticus.

"Speak," Albatron demanded.

"These four escaped," Vetticus said. "I was punishing them."

There was silence for a beat.

"Who is the girl?"

"Kraven's daughter," Vetticus answered.

"What is her purpose?"

Vetticus lifted his head to look at Albatron in confusion. "To teach Kraven a lesson in obedience."

Albatron's gaze shifted to me briefly before locking back on Vetticus. He stared at Vetticus for an uncomfortably long time and as each second ticked by, Vetticus seemed to shrink under his scrutiny.

"Inside," Albatron finally said.

He moved past Vetticus and disappeared into the house. Vetticus scrambled to his feet and quickly followed. I knelt in the dirt in a daze, staring across the space at Emersyn. She was still crying, the occasional whimper continuing to shred my sanity.

I saw Preacher move out of the corner of my eye. He groaned and struggled to his knees. We all still had guns to our heads but it was clear none of us were in any condition to stage an uprising. Atlas still was leaning heavily against the grill of the SUV. Nyx was the only one who seemed alert, albeit a little on the pale side.

There weren't any sounds coming from the cabin and there was an uneasy energy being shared amongst Vetticus' men. They kept glancing at Albatron's men who were still posted around the car. One of them stood at the steps to the house, facing out as though on guard. They all wore full tactical gear without any distinguishing features.

Finally, the door of the cabin squeaked open and Albatron strode out with Vetticus right on his heels looking grim and more than a little worried.

Albatron stopped at the bottom of the steps and pulled his gun.

Everyone tensed. Albatron leveled the gun at one of Vetticus' men and pulled the trigger. Before the man even hit the ground, he'd shot another one, then another.

Then his gun leveled at Preacher and before any of us could move, the shot rang out. Preacher fell.

Preacher.

I saw Nyx jolt in shock and my breathing picked up as anguish twisted inside me. But then Albatron turned to Emersyn.

"No! No...no—"

He pulled the trigger.

It took a moment to register as I watched blood pour down her face and then my ears were ringing, I was shouting and men were rushing to restrain me. It took several of Vetticus' men to beat me down until I couldn't see because of the dust and my breath was stolen from me.

Through the silence, I heard Albatron fire his gun again. I couldn't even see who that bullet was for.

"Stop playing around, Vetticus," Albatron said. His smooth voice slid through the silence and the anger that was loudly roaring through me. "Don't make me come out here again."

I heard car doors slamming and the rumbling of an engine rose and fell before silence descended on the clearing. I lifted my head to see Vetticus standing on the steps looking more than a little ruffled and pissed off. He bared his teeth in the direction the car had gone.

"What was that about?" One of his main guards asked.

Vetticus rounded on him. "Get rid of the bodies. Load the rest into the car." The cabin door squeaked again and slammed as Vetticus stormed inside, palming his cell phone.

I stayed down in the dirt and the men left me alone, moving about the clearing as they removed the bodies and made ready to leave. I lifted my head, my eyes automatically going to my daughter. A man was lifting her body into his arms and I staggered to my feet, stumbling over to try and get to her.

Nyx intercepted me. He grabbed me and pulled me down near the tire where Atlas was struggling to his feet.

"North, she's gone. We need to go," Nyx said.

"Vetticus went inside," Atlas ground out, wincing in pain but he stayed upright. "Now's our chance."

I looked once more at the blond hair cascading over the man's arm as he retreated towards the back of the SUV, then turned away.

Nyx was right. This time she was really gone.

She was...*gone.*

As quickly as I'd found her, I lost her again.

I spared one last glance towards Preacher's body as he too was lifted and dragged away, but I felt nothing but emptiness. Not even pain could reach me now. I turned away and we hurried as quickly as we could into the dark forest.

68

ATLAS

We were in a different kind of hell. After we'd gained some distance from the cabin, North shifted into SEAL mode and took over leading the way. It was like watching a wall fall into place in front of all the pain—both physical and emotional. I didn't want to think about everything I'd just witnessed. The darkness was all around us, just waiting for us to stumble and let it in. I knew if that happened, there would be no escape for us and that hell would be worse than getting caught by Vetticus.

Hours later, we staggered to a stop near a quiet stream. My back was numb and my adrenaline was going which helped dull the pain. Nyx knelt next to me near the stream and pulled off his shirt. Without a word, he dipped it in the water and tried to gently clean the cuts made from the whip.

I hummed in pain as the first drops of water hit and my shoulders shivered. To distract myself I watched North. He was standing on the other side of the creek, staring behind us as though he could see back into that clearing. There was no emotion on his face, just the dead expressionless mask of a man in survival mode. I couldn't take any more water on my back and I stood up. I hid a wince as I turned to Nyx.

"Let me see your hand," I said.

Nyx shook his head. "It's fine."

I scoffed. "Sure. You lost a lot of blood though."

His lips thinned but North spoke before Nyx could say anything.

"Let's keep moving."

His gaze didn't linger on us more than a brief second before he climbed up the far bank and continued through the trees. Visibility was low. The only light was from the moon as it filtered through the trees. The rest of the night we pushed past every limit we had to put as much distance between us and Vetticus as we could. Nothing mattered but our continual movement. Even if it was tenuous. We were free. And that drove me way past the point where

I was sure I'd collapse.

Nyx walked in front of me, clutching his hand to his chest. His breathing was ragged but he doggedly kept walking. North was several yards in front of us at all times looking like he had no end to his reserves. But I knew the comedown for us would be brutal. It was only a matter of time before we crashed.

As the forest began to lighten with dawn, my mind went back to Albatron. Even Vetticus was afraid of him. I mean, who kneels for someone like that? Then to just murder a bunch of people to make his point to Vetticus. There was a pang in my chest as I thought about Preacher. I'd grown really fond of the guy. To see him tortured and then abruptly shot dead was fucking with me. Not to even touch the things that happened with North's daughter. I shuddered, feeling my throat close with emotions.

Nope, not touching that either.

But who was Albatron? He was obviously the person behind Atrox and probably a shit ton of other dark avenues. Regardless of who he was, I knew he was now another name added to the list of people we needed to take down. Vetticus had killed the people we loved. But Albatron had been the nail in the coffin to seal the deal. And what had he been doing out in the woods? Why would he care about what Vetticus was doing with his personal Atrox team? All my questions just led to more questions—most of them I really couldn't care less about honestly but they were running through my mind all the same. If anything they were a welcome distraction.

"Let's stop for a minute," Nyx rasped.

The sun was well on its morning ascent and we needed a break. North waved his hand at a small rock outcropping nearby and continued on through the trees. Nyx and I exchanged a look before sitting down on the rocks. I sighed in relief.

"He's going to drive himself into the ground," Nyx muttered.

A low, quick whistle sounded through the trees nearby. We were on our feet and moving towards where North had disappeared. We came upon him crouched on the edge of a clearing. There was a small cabin—well, more of a shack—sitting in obvious neglect in the center. The door was hanging off its hinges and the forest was slowly encroaching on the structure. But what was most notable was the fresh tire tracks of a motorbike in the underbrush near the front door. I looked around behind us and through the trees as far as I could but there wasn't any indication someone was still in the area.

"How long ago?" I muttered.

"Last night? This morning?" North grumbled.

"Hard to say," Nyx murmured.

"Stay here," North whispered and before we could object, he was moving off to flank the shack. Nyx and I kept watch at the surrounding woods. The only access for a motorbike was down a small dirt trail leading off to the east.

We saw North edge his way up to the side of the building under the window and peek inside. Obviously seeing nothing dangerous, he signaled the all clear and we joined him at the front door.

The inside was small and decaying but clean. Fresh firewood was stacked against one wall and the smell of woodsmoke hung in the air. Nyx went over to the fire and stuck his hands near the coals.

"Not warm," he said. "Yesterday then. Or the day before."

I walked over to a shelf and grabbed at one of the canned goods sitting in the dust. I tossed one to Nyx. North was prowling around the other wall where a small cot sat. If you could call it that. The material was frayed and looked close to disintegrating at the slightest touch. The one blanket was moth eaten and raggedy. Under the cot were a few old but clean shirts.

I grabbed a hunting knife from the small assortment of kitchen tools. The blade was slightly rusted but it was still sharp. I sat down in the one wood chair and started sawing open a can of food.

"No fire," North grunted.

He had pulled the shirts from under the bed and was busy ripping them into strips. Nyx grabbed the tea kettle and headed for the door presumably to grab water from the nearby stream we'd passed.

North and I worked in silence until Nyx returned. I opened three cans and handed one to him and one to North before digging in with my fingers. It was beans, probably expired, but I didn't care.

"What's the plan?' I asked, looking over at North.

"We head down the mountain. Try and find a town or something."

North saw Nyx was done eating and took his bandaged hand into his lap, unraveling the crude dressing. Nyx tried to pull his hand away but North gripped his wrist firmly.

"Don't be stupid," he growled. "If it gets infected, you're fucked."

Nyx scowled at his hand but stopped struggling. When North peeled away the final piece of bloody fabric, Nyx looked away in obvious distress. My eyes landed on the bloody stump where his pinky finger had been. It was still slowly bleeding.

Anger flooded me and I looked up to see Nyx watching me. I knew better than to say anything but I held his gaze while North cleaned the wound and wrapped it in a clean bandage. When he was done, Nyx muttered a thank you. North stood up and approached me next, jerking his finger to get me to turn around. I hesitated too but I knew that look on North's face and knew arguing was useless. North cleaned my back and handed me one of the shirts he hadn't shredded.

"I wouldn't put that on yet—might be best to let those air out. Some of them look like they need stitches but we don't have anything for that. Just make sure they stay clean."

"Yes, sir," I muttered.

North cleaned a few of his cuts and sank down onto the cot again. He leaned back against the wall and closed his eyes.

"I'll take first watch," I said.

I grabbed the knife and pulled the chair closer to the door so I had a good view out the front then settled in. I didn't know if Vetticus would be hot on our heels or what kind of resources he would deploy to track us. Would he send some of his drones out? Were these tire marks part of that search party?

I didn't know. All I did know was that we weren't going back.

I'd do whatever it took to ensure we got out of this.

69

THERON

A month passed, and we still hadn't wandered into civilization yet. We looked like an extension of the wilderness—our clothing cut and torn, hair scraggly and dirty with rough beards on all our faces. We hadn't seen any sign of Vetticus but I wasn't surprised because now, he had to contend with three military trained men who had the upper hand and who didn't want to be found. I had no intention of ever letting him find us.

Nyx's hand was slowly healing. The process hindered by lack of nutrition and proper care. Atlas' back was no longer open wounds but I could tell the skin was still sensitive and because I couldn't stitch it up, he was sure to have some wicked looking scars.

But overall, we were alive. We were surviving. And that was all that mattered. It was the only thing I allowed myself to focus on. I couldn't afford to think about anything else or I knew I wouldn't be able to pick myself up and go on.

We were always hungry and expended massive amounts of energy walking every day so we had nearly no fat on our bodies anymore and our pace was slow. We caught what game we could—usually rabbits, once a porcupine. After the first clear night, it rained almost every day so we had plenty of water. We rarely spoke, operating off hand signals if needed but I could tell we were all nearing our limits. Our bodies just weren't holding up well enough with such little food.

I called a halt midday and Atlas collapsed onto a tree stump, his head in his hands. Nyx leaned against a tree, staring off into the greenery with a dull look of someone working on autopilot.

Suddenly, Atlas' head whipped up. "Do you hear that?" His voice came out raspy and hoarse from lack of use.

"A car," Nyx said.

Nyx and I followed him through the trees until we saw a break through the forest and an old beat-up pickup truck was rolling down a furrowed dirt road. We followed the truck through the forest for a few miles until the trees abruptly ended and the road spilled out across a valley with mountains far in the distance. The truck was headed towards a farm that sat about half a mile from where we crouched at the treeline.

"We'll wait for dark," I said and made myself comfortable in the shadows of the trees. I watched the truck come to a stop in the yard and a woman got out, two paper bags clutched to her chest as she lugged her groceries into the house. The farm looked like in the past it had been well kept but now had the hint of neglect tugging at its edges. The garden was the only thing that looked taken care of, having been recently weeded and trimmed, but the yard needed a mow, there was fencing in one pasture that needed repairing and the barn looked like it hadn't been swept out in some time. A few horses sat in the backfield, a few sheep and goats in another near the house and there was a chicken coop on the side yard.

The house was a two story old style farmhouse with peeling white paint and a bench swing on the wrap-around porch. The place held a nostalgic feeling about it as well as an underlying sadness I couldn't place. We sat watching the house the entire afternoon and didn't see anyone but the woman. No kids, no men—just an old hobbling german shepherd who emerged when the woman returned home and hadn't moved from his spot laying on the porch steps.

When night finally came, we carefully approached the house in the cover of darkness and split up. Atlas took the barn and Nyx and I flanked the house. There was a single light on in one of the upper windows which I assumed was the woman's bedroom, otherwise the house was dark.

The backdoor was unlocked, alluding to the level of security the woman felt by being this far out in the wild. She must be a comfortable distance from any neighbors or towns to not feel any threats. We met Atlas back at the barn. He had a basket full of vegetables from the garden.

"There's a well," he whispered.

Nyx nodded and moved off to fetch water while Atlas and I entered the barn and headed towards one of the far stalls. The barn didn't look used in a while, with cobwebs heavy in the corners and the straw smelled of mildew, but it was relatively dry and I was thankful for a warm shelter as the rain started up again outside.

"It's a feast," Nyx said when he came back, eyeing the food hungrily. I agreed and for the first time in a month we went to bed with full stomachs.

For the next week, we settled into a routine. An hour before dawn, we'd head back to the treeline to watch the house during the day, then creep down and raid the garden and well before sleeping in the barn. If the woman noticed, she gave no signs of it. Her daily routine consisted of letting the dog out, having coffee on the porch and then she'd do some farm chores such as weeding the garden, taking care of the chickens and livestock, and a few other odd jobs before she'd move inside the house and we wouldn't see her again.

As we sat down in our stall in the back of the stable on the seventh night; I bit into a carrot and nodded towards the house.

"I'm going inside tonight," I said.

"Do you think that's a good idea?" Atlas asked.

"I want to see if we can get a read on where in the world we are. The truck doesn't have a license plate."

Nyx nodded. "See if you can find some more food. Veggies are good and all but I'd love some fresh bread—with butter...or some meat." He moaned at the thought and Atlas scoffed under his breath.

"Always hungry," he muttered.

"Aren't you? I can feel my stomach kissing my spine. I feel like someone could come along and flick my forehead and I'd tip over."

I waited until the dead of the night, almost late morning to ensure she was well and truly asleep. We were pretty convinced she was alone on the farm at this point but I still palmed the knife we'd found that first day in the shack—just in case—as I crept to the backdoor.

I carefully edged the door open just enough to slip through, thankful it didn't squeak on its hinges. The back room was a mud and laundry room. It was mostly women's shoes but there were a few men's boots laying dusty underneath them. They didn't look recently used and there was only women's clothing on the washer and dryer, confirming my suspicion that there was a man of the house but he hadn't been around in some time. The next room was a sitting room on one side and a dining room on the other. Both were comfortably furnished with old, handmade wood furniture.

A floorboard creaked as I was leaving the sitting room for the kitchen and I froze, wincing at how out of the ordinary it sounded in the dead stillness of the house. I waited an excessive amount of time before moving again and made it into the kitchen in relative silence. It was a rare, clear night, so the moonlight filtered through the windows cast just enough light to see by.

I pocketed an apple sitting in a bowl on the counter and my mouth watered an embarrassing amount when I saw muffins sitting on a cooling rack. I grabbed one of those and bit into it, suppressing my moan of pleasure as the sweetness of wild blueberries exploded in my mouth. I saw some papers on a small desk and went over, sifting through them. I could barely make out what anything said, and I was holding up an envelope to the window to see the return address when the kitchen exploded with light.

"Don't fucking move." The woman's voice said from behind me.

I held up my hands and carefully turned to see her holding a .357 leveled at me. Her eyes scanned me quickly, lingering on the faded, torn up camo pants I wore before jumping to my face. There was fear there but also a steel resolve I recognized—she would do what she had to.

"I'll shoot," she hissed.

"I have no doubts about that, ma'am," I said softly, hands still up.

"What are you doing in my house?"

"I'm just passing through—"

"From where?"

I didn't answer, and she scowled. She looked like she was around our age, late thirties, with blond hair in a messy bun and a long t-shirt down to her knees. I kept my eyes on her face, knowing I looked fearsome having not shaved in some time and so filthy I probably looked like a wild animal.

"Get out," she growled.

I opened my mouth to say something and the barest twitch of her trigger finger was the only warning I had before she shot me. The gunshot rang out loud in the enclosed space and by some fucked up luck; I was mid step to the side, meaning the bullet barely grazed my arm. But now I had to move, so two steps brought me to her and I grabbed the gun, quickly shoving it up and flicking the cylinder. The clink of bullets falling echoed through the kitchen.

Before I could grab her other hand, I felt the bite of steel in my side, catching her wrist in time to avoid her shoving a knife into my ribs. I hissed at the pain and quickly turned her, slamming her wrist against the counter as I pressed her body against the island.

I happened to glance up in time to see Atlas and Nyx at the side door and before I could shake my head to stop them from coming in and making things worse, they opened the door, pulling the woman's attention.

"Stop," I barked.

They froze just inside the door, quickly looking over the situation.

The woman was shaking in my arms, vibrating with a potent mix of fear and anger but at the sight of Nyx and Atlas, she stopped struggling, seeing the situation for what it was. She was no match for three men.

"Let me go, please," she whispered, her words hitching in her throat.

"We're not going to hurt you," I said. "Like I said, we're just passing through."

"What do you want?" She hissed.

"Food mostly," Nyx said, trying for a grin but with his beard and how dirty he was, it didn't come across well. He must have seen the look on my face because he smoothed a hand over his beard and looked at the woman sheepishly. "Sorry for scaring you, ma'am. We don't usually look so—wild. I don't know how people have beards—this thing itches something horrible."

"If I let you go, will you promise to behave?" I asked. I could feel the blood dripping down my side and my arm and I needed to see the damage she'd done. "Let go of the knife."

She hesitated but the hand I had pinned slowly relaxed and I grabbed the knife and tossed it to Nyx. He caught it and put it in his belt. I nodded to the gun and Atlas carefully stepped forward and picked it up, checking to make sure it was empty and shoving it into his belt.

"Please don't—don't take that," she pleaded.

I stepped back away from her as Atlas held up his hands.

"Just holding it for you," he said. "I'll give it back when we leave."

"She got you good there," Atlas nodded.

I pressed my hand to the large cut on my side. It would need stitches. She looked at me with no regrets and folded her arms across her chest. I glanced at Nyx, silently ordering them to watch her. He nodded, and I moved over to the sink, pulling my shirt off, I grabbed a towel and held it to my skin. Atlas moved over to where the papers were that I was looking at.

"What's your name?" Nyx asked, leaning against the counter.

She stepped away from Atlas who was now a little closer to her, eyeing him warily and looked back at Nyx, frowning but resigned.

"Macy," she grumbled.

"We're in Canada," Atlas said, holding up a letter.

"What? Of course we're in Canada," she scoffed.

"What's the closest city?" he asked her.

She looked at him like he'd suddenly sprouted several heads.

"Hell's Valley," she said. "But it's a good three hours from here. The closest town is Banks."

"Do you have a first aid kit?" I asked.

She made to move, and I held up a hand. "Just words."

Her lips pressed into a thin line and she glared at me before jerking her head down the hallway.

"Hall bathroom, under the sink."

"Thanks, Macy," Nyx said, leaving to retrieve it. He came back and brought it over to me. As I pulled the towel away Nyx chuckled and turned to Macy. "Needle and thread? You got him pretty good."

He flashed a smile that usually would melt any woman, but in his current state it did nothing but make her blink at him in irritation.

"Dining room hutch," she said.

Atlas pulled out a chair from the kitchen table and nodded to it.

"Have a seat."

She hesitated, but he didn't break eye contact and she finally did as he said, watching each of us with her hands clutched in her lap. Nyx came back with a sewing kit and we got to work sanitizing a needle and thread. Nyx did the first stitch, and I heard a soft scoff. We both looked over at her.

"That's not how you do it," she said.

"I've stitched up plenty of people," Nyx said indignantly.

"I'd hate to see the scars they have now," she retorted. She stood up, and we all froze but she held her hands up and came over. "Give it to me."

Nyx hesitated.

"I'm a nurse, asshole," she snapped.

He hid a smile and held up his hands, stepping back. Macy washed her hands and then jerked her chin at the counter.

"Sit," she demanded. I hopped up, and she took the needle and thread. The first dig of the needle made me grit my teeth and glare down at her.

"Oops," she muttered.

"He probably deserved that," Nyx supplied from over her shoulder.

She stopped. "Do you mind?"

"Okay, okay," Nyx moved away, giving her space and her rough handling stopped. I saw her eyes rove over my body, taking in the other scars and the brand on my chest.

"Military?" She asked, doing another stitch.

"Retired," I said.

"Those don't look retirement issued," she grumbled.

"You don't want to know," Nyx said. He hopped up on the counter near the sink, swiping a muffin. "Do you live here alone?"

"That's literally the worst question to ask a woman," she said dryly. "And besides, don't you already know that answer? You've been spying on me for a few days at least."

"Touche," Nyx said.

Atlas emerged from the living room on the other side of the kitchen.

"Who's the Marine in the pictures?" He asked. I watched her stiffen beside me. She made a few more stitches, and I watched her lip tremble.

"My husband," she said.

"Where is he?" Atlas demanded.

"Not here," she said shortly.

"What does that mean?" Atlas continued aggressively.

"Come on, man," Nyx said.

"No, I need to know if some Marine is going to suddenly bust through that door," Atlas insisted.

"He's deployed," she said louder.

"He left you here alone?" Atlas continued. "In the middle of nowhere?"

"Jesus, At—" Nyx started.

"Knock it off," I barked. "He hasn't been home in some time—she's telling the truth. Just leave it alone."

The kitchen settled into silence as she continued her stitching. Her lower lip trembled but her hands stayed steady. Twenty stitches later, she snipped the thread with a pair of small scissors and grabbed a bandage, pressing it firmly against my side. She moved to my bicep to check the bullet wound but I knew it was a graze before she even said anything.

"This one just needs a bandage," she muttered.

A moment later, she stepped aside. "Done," she said.

"Thank you," I met her gaze, and she nodded before turning to the sink to wash away the blood.

"Macy," I got off the counter and stood behind her, waiting for her to turn around. When she did, she pressed herself back against the sink but met my gaze solidly with her own. "We need your help. If we could clean up, refuel and get a ride into town, we'll be out of your hair."

She looked around the kitchen at us, presumably seeing if her instincts told her she could trust us to keep to our word.

"You'll just take it, even if I say no," she grumbled.

"Yes, but we won't hurt you either way," I said. "You have my word on that."

"Fine, in the morning I'll drive you into town," she sighed. "You can use the bathroom down the hall."

"Until then, you'll hang out where we can see you," I said. "I'd prefer to not acquire any more scars while I'm here."

She glared at me briefly before nodding curtly and moved towards the coffee machine which sat near Nyx.

"Then I guess I'll start some coffee," she grumbled. Macy watched Nyx warily as she approached but he was busy eating another muffin.

"These are really good," he said, his mouth full. She finished filling the coffee pot. Soon the room was wafting with the smell of coffee and Atlas had gone to clean up in the bathroom. We stood around the kitchen awkwardly while the coffee brewed and the sound of the shower kicked on in the hall. Nyx jumped down from the counter and pointed to the fridge.

"Mind if I make some breakfast?" He asked.

She nodded and resumed her seat in the kitchen chair. Nyx gathered some eggs, bacon, spinach and a few other ingredients and set to work whipping up some sort of omelet with toast and jam. We both watched him while the first omelet cooked and the bread was toasting. He poured three cups of coffee and handed one to me and one to Macy. She looked like she was still trying to come to terms with the fact she had three strange men in her house and one of them was cooking in her kitchen but she nodded her thanks and sipped from the mug, not bothering with any creamer. Nyx took a sip of coffee and gave an exaggerated moan of pleasure.

"Fuck, I've missed coffee," he said.

"I didn't know you could cook," I commented.

Nyx shrugged. "I'm a man of many hidden talents," he winked at Macy.

"That just looks creepy," Atlas said, appearing in the doorway. "Don't do that while you look like a wild animal. You'll scare her."

Nyx flipped him off, flashing him a purposefully exaggerated grin before turning back to breakfast.

"Since when can you cook?" He asked, coming over and taking the cup of coffee Nyx offered. Macy's eyes followed him as he did. He was shirtless, in nothing but a towel. He'd shaved and cut his hair shorter again, throwing it up in his usual bun.

"Why is everyone so surprised? These hands are used for more than killing you know," he scoffed. Macy choked on her coffee, and Atlas sighed.

"Go get cleaned up," he said. "I'll finish breakfast."

"Don't ruin it," Nyx said. His eyes slid over Atlas' body as though he couldn't help himself any longer. "The bacon should be done in the oven in a minute."

"You make bacon in the oven?" Atlas asked.

Nyx's gaze shot back up to Atlas, and he shoved the spatula into his chest, a heated gaze jumping between the two as Nyx's fingers came into contact with Atlas' bare chest.

"Everyone knows you make bacon in the oven," he muttered.

They continued to stare at each other. I cleared my throat. Nyx blinked and shook his head as he stepped away and headed towards the bathroom. Macy's mouth was parted slightly, entranced by what just happened and probably also by Atlas who was looking like a viking god in nothing but a towel. He looked even more fearsome with the freshly healed whip marks on his back.

An hour later, I came out of the bathroom in a towel carrying an armload of all our dirty clothes into the laundry room. Macy saw me and sighed.

"Just throw those out. There's clothes in that closet you can look through."

Once we were all clean and clothed, breakfast was laid out on the island. We dug into the food and Macy nibbled on a piece of bacon; her legs now tucked up under her on the chair and her second cup of coffee in hand.

"This farm seems like a lot of work for one person," Nyx commented in between bites.

Macy nodded. "It is."

"How long has your husband been deployed?" I asked.

Macy's face fell again. "It's been four years. He's MIA—no one knows where he is—" Her voice broke and I frowned.

"I'm sorry to hear that," I said. "Do you know where he was stationed?"

"The last I heard, he'd disappeared somewhere in Syria. That's all they'll tell me."

I nodded. If he was MIA—missing in action—chances are he was either dead or had been taken by the enemy and was being held. Neither option was pleasant to think about.

Dawn began to break just as Nyx and Atlas finished cleaning up the kitchen. Macy was watching them curiously.

"Are you guys in some kind of trouble?" Macy asked.

"Better if you don't know," I said. "Do you have a map of the area?"

She nodded and disappeared down the hall only to reappear a few minutes later with a few folded up maps. She spread them out on the table and I ran my hands over them to smooth them out, my fingers tracing the mountains as I got my bearings.

"We're here," she supplied, pointing to a spot on the map.

I followed the forest back the way we'd come, tracing my finger over the forested area. I stopped on an isolated area with enough land for Vetticus to run his operation. The estate had to be somewhere in that area. I looked back at where this farm was and traced it to the nearby cities and towns.

"Can I keep this?"

She nodded. "Are there other farms around here?" Atlas asked.

"Yeah, they're spread out along this valley," Macy said, tracing a part of the map. Atlas met my eyes over the table, concern written all over them. Vetticus would surely check the farms. I didn't want to bring that trouble down on Macy. If I was him, I'd be busy sweeping all the farms in this valley knowing if we made it, we'd pop out somewhere around this area.

"We've already been here too long," Nyx said.

I nodded. A week here was pushing it. "Can you take us into town?"

She nodded. "I take it you want some supplies..." It wasn't a question but I nodded all the same.

"And any guns or weapons you can spare—minus the one Atlas is keeping safe of course."

An hour later, we had three packs full of supplies, clean clothes and best of all—two 9mm handguns and a rifle. Macy had been hesitant to part with the weapons but she knew I'd steal them regardless so I let her take her time choosing which ones.

We piled into the pickup, Nyx and Atlas in the bed and I sat in the passenger seat while Macy turned the key and the truck rumbled to life. We were just pulling out of the drive when a radio crackled in the truck and then a voice came through.

"Macy, come in, Mace. Over."

"Who is that?" I asked. I snatched the radio before she could grab it.

"He's my neighbor on that side," she said, waving her hand off down the valley. "He helps me out here and there."

"Macy, come in—" The radio cut out. "—men—guns—"

I heard Nyx curse through the open back window.

"Drive," I said to Macy.

She pulled out of the front yard and turned the truck towards the road leading into the woods. The radio crackled again but the warble of the man's voice couldn't be understood. Macy's hands gripped the wheel tightly and her face was lined with worry.

I handed her the radio. "Pick it up. Don't mention us."

She nodded. "Finn, I'm here. Are you okay? Over."

"Thank god—Mace—men—"

"I can't hear you, Finn."

"They're—down the valley—headed for you. Run—"

"Are you hurt? What happened?" No answer. "Finn!"

She turned wide eyes to me. "I think something is wrong."

"How far away is his property?"

"Five miles, maybe?" Macy said.

"Do not stop this truck no matter what," I commanded. I pulled my gun around and checked it as the truck bumped along the road at a steady pace.

"They're after you," she said, glancing at me.

"Yeah—watch for drones!" I called out over my shoulder. Atlas already had his rifle up and ready while Nyx looked out over the forest surrounding us.

"Are you guys criminals?"

I watched the road ahead as it wound through the trees.

"No, it's not the law that's after us."

"Who is it?"

"Something worse."

"And now you dragged me into it?" Her voice was borderline hysterical now.

"You heard your friend," I said. "They would have come through this valley looking for us anyway and done god knows what to you."

"So, what, I'm lucky it was you?" She scoffed. "The lesser of two evils or something?"

"Last I checked, I'm the only one who got hurt in the last twelve hours," I said dryly.

Her mouth snapped shut at that and pressed into a thin line as she focused on the road. Besides urging her faster, no one spoke for the rest of the drive down the dirt tract. When we pulled out onto a two lane paved highway, Macy pushed the truck well over the speed limit and we sped off towards town.

The drive into town was a nerve-wracking hour where any moment I expected a drone to come down on us but we made it without incident. The town of Banks was a sleepy backwoods town with two street lights and a quaint downtown strip with stores, restaurants and one gas station. Macy pulled into a vacant lot behind a store before entering the main streets.

"Everyone knows everyone, you'll stick out," she said.

I got out of the truck and slung a backpack over my shoulders. Nyx and Atlas hopped down and I walked around to the driver's side.

"Is there a place you can stay for a few days? You shouldn't go back to the house right away." She frowned at me but after a moment nodded. "Thank you for the help, Macy."

"Sure," she sighed. "Sorry about all that," she grumbled, gesturing to my side.

I flashed her a quick smile. "He's right—I deserved it." I grew serious again.

"You should forget you ever saw us. For your safety, we were never here, understand?"

She looked between the three of us and nodded. Atlas pulled the revolver out of his pants and handed it to her. He gave her a curt nod and Nyx waved as she pulled out of the lot and gave us one last look in her rearview mirror before she turned a corner.

"Now what?" Atlas asked.

"I have no intention of staying here," I said, looking around. "We need to find a car."

We saw a truck parked in the next lot and walked over. It was unlocked. Nyx went to dive under the steering but Atlas dropped the visor and the keys fell onto the seat.

"No one locks their shit in these kinds of places," he said.

We climbed in and Nyx took off while I spread out the map on the dash and gave him directions.

"Where are we headed?"

"We're actually a few hours from a friend of mine," I said.

By a few hours, it ended up being eight and since we didn't have money for gas; we ended up running out with two hours to go. We were on a two-lane highway deep in the mountains on the other side of the valley and after consulting the map; we ditched the truck and struck out on foot.

70

THERON

I smelled the smoke first. We walked up the dirt road a bit further, and a rustic farmhouse with smoke rising from the chimney appeared around the curve. Looking up, I noticed security cameras in the trees and around the clearing where the house sat away from the treeline. Atlas and Nyx stayed at the bottom of the steps while I went and knocked on the door.

The house sat quiet, so I knocked again and edged closer to the window. I was attempting to peek inside when I heard a small explosion from around back. I trotted down the porch and as we came around the corner, I saw a man feeding a burn pile with gasoline. A lot of gasoline.

"Jesus—" Nyx said in alarm. "Does he know—"

"Yes," I said dryly, watching as he tossed the canister into the flames and caused another small explosion.

"Can't help yourself, can you?" I called out.

The man turned quickly, his hand going to his sidearm as he squinted through the smoke.

"Well, fuck me!" A grin transformed his face as he walked over to me. He ripped off his clear protective glasses, revealing blue eyes glinting from the high of the fire he always loved to play with.

"North! What the hell, man?" He clasped my forearm and thumped me on the back before pulling away and looking me over. "I heard you were dead! I mean—you look damn close—should've known though, you're harder to kill than that. Stubborn bastard." He hugged me again, his excitement potent.

I chuckled. "It was a near thing this time."

"I take it there's a hell of a story behind it too."

"A dark one, if you'll have us?" I asked.

The grin took over again, and he spread his arms wide, encompassing the property. "Like I told you way back when—my family's property is always a good place to start if you're lookin' for me. You're welcome anytime!"

"This is Nyx—Atlas," I said, pointing respectively to the guys.

"Trent Knight," he extended his hand with a grin. "Or as some people like to affectionately call me—Pyro."

After I showered and borrowed some of Knight's clothes, I stood out on the front porch. The forest air was fortifying, and I took one deep breath after another, letting the calm and safety seep into my being. But with that came the grief and distress as the reality of what we'd just gone through shoved its way to the front. I closed my eyes, gripping the railing and fighting it back down. Unfortunately, when I closed my eyes all I saw was Emersyn's face and feel the blade in my hand—

The door opened behind me, thankfully interrupting my thoughts and Knight walked out. He leaned against the railing facing the house, studying me openly.

"I'm sorry to hear about your family, North," he said quietly. "Cap said you were in the fire too or I swear I would have—"

"I know," I looked over at him briefly. "It was a professional job. They didn't want any loose ends."

Knight nodded and turned to lean his forearms on the railing, looking out over his front lawn.

"They're all dead," he said. "We're the last ones. Cap died last year—suicide."

I nodded, unable to feel anything but a dull melancholy. We'd served together for a while and like any crew who'd gone through some shit together, we'd been tight. After the military, we'd gone our separate ways, keeping in touch here and there but life has a way of fucking over people that have seen the shit we'd seen. And once your friends started dying by their own hands, it was like having survivor's guilt all over again.

"How long have you been out here? The last time we talked, you were contracting I think."

"Yeah, I did that for a bit," he said. "But I needed a break. Pops died a few years back, so I figured it was the perfect time to come out here and see to the property. I was going to sell it actually, but I don't know—we all have our demons, mine are just less noisy out here. It ended up being the perfect break and I just haven't been able to bring myself to go back to civilian life yet."

I nodded. I could understand that. Knight straightened and put his hand on my shoulder.

"I'm really glad you're not dead," he smirked. "Let's go inside. We'll eat and you can tell me about everything—or at least who we need to kill."

It was late into the night by the time we finished telling Knight everything that had happened. Or at least everything we wanted to share. The conversation wound down, and we sat sipping whiskey and staring into the fire Knight was subconsciously poking at.

"I don't even know what to say to all that," Knight said after a moment. "I'm glad you guys got out. Do you have a plan to take him down?"

"Maybe." I threw back the rest of my whiskey and leaned my forearms over my thighs, watching the coals reflect in Knight's eyes. "Do you still have it?"

A slow smirk spread across his features, and he nodded once before standing up and leaving the room. He was only gone briefly before he came back and tossed a folder down on the coffee table in front of me.

"I looked into it a few years ago, but without you and the rest—" He shrugged. "It just didn't feel right."

"What is that?" Nyx asked, leaning forward.

I opened the folder and spread the papers out, looking for one in particular. Once I found it, I put it in the center of the table and Atlas reached for it.

"It's a map," he said.

"Not just any map," Knight said. He went around refreshing everyone's whiskey before sitting in an armchair next to me. "A treasure map."

Nyx laughed but when he saw neither Knight nor I laughing he stopped.

"You're serious," he stated. "Treasure? As in gold?"

Knight nodded. "During World War II, some Nazis hid a vast amount of gold in the Austrian mountains. The myth is they sunk it in a lake, but that map says otherwise."

"How much gold are we talking about?" Atlas asked.

"5.6—" I paused. "Billion."

"How come no one has found it yet?" Nyx asked incredulously.

"Everyone thinks it's in the lake," Knight shrugged with a grin. "No one can get to it."

"It's also dangerous," I added.

Knight barked a laugh. "Oh yeah, there is that too."

"Mysterious deaths mostly," I said.

"People would go searching for the treasure and either die in an accident," Knight emphasized 'accident.' "Or by a bullet. The area is off limits so there are usually some trigger-happy contractors hanging around and oh yeah—to top it all off the area is extremely treacherous."

"Only one access road in and out," I said.

"Why didn't you guys go after it before?" Atlas asked.

"I had a family," I shrugged and looked down at my whiskey and swirled it around in the glass, feeling the ache in my heart that was always there when I thought of what was and what could have been. I shook it off and looked back up at him. "Now—I want to build a fucking empire. I want to become untouchable and then I want to take down Vetticus, Albatron and Atrox. This money would expedite that process. If I have to do it the good old-fashioned way, I will. But this would give me a good jumping off point."

I looked between Nyx and Atlas. "I understand if you both just want to move on—"

"Oh no," Nyx said, shaking his head, his face hard with suppressed anger. "I'm in. For all of it. I want to take that fucker down."

Atlas nodded. "Whatever it takes."

Knight chuckled. "And count me in too—I was starting to get bored."

"Where did you guys get the map?" Nyx asked.

"Knight and I went to Salzburg on leave one year—got drunk with some Austrians and they started talking about the local lore. One of them told us about a map their family passed down for generations that shows where the Nazis dropped the gold. Knight ended up winning the map in a bet with one of them, with the stipulation that if we ever went after it, we had to call him and include him in the job."

"Why didn't he ever go after it himself?" Atlas asked.

"Apparently he went looking for it a few times. Had a few close calls and gave it up. He's already filthy rich on his own—family money—so he was doing it mostly for the thrill of it. Said he might as well let someone else have a shot. He's an ex-Jagdkommando, Austria's special forces, so he knows the country and he's also just a hell of a guy to hang with."

"Should I hit him up then? It's morning over there right now," Knight said.

I nodded and Knight pulled out his phone and shot off a quick text before he stood up.

"Well, I'm off to bed. Those bedrooms down the hall are all available. Help yourself to anything of course—my house is your house and all that."

Nyx and Atlas murmured a thanks, and Knight nodded and walked past my chair only to put a hand on my shoulder. "It's really good to see you, brother."

"And you, thanks for having us," I said genuinely. "Truly—coming here disrupting your peace—"

"Nah," Knight shook his head. "Like I said, I was getting bored and being your friend is always an adventure."

Once Knight went upstairs to bed, Nyx, Atlas and I all had one more drink.

"How long did you two serve together?" Atlas asked.

"We went through BUD/S and SQT together," I said. "Then we were assigned to the same team for a bit. Got pretty close—you know how that goes."

I'd seen gruesome and traumatizing shit with Knight and the others on my team. I was never the best at regulating my emotions. I was either running hot—buried in training and instincts that take over during a stressful raid—or compartmentalizing everything I'd seen and done after the fact. Why would I deal with any of it if I was just going to go out and do it all over again?

Overtime, my personality just let that be the standard and none of it bothered me anymore. The killing and violence were all just the dark side of human nature that I accepted and understood. It was my job. And like any job—it became my life and desensitized me to things that should have appalled and horrified me.

My feelings for the people I surrounded myself with became my weakness and caused my emotions to get the better of me. Love hurt too much and protecting what belonged to me implied a shortcoming on my part when I failed.

Both were unacceptable to me but overtime, I learned how to be the best, to execute at the highest level possible so that my chances of failure were low. Love was pushed out a long time ago because I couldn't control love. I'd found if I threw myself into making sure I was the best and my team was the best, I could protect those I had become attached to.

It always made me think, did I really love? Maybe in my own way but love implies vulnerability and openness—two things I was not good at. Even with Whit and the twins, I'd said the words and I would do anything to protect them because they were mine, but there were times Whit would look at me and I knew she was hoping for more.

I slept for a few hours before the nightmares started. After waking up in a sweat for the third time, I gave up on sleep. The bedroom I was in had a door leading out to the back porch and I slipped out the door and sat down in an old wooden chair looking out over the yard. The forest was alive in the early hours of the morning but it was peaceful.

"Figured I'd find at least one of you out here." Knight materialized by my side and took up residence in the other chair.

"You know how it goes," I said.

"Why do you think I'm out here with you?" He chuckled. "I've hiked a lot of these woods because exhaustion is the only thing that seems to help—and trust me, I've tried everything."

We sat in a comfortable silence for a while before Knight sighed heavily.

"Do you ever think about ending it?"

"Every day," I answered truthfully.

"I almost did it once Cap was gone," Knight said. "I hiked out to this vista about five miles from here and sat with my gun to my head for hours arguing with myself."

"Why didn't you?"

Knight leaned forward and rested his arms on his thighs. "Just seemed like a waste of a bullet." He barked a laugh. "In the end, I didn't even think I was worth that." He looked back over at me. "Why didn't you?"

"My family kept me alive. Then after they were killed, every time I thought about it—I'd see the twins..." I shook my head. "If I ended it—I'd end my suffering, and that didn't seem right. My family deserves retribution in this life and no one can give it to them but me. Until that's done, I don't deserve the peaceful oblivion of death."

Knight nodded. "Well, I know you'll get him—being on the wrong side of you would be nothing short of terrifying."

His phone dinged, and he pulled it out, grinning as he read the message.

"Our Austrian friend is in."

"When do you want to head over there?"

"Few days?" Knight shrugged. "We should put a plan together and then fly over and finalize it."

"Agreed. Tell him we'll be in town by next weekend. Do you have enough firepower?"

Knight didn't look up from his text as he scoffed. "That's embarrassing you even have to ask me that."

I laughed quietly. "I knew you had your personal collection. I didn't know you'd started stockpiling."

Knight put his phone away and sat back again. "It's a recent development. I started doing a few small deals here and there and ended up amassing a small inventory. One of those deals owes me a favor which is how we're going to get overseas—he can fly us."

"If we don't find the treasure, I'm going to owe you big for this one."

Knight shook his head. "No sir, you're forgetting about that op where you stopped me from getting my head blown off—twice! A few guns and a lift in a plane are hardly satisfactory exchanges," he scrunched up his face. "Or maybe for my sorry excuse for a life it is, I don't know, I'll let you decide that." He grinned over at me. "Besides, I was literally doing nothing with my life until now so don't worry about it. You've brought purpose and excitement back into this old soldier's life, I appreciate it."

"Who are you calling old?" I grumbled good-naturedly.

Knight laughed. "I feel old."

"We're the same age!" I insisted with a grin in his direction.

"Tell that to my back," Knight said in amusement.

Later that morning, I found myself alone with Nyx in the living room. I was standing in front of one of the terrain maps we'd pinned up on the wall and he was looking over one of the historical documents we'd pulled from the internet.

"So this empire," he said. "Tell me more."

"It'll be a private military company," I turned towards him. "Legal operations with teams around the world. I also have plans for a nightclub that will be a front for illegal arms dealing."

"You've really thought this out."

I turned around to look at him. "What else was I supposed to do for the last few years? On the outside it'll look like I'm after money and power—like everyone usually is—but it's all a smokescreen for my real plan."

"Revenge," Nyx said.

"I want you to be my second," I said. His eyes snapped to mine. "And I want you and Atlas to both take over the nightclub and help me put together a personal team—separate from the *Northern Tactical* employees."

"*Northern Tactical?* Fitting." Nyx smiled. "What will the personal team do?"

"They'll be our core team we'll use to get our revenge but we'll build up *Northern Tactical* to be a well-oiled machine and then we'll have money and resources coming in regardless of whether this treasure thing pans out."

I had nothing to my name anymore. Not even the clothes on my back were mine. Vetticus had taken everything but this time, I was going to be impenetrable. I'd build an empire, so it wasn't just one man he had to take down but a global enterprise. I wanted unlimited resources available to me. I didn't want money or support to be in short supply.

"Are you ready to play the long game?" I leaned over the table, resting my hands on the worn wood. "Because this won't happen tomorrow or even next year. I don't want sloppy. I don't want a thrown together mission. I want complete annihilation."

"I'm a patient man," Nyx said. I heard someone scoff behind me and turned to see Atlas walk in and smirk at Nyx.

"You're not, but I am," Atlas looked at me and winked. "I'll keep him in line."

That evening, Knight fired up the smoker and BBQ while we drank whiskey and beer on the back porch. Nyx was snooping around the perimeter when he pulled out a football and sent it soaring towards Atlas' head.

"Fucker," Atlas shouted as he barely batted it away in time to avoid spilling his drink. He put his drink down and they threw the ball back and forth. Soon the four of us were involved in a rowdy game of tackle football while the meat cooked.

By the time dinner was ready, we were panting and covered in sweat and dirt but the atmosphere was light and I was happy to see Nyx, Atlas and Knight so relaxed. I collapsed onto the stairs to catch my breath and realized for a moment I hadn't been stuck in the shadows. As Knight took the meat off the grill and the sound of Nyx and Atlas laughing at something drifted over me, I realized for the first time in a long time; I felt...hopeful.

The guilt immediately assaulted me. How could I be hopeful and positive when my family was gone and when I had so much death and destruction still ahead of me? People say to capitalize on the small moments—whatever you can get in the times in between—but sometimes I didn't think I deserved to feel good.

I had people to protect, people to kill, there wasn't time to focus on anything else. Even so, as I watched the light fade across the yard and tint the tops of the evergreens gold in the setting sun, I was able to draw in a full breath and maybe that's what these moments were for. To pause, catch my breath, and be thankful we'd all seen another day.

71

THERON

The nightmare dissolved and I lunged from the bed. I tore the lamp off the nightstand and smashed it onto the floor. I pulled the bed apart until the room was filled with down and feathers. I was unable to control myself. The visceral emotions clawed their way out of me, needing a release. My fist repeatedly slammed into the wall until the plaster was broken and smeared with my blood. I knocked the dresser over, pulled out drawers until the room was destroyed and I couldn't see through the tears. Sobs wracked my body until I was shaking uncontrollably.

The grief ripped through me—I missed them so badly my heart physically ached in my chest. But with it was also the rage at myself—I'd failed them.

I'd fucking failed them. And I'd hurt Emersyn and watched her die.

At some point the door must have been forced open because Nyx, Atlas and Knight were standing in the doorway. I slid down the wall, my head in my hands as I sobbed, unable to stop.

"I failed them," I gasped over and over again. "I couldn't save them."

Nyx knelt next to me and grabbed me, Atlas on my other side, and they held me while I broke apart. I never had the chance to grieve. I'd been thrown into a situation that required my composure, my leadership and for my emotions to be boxed up and put away.

Then I'd had to hurt my daughter—*fucking hurt her*—and watch her die...

Now, it was all crashing down around me.

The failure, the sadness, the broken heart—I felt it all viscerally and painfully. I couldn't breathe—I didn't want to live, but I knew I couldn't die either.

I don't know how long I sat there with Nyx and Atlas by my side but as my breathing steadied; I leaned my head back against the wall and took in the destruction of the room. Nyx relaxed and sat down next to me Atlas moved to sit across from us, leaning against the knocked down dresser that was cracked on one side.

"Fuck," I muttered. Some guest—destroying my friend's house. Before I could apologize, Knight spoke up.

"Mine was the kitchen." I looked up and saw Knight leaning against the doorway. "One night I lost it and destroyed the kitchen. Glass everywhere," he gave me one of his rueful smiles and shrugged. "Felt good at the time. It's just stuff."

"Now do you want to talk about them?" Nyx asked.

I never knew what people meant by heartbreak until now. The grief was so strong, the rage so potent—I could feel it as a tangible, solid thing inside me, but I nodded, needing an outlet.

"I was married," I said. "We had twins. Cole and Emersyn—Emy—"

I told them all about how I'd met Whit. I talked about how much of a handful the twins were but also how much fun it was to see the world through their eyes. I talked about the adventures we'd go on as a family and how much I didn't realize they'd helped heal me after being around so much death.

Then I told them about the lake house.

By the time I was done, my voice was hoarse and I was exhausted, but I felt much better. They deserved to know everything because I wouldn't stop until Vetticus was destroyed.

"There is nothing I won't do to get my revenge," I said. "Nothing is more important to me." Nyx nodded and when he stood up he held out his hand to help me to my feet.

"I wouldn't have made it through Atrox without you," Nyx said, gripping my forearm as I stood. "Even if that wasn't the case—even if I didn't owe you everything and then some—I have a score to settle with Vetticus. I'm not going anywhere."

Atlas put his hand on my shoulder. "We're with you till the end."

Since none of us could go back to sleep after that, Knight threw some water in a pack and herded us all outside, claiming there was something he wanted to show us. Five miles later, amidst complaints from Nyx on walking this far on an empty stomach, we broke through the trees and arrived on the top of a bluff. Before us was a vast blanket of forest touched by pinks and golds as the sun broke the horizon. A sense of peace swept over me. Knight handed me a water bottle and nodded behind him.

"There are a few cool spots over that way," he winked at me before he went and settled on a rock he'd obviously visited many times before.

I wandered around the bluff and eventually found a spot I liked. I sat down and watched the sunrise over the forest, letting the calm settle into my bones. It had been a while since I'd felt safe and I probably wouldn't feel that way for a long time to come. The path forward was bloody, dark and merciless.

Violence was in my blood. Preacher had been right in his worry—it was easy to lose yourself to the darkness and I'd lost a part of myself to Vetticus. Although truthfully, I was beginning to wonder if I'd ever really found it again after my last deployment. It was easy to see blood as the path to redemption. My humanity was questionable now, what would it be once all of this was over? All I knew was that humanity was just one thing I'd sacrifice for retribution.

I put three stones on top of each other and once more put my family to rest, but with closure this time. With love and grief and heartbreak and with the promise that I wouldn't let them down again. I kissed my fingertips, brought them to the stones and sent one last yearning of the heart out into the universe. If there was a heaven, I wasn't under any illusions that I would join them, so this was my goodbye. I rose and went to find Nyx.

I found him glaring into the sunset with a pile of broken sticks in front of him. I sat down next to him and let the silence stretch for a bit.

"I'm just so angry," Nyx finally said. "He's made me question everything—"

"What do you mean?"

"What if what I have with Atlas is only because of what Vetticus did to me?"

"Do you love Atlas?" Nyx hesitated then nodded and the anger fell off his face slightly at the admission.

"I do. I-I don't think I'm gay. I think we're just us, you know? I can't imagine being with other men except for him—and you." He flashed me one of his rogue smiles and I chuckled.

"You know I don't lean that way. But if I did—you and Atlas would be it," I grinned. Nyx shrugged good naturedly and the rest of the anger fell away.

"It was worth a shot."

"I like to share though," I said. "Watching you both with Red and sharing her was hot. I wouldn't mind having that kind of situation one day."

"Maybe we'll find a girl for all of us at the end of this," Nyx said.

"Maybe," I echoed. We sat in comfortable silence for a bit.

"Are you okay?" Nyx asked me.

I nodded. "Yeah. I wasn't able to grieve for them properly. Vetticus took that away from me too. And then with everything that just happened..." I shook my head. "It was all bound to come out sometime."

"I think what I'm most angry about, isn't that he did what he did, but that he made me question myself," Nyx said. "He made me hate myself."

"Do you? Hate yourself?"

Nyx frowned down at the stick in his hand but his thoughts weren't on it. He broke it apart into a few pieces then sighed heavily.

"Not like before. You and Atlas helped with that. But I don't think this is an overnight kind of thing."

"No, it's not," I agreed. I clasped him on the shoulder, then rose and went to find Atlas.

Atlas wasn't watching the sunrise. He was sprawled out on his back with his shirt over his face and one arm behind his head. I lowered myself down next to him. Atlas moved his shirt and sighed.

"Do you think he'll come after us?"

"I don't know," I said honestly.

"I'm not going back," Atlas said vehemently. Atlas sat up and draped his arms over his knees, hanging his head.

"I've never felt that close to destruction before," he said quietly. "So out of control."

I reached over and grabbed his neck. "Look at me," I commanded.

He lifted his head and I saw the haunted look in his eyes along with despair for things that he would never forget.

"I won't let him take you, understand?" I said fiercely.

He searched my eyes for a long moment then nodded. I released him and looked out over the forest.

"Like I said—I'll bide my time. I want us at full strength with resources and support." I looked over and flashed him a dry smile. "The three of us aren't just going to go in rogue and hope for the best." That got a smile out of him and I saw some of the tension leave him.

"I don't know how I'm supposed to go back into the real world after this," he said dryly. "This is worse than a deployment."

I didn't have anything to say to that because I agreed. We were prolonging things by coming first to Knight's house and then doing the Austria operation, but after that we'd have to head back into the real world—back to civilization when we were far from civilized. We sat in an easy silence for a time until I got to my feet and dusted myself off.

"You should go find Nyx," I said.

72

ATLAS

I found Nyx sitting near the edge of the bluff. He was leaning over his knees with a frown on his face as he looked out over the valley. I sat down next to him, my shoulder brushing his lightly as I leaned back against the rocks. I saw him stiffen at the contact and could practically feel the nerves radiating off of him.

"I never told you what Vetticus took from me," I said.

Nyx looked over his shoulder at me.

"It wasn't really the place to talk about things like that," he said dryly before looking back out at the view.

"Yeah, but I want to tell you now," I said. "I think it's important."

He didn't say anything and I collected my thoughts, preparing myself to talk about something I'd avoided even thinking about because of how much it hurt.

"I was married," I started. "I had a beautiful wife, Nova. She was my soulmate in every way."

Her face flashed in my mind. The killer smile that pulled her dimples out and lit up her eyes. Those same eyes that teased me with the way she always looked at me so suggestively, like she didn't want to go one more second without being in my space. I swallowed past the lump in my throat as the thought of never being able to touch her again assaulted me.

"She was bi," I continued. "And we'd always discussed opening up our relationship at some point. A polyamorous lifestyle appealed to us so one day we just went for it. We had a lot of fun both together and separately and then she met another man and fell in love. His name was James."

James. An artist with the body of a god. Where I was rough edges with the ruthlessness of a viking, he was all masculine grace covered in the dark paint palettes he used to create. He always reminded me of a rogue pirate with his black hair he wore pulled back in a low ponytail and the gold rings all over his fingers. Just the thought of how those hands had once felt on me was enough to make my words stall.

I cleared my throat and went on. "I was okay with her feelings because our relationship only got stronger and there was plenty of love to go around. I never felt neglected or like she was pushing me aside. In fact, it was the opposite. We started having threesomes together—of course that was really hot—having my wife in between us while we made her fall apart. Well, I guess you know—"

I chuckled, but it came out gruff and suggestive. I couldn't help but feel turned on as I remembered Nyx on his knees behind Red, making her moan around my cock. I saw the tips of his ears heat and smirked, knowing a similar thought was in his mind.

"Anyway, the more we hung out, the more I started having feelings for James. He wasn't bi, neither was I—I didn't think. At least I'd never had feelings for a man before, and still didn't during all of this. It was only him because I'd fallen in love with the person he was. Turns out, he'd started developing feelings for me too in the same way. It started with just exploring more with him during threesomes but then we all started hanging out together outside of the bedroom and when James eventually told me he loved me, I returned the sentiment."

One evening, Nova and I showed up at James' studio where things quickly escalated. Before we knew it, we were all naked with paint flying everywhere. Later, Nova was in the bathroom and James and I were laying together on a giant canvas drop cloth, the paint drying and flaking off our bodies. He propped himself up on his elbow and looked down at me. I remember grinning at how haphazard he looked with dark greens and blues all over his face and his hair sticking up as the paint dried it in crazy places on his head.

I reached out and smeared a streak of green across his jaw, thinking it was the same color as his eyes. He caught my hand and entwined our fingers then his gaze swept across my face and dipped to my lips before he met my eyes.

"You speak to a part of me I didn't know existed," he said quietly. Happiness flooded through me and his eyes caught on the smile tugging at my lips. He returned it. "There are no other men who catch my eye or make me feel the way you do when you look at me. There wasn't before you and there won't be anyone after you."

He brought my fingers to his lips, not even caring about the paint that covered them.

"I don't know what you'd call that and I don't care. All I know is that I love you—deeply, completely and with everything I am." His voice had grown gruff with emotion and his eyes searched mine. "Tell me you feel the same," he whispered.

Intensity rushed through me leaving me aching with a love I couldn't even begin to express. Even if I had a way with words the way he did, it wouldn't come close. I sank my fingers into his hair.

"You're mine—that's what I know. It scares me sometimes, how deeply I feel for you—like because I'm a man I'm not allowed to love another man. But I do love you, my pirate," I huffed a laugh. "Completely and without restraint. My heart is yours."

"And Nova's," James grinned.

I returned the grin and nodded. "You both hold my heart," I whispered, and pulled him in for a searing kiss.

I came back from the memory, tears stinging my eyes. Nyx seemed to know I'd gotten lost for a moment because he didn't look back at me or speak but his hand dropped to my thigh in a move that felt right to us both because he kept it there.

I took a deep breath and quickly ended the story. "Long story short— we all moved in together and eventually we unofficially all got married. He married her, I married him and we were one big happy throple."

Nyx seemed to process it all for a moment. "And Vetticus took them both away from you?"

"Yeah, similar to T's story," I said quietly.

"I'm sorry," Nyx whispered.

"Me too," I said sadly. "He's taken so much from all of us. I want this as much as North does and I don't think I can move on until Vetticus gets what he deserves."

"I understand," Nyx said, sounding almost disappointed. Heat rushed through me at the thought of how he might have taken that the wrong way.

"I mean, I can't live a normal life—or even try to be content—until he's gone," I tried to explain. "But, I-I feel something here that has started to feel like more than just a friendship," I ventured, nervously. "I don't know if you feel the same and I don't want to make things weird—"

Nyx turned to me and grinned. "So you're saying you want to live a discontented life with me?"

"Fucker," I said easily, hiding a grin and shaking off his hand on my leg as I drew my knees up so I could sit even with him. He chuckled and looked away as though he couldn't hold my gaze for very long.

"I don't know how to do any of this," he said.

"And you think I do? What with all of my vast experience with men?" I scoffed.

The sarcasm dripping off my words pulled another laugh from him.

"Look at me," I said. He slowly turned those dark eyes on me, and I saw a vulnerability he rarely showed.

"I'm not making it up, am I?" I asked.

He hesitated the barest second, and I watched the emotions rage across his face before he slowly shook his head. Relief washed over me and a half smile pulled at my lips.

"Good, so I wasn't imagining you staring at my dick when we were fucking Red."

That earned me a genuine laugh from him and he ran a hand through his hair, the tension gone.

"I couldn't help it and I don't know what that means," he said without any trace of embarrassment. "I understand perfectly when you said you and James weren't bisexual—you just loved each other—it should be allowed to be that simple." He looked at me again and cocked his head as though he was allowing himself to really study me for the first time. "I feel a similar way for you, I think."

His face fell, and he looked away. "But I'm afraid that what Vetticus did has tarnished that."

"What do you mean?"

Nyx dug into the ground between his feet with a stick. "I don't know, what if it's all just trauma?"

I nodded. "I guess you won't know unless you decide to explore it more."

"I don't want to use you as an experiment," he scoffed.

"I don't know, I might enjoy that," I said darkly, my voice dropping low.

His back stiffened, and I watched him try to repress a shiver. His eyes flicked to me briefly, and he bit his lip to hide a smile. My eyes dropped to his mouth, thinking how much I wanted his lips on mine so I could tug his lip between my own teeth.

I looked away before more dirty thoughts could invade. We had nothing but time now and if that's what he needed, it would be hard—no pun intended—but I'd give it to him.

73

NYX

We can drive in or walk in, but we'll obviously need to get a lift out," Knight said. We were all huddled around the dining room table where documents were strewn about. We'd been planning for several days already and a solid plan was beginning to come together. Now Knight was looking at North with a pointed look. North returned it for a moment before a slow smirk crossed Knight's face and North's eyes narrowed.

"No," North stated. "Absolutely not."

"Come on, North," Knight chuckled. "You know she's the best."

"I don't care."

Atlas and I looked at each other then back between Knight and North.

"She?" Atlas asked, eyebrows raised.

"Rebel Madigan," Knight said, looking like he was enjoying this way more than he should.

North scowled and shook his head. "Find someone else."

"Mads is the best," Knight stated.

"No."

"Well, she's the best, and she's the only option," Knight shrugged.

"You already contacted her didn't you," North grumbled.

Knight ignored him and turned to Atlas and I.

"Mads was deployed with us—frankly one of the best pilots I've ever come across—she and North had a...thing," he chuckled.

My eyebrows raised, and I looked over at North with a grin. He scoffed and sat back in his chair, arms crossed over his chest as he glared at Knight.

"It was a very long time ago—before Whitney," North said begrudgingly. "I was young, wild and a soldier with nothing to lose—didn't last very long."

"What happened?" I asked.

"She started doing drugs, fell in with some bad people. We broke up—I started dating Whitney—then Mads asked for my help with something, nearly got me killed when I gave it. I told her that was the last time I'd bail her out of her shit. Shortly after that was when I found out Whit was pregnant and I never heard from her again."

North looked over at Knight. "I'm surprised she's still alive honestly."

"Well, she is—she surfaced a few years ago and reached out to me. She came to your funeral by the way."

"Touching," North scoffed.

"Does anyone know a techie?" Knight asked, changing the subject. "My go-to has disappeared recently."

"I think I might have a tech guy we could use," I said. "He has a military background but is a killer programmer and hacker. Can I use your computer Knight? I'll reach out to him. Speaking of—we'll need phones."

Knight nodded and disappeared.

"I have extra phones too," Knight said when he returned.

He handed me his laptop and distributed three phones to Atlas, me and North. I popped open the laptop and logged into my email, not bothering to look at the thousands of messages I'd amassed over the years I'd been MIA. I drafted up a quick email and sent it off before putting the laptop aside.

It felt weird having a phone after all this time. I took a few minutes setting it up while I listened to Knight and North bicker about this Mads character. I was eager to head out to Austria. I mean, who wouldn't be excited for a treasure hunt? A thrill rushed through me at the prospect of finding that much gold.

5.6 *Billion*. That was a lot.

It certainly would set us up for success.

My missing finger caught my eye and anger hit me hard and fast. I shoved it away but it was a constant reminder of how much Vetticus had taken from me. I had my own vendetta. I didn't care how long it took—I would see Vetticus brought down. I wanted to see him crawl across the ground and clutch at my boots.

I finished setting up my phone and was about to put it down when I noticed a new email notification. It was West—the tech guy I'd contacted.

That was fast. Although he was always on his computer so it made sense.

He was in.

By the end of the week we had a plan in place.

We all stood in the living room which looked like a tornado had run through it with the amount of papers strewn both across the table and pinned up on the surrounding walls.

"Everyone is confirmed to meet us in Salzburg," Knight said.

I pulled down the terrain map and folded it up along with a few of the other documents and maps before sticking everything in a plastic bag. Knight pulled out passports and documentation for each of us and handed them out.

"Plane leaves tomorrow morning," he said. "Weapons are this way."

We followed him down a hallway and eventually down a flight of stairs into his basement where behind a vault style door lay an armory.

I actually gasped. I didn't know where to look first. The firearms were backlit on the walls in various models and calibers. It looked like a scene out of a spy movie. Atlas made a beeline to the sniper rifles lining one wall.

"Damn, Pyro," I said, throwing my arm around Knight. "Holding out for an apocalypse?"

"Can never be too prepared," he chuckled. "Help yourselves to anything. Ammo is through that door."

I couldn't help rushing towards the far door. I pushed it open to reveal an equally large room with pallets of all different caliber of ammo.

"Fuck," I exclaimed.

"Like kids in a candy shop," North chuckled.

"Don't act like your trigger finger didn't just get real itchy," Knight laughed.

North walked over to the handguns and picked up two .45s. Checking them over, he grabbed an AR and a few knives for good measure before heading in to stock up on ammo. Atlas was already gathering up rounds for his rifle and other selections. But I'd seen something even more enticing.

I was hoisting up the RPG when I heard North from the other room.

"We're not taking that with us," he said loudly, not even looking up from the box he was rifling through.

"There is always a use for one of these," I insisted.

"No," North stated.

"Party pooper," I frowned and reluctantly put it down.

Knight walked past me and hit my arm. "Check this out."

He pushed open another panel.

"Holy shit," I breathed. Knight pulled out a freakin' flame thrower. I knew I liked this guy.

"This is my baby," Knight said.

"You're not bringing that either," North called.

"Don't listen to him," I whispered loudly.

"You'll light the entire forest on fire," North insisted.

"I will not," Knight argued. "I managed not to set this one on fire."

"That's not what I saw," North chuckled.

"Fine, I didn't burn the entire thing down," Knight amended.

We spent the next few minutes packing duffle bags with additional weapons and ammo before heading back upstairs—sans grenade launcher and flamethrower—amidst complaints from me and Knight. I looked over at Atlas who looked just as happy as I did lugging a duffle of firepower up the stairs. We deposited the bags near the door. I watched his muscles bunch and ripple under the t-shirt stretched across his broad shoulders.

This entire week I'd been stepping carefully around him because I didn't know what to do. I was attracted to him—there was no denying he was one hot viking piece of ass—but I still had to get used to the fact that if I wanted to touch him...I could. No one was watching, well besides North and he'd probably enjoy it.

We could be intimate. But for the first time in my life I was terrified. More terrified than if a gun was pointed at me. This was different and yes, it's definitely fucked up to not be afraid of death but terrified of intimacy—I know that.

It was also fear of the unknown. I was afraid of what could change if I crossed the line. What if we tried to be something and it didn't work? We had a plan to execute and I didn't want anything to get in the way of that.

My eyes traveled up his chest and clashed with a pair of intense green eyes glimmering with humor. I could feel a blush creeping up my neck.

Fuck me—how come he always made me feel like a teenager with a crush?

A low rumble of a laugh escaped Atlas and I quickly looked away, dropping the bags and turning away. I physically felt the air shift as he came up behind me.

"You can look you know," he said gruffly. "I won't tell anyone you're checking out a man."

"Maybe I was, maybe I wasn't," I shrugged. "What are you—"

I turned to smirk at him but I hadn't realized just how close he was to me and my shoulder bumped into his chest, bringing my face inches from his. My eyes dropped to his mouth as his lips curled into a rogue smile. I lost the ability to breathe. The air between us rippled with static tension.

"What am I going to do about it?" He finished the sentence I couldn't seem to get out. "I can think of a few things."

My lips parted, whether to say something or close the distance and kiss him, I will never know, because Knight appeared around the corner.

"What do you guys want to—oh shit, sorry," Knight chuckled.

I stepped back to put some distance between Atlas and I like we were a pair of teenagers caught doing something we weren't supposed to.

"My bad," Knight went on, his grin a mile long. "Just was coming to see if you guys wanted whiskey but now I'm thinking we should take a few shots of tequila—"

Atlas laughed and strode over, punching Knight playfully in the shoulder.

"Tequila just makes me want to fight—or fuck."

He turned and winked at me before throwing an arm around Knight's shoulders and leading him back into the kitchen.

"Fifty-fifty—I'll take those odds," Knight said, his voice fading as they bantered their way out of the room.

I let out the breath I'd unintentionally been holding. I ran a hand through my hair and shrugged my shoulders, trying to alleviate the tension I felt as though my skin was too tight on my body.

God, this was confusing.

Fuck it. Since when was I ever hesitant about fucking shit up? In true Nyx fashion, I was always one to mess around and find out—ask forgiveness, not permission, that sort of thing.

Why would this be any different?

74

THERON

SALZBURG, AUSTRIA

We were standing in a warehouse in Salzburg. Weapons were strewn around tables mixed with the maps of the terrain. A disassembled AR sat in front of me as I cleaned it under the dingy lights. Nyx strode across the main floor with another man in step behind him, a duffle bag slung over his shoulder.

He pushed shaggy brown hair out of his eyes and looked around the room. He looked like a tech version of Bruce Wayne—tall, muscled and calculating.

"Guys, this is West Blackwood," Nyx said, clasping the man on the shoulder. He pointed us out in turn for introductions. "That's Atlas Sterling, Trent Knight and Theron North."

Knight walked over and took his bag, shaking West's hand.

"Welcome to the team," Knight grinned.

"Thanks," West said. "So a treasure hunt, huh? That's a first for me."

Before anyone could answer, I heard a motorcycle rumble to a stop outside the warehouse doors and looked over at Knight.

"She's here," I sighed.

A moment later the door slammed and the storm herself sauntered across the room. All black leather hugged lethal curves and aviators flashed as she pushed them to the top of her head. Dark auburn red hair fell down her back in tousled waves, messy from her helmet. She smirked around a cigarette smoking gently between her lips.

"Hello boys," she said, extending her arms out.

Blue eyes flashed with amusement as she took in the room. Her gaze lingered on Knight before fastening on me. Dragging her eyes down my body and back up she stopped in front of me. We stared at each other. I took the cigarette from her lips, took a deep pull and exhaled the smoke into the space between us before I dropped it and stubbed it out with my boot.

"Hello, Mads," I said. "You look good."

The smirk widened. "So do you, T," she said.

We stared at each other for another moment before she winked at me and walked over to Knight, throwing her arms around his neck. He lifted her up and twirled her around, kissing her cheek lightly before setting her back down.

"Hey, gorgeous," he said. "Glad you could join us."

"I'm sure not everyone is as excited," she said dryly, flashing a look in my direction.

Knight chuckled. "Well, you know how convincing I can be."

She barked out a laugh. "Nah, there's just no denying I'm the best."

She looked around at the others and I could see her hungrily assessing them.

"Aren't you going to introduce me?" She asked no one in particular.

Nyx stepped up, holding out his hand and flashing her a charming grin.

"Nyxon—but you can call me Nyx," he nodded across the room. "That brooding hottie is Atlas and this is West."

Atlas didn't move but nodded to her from where he was leaning back against a table, cleaning a sniper rifle. West waved a hand without turning around, concentrating on setting up his computer.

"Lively bunch you have here," Mads said with a look back at me. "Is this all of us?" As if in answer, the door slammed again and a tall man in a light blue t-shirt and jeans with combat boots strode into the room.

"Knight, you bastard," he said with a grin. "I didn't think I'd ever hear from you again."

"Can't get rid of me that easily," Knight laughed as they embraced. He turned to the group and gestured to us again. "Everyone—this is Lachlan Frey—former Austrian special forces and the town drunk."

"I seem to remember you matching me shot for shot," Lachlan said, shaking hands with everyone. "North—good to see you again, man."

"That must be why he doesn't remember," I said dryly. "Good to see you, Lachlan." I watched Lachlan's eyes land on Mads and instantly his smirk turned feral. He took her hand and stepped closer.

"Ah, and who might this be?"

"Rebel Madigan," she said, looking at him with equal curiosity. "I go by Mads."

"A dangerous name—" he let his gaze sweep her lazily from head to toe.

"For a dangerous woman."

In all my years of knowing Mads, this was the first time I'd ever seen pink tint her cheeks.

"Wow," Knight said, catching on to what I saw. "I think you're the first person to ever make her blush."

"Fuck off, Pyro," Mads said, not looking away from Lachlan.

"Okay, well if you two are done eye fucking each other, we have work to do," Knight snickered.

We gathered around one of the center tables where I'd spread a map. We'd already sent the other documents and historical information to them earlier so they could familiarize themselves with what we were going after.

"Besides environmental logistical problems," I said. "There are the contractors to contend with. Lachlan."

"Yeah, there's a company that services that area. They're hired by the government. Nothing much happens out there besides the occasional tourist so as you can imagine that's a recipe for a trigger happy finger."

"How many?" Mads asked.

"Hard to say, but I did take a peek around there a few days ago and it looks like they built a semi-permanent compound on the border of the mountains to make rotating the shifts easier so we have to anticipate plenty of company."

Lachlan held Mads' gaze again for so long I finally cleared my throat to get his attention.

"Anyway—" He turned a wide smile on me. "Should be fun. There are some access roads once you make it into that area but there's only one leading in and out. The terrain is difficult so let's hope we can stick to the plan and don't have to improvise."

"Alright, West will hang back and operate the drone so we have constant eyes in the sky," I said. "When we find the gold, it's going to require multiple trips to the loading point. We'll take out the two outposts here and here—" I pointed to the map. "Lach, you said the shifts are twenty-four hours so we'll have at least that before they're alerted that something is wrong and send backup."

"Helo will be multiple trips," Mads said. "The bird can only hold so many kilos at a time, but what we need to talk about is the weather."

"There's a storm coming in," Lachlan agreed. "I don't think it'll hit until we're out of there but—" he shrugged.

"I can handle it," Mads smirked. "But the helo has its limits."

"It's your call," I said. "If we delay, it'll be a few days until it looks like the weather clears."

Mads turned to Lachlan. "This is your country. What do you think this storm will look like?"

"We have thunderstorms frequently—one of those could be a problem. Little snow up at altitude...maybe hail. But if it's just a rainstorm, nothing you couldn't handle I'm sure." He winked at her and she smiled back.

"It doesn't look like it's a thunderstorm, more like rain showers and maybe some snow higher up." She dragged her eyes away from Lachlan. "If I see anything concerning, I'll let you know."

75

THERON

Looking out of the helo, I scanned the terrain below us. It was mountainous and densely forested with hardly a break in the trees. We weren't going to fly anywhere close to the lake in order not to alert the security presence there. I looked over at Nyx, Atlas and Lachlan. I could see the readiness I was so familiar with on Atlas' face and the set of Nyx's jaw told me he was dialed in and already in go mode.

"DZ coming up in two," Mads said over the radio.

"West, do you copy?" I asked.

"Loud and clear," he said.

Knight picked up the drone he'd sent with us and powered it on, adjusting a few settings.

"Drone is live," he said.

A small gap in the trees appeared below us and the bird hovered there. I looked down. It couldn't even be considered a clearing but would work. Knight strapped the drone to his chest while Atlas released the rope.

"Ready when you are," Mads said.

Atlas dropped down the rope, followed by Nyx, Knight and Lachlan. I went last and as soon as I hit the ground the helo dipped off, the sound of the rotors disappearing quickly. Knight launched the drone and I signaled for the others to fall into line.

Based on the maps we would head south towards the lake and loop around to where the caves were on the west bank. The lake was steep on most sides with the forest encroaching on it aggressively. This was why it was so dangerous to dive there—trees would fall into the water and sink to the bottom forming a layer of logs waiting to trap even the most experienced divers. The rumors of the gold we'd found online said the treasure had fallen below this level to the sand below but no one was able to reach it. Now we knew better and if the map was accurate, we weren't headed into the lake.

The forest was alive with birdsong but the ground was dense with underbrush and our pace was slow and tedious. We'd been on the ground for about an hour when I signaled for a halt. I heard something through the trees and signaled as much.

"First guard house is a hundred yards east of you," West said in my ear.

I turned to the men and motioned for Nyx and Knight to come with me and Lachlan and Atlas to sweep around, merging on them from two sides. Lachlan and Atlas disappeared silently into the trees and Nyx and I continued to advance.

"Man, these guys look bored," West said. "Two outside—guns are propped against the cabin. Scanner shows three, maybe four inside. Little over-staffed if you ask me."

I made it to the edge of the treeline and saw a crude cabin in a clearing. Two of the guards were throwing a football around, their banter filtering through the trees to us. I couldn't see much through the dingy window to confirm what West said but I wasn't worried about it.

"Lach, Atlas—take out the two outside, Nyx and I will head into the house. Knight watch the treeline. Knives only."

"Copy," Atlas murmured.

"Go," I said.

I circled around the house, went up to the back door and inched it open. I signaled to Nyx—two at the table, one in bed, another looking out the window.

I crept inside. I stood behind the man at the window and a floorboard creaked. He went to turn, but I already had a hand around his throat, covering his mouth and then my knife was shoved up into his head, killing him. The second man lunged up from the table with a shout, lurching towards his gun. Nyx had already dispatched his partner at the table and was on the one in bed just as I neatly slammed the last one against the wall and killed him quickly.

We walked outside and Knight fell into step with us. Lachlan and Atlas faced the forest, the other two men dead at their feet.

"Move out." I headed back towards the trees and we swept into the shadows as silently as we'd arrived.

"Second guard house, mile out to the east," West said. "This is a barracks—I count twelve men."

I signaled to move closer. This building was better constructed and there were two vehicles parked along one side. There wasn't anyone outside so Nyx, Knight and I quickly made our way to the door while Atlas and Lachlan circled to the other side. I poked my head up to look through the window and signaled to Nyx and Knight.

Five.

I pulled the door open and we rushed inside. The men jumped up in surprise but Nyx and I had already dispatched one each before they could even draw their guns. I rushed one, shooting him in the head quickly, then stabbed another as he pointed his gun at my face. We advanced down the hallway.

I heard the occasional shout from the other end of the building but otherwise it was quiet. Knight and I went into the first room where two men were sleeping. I shoved my knife into the first one's neck while Knight did the same to the other then we moved on.

With ruthless precision we efficiently and quickly cleared the building room by room until we met up with Atlas and Lachlan in the middle. We made our way outside and I motioned for everyone to spread out and clear the rest of the area. I didn't want anyone raising the alarm early.

"Knight, rig the trips in the road," I said.

Once done, we headed off through the trees in search of the caves.

We got to the caves that overlooked the lake and while Atlas kept watch, the others followed me into the mouth of the largest opening. I pulled out my flashlight and followed the winding path down into the darkness. We searched and searched but an hour passed and we still hadn't come upon any gold. When one passageway became too narrow to continue, we doubled back and chose another tunnel.

Another hour passed.

"Are you guys lost?" Atlas asked. The comms connection crackled with static as we ventured deeper under the rock. None of us found it funny. It was claustrophobic and oppressively quiet underground.

After the third hour, my frustration grew and I stopped to gather my bearings. We'd explored the majority of the passages that branched off of this cave with nothing to show for it besides us growing increasingly more dusty as the minutes ticked on.

"There's another cave entrance a few yards from where we came in," Lachlan said. "We'll check that one."

Another few hours of cave exploration passed and I was beginning to think the map was wrong until my flashlight swept over a wall and I saw a large fissure extending high above our heads. I almost walked past it, but something made me stop and I examined it further. It wasn't a fissure, someone had caused a cave in.

"Here," I said.

I handed the light to Knight while I climbed up the boulders and peered through the gap in the stone.

"We need to get back there," I said.

Together we moved enough rocks to allow us to squeeze through to the other side. The passage was narrow and claustrophobic but it quickly widened into a shelf overlooking a pool that glistened darkly a few feet below us. A dim glow emanated from crystals on the ceiling, casting a blue sheen on the water revealing what we'd been looking for. At the bottom of the pool, our beams of light caught on the trove gleaming in the depths.

Gold bars.

"Bingo," Nyx said excitedly.

"I'll be honest—I was worried it didn't exist," Lachlan said ruefully.

"Well, let's get swimming," Knight said. "Nyx, Lach—widen the passage. North and I can start diving."

I stripped off my gear and put on a waterproof headlamp and goggles that had been a random afterthought—a 'just in case' I was now glad to have. I dove into the water with Knight following. It was deeper than it appeared, maybe about ten or eleven feet deep. I got to the bottom and swept the light over the sandy floor. My excitement flared and I looked up at Knight giving him a thumbs up—there were hundreds of boxes down here.

I ripped one open and gold bars flashed. Now we just had to get it all out and we didn't have a lot of time. I surfaced and grabbed the rope we'd brought.

Knight's head popped up next to me. "It's beautiful—there's a lot there."

"Yeah, we have a lot of work to do."

We worked quickly raising crates of gold bars from the bottom of the pool. The boxes were stamped with all manner of World War II distinguishers. Knight and I took turns diving while Nyx and Lachlan pulled up the boxes and an hour later we had a fair haul clogging the ledge. We loaded the truck with as many crates as we could and drove out to an overgrown landing strip we'd designated as the extraction point.

"Two minutes," Mads said over comms.

We heard the chopper overhead and a net dropped down. We loaded the crates and Mads flew away. We repeated this process a few more times before darkness fell. We called a halt for the night and made camp near the caves.

"Movement in the main compound," West said. "They're getting ready for the shift change."

"Don't these people report in or something?" Knight muttered.

Lachlan chuckled. "It's a good thing they're so lax. It's giving us plenty of time." We'd retreated into the cave a ways so we could light a small stove we'd brought. I sat with my back against the wall, waiting for West's report.

"They know something's wrong," West's voice came over comms.

"Sleep in shifts," I ordered. "We're up and moving in—"

An explosion boomed through the forest. It was so powerful it brought a sprinkle of dirt and pebbles down on our heads. It was the trips Knight had set. I glared over at Knight who looked at me sheepishly and shrugged.

"Oops..."

"Fucking Pyro," I muttered.

76

ATLAS

We rotated sleeping and an hour before dawn, we started again. It was exhausting work. Diving, lifting and hauling crates of heavy gold was tedious and depleting but we doggily pressed on. The security contractors hadn't organized a search party until dawn and so far they weren't anywhere close to us. West was keeping us apprised of their locations. We were enroute to the pickup location to drop another load off with Mads when West came over comms sounding concerned.

"There's a plane inbound to the landing strip," he said.

"Let me know what they do," I said, picking up the pace.

"Okay, that's a lot of men," West said. "You guys need to get out of there."

"How many?" I demanded in irritation.

"Thirty."

"Safe to say we pissed them off," Lachlan said around a cigarette hanging out of his mouth.

"There should be another road about ten yards on the right—take it," West said.

Lachlan veered off when the overgrown track appeared and we wove through the trees. The ground was uneven and bumpy making our pace slow considerably.

"There's a potential new extraction point a few miles down this road but you'll have to carry the crates several hundred yards—it's too dense for the truck," West said.

"Copy that."

"Oh shit," West said.

"I really don't like hearing you say that," Nyx grumbled.

"They have dogs."

"Ah man, I'm telling you right now I'm not killing any dogs," Nyx griped from the back of the truck.

We reached the end of the road, although I wouldn't call it that because as we got deeper and deeper into the woods the truck scraped trees and finally landed in a rut and Lachlan couldn't drive any further.

"End of the line," Lachlan said, turning the truck off.

I jogged through the trees behind North to check out the clearing West directed us to. It was small and slightly boggy but it would work. We spent the next hour shuttling crates and stacking them in the clearing for when Mads would come pick us up. As we worked, clouds rolled in and I looked up when the first drops of rain hit me.

"They've picked up your trail," West said. "You have about twenty minutes before they're on you. I think they know about this place—they're breaking into groups to swing around. Oh shit—"

"West—" Nyx growled.

No answer. They must have taken out the drone.

"We need to lead them away from here," North said. "Lach, Nyx—continue moving the gold. Be ready for Mads—Knight, Atlas, with me."

We crossed over our trail several times to hopefully disorient the dogs and Knight set a few trip wires. The forest here was dense and horrible for long range. Someone could be almost on top of you before you saw them with the way the trunks crossed and overlapped when you tried to see deeper into the woods. I heard the barking before I saw the dogs.

Two explosions thundered through the trees in quick succession.

Then we were getting shot at.

I got separated from Knight and North. Pain bit into my side but the adrenaline soon dulled it and I quickly shot two men coming up through the trees.

"Mads is here! Back to the bird!" Lachlan shouted over comms.

I turned to head back to the extraction point when a dog hurtled through the trees towards me, catching me off guard. Somehow I avoided the gnashing teeth and quickly climbed up into the dense canopy of the nearest tree. I hopped to the next tree, then the next until the dog was left behind.

"Atlas, where are you?" Nyx's voice sounded strained over comms.

"One of the fucking dogs treed me," I panted.

I sprinted through the forest, only to come up on the enemy at the treeline. I quickly took out as many as I could before I had to skirt around to find cover. Thunder crashed and I hadn't even noticed how dark the sky had become. Being under the dense forest canopy had shielded us from the weather but now I saw the truth: the storm was here.

I crouched at the edge of the trees as the rain fell harder. The rest of the men were already in the helo and there was a rope dangling to the ground with at least half of the last load of gold not loaded into the netting. I could make it if I went now. I looked down the treeline and dread settled in my gut.

Oh no.

I gave up on the idea of making the rope.

Instead, I raised my rifle, hoping I could get the shot off in time.

77

NYX

They have a RPG! Get out of here!" Atlas shouted over comms. The rain fell harder and North grabbed onto my vest to keep me from falling out of the doorway. The bird was listing and shaking with the wind as the storm picked up intensity.

"We have to go!" Mads shouted, an edge to her voice I didn't like.

I looked out towards the treeline but couldn't see anything in the shadows. Bullets peppered the side of the helo and I fired back.

"We're not leaving—" I shouted.

"North, we have to go! Now!" Mads shouted. "Cut the rope!"

"No! We're not leaving him down there," I yelled.

"Go! Now! Now!" Atlas' voice was frantic. "Cut the rope!"

Lachlan released the rope holding the gold and it fell away. At the same time Mads dipped the bird hard to the right just as an explosion rocked us. Warning sounds filled the space but Mads quickly corrected and dipped low over the trees. I slammed my fist against the side of the doorway.

"We'll come back," North said.

I cursed viciously and scowled out at the shivering trees lashing in the wind. Atlas was down there with the enemy. Alone.

He's a SEAL. He can handle it. He was trained for this.

My mind tried to reason with me but my heart was not letting me be comforted by it. I could feel North watching me. Probably making sure I didn't bail out of the helo. I would have if we weren't already so high up. The storm pulled and yanked at the bird but I didn't care about my safety.

"Atlas, come in," I said.

"I'm here."

I closed my eyes in relief.

"You guys good?" He asked.

"Yeah—Mads has some mad skills," I said dryly.

Atlas chuckled and I felt better being able to still make him laugh. My attention turned to Mads who looked like she was in heaven as she glared out at the storm and took the challenge head on.

"Hang in there—" North said. "We'll be back as soon as the storm clears."

North pulled off his pack and stuck a few more items into it before he positioned himself near the doorway and looked down.

"We dropped you a pack with supplies and ammo about three klicks west of you," North said. He dropped the pack and we both watched it fall into the forest below.

"Copy that. I'll be fine."

Lachlan was busy looking at a map spread out over his thigh. He stabbed a finger at a location and shoved the map at North.

"New extraction point—30 klicks west, around the other side of the lake. Has a burned out tree," North relayed.

"We're almost out of comms range," I said grimly.

"I'll reach out when we're back in range," North met my gaze. "Be safe out there."

"Copy that. Fly safe—over and out."

Worry made nausea churn in my stomach, made worse by the bumpy ride. By the time we landed back at the hangar where we'd moved our base, I was filled with pent up rage. I jumped from the helo, yanking gear off as I went. West stood up from the computer, watching me warily as I stormed through the space towards the back.

"What happened?"

"Atlas is still back there," North said from behind me.

West's face fell.

"He'll be fine, Nyx," West called after me. "You know he will."

I didn't answer. If it was anyone else, I wouldn't be this bent out of shape. But this was Atlas. The man I'd been with for the last three-ish years. We'd tackled everything together and I couldn't remember the last time we were apart for longer than a few hours. We never left anyone behind.

If I lost him before I could explore whatever these feelings were...I bared my teeth at the thought, pacing along the back wall as I jerked my gloves off.

North came over, just watching me with arms crossed over his chest. He wasn't even out of his tactical gear yet, AR still slung over his shoulder.

"Nyx."

I didn't answer, still pissed at him for making the call even knowing it was the right one. Any further hesitation would have gotten us all killed.

"Nyx."

I whirled on him. "I thought we never left anyone behind?"

North's eyes narrowed and his lips thinned.

"He's a SEAL. Have some faith in him for fucks sake," North said irritably. "Come help stack the gold."

78

ATLAS

I signed off with the team and made my way back through the trees. I planned to head towards where North had dropped the pack for me and then make a plan from there. Being here with the enemy until the storm died was not ideal, but it was the reality of the situation so I'd have to make it work.

Darkness was already falling, faster with the storm clouds sitting heavy in the sky. I looked around and jogged deeper into the woods. I hated to admit it but this was where I was in my element.

Alone. Working off adrenaline with only my training and instincts to rely on for survival. The thought of Nyx crossed my mind—I knew he was probably freaking out and livid at having to leave me behind but it would have been worse if they'd tried to stay. Much worse. In fact I'd probably be the only one still alive if they'd stayed.

Pushing Nyx out of my head, I focused on the present. I couldn't afford to slip up here and be distracted when I was vastly outnumbered.

I made it to the area North said the pack would be and after searching for a few minutes, found it snagged on some branches ten feet up in a tree. I looked around carefully before slinging my gun across my back and scaling the branches. Once back on the ground I took inventory. I had my rifle and plenty of ammo thanks to the supply drop. The pack also had a water filter, a few energy bars, a first aid kit and a tarp. In one of the pockets was a compass and one of our terrain maps.

I studied the map briefly, orienting myself and then took off through the trees again, headed west towards the new drop zone. For the first few miles I didn't run into any issues but then my luck ran out.

I don't know what made me duck down, instinct or something else, but a bullet bit into the tree where my head had been. I rolled behind a stump just as another few peppered the ground around me.

I'd barely made my feet again when two men rushed me. I shoved the first one past me and wrapped the second in a choke hold. I twisted just in time to have him shoot the first one, then snapped the other's neck.

I knew it would take me most of the night to reach the new pickup spot, but I also didn't want to lead the enemy to it. To avoid this, I headed back towards the guardhouse we hit first, hoping to pick off a few more and get me on more even footing. It was on the way to the new extraction point anyway and I'd be able to raid their guns and ammo in the process.

The rain was still pouring down, making my hearing untrustworthy and visibility in the dark was nearly nothing. I needed to find a place to hole up until morning. I found a shallow cave under some tree roots and wedged myself back in the deep shadows, hoping it would be enough. I ate an energy bar, drank some water falling off the leaves and settled back to wait for daylight.

79

ATLAS

The next morning, the rain hadn't let up at all but the grey of dawn was a welcome sight. I carefully extracted myself from my hide, stretching stiff muscles and working a kink out of my neck. This had all been a lot easier when I was younger but I didn't have time to think about the discomfort.

I made it to the guardhouse mid morning. My plan was to raid the weapons and then pick them off from the treeline, but as I was exiting the structure, I heard the men approaching through the trees.

I grabbed a few of the rifles I'd found and leaned them against the wall under the two windows, then I posted up at one and started picking them off. That was working until they got smart and circled the cabin. A group of them rushed the door. I dropped the first few with my rifle before I had to use my knife.

I slammed it into one man's chest, getting a sharp hit to my side by another. A third shoved me against the wall and I blocked his knife just in time, redirecting it into his buddy. I fought my way viciously out of the guardhouse, grabbing the last man standing to use as a shield. I stumbled out of the shack with him in front of me, a knife pressed to his neck. I looked around for any enemies in the trees but no bullets came.

"You're dead—" the man rasped.

"Shut up," I muttered. I made the treeline and quickly slit his throat, disappearing into the trees before he'd even hit the ground.

A few minutes later, I emerged from a particularly dense part of the forest to see the lake sitting dark and ominous ahead of me. I didn't have time to admire the view before a weight slammed into me and I pitched forward, tangling with my attacker as we slid down a small slope.

I lost my pack and my rifle in the fall but came up with my knife and immediately got the upper hand. But he was better than the others had been and quickly dislodged me. We broke apart and circled each other, looking for a weakness.

We clashed again and rolled through the mud, ending on the edge of a large drop. Pain blossomed at my side and then the man was on top, his knife pressing down towards my neck. The pain just served to piss me off and I let the rage take over—I wasn't going to die here. I lunged up and let the fire fuel me through the next few moves. I gained the upper hand only to feel the ground give way at my feet.

We fell together down a steep drop.

I hit trees and rocks on the way down, each one feeling like a punch to my body. When I finally came to a stop, I lay on my back gasping for air before pushing myself to my side. Looking for my enemy, I dipped my head in relief when I saw him impaled by a broken tree, still twitching in death but no longer a threat.

I stood up and stumbled as my body acclimated, and my breath returned. I looked up. My pack and my rifle were somewhere up there but there was no way I could climb back up. I muttered a curse and wiped the mud off of my face as best I could. At least I still had my knife and a handgun with one extra clip. It would have to be enough.

The rain was still coming down, but it wasn't as intense as before and the clouds didn't seem as heavy. I hoped that meant rescue was only a few hours away although I had a trek still to reach the clearing where the helo would pick me up. I debated just swimming across the lake but quickly decided against that as I would be exposed and the weather was not exactly prime for a dip in the cold alpine water. I raided the body of the man but didn't come up with anything besides a few clips of ammo that were the wrong caliber. I cleaned my knife, made sure my gun was in easy reach and headed off into the trees keeping the water on my right.

For the rest of the day I put every bit of my skills into play. I created false trails, set up traps and basically wreaked havoc on my pursuers. By the end of the day though, I was hungry, exhausted and still hadn't heard from North. The rain had stayed steady all day and to make things worse, the temperature had dropped. As the forest darkened, I knew I would be spending another night under the trees.

I was about to find a place to hole up for the night when pain slammed into me. I went down on one knee as a knife was pulled out of my side.

"All this commotion over one fucker." The man kicked me all the way down to kneel in front of him. He wiped his knife with my blood on my shirt and pressed it to my neck. He ripped my comms unit out and disarmed me, tossing the gun to his partner who emerged from the trees. Ten more men quickly surrounded us.

"One guy taking out almost half of our team," his partner said with a shake of his head. "I'd recruit you if I didn't have to kill you."

"Not interested anyway," I panted.

"Yeah, you'll be wishing you had that choice soon," he sneered.

Zip ties were pulled tightly around my wrists, restraining them behind me. They yanked me to my feet and dragged me away.

80

THERON

I stood just inside the hanger doors, watching the rain and hail pound down on the tarmac. Nyx was next to me. He'd been standing here for the better part of the day, glowering at the rain. I didn't like the delay either. Another day of this storm meant another day we couldn't get to Atlas. The wind made flying anything impossible—even a drone. Nyx had his arms crossed over his chest, his body tight with nervous, restless energy.

"He's fine," I muttered.

"I need you to stop saying that," Nyx snapped.

Knight came up to stand with us. "The weather looks like it will let up a little tomorrow morning."

"Hey!" West called. "Food's ready!"

I turned with Knight and headed over to where we'd set up a table and some camping chairs around a fire barrel. Mads appeared from where she'd been tinkering around with the helo.

"Did a few fun things to her for tomorrow," she grinned. Strands of hair were coming out of her ponytail and she had grease all over her face. We sat down and ate. All of us except for Nyx who refused to leave his weather watch.

"Do we have a count?" I asked once we were all done eating.

"We have about five billion," West said.

Mads whistled low, her eyes glowing in the firelight.

"That means there's still a lot left though," West continued.

"Some of it's still in the cave—some of it's hanging out in that clearing," Lachlan said.

"When we grab Atlas we'll have to assess things and see if we can finish things out or if it's too much of a risk," Knight said.

A few hours later, the hanger was quiet except for West's gentle snoring happening on the couch. Lachlan and Mads were messing around cleaning a few guns while Knight and I were sipping on beers around the fire.

Mads put down the gun and I watched her exchange a glance with Lachlan before she turned and sauntered off towards the restroom.

"I'm going to take a shower," she said.

She tossed a look over her shoulder, encompassing Lachlan, then Knight, then myself. Knight's beer stalled at his lips. Mads smirked and pulled off her t-shirt as she resumed walking across the room. Her hands went around to the back of her bra. She unclasped it with a flick and let it drop. She didn't turn around again but Lachlan didn't even spare us a glance before dropping the gun in his hand and following her. Knight looked at me, drained his beer and stood up.

"Could be fun," he shrugged and headed off to join them.

I debated whether I was going to head back there but Mads *was* a lot of fun in bed. I finished my beer and set it aside as I made my decision.

Opening the door to the bathroom, the shower was already running filling the small space with steam. Clothes littered the ground and I already could hear sighs of pleasure as I pulled my shirt over my head.

Once all my clothes were off I rounded the corner of the large shower stall and saw Mads between Lachlan and Knight. Lachlan was kissing her while Knight was pressed against her back, his fingers playing with her nipples.

I stepped in close and as my hand slid across Mads stomach, her eyes opened and jumped to mine. I found her clit and started rubbing slow circles. She hummed in pleasure and leaned back against Knight who kissed her neck.

Mads had her hand wrapped around Lachlan's cock, stroking him. She leaned in and brushed her lips against mine in a tentative ask. In answer my tongue sought out hers. It felt good to kiss someone on my terms again. I'd refused to kiss Red—and Vetticus—but I didn't want to think about that now.

Mads' hand found my dick and I quickly hardened at her touch. She pulled away from my kiss and turned her head to find Knight. I watched them make out while Mads ran her hand up and down my length. I dipped my fingers down, feeling her wetness that had nothing to do with the shower. Pushing two fingers inside I hooked them and she moaned against Knight's lips.

Two other fingers joined me inside her and she broke the kiss, panting as she turned to Lachlan. The three of us worked her towards the edge as she writhed between us. The sounds she made were making me painfully hard and I enjoyed seeing every nuance of pleasure bleed across her face.

When she came, she gasped and shuddered. "Oh god...yes—fuck."

After the waves dissipated, she dropped down on her knees and looked up at me. Her eyes half hooded in pleasure, she let a smirk pull at her lips before wrapping them around the head of my cock. I groaned as she sucked me into her mouth, her eyes never leaving mine.

One of her hands found Lachlan's cock, the other Knight's and soon the three of us were the ones panting in pleasure. My hand twisted in her hair and she took me deep into her throat, no gag reflex in sight. She did it again and then moved to Lachlan's dick, taking him into her mouth and deepthroating him while she rubbed Knight and I. It was incredibly hot seeing her suck on another cock. We were so close together, she pulled off Lachlan and trailed her tongue over my head as she turned to Knight. She took both of our cocks in her hand and swirled her tongue over first mine, then his, then back again—over and over until I couldn't take it anymore.

"Lachlan, sit on the bench," I rumbled. Lachlan did as I asked and I pulled Mads up to her feet. I led her over to Lachlan.

"Sit on his lap, darlin'," I said in her ear, planting a kiss on her neck.

Lachlan ran his hands up her sides as she straddled him and sank down on his cock. Both of them groaned in pleasure at the sensation. Mads dipped her head to kiss him while Lachlan gripped her ass, spreading her cheeks as he moved her hips.

"Are you going to take the three of us like a good girl?" Knight rasped.

He'd come up behind her. She stopped kissing Lachlan and looked over her shoulder. Knight stuck his hand out.

"Spit," he commanded. Mads spit in his hand and he brought it down to his cock, using it as lube.

"Fuck her pussy with Lachlan," I rasped. My hand was stroking my cock as I watched Knight push against her pussy from behind. Mads whimpered and leaned forward into Lachlan, a gasp escaped her lips as Knight forced his head in with a groan.

"Damn, you're tight with two dicks, sweetheart," he panted. Lachlan withdrew slightly and they both shoved forward and buried their cocks in her pussy.

"Fuck," Mads stammered, breathing heavily. Knight was pressed against her back, groaning as she relaxed to accommodate them. Lachlan threw his head back against the tile with a moan.

"Fuck, you both feel good," he murmured.

Mads shifted her hips around, impaling herself even further. Knight withdrew just slightly and then shoved forward again—both Lachlan and Mads groaned. He did it again and set a steady pace until he was panting and

Mads was shaking, her sounds of pleasure growing louder.

Knight spit in his hand, not breaking his thrusts and his fingers disappeared between her ass cheeks. A high pitched whimper escaped Mads.

"Oh god—oh fuck, fuck..." She whined. It wasn't long before she was bucking against them, lost to the sensations and with a cry she was coming. Hard. Her cries echoed off the walls and Lachlan cursed, his fingers digging into her hips as he thrust up, matching Knight's pace. It seemed to go on for a long time, her orgasm flowing through the four of us in waves.

"Take her ass, Knight," I rasped.

Knight pulled out. One hand grabbed her hip, the other twisted in her hair and then he was pushing forward again, this time into her ass. She pushed back, her eyes closed, utter rapture on her face. A moan escaped as I watched Knight's cock disappear into her ass. He pumped in and out a few times until Mads was gasping again. Lachlan's hand went up to her throat and cut some of her air off.

"I want you choking on North's cock, pretty girl," he growled.

She nodded frantically and I put one leg up on the bench. She bent down and sucked me into her mouth. The blow job was sloppy and soon the only sounds were the moans of pleasure and skin against skin. The build was steep as the four of us worked our way towards the release. Mads came first, crying loudly and choking on my cock as her orgasm slammed into her.

I was next. I could feel it racing up my spine, so strongly I shuddered and gasped. I grabbed her head, holding her head down as I came deep in her throat with a curse.

I pulled out of her mouth just as Knight and Lachlan detonated together. They came at nearly the same time, which set Mads off again. She threw her head back against Knight and shook with the aftershocks, then slouched against Lachlan's chest as she caught her breath.

Knight's hand slammed against the tile near Lachlan's head as he heaved in air, his shoulders shaking as he came down. Lachlan's head rested against the tile, eyes closed, his hands still on Mads hips.

"God, that was fucking hot," Mads breathed, finally able to speak.

Knight pulled out of her and she climbed off and stood under the spray, her eyes barely open. She looked freshly fucked and satisfied, flushed and beaming with pleasure.

"I agree," Lachlan said. "Great idea, sweet cheeks."

He stood up, slapped Knight on the ass and reached past Mads for the shower gel.

"Who you callin' sweet cheeks?" Knight laughed as he stole the soap from Lachlan.

Lachlan smirked. "Both of you."

A rumble of a laugh escaped and I shook my head as I left the shower, leaving them to it. It had been nice to just let go and be present in the moment—at least for a little while. But as I exited the showers, a towel slung low on my hips, I saw Nyx. He was still standing looking out at the storm and it was a sobering reminder of our reality.

81

ATLAS

I lifted my head off my chest from where I'd been dozing—or unconscious—not sure which. Probably a little of both. The men had brought me back to the main compound where they'd roughed me up and tied me to a chair then left me in a concrete room with no windows.

I had no idea what time it was or whether the storm was still raging outside. Blood had dried in streaks down my chest from several cuts on my face and a split lip but otherwise, I'd definitely gone through worse. It probably hadn't been smart to start laughing at them, but compared to the treatment I'd received at Atrox, this was like a spa day.

The only concerning things were the stab wound in my side and the large gash that ran down my chest. Both hurt like a bitch and the stab wound was making it hard to take a full breath.

The door slammed open and I looked up to see three men file into the room. The first two were the ones who'd spoken to me in the woods, but the third was obviously the leader. He had red hair buzzed short and a handlebar mustache surrounding a mouth chewing on a cigar. The man stared at me for an almost uncomfortably long time, like he was trying to make me speak first or intimidate me. He wasn't going to achieve either one of those things so I just stared back at him with a bored look on my face while I waited him out.

"I would ask what a military man is doing out here in the middle of nowhere but the crates of gold we discovered answered that question for me," he said finally. "What's your name, soldier?"

"Does it matter?"

The man shrugged. "Or I can just call you asshole."

"That fits him better." I looked over at the man who had spoken and shrugged as best I could.

"Suit yourself."

The man stepped closer, looking me over before meeting my gaze again.

"Where's the rest of the gold?" He asked.

I leaned forward slightly like I was going to tell him. "Go fuck yourself."

The man blinked and barked out a laugh.

"You know—you have some balls. Taking out as many of my men as you did and then sitting here giving me attitude—big balls." He patted me roughly on the cheek and chuckled.

I didn't answer. He shrugged and pulled his knife out of his belt.

"Here's the truth of it—I have your comms unit. When your friends reach out, probably soon now that this storm is letting up—they're going to find you unavailable. I'm going to demand the rest of the gold from them in exchange for you..." He smiled but it didn't reach his eyes. "But we both know you're not leaving here alive. So you might as well save yourself some pain by just telling me where your little hideout is and we can make all of this real easy."

I shook my head, trying to hide a smirk and failing.

"Talk about balls—you don't even know who I am," I scoffed. "Making a threat like that—let's just say this isn't going to end well for you."

The man blinked at me then tipped his head back and laughed. It went on before he dashed his hand over his eyes, a few laughs still rocking him.

"Seriously, I really wish I didn't have to kill you," he said.

Before I could blink, he whipped his hand out and drove the knife into the back of my hand where it rested on the arm of the chair. Pain roared through me and my breathing picked up as I growled my displeasure.

The door opened and a man stuck his head in. "Sir, they've made contact."

82

NYX

Atlas, come in," I said. We were finally in the helo headed back to the extraction point. The night had been long and the morning too while I waited for the storm to let up enough for us to fly. It was still drizzling but the wind had died down and that's all we cared about.

"Atlas—"

"Ah, so that's his name."

North sat up straighter as a voice that definitely wasn't Atlas came over the comms unit.

"Who is this?" North demanded.

"You can call me Roland."

"Roland—it seems you have something of mine," North answered.

"Well isn't that convenient," Roland said. "You have some gold I'm dying to get my hands on. How about a trade?"

"That's not going to happen," North said.

"We're in quite the pickle then," Roland said, his smirk audible through the line. "How about if you don't tell me the location of the rest of the gold, I kill your man."

"The way I see it, you kill him, you don't get the gold regardless."

"Are you that kind of man? Are you willing to test that theory?"

"Here's the thing, Roland. You kill him—I come after you. You don't—I still come after you," North's voice was deadly. "Either way, you've already pissed me off." There was silence over the comms. It stretched for so long I started to get nervous, then Roland came back on.

"Sounds like you've made your choice then. See you soon."

The line went dead and dread filled me. I hoped we weren't going to be too late.

Mads dropped us into the woods near the compound. Lachlan and Knight went one way, while I went the other with North. I could hear the helo take off towards the compound. This time West had joined us and he and Mads had some surprises for our new friends.

"In position," Knight said over comms.

"Copy—hold for the signal," North said.

I was crouched with him on the edge of the treeline, the compound in view across a small clearing. It was a large two story concrete establishment.

"Missiles away—" Mads voice said. "Impact in three...two...one..."

The explosion as the missile hit the line of vehicles near the building was enough to rock the ground around us and I could feel the fire radius from all the way across the property. Chaos ensued. Men were running everywhere trying to get eyes on the helo but the forest limited visibility and Mads was already out of range. Using the distraction, North and I took off across the space headed for the building. We cut through the chaos with ease, dropping anyone who was in our path. We were able to reach the front doors before anyone even started shooting at us and by then it was too late. North and I swept into the rooms, clearing them one by one.

I was in my element—no distractions, no noise in my head—this was after all what I'd been conditioned for. Except this time, I was emotionally invested in the target.

"Second missile impact in three...two...one..." Mads said.

We heard another explosion rock the grounds followed by machine gun fire. North and I were in a hallway when three men burst from a doorway on our left. The gunfire in the space was deafening but I dropped one, North the other while the third dove back the way he'd come. I edged around the doorway, slowly revealing the room while North watched our backs.

I went down low and bent around the corner to shoot the man in the leg. He grunted and fell to his knees. North held him at gunpoint.

"Where's the prisoner?" he demanded.

I watched the door near North's shoulder. North jammed the butt of his AR into the man's face but the man just sneered and spat at North's feet. I bared my teeth in irritation but North was already moving, his knife in his fist.

"Last chance," he snarled as he brought the blade up.

"Fuck you," the man hissed. North shoved the knife into his neck and ripped his comms unit from him so he could listen to the enemy chatter.

"Knight, Lach—report in," North said.

"Clearing the east wing now. No sign of Atlas," Knight said.

North appeared to be listening to the enemy comms for a moment. "They're regrouping. Clear an escape route—we're headed to the lower level."

"Copy," Knight answered.

83

ATLAS

The explosions sent shockwaves through the structure. Chunks of concrete and rubble fell from the ceiling of the room, dusting my head with debris. Roland was barking orders over comms and I couldn't help the laugh that bubbled up.

"Something funny?" Roland snapped.

"I warned you," I rasped.

Roland and his two men had spent the evening and most of the morning torturing me for information. One of my eyes was nearly swollen shut, I had a split lip and more cuts on my chest than I wanted to think about. The knife was still impaled in my hand, anchoring it to the arm of the chair.

"You're as good as dead," I chuckled.

Roland scowled and backhanded me with his pistol. I spit out blood, baring bloody teeth at him. He leveled the gun at my head and I met his gaze, seeing the truth there. He was going to pull the trigger. Suddenly, he cocked his head, listening to something and the gun dropped.

"Let's go!" He barked and I found myself alone.

I immediately rocked the chair back and forth. It tipped over backwards and I heard, and felt, the wood crack and break. I cursed viciously as it jarred the knife in my hand. I got my other hand loose and quickly untied my ankles.

Now I was just left with the hardest part. The knife was stuck into the piece of wood and I knelt on the concrete, wrapping my fist around the hilt. Taking a few deep breaths, I psyched myself up and muttered a countdown under my breath.

"Three, two, one..." I growled and yanked the blade up.

I hissed in distress, pulling my tattered shirt over my head and binding it as best I could. I heard the door and grabbed the knife, launching myself at the wall near the door. I saw the barrel of the AR first and knocked it down as I brought the knife towards the man's throat.

"Fuck!"

It was Nyx. My momentum sent him and I crashing into the wall and I just barely diverted the kill blow in time. The knife hovered at his chin while North's AR leveled at my face.

"Jesus—" Nyx breathed, dropping his AR to his side as he steadied me with a hand. "You look like shit."

"Gee, thanks," I grumbled, even as my lips twitched into a half smile.

North's gaze swept me from head to toe. "You good?" he asked.

I nodded. "Yeah—did you meet Roland yet?"

Nyx shook his head. "Not yet," he growled. "I'm looking forward to it though."

He pulled out a handgun and thrust it at me. I nodded my thanks and we fell in together at the doorway. We were immediately thrown into the fight in the hallway.

"We have Atlas—headed up," North said. I couldn't hear the reply but we advanced down the hallway towards the stairs.

"They have Roland," North said a moment later.

We stepped outside into the overcast but bright afternoon to absolute destruction. A giant crater sat in front of me where one of Mads' missiles had leveled the forest. One entire wing of the building was gone and there were bodies everywhere.

Out on the lawn, Knight and Lachlan stood with Roland and a few others kneeling at gunpoint. I could hear the helo approaching in the distance.

North walked the line of men. "You Roland?" he asked.

Roland looked a little beat up but there was nothing but anger in his eyes and he looked North up and down.

"Does it matter?" he scoffed.

North gave him one of his lethally cold smiles. "No. See, I don't like it when someone touches what's mine without permission—"

"You killed my men first," Roland said petulantly.

"Do I look like a fair, reasonable person to you?" North interrupted.

Roland pressed his lips into a thin line and shook his head.

"Good—at least we agree on that."

"If you're going to kill me, just do it—quit yappin'," Roland grumbled.

"Oh I'm not going to kill you," North said.

He stepped aside and nodded to me. Roland looked confused and irritated until I stepped up to him with a grin and realization dawned on his face.

"Who are you people?" Roland asked.

"Someone you shouldn't have pissed off," I shrugged. "Told you this wasn't going to end well for you."

I leveled the gun at him and pulled the trigger.

Knight and Lachlan took out the rest of the line. The helo was deafening as it hovered above us and a rope snaked down. I looked up to see West hanging out the door.

"Talk about valet service," Lachlan chuckled. He gestured to the rope and smirked at me. "After you!"

84

NYX

Once back at the hanger, I stormed into the bathroom after Atlas and threw the door shut. He whirled to face me, his eyes narrowing when he saw whatever was written all over my face. I slammed my palm against his chest and backed him into the counter.

"What the fuck were you thinking?" I snarled.

"Nyx—"

"Risking your life? Are you fucking serious?" I seethed.

"They had an RPG—"

"I don't care!" I shouted, chest heaving.

I turned away, running my hands through my hair. The bathroom was too small to pace. Atlas touched my arm.

"Nyx—"

I whirled towards him, my emotions all over the place. A half step brought me back into his personal space. I meant to shove him again but I just gripped his shirt in my fists as anger and something else swept through me.

"Reckless asshole," I growled.

"Strange way of saying thank you," Atlas breathed.

"I didn't ask you to do any of that," I said harshly.

"Don't tell me I can't bleed for you," Atlas rumbled and his eyes darkened.

The tension simmered between us. My eyes dropped to his mouth.

Then all thought left my mind as I crushed my lips against his.

He froze for a half second before his hand went around the back of my neck yanking me closer. Our teeth clashed and his tongue sought mine in a tangle of angry passion turned desperation to shrink any remaining space between us.

My hands clutched his shirt, but that wasn't enough. I ran them down his chest, gripping the bottom. I ripped the fabric up and over his head. My hands went to his sides, nearly scalding myself on his bare skin, and he hissed against my lips.

I immediately drew back and looked down. He had a long cut that ran down his side and halfway across his stomach. A low growl rumbled in my throat but instead of stopping, my hand pressed against it and I watched my fingers turn red with his blood. My eyes jumped to his as I pressed my hand against his wound and leaned closer. We were both panting and I could feel his breath against my skin.

"I live to bleed for you," Atlas rasped. "It's impossible not to."

My jaw clenched and my fingers curled into his side. Atlas leaned into me. His hand on the back of my neck tightened as I pushed his limits but only the tick of his jaw gave away any sign of pain.

"Then I'll be your pain—there can't be one without the other."

He shoved his body against mine and drove us back against the door. My hand, slippery with his blood, wrapped around his waist and I yanked him into me. Our lips met again. Pleasure shot through me as he rocked his hardness against mine.

Atlas grabbed the neck of my shirt and ripped it off me so he could run his hands up my chest before slamming them against the door beside my head. His lips moved to my jaw, then my neck, then my collarbone. There he bit me hard enough to draw blood at the same time his other hand swept up my thigh and palmed my cock. The sensation nearly had me seeing stars, and I threw my head back against the door with a groan.

"I want to get lost in your shadows," Atlas murmured. "Show me how they like to play."

He lowered himself onto the dingy tile floor and his fingers did quick work of my pants, dragging them forcefully down. I grabbed my cock, stroking it once before Atlas yanked my hand away and replaced it with his. It was rough and so different from when a woman handled me.

Different in all the best ways.

His eyes met mine and I slid my hands into his hair and pulled him forward. Anticipation made a thrill rush through me at what he was about to do. He took me into his mouth and I didn't know how I was going to last any length of time.

I hissed a curse as the picture of him on his knees and his warm mouth taking me deeper nearly was my undoing. I hit the back of his throat and when he swallowed I definitely saw stars. I thrust my hips and pushed deeper down his throat. I couldn't hold back. My hands pushed through his hair and he let me set the pace as his hand found my balls and I let out a breathless curse.

"Fuck, Atlas," I gasped. I wasn't going to last long as embarrassing as it was to finish this fast there was no stopping the wave rushing towards me. My hips faltered and I opened my eyes just in time for ours to clash as I came. I groaned as I emptied down his throat. He sucked every bit of come from me until I shivered with sensitivity.

Atlas looked up at me smugly and his tongue darted out to lick his lips. Entranced, I pulled him to me and tasted myself on his tongue as we kissed again.

I trailed kisses down his chest and over his abs as I sank to my knees. I was suddenly nervous. I'd never given another man a blow job before. Atlas smirked down at me as he leaned back against the counter. His fingers drove through my hair and fisted it, pulling my head back so I had to look up at him.

"You'll know what to do," he said quietly.

I wrapped my hand around his length and swirled my tongue around his tip, tasting precum and humming in pleasure. Who would have thought I'd enjoy this, but maybe it was just because it was Atlas. I slipped him into my mouth and sucked his head, slowly working him deeper. I refused to gag, although something told me he'd like that. I gripped his hips and sank deeper, feeling him hit the back of my throat, I swallowed, eliciting a groan from him. As I withdrew, I sucked him to the tip and started up a steady pace.

Atlas grip tightened in my hair as his breath caught in his throat. I filed away every gasp, moan and clench of his fingers. I soaked in his pleasure. Soon he was panting and rocking his hips forward. I'd adjusted enough that I took his other hand and put it on my head. He got the hint and his grip tightened and he increased the pace.

"Fuck," he gasped.

Atlas fucked my mouth but I could tell he was still holding back. I growled around his cock and looked up at him, my gaze dark and provocative. He moaned and gave a breathy laugh.

"First time and already like it rough," he panted.

In answer I fondled his balls and tugged on them gently. He gasped and set a rougher pace than before. My eyes watered but I could feel myself growing hard again at the look on Atlas' face. My fingers slipped back and rubbed the spot in between his balls and ass and his movements stuttered. A groan escaped him and with hooded eyes he met mine again.

"You want my come down your throat, my dark one?" He growled.

I gripped his thigh harder in answer and with a soft cry of pleasure he broke. The taste of his come burst across my tongue and I let it slip down my throat, greedily swallowing it all. Atlas' head tipped back and his hand lay against my neck as he caught his breath.

I looked us over as I stood up. We were covered in blood and our clothes were either ripped or bloody on the dirty floor. I leaned over and turned on the shower, looking over my shoulder in time to see Atlas' gaze sweep over me.

"Keep looking at me like that I'll be ready for round two real quick," I joked.

He gave me a dark smile as he pulled me into the shower with him.

"It looks like you already are."

I was about to open the bathroom door when Atlas' arms snaked around me. He pressed his body up against mine. Even after messing around in the shower together, it was like I couldn't get enough—I could feel myself reacting to his touch.

"So have you decided?" He asked against my neck.

"Decided what?" I turned enough to look him in the eye. A smirk danced across my lips and warmth filled me as I saw his gaze drop to my lips.

"If I'm just an experiment."

Something about his tone made me hold the joke I was about to say. There was something in his eyes that demanded honesty.

"None of what we just did felt like an experiment," I said.

I grabbed his jaw and pulled him in closer to press my lips against his in a kiss that was sweet, intimate and much too short.

"I'm all in," I whispered.

When Atlas pulled away, he gave me a rueful smile.

"You know they're going to give us shit when we go out there."

I rolled my shoulders back and turned the doorknob. "Don't I know it—you better not tell them I barely lasted two minutes or I'll never hear the end of it."

I flashed him a smile, and he looked at me smugly. "What can I say—I'm just that good."

85

THERON

A FEW MONTHS LATER
NEW YORK CITY

Nyx and Atlas stood on either side of me on the sidewalk. Cars rushed by, horns blared and people strode by without paying us any attention. We'd spent the last few months getting our lives back together. Lachlan decided he wasn't done having fun with us, so he was finalizing things in Austria before coming to join us in the states. Knight was finishing up some contracts and then he'd do the same. Turns out West enjoyed himself too because he'd flown back with us and was now our tech guy.

The team was coming together.

With the gold, we'd purchased a massive estate and the office tower we stood in front of now. I stared up at the skyscraper rising into the sky. It was a beautiful display of windows and iron flourishes.

"I never thought I'd call a building beautiful," Nyx said. "But she sure is pretty."

Atlas chuckled from my other side. "A blank slate too."

He was right. It was a new development just finished and all the floors were empty, just waiting for someone to come along and apply their own vision to it. I took a moment to take a deep breath and revel in the moment. I rolled a set of keys in my hand.

It was mine. All of it.

My eyes continued to trail up the building, settling on the last piece of construction going on at the very top.

The business name.

The workers were just finishing the final letter of the sign.

NorTac. Northern Tactical was officially a reality.

"And so it begins," Atlas murmured.

"Hoorah," Nyx said. "Now let's go celebrate. We need to christen your office with whiskey."

It was time to build. It was time to plan. And one day, it would be time to execute and show Vetticus just how much of an enemy he'd made in me. We were free, there were no rules, and it was time to play one last dangerous game. *Our game.*

ABOUT 3 YEARS
BEFORE PRESENT DAY

Vengeance is in my heart, death in my hand,
Blood and revenge are hammering in my head.

WILLIAM SHAKESPERE

86

THERON

MOSCOW, RUSSIA

We were fresh off a job as we pulled into the loading bay of a NorTac warehouse in Moscow. The blood and dirt had barely dried on us as we all climbed out. Nyx popped the trunk and I walked around, tearing off my vest and tactical gear with a sigh of relief. I frowned as I watched Atlas round the vehicle.

"That probably needs stitches," I said, nodding to a nasty gash on his jaw from where someone had caught him with brass knuckles.

"Yeah, hurts like a bitch," he grumbled. He pulled off his gear, followed by his t-shirt and looked down at the bruises littering his ribs. "Probably a broken rib too."

"Need to work out those abs more," Viktor teased.

"At least I have abs," Atlas fired back.

Viktor's twin, Konstantine, appeared around the other side of the car and chuckled as he socked Viktor playfully in his stomach that very much already had a six pack.

"I've told him he needs to follow my workouts."

Viktor replied in Russian which turned into good natured bickering between the two of them. Or at least I thought it was good natured—my Russian was still elementary at best.

As the years passed, together with Nyx and Atlas, we built up Northern Tactical to be a global enterprise. Lachlan and West joined us full time and a few years later, we were operating heavily in Syria and that's where the rest of our team rounded out.

Knox Taylor—Macy's husband—we found rotting away in a Syrian prison. I'd sent someone back to check on Macy a few years after our escape. She'd avoided Vetticus although she did say that he terrorized the area for a few months, convinced we were hiding out somewhere. I couldn't stop thinking about her missing husband and as thanks for helping us, I decided to put some resources into trying to locate him. After we rescued him, he moved Macy to New York and became a part of our team.

After that, we were hired to do a security job in Syria. The Russians attacked and that's how we met the Volkov Brothers. They were taken prisoner during the attack and I decided on a whim to break them out. Well, it wasn't a whim. I knew who they were and I knew I wanted that favor owed to me when I got back to the states. They were Bratva royalty and having the Russian mob owe me a favor was very appealing.

Once we'd stripped off all our gear, we headed into the warehouse, Viktor and Kon led the way towards the most recent shipment ready for one of our Russian contractors. Demetrius was standing at a pallet with a gun case open on top of the merchandise. He turned at our arrival.

"*Privet, droog moy*," he grinned, greeting me warmly.

When I'd met Demetrius Volkov, I'd just killed his previous arms supplier and inserted myself as the replacement. Demetrius wasn't too happy about that and was going to kill me when the twins arrived just in time and told their brother who I was. At the time, Demetrius was the new leader of the Bratva and although he grudgingly accepted the terms of our agreement then, over the years we ended up becoming close and partnering on many ventures—of which included dealing illegal weapons.

"What do you think?" I asked. I picked up the gun and checked it before handing it to Demetrius to look over.

"I think these new modifications are exactly what the client is looking for."

"Good—those pallets over there should be the rounds requested."

"We have a truck arriving in an hour," Viktor said after a brief conversation with one of the workers nearby.

Now that business was settled, Demetrius gestured for the guns to be secured and walked with me towards the entrance of the loading bay.

"How long are you here for?" Demetrius asked.

"We fly back to London tomorrow afternoon."

"Then I insist you come out with me tonight," he said. "I want to show you the club and run some ideas by Nyx and Atlas."

Later, back in our hotel room, I was getting ready to head out to meet everyone for dinner when my phone rang with an unknown number.

"North," I answered.

"Hey buddy."

"Knight," I said, recognizing the voice. "You back in civilization?"

"Yup—phone was a casualty of the job."

"How did it go?"

"Pretty smooth—got everyone out alive. Listen, I'm on my way to Paris and I need you to meet me there."

"What's in Paris."

"Have you heard of Gabriel Griffin? Deathwing? I met him a few months ago. Fucking freak of nature, man. Our teams collided during an op and when I tell you I've never seen someone as psychotic as him, well, maybe you—but anyway, he called me just now and said he needed to get into contact with you. Urgently."

"What for?"

"He wouldn't tell me over the phone. He deals with anti-trafficking organizations. He's making a name for himself as the *angel of death*—cheesy, but whatever. We don't choose our reps, you know? He comes in and basically annihilates these rings. If he has something he wants to show you—I'd go. Immediately because it's probably important."

"Alright, I can leave tomorrow AM. Text me the meetup details."

"I'll come get you from the airport."

"Even better."

87

THERON

PARIS, FRANCE

The next day, Knight picked me, Nyx and Atlas up at the airport.

"Hey man," Nyx said, greeting Knight warmly. "It's been a minute!"

"Tell Cal to fuck off and come work with us," Atlas grinned.

Knight laughed. "You know I work best as a free agent. But I'm here now—I'm sure you have some trouble for me to get into."

"Always," I chuckled and embraced him hard. "Good to see you, brother. Now, what's all this about Deathwing?"

"Load up—all I got is an address."

Knight drove us out to an abandoned house on the outskirts of town. It was dark, foreboding and just the look of the place was heavy and ominous. We all stepped out of the SUV and a dark haired man in tactical gear and an AR slung across his shoulder walked out to meet us. He greeted Knight with a friendly albeit serious demeanor then his sharp green eyes swept over us quickly. He held out a tattooed hand to me.

"Gabriel Griffin," he said. "You must be North."

"I am—this is Nyx—and Atlas." Gabriel shook their hands. "So, why am I here, Gabriel?"

He nodded towards the house. "There's something you need to see."

The house was obviously some sort of boarding house but it was run down and filthy. I stopped in the entrance of the living room, equal parts dread and disgust made my skin crawl.

"What is this place?"

"It was a boarding house for children," Gabriel said.

"Children?" Nyx echoed incredulously.

A chain ran from the wall to a mattress in the corner where it was obvious a sheet covered a body far too small to be an adult. Atlas cursed softly.

"This way." Gabriel led the way upstairs, a sad look cutting through his stoic features. The deeper into the house we got, the worse it seemed to be. Every room held new horrors. Gabriel finally stepped into one of them and walked over to the far corner. We walked past rows of crudely constructed wooden beds with threadbare mattresses and thin sheets. Each bed had a chain attached to a collar and my stomach turned. A few small toys and books were strewn across the floor and the windows were broken, letting the harsh winter air tear through the bars covering them.

"Over here," Gabriel said.

He dragged one of the beds away from the wall and pointed at something carved into the wood near the floorboard. It was a name. I bent to look closer at it and my heart stopped in my chest.

"No," I said.

I fell to my knees, my legs no longer able to hold me up. I reached out my hand and ran my fingers over the letters. "No, it's not possible."

My voice sounded far away.

"She's...dead—"

I couldn't finish speaking, I'd run out of air.

I couldn't breathe.

My vision narrowed and I couldn't bring myself to pull my hand away from the letters carefully and deliberately carved into the wood. They were traced back over with red making it stand out.

Emersyn North

Papers sat near the carving and I grabbed the closest one with a shaking hand. There was an EN in the corner as though she'd signed the artwork.

My vision blurred.

I stood up and stormed out of the room. I needed to get out of this house.

I threw open the back door and lurched into the yard, immediately throwing up in the overgrown bushes. I took great heaving breaths to pull myself together and sat down heavily on the back steps. I stared at the drawing I clutched in my hands.

It was of *Little Red Riding Hood*.

She was alive.

My daughter was alive.

88

THERON

*I*t wasn't possible.

I saw her get shot. This just couldn't be real. But even as I thought it, I knew in my gut it was my Emersyn—the *Little Red Riding Hood* drawing solidified it. She'd been alive that night in the woods.

And I left her.

I didn't even feel the drops as it started to rain. From my position sitting on the steps, I was quickly soaked. I'm not sure how long I was outside before Nyx came out and put a hand on my shoulder startling me.

"Come on, Griffin is taking us to his safe house. We can talk about what to do next. This place creeps me out."

I nodded and climbed to my feet, wiping rain off my face. I didn't go back into the house though. I couldn't face the darkness there and instead made my way around the side. Knight was already loaded up in the SUV and Gabriel was in his vehicle with the rest of his team. The drive over was silent and heavy. The men knew better than to say anything.

When we got to the house, I changed into dry clothes before finding everyone sitting on bar stools in the kitchen while Gabriel threw some food together and handed out beers. I sat down and drank half of the bottle he handed me in one go. He looked at me with a ghost of a smile on his lips before he reached into a different cabinet and grabbed a bottle of whiskey and a shot glass.

He slid both in front of me without a word.

The guys were talking amongst each other as I threw back two shots back to back. There was too much noise going on in my head. How was she still alive? What happened after I'd run?

I left her.

"How do you find out about these boarding houses?" Atlas asked.

Gabriel handed sandwiches out to everyone before leaning back against the kitchen counter and taking a sip of his own beer.

"I have informants, sometimes I'll interview girls if they escape or we rescue them. Sometimes I go undercover if it's a big ring."

"How did you even find her name?" Nyx asked.

"We go through every grooming house with a fine-tooth comb. You never know what evidence the traffickers will leave behind or what clues the girls will leave. Often it's their journals, or drawings or like in this instance a name on a wall—that leads us to rescuing them. My men will continue to go through that house board by board until we're done then we'll burn it to the ground."

He took another sip of his beer. "You have to remember, sometimes these girls just up and disappear from their families, so any evidence we find, we try to get the information out to the families if possible so they can either have hope...or closure."

I took another shot.

"Where do the women go after the boarding houses?" Nyx asked.

"The auctions usually, or a middleman. Some auctions are for rich individuals but there are also ones that center around—" he paused as though trying to think of the correct words. "—destination experiences I guess you could call them. There are a few islands and private resorts that supply women to their patrons for a price. They usually cater to certain kinks, illegal ones mostly."

"How do I find Emersyn?" I asked.

I poured another shot.

"The boarding houses usually distribute to the same places. The difficult part will be if she went straight to auction because the records after the auction house are vague at best."

Gabriel finished his beer and set the bottle down.

"I have to warn you," he said. "I spoke to one of the girls from this boarding house and she said Emersyn aged out shortly after she got there. I couldn't get an accurate timeline—could be months, could be years, time turns into your enemy when you're trafficked—if I had to guess though I'd say over a year ago. There's something else you should know—the girl mentioned Emersyn had a scar running down the side of her face. This was why she remembered her and also why Emersyn aged out because I guess none of the usual buyers wanted to buy her."

The silence was so heavy I could feel myself choking on it. I must have paled significantly because Gabriel's usually passive face grew concerned. I shoved off the bar stool and threw back another shot.

"North—" Nyx said, but I held up a hand.

Yeah, she'd have a scar—

I fucking put it there.

It was my fault. All of it.

I left her.

"What are the odds of finding someone?" My voice came out hoarse.

Gabriel hesitated but shook his head. "Not ideal. There are a lot of variables." I could still feel the knife in my hand. Her shaking sobs assaulted me anew. I closed my eyes briefly and shoved the memory away.

"Can you get me the records from the boarding house?" I asked.

"I'll have my men bring them over tomorrow morning. This particular boarding house we've been watching for a while, which is why I say it had to have been over a year ago that she was there because we've been sitting on this one for nearly eight months."

I nodded and stood up, leaving my sandwich untouched. I grabbed the bottle of whiskey before heading towards the back of the house where I'd seen a patio with some chairs. The alcohol sat like a weight in my stomach, heavy and unyielding. I collapsed into a plastic chair. It protested as I sagged forward over my forearms, bottle dangling between my legs. I took another drink and leaned back.

I'd thought she was dead for so long. I saw it happen.

But you didn't confirm it. You should always confirm it.

What if this time she was really dead? What if she died before I could get to her? I didn't know what I would do if we found out she was actually dead. It would be like losing her all over again except the guilt would drown me. I had a decade of time available to me to search for her if I had known she was out there.

I took another drink, trying to drown the sick feeling but it only made me feel worse. I heard the door open and Knight settled in a chair next to me, reaching for the bottle. I let him take it and we sat in silence drinking for a while.

"She must hate me," I said finally, staring off across the sloping lawn of the safe house. "I–I hurt her and then—abandoned her." My voice broke. "I could have been spending all of this time searching for her!"

I stood up, fury rising in me as I paced the length of the stone laid patio.

"You didn't know," Knight said.

"No, but I should have," I snarled. "I–I saw him shoot her. I saw him shoot her in the head, Trent."

I paced some more, trying to keep my emotions at bay but like the storm rolling in above us, it was getting harder to hold it all in.

"What kind of father gives up on their kid?" I stopped, my back to Knight, running a hand over my face to get rid of the tears silently falling. "I fucking failed her."

"You haven't failed," Knight said.

"Yes I have...too many times to count," I growled. Knight came to stand next to me and I took the bottle he extended my way.

"Well, now you have another chance," he said.

"What if she really is dead this time?" I muttered after taking a sip.

"Then nothing changes and you continue with your plan for revenge."

"It'll be like losing her all over again."

Knight nodded. "Probably."

"You're a great pep talker, you know that?" I grumbled, handing him the bottle back. He laughed and nudged my shoulder.

"You know it's not one of my strong suits."

"But you're always there for me anyway," I sighed.

"You're stuck with me, old man," Knight said, taking a long drink.

"Fuck, are we old?"

"Nah, although missions hurt more now, that's for sure," Knight said. "I'd kill for my twenty-year-old body again. That thing was resilient as fuck! I could sleep on the hard ground for a week and then go get in a fight."

My lips turned up in a smile but it didn't reach my eyes.

"We look damn good for fifty though," Knight smirked.

I took another drink, realizing with a jolt that I'd turned fifty and hadn't even stopped to acknowledge it. I'd been going full speed ahead for the last decade and now that I knew Emersyn was alive, it was just one more thing on my plate.

"We'll find her," Knight said. "And then we'll kill Vetticus...and anyone else who needs to die."

He turned to me and put a hand on my shoulder.

"You accomplished what you set out to do all those years ago when you showed up on my doorstep with a vendetta and a dream. Now you have an empire, you have the financing and firepower. But most importantly, you have us—and we're ready."

89

THERON

The next morning, a little hungover but feeling more like myself, Deathwing showed us into his war room. Several men stood upon Deathwing's entrance.

"This is Theron North and some of his team." He gestured to his men. "This is Kyllion—my second. Seven, Lincoln—and Rune is behind the computer there. Rune, pull up the boards." An electronic evidence wall appeared on several huge screens along one wall.

"Makes it easy to transport when it's digital," Rune said when he caught West's jaw dropped. West had joined us this morning and the rest of my team was expected later this afternoon.

"Looks like the paper one visually—" Rune continued.

"But so much better," West said in awe.

Deathwing gestured to Rune. "West, have Rune set you up with anything you need."

He pointed to three images posted at the top of the board he'd pulled up.

"This is Greg Mahoney, Alex Palmero and an organization we don't know much about yet that we call the Faceless. There are more—rings and secondary people—but this seems to be the biggest ring and the main players we encounter the most. Mahoney and Palmero are ghosts and spook easily so we've been targeting the grooming houses. Taking down an auction is nearly impossible. They just pop back up again. Until we chop off the head, targeting those doesn't make a lot of sense. Mahoney is part owner of the Red Auction and Palmero runs adventure style businesses."

A list of establishments appeared under Palmero's photo.

"We'll look through the documentation from the boarding house and see if any of these pop up."

We spent the rest of the morning combing through the documentation and adding to Deathwing's evidence board. By the end of the day, we'd finished going through everything and I didn't feel any closer to knowing where Emerysn could be.

"This is the problem with trying to find an individual," Deathwing said. "They don't use names, usually just numbers or maybe nicknames. It looks like over the past year, they've sold girls off to Palmero, Mahoney and a long list of middlemen—not very helpful when we don't know her number or nickname."

I stood in front of the evidence board, looking over it thoughtfully. My gaze hovered on the names under Palmero's photo and then at the ones under Mahoney.

"Does Mahoney ever frequent any of Palmero's businesses?" I asked.

"Yes, we have reason to believe they are partners in a lot of their ventures," Rune said.

"What are you thinking?" Deathwing asked, coming up to stand beside me. I pointed out a few names on the board.

"I'm not going to find her knocking down doors of grooming houses or middlemen. There's too many. I need to learn more about the key players."

Deathwing nodded. "We haven't attempted going undercover with this ring yet. Both men are extremely wary of strangers and tight with their inner circles. The Red Auction is invite only and a lot of Palmero's establishments are too."

"Do you have information on each of these?" I asked, pointing to the lists of businesses.

Rune pulled up another evidence board on another portion of the wall. I walked over and saw the list was drilled down in more detail. There were a few islands, a resort, a few sex clubs...

"What's this place?"

"It's an island Palmero owns. He runs one of his adventure style businesses there—it's not invite only so we could get you in."

"West—" West nodded and turned to his computer.

"What about this one?"

"That's Palmero's main business. It changes location every event and is always in a remote area of the world. It has experiences the buyers can participate in and is invite only."

"And this one?"

"The Warren. It's not either of Palmero's or Mahoney's but we have it on there because they both sell to him," Rune answered. "His name is Cooper. We don't know much about that spot yet because of its remote location and relative newness to the scene. I've hacked Mahoney's flight plans though, and he is attending the next auction there."

"When is the next auction at the Warren?"

"A few weeks," Rune said.

"I want in on that too," I decided. I looked over at West again.

"I got you, boss," he said.

I turned back to Deathwing. "I can get close to these two which would also give me access to the auctions which it sounds like is where Emersyn is eventually going to end up. I can also lay some groundwork so we can eventually take them down for good."

"You'd be willing to do that?" Deathwing asked.

"I need to find my daughter, Gabriel," I said. "And then I plan on taking down anyone and everyone who ever thought they could take something of mine away from me."

"What does this mean about Vetticus?" Nyx asked.

"Vetticus?" Deathwing asked.

"He's the one responsible for Emersyn being in this situation in the first place," I said darkly. "He took my family and my freedom away from me and until yesterday I thought my daughter was dead. Everything I've done for the last ten years has been to take him down. It's all connected."

Understanding crossed Deathwing's face, and he nodded.

"So we secure your daughter and then go after him."

"We?"

Deathwing smirked, a rare sight. "I think you're stuck with me for at least the foreseeable future, North."

I matched the look on his face and nodded once. "Can't say I'm mad about that, brother."

PRESENT DAY

There will be killing till the score is paid.

HOMER, THE ODYSSEY

90

KAELIN

The silence descended on us, heavy and potent as Theron stopped talking. I watched him throw back the rest of his whiskey and walk over to stand on the terrace looking out over the pool and the rest of the back property. Hours into the story we'd ended up outside—Graham, Theron and I.

And hours is what it took for him to finish telling us everything. My cheeks were wet with silent tears. I tried hard to keep them discrete but there was so much horror in his past, my heart broke with each passing hour.

Graham was tense in his chair, leaning forward heavily on his arms and staring at the concrete between his feet. He knew revenge intimately and I wondered if his own past was rising up from the depths to linger. I didn't even know where to start with trying to wrap my brain around what I'd just heard but I did know that all I felt was a deep ache in my heart for Theron.

He'd introduced himself to me as Kraven but the man who I'd met in the Warren was continually evolving until I really did not know who stood before me now. Theron wasn't who I thought him to be and now that I knew everything—I didn't even know where to begin or what to say to him.

I knew enough to know he wouldn't want sympathy from anyone but it was undeniable that what was going on now was big and very important. I was still a little angry he hadn't asked me to help, but I wasn't about to make it about me.

My eyes bore into Theron's back, noting despite the heaviness of the story he still stood strong and sure, carrying it all with resolve and confidence in his desired outcome.

"I don't even know what to say," I admitted honestly. "So this is what's been going on lately?"

Theron nodded. "We kicked everything off recently by taking out the Atrox board members. We then eliminated the map architects—shut down most of Vetticus' supply lines and we located his partner, Albatron. It's all coming to a head soon—it's time I finish what he started all those years ago."

"So—you think Greg has your daughter?"

"I doubt he knows who she is—or let's hope he doesn't and she's just some number to him—but yes," Theron said. "She's somewhere in the system and Deathwing and I have been trying to find her for the past few years."

"The Warren—" I choked on the word.

Theron turned and took a step towards me. He pushed a strand of hair out of my face, his knuckles brushing against my skin.

"The Warren was all show—mostly," he added with a dark smirk. "You still captivated me and I wasn't expecting that. You should know by now I take what I want—I like control and pushing people's boundaries—but I was telling the truth...I tried to get you out, later. I called Cooper."

I looked up at him, absorbed by the intensity of his gaze.

"T—I'm so sorry—"

His lips sealed over mine and the words died on my tongue.

I knew he didn't want to hear them anyway.

FLASHBACK

THERON

THE WARREN

Palmero's island adventure had been a bust. It was nothing but a place for rich businessmen to legally act out their fantasies. I hadn't seen any trafficking signs there and I hadn't run into Palmero or Mahoney. Now, I was on my plane again but this time I was headed for the Warren. Nyx and Atlas had accompanied me on the plane ride and as we began our descent, I looked out the window at the vast expanse of forest.

"I guess that's one way to ensure your business isn't discovered," Nyx muttered. "Having it in the middle of the wild."

Atlas looked up from his phone. "What's your budget in there?"

"As much as it takes."

Atlas ran a hand over his face. "This is going to be expensive..."

Nyx shrugged. "I mean, since you have to go in and act like you belong there, you might as well have some fun."

"He's going to be raping someone," Atlas said dryly.

"Wellllll," Nyx said. "I mean, the way T does it...at least it's not violent."

"You're justifying this?" Atlas asked, but he was trying to hide a smirk. "After everything all of us have been through?"

"Well, it's not like he has a choice really—he has to make Mahoney believe he's just like him. They have to become besties. And look, T is probably going to be the best thing to happen to some poor girl in there. I saw West's notes on the Warren, I know what kind of dark shit he's about to walk into," Nyx shrugged. "I'm just saying, he's not going to beat his woman to death. Which, unfortunately, I saw is a kink in the brochure. This place has very few rules."

Atlas chuckled. "I guess Red did have a pretty good time and you could consider that rape," he shrugged.

"Exactly!" Nyx exclaimed. "What was it you said one time, T? Manipulate the body and the mind will follow?"

"Something like that," I chuckled.

Shortly after that we landed and I said goodbye to the guys. A sharply dressed man flanked by two armed guards was waiting for me when I disembarked the plane. A blacked out jeep sat behind them gleaming in the sunlight. I threw my aviators on as he walked over and extended a hand.

"Kraven," I nodded and shook his hand. "Welcome to the Warren. I'm here to show you to the facility and get you all checked in."

He took my luggage and we all piled into the jeep which took off down a manicured dirt track through the trees. The drive was maybe five minutes before we pulled up in front of an iron door set into a cliff face. Beautifully crafted forest designs ran from top to bottom and two additional armed guards stood sentry on either side. I followed the man through the door and into a warm, welcoming reception area. He handed my luggage off to another porter and walked around a counter to a computer. A few clicks and he pointed to the counter in front of me.

"Extend your wrist for me there, please. This is a temporary tattoo which will serve as your access key to all necessary areas in the facility."

I did what he instructed and he hovered a device over the inside of my wrist. A white tattoo of a running rabbit appeared. I raised my eyebrows at the man and he chuckled.

"You'll find the owner of this establishment has a specific sense of humor," he said dryly. "Don't worry, it will fade by the time you leave at the end of the week."

He placed an ipad in front of me that had documents pulled up.

"You should have already received a copy of these and signed them, I've pulled them up for you to look over once more. At this time, I do wish to remind you, this place has very few rules and what you may see here could cross over any moral codes you may have. This is a safe place for our patrons to explore their desires without fear of repercussions. This includes accidental—" he gave me a look like accidental was a loose term here. "—death of one of our rabbits. We assume you are here because of your own deviant desires but if this isn't what you expected, now would be the time to back out."

I gave him a look that had a grin ghosting over his face as though that was the usual response to his script.

"Very well. There is a reception dinner tonight and the auction is tomorrow morning. Is there a phone you wish to check in during your stay? Any device connected to the outside world is prohibited. There is a media room you may visit at any time to use it if you'd like but it cannot go outside of that room. We have jammers to ensure this rule is followed."

I shook my head. I'd left my phone with Nyx and Atlas. The tracker I had in me would alert them if I was in distress or needed extraction.

"Everything is included during your stay—including drinks and food and use of all of our many facilities. We understand this place can be quite the maze to navigate so anytime you need directions, you can go up to one of the monitors on the walls and scan your wrist. It will pull up a menu with options on it, including navigation."

He clicked a few more buttons. "It looks like your auction contribution is in the holding account. After the auction, you will sign over whatever amount you bid. If you don't see something you like during the auction, we can select something to your liking from our inventory. We already have your STI panel results and general health screening. If you'll just ensure all of the documentation is to your satisfaction?"

I scanned the iPad, signed and handed it back.

"You have access to your rabbit during designated times and while we do have an itinerary such as dinners, cocktail hours and such, you are more than welcome to pick and choose what to attend. However, I highly recommend attending some of the group events. Watching and sharing is encouraged. Finally, our staff already know who you are and have your preferences memorized as far as food and drinks go. Don't hesitate to ask them for anything."

He put everything away and fixed a customer service smile on his face.

"Any questions?"

I shook my head and he gestured to a door behind him. "Then if you'll follow me, I'll show you to your room."

I walked into my room and discovered the porter had already neatly put away my bags. It was a modest room but with all updated fixtures, a large shower and king sized bed. It felt like a high end resort room, only without the view.

Following the directions the man left with me, I headed for the cocktail lounge. When I walked through the door, I would never have thought this place was underground. It looked like any upscale, dark and sultry speakeasy with black walls, charcoal furnishings and a deep mahogany bar that stretched across one wall with the alcohol bottles alluringly backlit. Soft modern jazz music was playing, providing a relaxed but not lethargic atmosphere. All the seating was comfortable couches, lounges and armchairs surrounding low tables of dark wood. Soft, dim lighting on the wall, interspersed among provocative artwork pulled the entire space together.

"Old fashioned, sir?" The bartender asked.

I nodded and leaned back against the bar, looking over the men already in attendance. A boisterous laugh cut through the general low level of noise in the room. It belonged to a man with a buzz cut in a grey button down with sleeves rolled up and dark dress pants. He noticed my attention and excused himself from the group before walking over and stopping in front of me.

"Cooper," he said, extending a hand.

"Ah, you must be the one behind this white rabbit I have to have on my wrist for a week," I said, amusement in my eyes as I shook his hand.

Cooper laughed. "You know it's funny—the Warren—rabbits—cute, huh? You're Kraven, right?"

"Yes I am." My drink arrived and I grabbed it, taking a sip.

"I want to talk to you at some point about a possible contract."

"You go through a lot of ammo here?" I asked, fixing him with a skeptical look. He laughed again.

"God no, not here. I'm partnered with another company who is always looking for additional suppliers and they go through hundreds of thousands of rounds per month."

"Sure, but I don't make business deals on vacation," I said, winking at him.

He clasped me on the shoulder, that amused grin still on his face. "Of course, of course! Just wanted to put it in your head. We can set up a time to discuss later. What do you think of the place so far?"

"I have to say—having the staff know my preferences is great," I said, lifting my drink to him.

"Only the best for my clients," he chuckled. "And that extends to the product. I'm sure you'll find something to your liking here."

"I have no doubts," I agreed.

"Come with me," Cooper said, gesturing as he turned. "I want to introduce you to some people. Part of the fun is networking at these things."

He led me back to the group of three men he was originally talking to.

"Sorry to interrupt gentlemen," Cooper said. "I wanted to introduce you to Kraven. It's his first time here so I expect you repeat offenders to show him the ropes."

He pointed to a large man, more round than tall with a balding head and beady black eyes. "This is Paul Johnson." His finger jumped to the next man wearing an all black suit with black rings and tattoos peeking out on his hands and up his neck. There was a cruel twist to his mouth that looked permanent. I instantly didn't like him.

"Roger Holdings," Cooper said. Then he pointed to a swarthy forty something man in a crisp suit and calculating brown eyes. "And finally, Greg Mahoney." The man nodded politely, his fingers curled around a martini glass as he studied me. "I'll let you guys chat—dinner will be served shortly."

"What line of business are you in?" Mahoney asked.

"Weapons mostly." I took a sip of my drink. "Some contract work."

"Ex-military?"

I nodded. "Yeah—emphasis on ex. Apparently I enjoy killing people too much." The men chuckled. "What about yourselves?"

"Finance," Johnson said.

"Imports and exports," Roger said. So drugs basically.

I turned to Mahoney. "I deal in people."

There was no smirk, no underlying smugness, he was just stating a fact.

"Most of the product here is courtesy of Mahoney," Roger said.

"Some of the best in my opinion," Johnson offered. "Heard of the Red Auction? That's his."

"I've heard of it," I nodded. "Have to say it does seem intriguing."

"Pretty exclusive," Roger said.

"Knock it off, Roger," Johnson said. "Greg is right here and can invite anyone he wants."

"I respect a man who's tastes are as black as my own," Mahoney said. "But forgive me if I'm wary of strangers."

"That makes two of us," I said easily. "I'm not asking for an invitation."

"It's not that—I just have to be assured you are who you say you are," he shrugged and took a sip of his drink. "Can never be too safe these days. But I'm sure after this week I won't have any doubts."

"You're lucky voyeurism is a kink of mine," I said. Amusement flashed in my eyes as I turned on the charm. "I plan on taking my purchase out to the forest first. You're welcome to watch the show."

"The first meeting is always the most exciting," Mahoney chuckled. "I'll take you up on that."

92

THERON

Kaelin held out her hand for Graham as I went to lead her inside. I felt empty after wandering around in the past and all I wanted was to bury myself in Kaelin and forget again—at least for a little while.

Graham shook his head. "You two go—I need a few."

Kaelin kissed him on the cheek and I touched his shoulder, then I was leading Kaelin upstairs to my bedroom.

The minute the door shut, my hand was around her neck and I pushed her against the back of the door. My lips hovered over hers, sharing air but not quite touching.

"I'll admit I deserved that slap earlier," I murmured dangerously. "But if you ever do that again, you won't like what happens." I nipped at her bottom lip and stared darkly at her, tightening my grip around her neck in warning. "Understand?"

"Yes," she gasped.

Her eyes fluttered as I cut off more of her air. I released the pressure and captured her lips, claiming what was mine. The kiss was searing yet I could feel how wet her cheeks were. I loved her for not giving me sympathy. I loved how she didn't berate me, lecture me or try to turn me away from my path. I loved that she wanted to help—although I hated that part too because I wanted to protect her from people like Vetticus. Especially after everything she'd been through. I loved her confidence in me—

I loved her.

The realization slammed into me. I grabbed behind her thighs and lifted her into my arms. I brought us over to the bed and fell onto it with her underneath me. The love was a physical ache in my chest. It was a yearning to be consumed by her. To live in every part of her being so we were never apart. It was the pull of possession and the ache to never let go. Her fire could burn me and I'd be thankful because it meant she was mine.

We tore each other's clothes off. I couldn't stand any barriers between us. The passion was potent as our kisses went from frantic to deep and soulful.

"I want you," Kaelin breathed against my lips. For once there was no foreplay. Our need to be one overrode everything as she writhed beneath me, begging me again. "Please, T. I need you."

My hard cock pressed against her pussy and I pushed forward—once, twice and then I slid inside her. She sighed in pleasure and kissed me again, her tongue finding mine. I began to move, withdrawing inch by inch, reveling in the friction, the feel of her—not quite wet but getting there. She sucked on my lip and I groaned.

"I will never stop wanting you," I murmured.

My hand slid up her chest and settled on her throat.

"You're mine—now and always." And I meant it with my heart this time.

Her eyes found mine and the green in them was nearly gone—consumed by black, by the shadows—mine—ours. It was a call to my darkness as it bled into hers. We were one and the same and she was calling me home.

Our breathing grew ragged and I couldn't drag my eyes away from hers as we breathed in each other's air. The pleasure erased any and all barriers until all I could see was her vulnerability. The side of her she'd continued to show me, again and again, when all I'd done was push her away. A potent wave of regret washed over me. I wanted to say something to her—to tell her the truth I'd known for a while—but still it stalled in my throat. The words too unused to come easy.

I buried my face in her neck and dragged my lips down to her throat as I picked up the pace. The sounds she was making drove me into a feral state. Her nails dragged grooves down my back as she wrapped her legs around me and pulled me deeper.

I could feel her getting close. The way she clung to me, the way her pussy milked my cock as she chased that feeling of fullness. The way her moans increased as she couldn't contain the pleasure any longer. I was on the edge too—barreling towards it, out of control but this time I was ready. I was willing to fall.

We crashed over the edge together. Her walls contracted around me as she cried out. First a curse, then my name. It was my name that tipped me over a second later and we rode the high that seemed to peak and go on forever.

There was no other state but this—there was nothing else but us.

I rocked into her through it all, slowing as the waves finally receded. I tried to hold my weight off of her but my heart was pounding in my chest as I caught my breath. Her arms stayed glued around me, her face buried in my neck. She went slack underneath me but not before she planted a small kiss on my neck and hummed in pleasure.

Her heart beat against my chest with a fervor that matched my own and I knew the truth: there was no going back—she'd consumed me.

Mind, body—and heart.

93

THERON

The text sent chills racing through me.

Nyx: HE'S HERE

I jumped out of bed and shoved on clothes. Kaelin looked up at me.

"What's going on?"

"I have to go," I said.

"Theron," she growled in warning.

"Don't leave this house," I continued. "West is here—" at the look on her face I paused and came around to her side of the bed. I took her face in my hands. This could be the last time I saw her but I didn't want to think about that and I wasn't about to scare her.

"I'm serious—do not leave this house. But—have West hook you up in his cave and anything you can do to help him I'd appreciate it. He can fill you in."

She lit up and nodded eagerly. "Thank you," she breathed.

I cut her off with a kiss. I went to pull away but she tugged me back for another and looked at me intently like she wanted to say something more. Instead she gave me a knowing smirk.

"Get a few hits in for me," she said. I grinned back as she echoed the words she'd said to me before the Red Rabbit job.

"Good bye, darlin'." I wanted to say more. I wanted to demand she stay safe and tell her how I felt all in one breath. But there wasn't time and saying those three words now was not how I wanted to do it. With a final look over my shoulder, I left the room and raced down the steps. I ran into Graham in the kitchen.

"He's at Elysium."

Graham grabbed his jacket and tossed me the keys to my Aston sitting on the counter.

"Let's roll," he said.

I dialed Nyx as I peeled away from the house, trying really hard not to exceed the speed limit through the neighborhoods.

"Jesus," Nyx answered. "I've been trying to reach you—"

"When did he get there?" I demanded.

"About five minutes ago. He's sitting at the bar with a few men. He's asking for you."

"Has he seen you yet?"

"No."

"Good. Tell Demetrius to clear the bar. Who's there with you?"

"Lach and Atlas," Nyx said.

"Wait for me in the back," I said. "I'll be right there."

The drive to the club felt like it took an eternity. Really it was only fifteen minutes, maybe less since I couldn't help running a few red lights the closer I got. I flew into the back parking lot of the club but the minute I parked, I turned to Graham.

"Are you ready for this?"

"I'm all in—Let's end this."

We walked through the back door of the club and Nyx and Atlas were standing there waiting.

"You good?" I asked them.

Nyx was practically vibrating with adrenaline but he nodded, looking more composed than when I'd spoken to him on the phone. Atlas looked as calm as ever and if I didn't know him as well as I did, I'd think this wasn't affecting him. Except I knew better.

"Lach and Demetrius are clearing the bar," he said.

I headed down the hallway towards the main floor of the club. The smell of alcohol, cigars and perfume from the dancers assaulted me as I rounded the corner and stepped down into the moody lighting of the speakeasy. Lach and Demetrius stood near the front door, speaking quietly to some of my men. But I had eyes only for the man at the bar. He turned and those sinister eyes that haunted me locked on mine with a slow sinister smile on his lips.

"Vetticus," I said, stopping in front of him.

He looked the same as he had a decade ago—the same lithe body, more business man than military. His hair was a little longer, a little grayer and his face had a few more wrinkles, but it was him—the man who'd stolen everything from me. The man who I'd spent every waking hour of the last ten plus years planning my revenge against.

"Kraven," he purred, stepping down from the barstool, he looked me over in appreciation. "Time has been good to you I see." He looked around at the bar. "You've built quite the empire for yourself—all while staying hidden for some time."

"Well, you found me," I said.

He chuckled. "Don't start thinking me a fool now, Kraven," he said condescendingly. "You wanted to be found."

I shrugged. "So did you."

He inclined his head, his smirk stretching to his eyes. "A great reminder of how much we're alike, don't you think? What did you say back then? We break people. Are you still a monster, Kraven?"

When I didn't answer, he gave me a knowing look before he turned his head to take in the space.

"Still trying to play house I see," Vetticus said. "You have quite the family unit going on."

His gaze settled behind me on Nyx and Atlas, and his eyes sharpened. Heat poured through me and I wanted to drag his attention away from them.

"Reaper, Phantom—good to see you two again."

"Can't say I share that sentiment," Nyx said.

"Go fuck yourself, Vetticus," Atlas growled.

Vetticus' eyes crinkled at the edges as he chuckled. He turned his attention back to me.

"Well, I'll cut to the chase," Vetticus said. "I'm here for you. So—here's the part where I say we can do this the easy way...or we can do this the hard way."

Vetticus motioned to his men who moved towards me.

Atlas stepped forward. "He's not going with you."

"I see we're choosing the hard option," Vetticus said easily. "I'm afraid you're outnumbered in this." He pulled his gun out and leveled it at Atlas, then looked over at Demetrius.

"Sorry, North," Demetrius said as he pulled out his own gun and pointed it at me. Viktor, Konstantine and a group of other Bratva stepped out of the shadows, guns pointed at my men.

"Demetrius," I growled. "Why?"

"A better business opportunity presented itself."

"What did he give you?"

"Stakes in the games—exclusivity," Demetrius shrugged. "It's always about money and getting ahead isn't it?"

"Fuck you—Viktor, Kon—seriously?" Nyx snapped.

He made to step forward and Viktor punched him solidly in the jaw. Atlas snarled but Kon pressed the barrel into his face and he stilled.

"Turns out your people aren't as loyal as you thought," Vetticus said, the false sadness on his face at odds with the glitter of amusement in his eyes.

"Cuff him." I heard movement behind me as two men came and yanked my wrists behind my back.

"On your knees," he said forcefully.

I could feel Vetticus' gaze boring into mine. The club was silent, the tension high. My jaw clenched as I slowly sank down onto the ground, my glare locked onto Vetticus. He stepped up to me, the smugness pulling at his lips as his eyes glowed with triumph.

"Ah, I always did prefer you in this position," he said. His hand caressed my jaw and I turned my head away. Vetticus just laughed.

"I told you I'd bring you to your knees before me." Vetticus basked in the moment as he stared at me, then seemed to catch himself and turned to his men, waving his hand over my shoulder. "Line them up."

"Vetticus, you have me," I growled. "Leave my men out of this."

Vetticus just looked at me with a condescending look.

"Come on now, Kraven—where's the fun in that? Besides, it wasn't part of the deal." His men moved towards Atlas, Lachlan, Graham and Nyx. They were restrained and forced to their knees off to one side. His men and a few Bratva stood behind them with guns to their heads.

"What deal?" Nyx asked, his attention jumping from Demetrius to Viktor who had his hand on his shoulder.

"Oh, that's right you wouldn't know," Vetticus chuckled. "You're all going to play in the next game."

Nyx's mouth thinned and his gaze turned murderous but he didn't make any other comments.

"My, my—this is a familiar sight," Vetticus grinned as he walked the line. He ended in front of me again and paused, slowly pulling brass knuckles from his pocket he placed them on his fingers.

"I've waited a long time for this."

He slammed his fist into my jaw. Once, twice—a third time and I collapsed to the ground. The men must have tried to move because I heard barked orders and a scuffle, then I was getting hauled back to my knees.

"Oh yeah," Vetticus exhaled loudly and chuckled. "It feels good to have you back." He walked over to Demetrius and slung an arm around his shoulders. Demetrius stiffened but his face remained unreadable, cold and calculating.

"I'm liking this partnership already," Vetticus said. "Alright, load 'em up! It's time to go!"

I was hauled to my feet and dragged towards the door. The others were given similar treatment but then I heard Vetticus speak.

"Wait," he called. "Bring the Reaper back."

Viktor and Kon shoved Nyx back down to his knees in front of Vetticus and he pointed his gun at him. "Vetticus!" I barked. I took a step towards them but the men hauled me back.

Atlas fought savagely to get free. "No!"

"I think you need a reminder of who's in control," Vetticus sneered. "Pity—but all is fair in love...and war."

Vetticus' finger settled on the trigger.

Demetrius stepped forward and put a hand on Vetticus' arm.

"A show of good faith," he said.

He aimed his own gun at Nyx and pulled the trigger.

Nyx fell backwards into Viktor and Kon and then chaos ensued. Atlas lost his mind. I viciously fought the men holding me—fury and panic rising.

No. No. No.

Atlas was yelling, the look on his face equal parts anger and agony. It took an additional two men to restrain him. Out of the corner of my eye I saw Graham putting up a fight but then go limp as they drugged him. Lachlan was colorfully cursing Vetticus out and struggling against his attackers but he soon was drugged as well. The Bratva obstructed the view of Nyx as Vetticus' men continued to drag me towards the door.

"I'll kill you!" Atlas raged. "I'm going to fucking kill you!"

I watched Vetticus shake Demetrius' hand, ignoring the yelling and general upheaval he'd just caused.

"Pleasure doing business with you. I'll see you soon."

Demetrius' hand snaked out, his eyes cold and dangerous. "Looking forward to it."

Atlas' raging fell silent as he was drugged and I watched as Nyx was dragged away. I felt a prick in my own neck and as everything began to go dark, there was only one thought running through my head: *This wasn't part of the plan.*

FLASHBACK

THERON

THE WARREN

I still hadn't bid on anyone. Greg, Johnson and Roger had all already selected their women and were eyeing me with various looks of curiosity mixed with apprehension.

"I remember my first time," Johnson chuckled as Cooper spoke about the last woman he was going to bring out.

"So many choices," Greg said. "It's hard to choose isn't it?"

I shrugged, swirling my nearly empty glass of whiskey in my hand as it dangled over the edge of the chair.

"Cooper will accommodate you with other options if—" I didn't hear the rest of Greg's sentence because a guard was leading the last woman onto the platform and I couldn't tear my eyes away.

Her eyes were so green I could see them from where I sat and they were filled with fire—more than the other women whose eyes were already dulled with defeat and abuse. I went still as the bidding started, enthralled with watching her fight against Cooper. His hands were all over her but the minute they slid into her pussy was the minute I pressed the button, my jaw clenching.

No one should be touching her but me.

I didn't know where the fuck that thought came from, but a feral feeling rose in me that demanded I make this woman mine. I felt like I knew her. Or something about her called to a part of me I didn't understand or had long laid dormant.

I sat up straighter in my seat, watching her struggle against Cooper. I wanted to be the one she fought against. I wanted to see what she looked like when she was made to come undone. I wanted to get burned by her flame as I coerced her into submission.

I hadn't felt like this about a woman in...over a decade. Maybe Whitney?

But even she hadn't touched this primal desire to claim.

The thought that I shouldn't get distracted from what I'd come here to do popped into my head but even that couldn't calm the obsession building within me. I was going to make this wildfire mine.

I stood in the forest, watching her take it all in. She hadn't noticed me yet and was looking like she couldn't decide if she wanted to bolt or stand around and see what happened next. I stepped out into the clearing.

"You're supposed to run."

She turned quickly, her gaze sweeping me from head to toe and back again, her eyes alight with fire and apprehension. I could smell the fear on her but also the anger that radiated off her in waves. I took a step towards her and she stepped backwards.

I smirked. "Ah, there we go." I took another step and so did she. "If you want a head start, I suggest you go now," I said.

A thrill rushed through me at the prospect of chasing her through the trees and I didn't need to look up at the gallery to know Mahoney was watching me. I was going to have to put on a show although how much of it was for his benefit and how much was the primal need simmering through me, I wasn't sure yet. I could tell she didn't like being told what to do. Her eyes narrowed on me as she quickly decided whether or not she wanted to obey me.

"If you don't run, I have this remote here and I've been told the shock is quite unpleasant. Or Cooper mentioned he has a punishment room we can start out in if that's what you prefer. So you can either run, or we can set my expectations there."

I didn't advance on her again but she got the message and I watched her turn and walk off into the trees. I chuckled at her display of defiance as she pushed her shoulders back and sauntered off, refusing to show me her fear. I was true to my word and waited a moment before heading off into the forest, following her trail easily.

What had started out as something I needed to do to keep up appearances was now something else entirely. I didn't want to catch her too quickly—the sadistic part of me wanted to rile her up so when I did catch her, she'd put up more of a fight. I needed Mahoney to believe I was as fucked up as him.

Right—that's why I wanted to do that.

A short while later I heard a sound in the bushes and Roger stepped out, looking like he'd gotten into a fight with his girl. I nodded to him, barely holding back my distaste for the man as he sneered at me.

"Having fun?" He asked. He nodded to the gallery above us. "Mahoney likes it when you rough them up a bit."

"I'll keep that in mind," I said dryly. I turned my back and walked off. Roger was the kind of person I usually wouldn't associate with at all. The lowest of the low. Someone with no strength of self and would do anything to get ahead. A man didn't have to be good, but trust was something I took seriously and I wouldn't trust Roger with anything.

I made my way through the trees and saw my prey watching another man fuck the woman he'd caught. I crept up and as she turned to go, snaked a hand around, covering her mouth.

"I didn't know my rabbit liked to watch," I said in her ear.

She stomped down on my foot and head butted me in the face in answer. I let her go, grinning to myself as I watched her take off. At least she was making this more fun than I anticipated. I let her think she'd put some space between us but instead I kept close and just watched her as she wandered through the forest. She was never frantic—never panicked, but she was still definitely afraid and when I finally made my move, I startled her so badly she shrieked and jumped away. My fingers just brushed her and she tripped herself up and crashed into a tree. I held back my amusement as I grabbed her and we went down to the ground with me straddling her. She tried to fight to no avail and her strength quickly bled away.

"Tired, love?" I panted with a triumphant smirk. I pressed my hips into hers, pinning her to the ground and ran a hand through my hair. Those killer green eyes glared hatefully at me and then her fist connected with my jaw. The surprise on her face was almost comical but I could tell she was afraid of how I'd react as she went still, waiting for me to retaliate. Instead I barked out a laugh and watched her face tint a pretty shade of pink as anger filled her eyes.

"You've never punched someone before have you?" I stated.

I grabbed her hand. Her wrist felt fragile, like I could break it just by squeezing too hard. She tried to yank out of my grasp but went still when I closed her fingers into a fist and tucked her thumb in. I brought her fist to my jaw.

"Do it like this next time," I said. I released her wrist only to regret it a moment later when she landed a solid punch between my legs. I hissed in surprise and released her enough that she managed to shimmy out from under me. I watched her scramble away and decided I was done playing. I grabbed the remote to her collar and pushed the button. She instantly collapsed as the electricity jolted through her. I stopped it just as quickly and she lay there gasping.

"Well that's definitely useful," I muttered as I straddled her again.

"Don't—touch me," she gasped. I grabbed her chin roughly between my fingers and leaned down towards her. She shrunk away from me, trying to disappear into the dirt under her at the look on my face.

"You can punch me in the jaw all you want, love, but you punch me in the dick again and I'll collar you until you don't know your name."

I watched her glare drop between my legs again and bared my teeth at her, raising the button up with my other hand and hovered my thumb over it. I released her jaw and undid my belt and zipper, pulling out my cock.

"I love the fire though, darlin'," I murmured. I watched her pale slightly and she struggled under me again. I let her escape me, but only so I could grab her ankle and pull her back, still conscious of Mahoney's eyes on me. She bucked and twisted but her struggles were weaker than before and I got a hand around her neck, squeezing hard enough her eyes shuttered. I pushed her knees apart and pressed my cock against her pussy, watching the fight leave her as she struggled to breathe. I loosened my grip and she heaved in a breath.

"Let's see what 5.5 million bought me," I growled. I pushed inside her and watched her eyes close. God, she felt good. Despite her protests, I could feel her getting wet around me. I increased my pace and she struggled again, trying to claw at me. Lost to the moment and the primal lust of taking her in the woods, I slapped her hard across the face and with a shudder she went still, tears leaking from her eyes.

My hand went to her neck again and her weak protests and struggles fueled me to the edge. After I came, I pulled out of her. The dark part of me reveled in her helplessness in that moment and I couldn't find it in me to feel guilty knowing it was a means to an end. I looked up at the gallery and saw Mahoney, drink in hand, watching with a lustful gleam in his eyes.

I redid my pants and brushed the dirt from my clothes as two guards came for her. I didn't linger but headed back into the facility. Despite the rush I'd just experienced, I frowned, irritated with myself for a different reason. This woman called to a part of me I didn't know still existed and I wanted to know why. She made me lose control. I wanted more—like a drug I couldn't shake the habit of. She made me forget about everything but what was happening in the moment. I wanted to capture her fire and drink it in.

I wanted to see what else waited for me in those twin green flames bent on my destruction.

95

THERON

I woke up in a dark space, strung up by my wrists dripping blood down my arm. Déjà vu rushed through me with the memories of the last time I'd woken up in a similar space. It was disorienting for a moment—until I remembered.

Nyx. No. It wasn't true. I refused to believe he was gone.

I heard a door slam and footsteps echoed ominously as they crossed the concrete. Vetticus appeared in front of me, looking me up and down.

"More tattoos, a few more scars—It's almost like you never left," he reached out and traced the one on my face from the Warren. "Still so easy to manipulate though—a bit disappointing honestly."

He moved just out of my line of sight and I heard something slide across a metal surface. He must have a table behind me and sure enough steel bit into my lower back.

"All these years and we're finally reunited," he said. "You know, I did look for you in the beginning." He stepped back around me, dragging the blade as he did, cutting deeply into my skin.

"But then I liked the idea of *you* chasing after *me*—kind of poetic, don't you think? You fought so hard to get away...only to want to find me again."

I looked down to see him raise a scalpel to my chest. His eyes narrowed on where his brand used to sit and he growled his displeasure.

"You cut it out?" He hissed.

I didn't bother answering, I'd cut it out after the Austria job. His eyes took on an intensity that I recognized and I closed my eyes, knowing what was coming. He dug the blade into my skin in a ferocious fervor making first one side of the V and then the other. He repeated the action several times until I groaned in pain.

"I have to admit, I didn't think you'd take this long." He sucked on his lip and shrugged. "But I guess life does tend to get in the way sometimes. That's okay—" He slid his fingers through my blood and grabbed my cock making the chains shiver as I jolted. Vetticus pulled out a syringe and almost lovingly let the needle glide into my neck.

"We have all the time in the world to catch up. Because what you don't seem to get—is the fact that I'm always in control," he murmured.

I braced for what I knew was coming and I gritted my teeth as the heat surged through me. All the cuts he'd made were fire on my skin and the intensity of the V was making me short of breath. His hand on my cock jerked me roughly and his other hand continued to make cuts randomly across my chest and abs.

"You're mine," he purred. "I plan on punishing you for leaving me and then we can start fresh." Against my will, I grew hard under his touch and the sensations of pain and pleasure warred viciously with each other until sweat broke out over my skin.

"Who do you belong to?" He asked.

I bared my teeth and met his gaze. "Never you," I snarled.

Vetticus' anger flared briefly, and he stabbed me in the side with the scalpel. He pulled it out and in quick succession did it four other times in different places. On the fifth, the relief didn't come when he pulled the blade out and he chuckled.

"Broke it already." He tossed the metal handle over his shoulder, sending it clattering off into the shadows. He pressed himself closer to me and his tongue swiped across my jaw and over my lips. I tried to turn my head but he pulled my lower lip into his mouth and bit down on it. The taste of blood burst over my tongue. He sucked the sting away as he kissed me. I let him do it, unable to move.

"Who do you belong to?" Vetticus whispered against my lips. He bit lightly along my jaw and down my neck before biting hard into my shoulder.

"Tell me, Kraven," Vetticus demanded.

"I'm going to kill you," I hissed instead. "Slowly...so I can savor it."

He huffed a laugh and stepped away, his own chest heaving. I could see he was turned on from his efforts. He was covered in my blood and sweat beaded on his forehead as he stared at me.

"Big words for a man who's at my mercy." He shrugged. "We'll try again, tomorrow." He moved a monitor into the center of the room. It showed my men in cells. "You'll be able to watch the game tomorrow night." He came over and roughly patted my face. "I'll make sure you get to see every single one of them die."

FLASHBACK

THERON

THE WARREN

Alright Greg," I said. "Five minutes. No cutting or damaging of my property." I added, my eyes jumped quickly to Roger. The display I'd just witnessed was disturbing to say the least. Roger had just cut up Johnson's girl in a horrific display of knife and blood play.

If you could even call it play. It was torture, pure and simple. I enjoyed the occasional pain and pleasure practice but this was at the expense of the woman who had to be taken away by the guards, barely conscious.

Now, Kaelin was sitting on my lap facing the men, legs spread on either side of mine. I'd been watching Mahoney eye her most of the evening and now was offering him a taste. Her head rested against my shoulder and I ran my hands up her thighs, settling there and feeling her take a few deep breaths after my denial of an orgasm.

I didn't want to share her with Mahoney—I didn't want anyone else touching her—but I knew I could use his interest to my advantage. If a few licks of her pussy built rapport, so be it.

Mahoney came and knelt between our legs, his hands sliding up the inside of her thighs. I heard him moan as he leaned towards her pussy.

As soon as his tongue touched her, she tensed in my arms. I willed my features blank, until his fingers slipped inside her and a sound of distress left her lips. Mahoney's eyes raised to mine and my message was clear—do that again and the deal was over. It was the longest five minutes of my life but once he was done, he sat back, licking his fingers.

"I can see why you spent the big bucks," he said.

97

GRAHAM

The drug made my thoughts slow to formulate as I returned to consciousness. I regretted coming back to reality immediately as the horror of what I'd witnessed hit me.

Nyx—that wasn't part of the plan.

I closed my eyes briefly, pushing the sadness down.

"Graham—" A familiar voice called to me.

I opened my eyes to see Tex in a cell next to me, crouched near the bars.

"Glad you're back with the living man," he said.

I looked around and saw we were in crude cells built into rock. We must be underground somewhere. I turned and Sakari nodded to me on my other side. Across the way was Knox and Lachlan next to Atlas who was still unconscious.

"Gang's all here—wait..." Tex looked around. "Where's Nyx?"

I struggled to my feet, using the wall as support and met Tex's gaze. I shook my head and his face fell. Lachlan was sitting with his head buried in his hands.

"Fuck, really?" he cursed quietly. "What happened?"

"Demetrius..." Lachlan muttered, lifting his head briefly but unable to finish the sentence.

Fucking Demetrius. We thought he was our friend, our ally. Sure, the whole plan was for him to turn North over to Vetticus but killing Nyx was definitely not part of it. I thought back to the conversation I'd been privy to.

"Come on, T," Demetrius said with a knowing smile. "I know the only reason you took over as my supplier all those years ago was for this moment. Hell, I'm positive that's why you saved my brothers in Syria if we want to go back that far."

North smirked. "It worked didn't it?"

"You're lucky you've grown on me," Demetrius said fondly. "Well, go ahead—let me hear it."

North barked out a laugh. "Demetrius, I'm calling in my favor."

The mafia boss chuckled. "I thought you'd never ask. I have to say, ten years is a long time to owe someone. I'm ready to even the score."

"After this I'll probably owe you," North admitted.

"I'm looking forward to it," he said. "So what's the plan?"

"The plan is to take down Vetticus piece by piece. Provoke him into action. He's been in hiding for awhile and the only way to get to him is to draw him out. We took down the board members, we have plans to take down the architects of the maps, disrupt his supply lines and finally lure Albatron into showing his face. He's the other big player."

"Where do I come in?" Demetrius asked.

"I need you to betray me."

Demetrius' eyebrows shot up. He leaned forward in his chair, steepling his fingers in front of him.

"Go on."

"Vetticus has only ever wanted one thing: Me. He won't be able to resist if you dangle me in front of him. I need you to turn me over to Vetticus—tell him where I'll be—pull him into making the first move. It's the only way we can get to him. Have him give you an Atrox team—then we can take him down during the next game. Knowing him like I do, he'll want the rest of my team too. If everything goes to plan, we'll all be on the inside for the next game and can take it all down."

"It wasn't part of the plan..." I muttered.

We were supposed to be taken, sure, but not killed. Vetticus had told Demetrius he was going to use us in his upcoming game. I'd heard the phone conversation shortly after the fight with Kaelin. North and I had gone to see Demetrius again.

"You're a hard man to get a hold of," Demetrius said.

"Well, when the Russian pakhan wants to get a hold of me, I make an exception," Vetticus said. "What can I do for you?"

"I saw the calling card you left at Elysium," Demetrius said. "I don't want to get caught up in a long standing feud. Bad for business you understand."

"Perfectly," Vetticus said. "But anyone associated with Kraven is bound to get burned eventually. I can't be held responsible for anyone caught in the crossfire." Demetrius paused and looked over the desk at me and North who sat listening quietly.

"What if I told you I could give you North?"

Vetticus was silent for a beat.

"I'm listening," he said.

"Like I said—I don't like things interfering with my business," Demetrius explained.

"I was under the impression you two were—friends," Vetticus said. "This would be a pretty big betrayal."

"We were. And it will. But I have to do what's right for me in the end and our partnership has...let's just say it's nearly run its course. I'm looking to explore other avenues."

"Let's hear the price then," Vetticus chuckled.

"I want exclusive rights to your supply line," Demetrius said. "With competitive commissions of course."

"Of course," Vetticus agreed. "Anything else? I can throw in an Atrox team if you're interested."

Demetrius smirked and locked eyes with North. "That would be acceptable—when is the next game?"

"You're in luck. It's in a week—I'll accept those terms—if you also throw in the rest of Kraven's crew. I think putting them in this next game would be very lucrative."

"Done."

"When do you want to do the deal?"

"He'll be by the club Elysium in two days."

I was pulled out of my thoughts as I saw Atlas stir in his cell. He surged up, stumbled to his feet, and frantically gripped the bars. He shook his head, trying to clear it and took a few steps, muttering to himself. He slammed his fist against the rock wall behind him, a sound of anguish leaving him.

"Atlas..." I said his name, but I didn't really know what to say to him.

He ignored me, turned his back to the bars and slid down them before burying his face in his hands. He went still and Tex and I exchanged a worried look. If this wasn't going to plan, was anything else going to go as planned? Or was this just a disaster waiting to blow up?

I'd been ready to help North with his revenge because I understood all too well how far someone was willing to go for the people they love. I had to go through what I went through for my brother—I understood why North had to do this. While some of what I did in my past weighed heavily on me, I couldn't imagine not having gone through with it. I didn't regret anything and I hoped North could say the same. Even though I asked him if it was worth it—that would be like trying to tell me the same thing after watching my brother get dragged away. It would be like trying to tell me to move on while I was holding his dead body. Men like us just didn't work that way.

"Now what?" Knox asked grimly.

"Now we find a way to get out before the game starts," I said.

FLASHBACK

THERON

THE WARREN

K raven!" I turned and saw Cooper jog to catch up to me. "Hey man, I can't have you killing my customers," Cooper said although he didn't look overly concerned. "It's bad for business."

I started walking again. It hadn't even crossed my mind to let Roger live when I saw on the cameras what he was doing to Kaelin. I'd run out of that room with murder on my mind.

"I warned him not to touch my property," I said.

"Technically, she's my property," Cooper said as he fell into step with me.

"Until I leave here, my 5.5 million says otherwise," I said dryly.

He chuckled and nodded. "That's fair—you know what you signed up for though. Some of the men who come here have...unique tastes in kinks."

"What did you think I would do when I saw him torturing her?"

"Join in?" Cooper smirked and shrugged. My lip curled in disgust and his eyes glittered dangerously like he'd caught me in a lie. "Why are you here if you're not a sadist?"

"Who said I wasn't?"

"Alright, I guess I don't know what you do behind closed doors but Kaelin doesn't have any marks on her."

I stopped and turned fully to him. "I don't need to make my woman bleed to derive pleasure from pain," I said with contempt. "Is this a new thing? Questioning your client's kinks?"

Cooper held up his hands. "Nah, man, I'm just making sure you knew what you signed up for."

"There are other ways to torture someone."

He tilted his head slightly and studied me for a long moment before nodding and the sly twinkle was back in his eyes as he shrugged.

"I suppose there's truth in that."

I turned and started walking again.

"Remember—she's not yours, Kraven," Cooper said.

I didn't turn back, but those words made something dark twist inside me. Something that I pushed away because in less than five days I shouldn't be feeling anywhere near as possessive as I felt about her.

"And no more killing!" He called louder before I rounded a corner of the hall.

Cooper was lucky I didn't string Roger up and play with him like he'd played with Kaelin. A slit throat and a quick death was me being merciful.

The brutality against the innocent I witnessed here was a kind of darkness you didn't come back from. But it was not in me to play savior—it never crossed my mind to save any of these women—that is until I saw a pair of livid green eyes storm onto the auction block.

The dragon inside me had taken one look at Kaelin and said: Mine.

I hadn't expected to get in this deep and I certainly hadn't come here for pussy, but now I found myself distracted—intrigued even. I wasn't a good man. I would always take what I want—and Kaelin was no exception.

"Heard Roger won't be joining us," Mahoney said.

We were standing at the bar in the cocktail lounge. It was our last night in the Warren and anxiety crawled through me at the prospect of leaving Kaelin here. I grunted in answer as I picked up my whiskey and took a sip. I watched Mahoney over the rim of my glass but he was smirking at me knowingly.

"He won't be missed," Mahoney continued.

I shrugged. "He touched my property without permission."

Mahoney's gaze sharpened on me and after a moment he inclined his head and regarded me thoughtfully.

"You and I are a lot alike," he said. "I think you would benefit from attending one of my auctions."

"Oh?" I tilted my head in amusement. "I thought you didn't take kindly to strangers?"

A rumble of a laugh escaped Mahoney. "This week has been very illuminating. I admire a man who can use his mind as a weapon, just as powerfully as he can use his hands."

We sipped in silence for a moment before Mahoney spoke again.

"We should get together for a drink soon," he said. "I'll be in Europe for a few months sourcing for my next auction. You should join me for some of it."

"Sure," I nodded. "Send me the details."

We talked for a few more minutes before I excused myself and headed back to Kaelin. I'd accomplished my goal—get close to Mahoney. I now had an invitation to not only the Red Auction but also to see more of his inner circle.

Mission accomplished.

Now, all I wanted to do was spend these last moments with Kaelin. I wish I could just walk out of here with her, but it wasn't going to be that easy. Cooper would protest—and my groundwork with Mahoney would go out the window. I would have her—it would just take a little more planning and I was nothing if not patient.

99

THERON

When Vetticus returned some time later, he came and stood in front of me. I'd been in and out of consciousness for hours. If he kept this up, I wouldn't be in any shape to fight my way out.

"You always did bleed so pretty for me," he said hungrily. "And I will never forget the night you truly submitted to me. You know—the night you hurt your daughter."

I glared at him with as much hate as I could muster. I spit blood onto the ground at his feet.

"You looked at me and that defiance was gone—snuffed out—" He sighed wistfully. "It was what I should have been doing since the beginning but silly old me seems to enjoy getting burned. Plus, I love a good fight."

He punched me in the gut and the air left me in a groan as I tried to double over but couldn't. I swayed in the clutches of the chains as he punched me again, this time in the jaw. Vetticus walked around me, delivering hits as he went.

"You belong to me. I want to hear you say it."

Another hit to the ribs.

"Who do you belong to?" He said louder.

A hit to the face. "Tell me, Kraven!"

When I stopped swinging, I lifted my head and leered at him, an unhinged laugh bubbling up. Vetticus' lip curled as I continued to wheeze in amusement.

"I will—never belong—to you," I gasped out.

Vetticus' lip curled in irritation and he walked back around behind me.

"I'll beat it out of you then," Vetticus said.

The pain that lanced through me made my back bow. He landed blow after blow, the whip digging into my skin and flaying it open with each hit.

"Who do you belong to?"

He yelled after each stroke and I soon lost count, going in and out of consciousness. When he finally stopped, I didn't realize he was back in front of me until his hand gripped my jaw and his crazed look swam into view.

"I don't know why you insist on making this so difficult," he ground out between his clenched teeth. "I was going to save this for later, but I have one more surprise for you," he panted.

He motioned to the monitor and a dual screen came up. One side showed my men in cells and the other—I squinted at it, willing my vision to sharpen.

"Fuck you!" I rasped.

Kaelin was in a cell, hands cuffed in front of her. I was relieved to see she didn't look like she'd been touched and the look on her face was calm and resolute. My hands balled into fists above me and the pain seemed a distant dull sensation as fury rolled through overpowering it.

"I thought you'd like that one," Vetticus said. "It'll be a pleasure to get rid of her in front of you. Or maybe I'll keep her as a pet—she did after all design the drones I love to use. Either way, I was right again...she does look good in a cage."

This time when Vetticus left, he released the chain, and I fell to the ground. The chain dropped heavily down around me as I landed in the pool of blood beneath me. I passed out for who knows how long. When I came to, I lay there and dug my fingers into the cut at my side where the blade of the scalpel had snapped off. I growled as pain lanced through me but I managed to pull it out and got to work picking the lock holding the chains around my wrists.

I pulled myself up using the table, toppling the monitor that still showed my men in their cells. Good, I wasn't too late. I needed to get them free before the games started.

The room spun dangerously. I hadn't expected to be this fucked up. I thought Vetticus would just take his rage out sexually instead of physically but there wasn't any way around it now. I stumbled my way to the door. I put my hand on the knob and took a few deep breaths as I gathered my strength, then I ripped the door open.

Two guards looked at me in surprise. I dropped them before they could alert anyone and yanked a comms unit off one to stick in my ear. Chatter assaulted me instantly.

"She fucked with the drones!" Vetticus raged over comms. "Bring her to me!"

An array of emotions hit me. First pride, then worry, followed by anger. I told her not to leave the house. But was I surprised?

No. Not at all.

One of the guards was about my size and I pulled his shirt and pants off, putting them on, then relieved them of any guns and ammo. I stood up just in time to see another pair of guards round the corner. I shot the first one but the second one shouted into his comms unit before I took him down.

Despite the guard sounding the warning, I made it down to the cells without incident. They were located deep into the mountain under the house. I took down the man guarding the door and lifted the keys to the cells off him. On the other side of the door, I let my eyes adjust to the gloom and followed the muted voices.

"What the fuck?" Knox exclaimed as I came into view. "North?"

"Hey boys," I rasped. Knox's cell door swung open as I unlocked it and I moved to Graham's.

"You look like shit," he said dryly.

My lips twitched in as much of a smile as I could muster. I clasped him on the shoulder as he walked out of his cell and quickly released Tex and Lachlan. Atlas was last and he was standing at the door of his cell, eyes haunted and empty.

"Atlas—"

"Let me out, North," he rasped. His voice didn't even sound like himself. The minute I unlocked the cell, he shoved past me and made a beeline down the hall.

"Atlas!" I called.

"Atlas, wait!" Lachlan said.

"I'm going to kill him," he shouted and then he was gone.

"Fuck," I muttered.

"What's the play, boss?" Tex asked.

I turned to look at Graham. "He has Kaelin."

100

ATLAS

I killed three guards who ran by as I stepped out of the stairs leading down to the cells. I slung an AR over my shoulder, shoved two pistols into my pants and loaded up on ammo. A calmness had settled over me the minute North let me out of my cell. I was going to kill Demetrius and then I was going to find Vetticus and kill him too.

Fuck North and his plan.

I was done.

Vetticus had stolen too many people from me. I would end him and then I would probably end myself. I didn't think—no I knew, I couldn't live without Nyx. As I made my way down the hallway, it was as though all my emotions had been switched off. I didn't feel fear, anger or even grief—just a solid resolve to remove anyone who stood in my way.

I fought through a few groups of guards who were obviously in disarray, running through the house. I didn't have a plan. I wasn't thinking. I was just executing—killing my way to my goal.

Nyx had been everything to me. We'd gone through so much together.

Too much for him to just be…gone.

Two guards rounded a corner and I took a few hard hits this time before I killed them. I pushed myself to my feet and there rounding the same corner was Demetrius with Viktor and Kon behind him. I snarled and raised my gun at him.

"You mother fucker," I yelled.

"Atlas—"

"No, fuck you! Why'd you kill him?" I could feel my calm exterior cracking. Emotions were bleeding through, forcing it wider. I felt raw, broken.

"Atlas, wait—"

"He's gone," I said, my voice breaking.

"I can explain," Demetrius said calmly.

"I don't want to hear it," I hissed. My eyes blurred with tears and I shoved the gun at him. "You were supposed to be on our side."

"Atlas," Viktor barked. "Put the gun down."

"Fuck you, Viktor," I cried. "Fuck both of you for turning on us...after everything we've been through—"

My finger tightened on the trigger.

"Atlas!"

I froze. *That voice.* The Volkov brothers were looking over my shoulder at who had spoken.

"Put the gun down."

I'd know that voice anywhere—but how—

I slowly turned around, the gun dropped loudly onto the ground and then I was rushing towards Nyx—who was standing at the other end of the hallway—very much alive. My hands found his face as though I didn't truly believe he was real.

"Fuck," I breathed and pulled him to me. We clung to each other. It could have been hours or only a few seconds before I was able to pull back enough to look at him.

"How?" I asked. "Demetrius shot you!"

"Well, obviously he didn't," Nyx grinned.

"You looked dead," I insisted.

Nyx chuckled. "Nice little improv there actually. It was obvious Vetticus was going to shoot me so Demetrius just pretended to. Luckily, Viktor and Kon were next to me because they pulled me backwards and one of them whispered 'play dead' in my ear—"

I didn't let him finish. My lips crushed his and I shoved him up against the nearest wall. He dug his fingers into my skull, matching my intensity. Tongue and teeth clashed as we tried to consume each other. Finally I rested my forehead against his to try and catch my breath. My hand grabbed under his jaw and my thumb caressed his lips.

"I thought I'd lost you," I murmured.

"That part killed me," Nyx said quietly. "I knew you'd think I'd really died. I was hoping you wouldn't do anything stupid but here you are, about to kill the Volkovs—"

"Yeah," I scoffed. "You got here just in time. I was going to do it too."

"I love you," Nyx chuckled and shook his head.

"What?"

"Everytime I say those words, they just fall so short of what I really mean."

"What do you mean?" I whispered, pulling back enough to meet his darkening gaze.

"You are more than just my partner, Atlas. You are part of my heart, part of my soul. I never thought I'd find a love like this—much less a love like this with a man," he smirked. "Even after all these years, I still don't know what this is—all I know is 'I love you' fails miserably to describe how I feel when I'm with you." He smirked at me and bit his lip playfully. "But since I obviously can't proclaim my love through an essay of words each time, I think 'I love you' will just have to suffice."

"I don't know...I kind of like the declaration," I grinned and pulled his lip out from his teeth with my thumb. "You know what that does to me, my dark one."

"And once again, we don't have time," Nyx chuckled.

"Then I'll save my declaration of love for later," I grinned. "But I hope you know I feel the same way—I love you—and there is no life worth living without you."

101

KAELIN

TWO DAYS AGO

What the fuck are you doing here?"
I drew my gun as I stormed into the War Room, leveling it at Demetrius who was sitting at the table like he owned the place. Viktor moved towards me but Demetrius held up his finger, his hands resting calmly on the table. His lips twitched, and he had the balls to look at me like something was amusing him.

"You betrayed, Theron!" Tears clouded my eyes and my voice wavered. "You—you killed Nyx!"

How did I know this? I'd gotten curious. I wanted to know where Theron and the other guys were going. So I did what anyone with my skill set would do. I hacked into their trackers, found out they were going to Elysium and then watched the entire thing go down. Unfortunately, it wasn't live—or I might have done something reckless.

Afterwards, I was devastated and pissed to say the least. I'd gotten up to search out West only to hear the front door open and see on the security feed it was none other than Demetrius himself. Now, here I was, gun leveled at the person I saw kill Nyx and give Theron up to who I can only presume was Vetticus.

Kon edged his way around the table, and my eyes flashed to him.

"Don't even fucking think about it," I snarled.

"I assure you, my dear, I did nothing North didn't ask me to do," Demetrius stated. "Although I will admit, killing Nyx was not part of the plan—"

"I can't believe you'd do this—"

Before Demetrius could respond, the front door slammed open.

"Honey, I'm home!"

I recognized Knight's voice and a moment later heard him speak from the doorway.

"Whoa, Killer—maybe not a good idea to take out the leader of the Russian mafia, yeah? We need him. Also, we've grown kind of fond of him—"

I turned just in time to see him wink at Demetrius.

Then another familiar face rounded the corner.

"Why is it every time I see you, you have a gun pointed at one of our own?"

Cal's dimples popped as his gaze swept me from head to toe and back again. Ghost appeared behind him and gave a little wave.

"He killed Nyx and betrayed Theron," I snapped, not finding any of this amusing.

"He did what now?" Knight looked over my shoulder.

"He betrayed Theron—" Knight waved his hand, disregarding my words.

"I know that part. What's this about killing Nyx?"

"If I may—" Demetrius said, but a voice from the doorway interrupted him.

"Man, I'll admit, it's very flattering to see you avenging my death, Killer."

I whirled around and there was Nyx, standing in the doorway, drinking a beer and looking at the gun in my hand with a crooked grin on his face.

"I'm very much alive, baby girl," he said with a wink. "You can put the gun down."

"Oh my god," I exclaimed. I rushed into his arms, colliding with him so hard he stepped back into the wall with a chuckle. I buried my face in his neck.

"Thank god," I breathed, my voice breaking. "Oh my god—fuck—Atlas must—"

His face fell as I disentangled myself from him.

"Yeah, no help for that I'm afraid. I just hope he doesn't do anything stupid until I can get to him."

"Okay, I missed a lot apparently," Knight said. "But now that we've established everyone is alive, we have some logistics to go over."

"Care to fill me in so I don't accidently kill someone I'm not supposed to?" I said dryly. The men exchanged looks.

"Oh no—don't you fucking dare shut me out," I said. "We're all going to sit down at this table and you are going to fill me in on everything because I'm involved now. We're beyond pretending I'm some damsel you need to protect behind your fortified walls."

"North will literally kill us if something happens to you," Knight said. "And I wish I was kidding."

My jaw clenched. "I don't think anyone here really understands what it is I do." I looked around the table in annoyance. "For example, how were you planning to combat the massive fleet of drones Vetticus has? I'd like to remind everyone that I designed them. West can't hack them. You need me."

"It's not that I can't," West said indignantly as he appeared behind Knight. "It would just take me more time than we have."

"There you have it," I said. "You're stuck with me." I sank down in the nearest chair at the table and looked across at Demetrius.

"I'm sorry I almost killed you."

Demetrius inclined his head, letting his grin appear. "I expected nothing less from you."

"Fine, fine, I always did like living on the wild side," Knight huffed, slipping into a chair next to mine. Cal shook his head in resignation and together with Ghost, Nyx and West, everyone took a seat around the table.

I pulled up a screen on a monitor on the wall and showed them a bunch of glowing red dots.

"Those are all drones," I said.

"Wait—" Knight said. "You mean to tell me you already hacked the drones?" I just stared at him until he ran a hand over his face and looked over at Cal.

"He's going to kill me," Knight grumbled.

"Okay, so that means you've found where Vetticus is holding them?" Cal sat up straighter.

I nodded. "Yes—" I turned back to the screen.

"Were you able to gain control of them?" West asked.

"Not exactly."

"What does that mean?" Knight asked, looking suspiciously at me.

"I can track them and hack into their live feeds, but—"

"Why do I just know I'm not going to like this," Knight said.

"I have to be on the inside to deliver the kill code," I admitted.

Knight looked over at West who held up his hands in surrender.

"Don't look at me, she designed them."

"They're military—they are meant to be impenetrable. Even my back door doesn't have the ability to deliver a complete kill code. It would take me a lot longer to truly hack them. It's faster if I can just get inside and take control there."

"No," Cal stated.

"Yeah, I have to agree," Knight said. "North will kill us. Have I mentioned that already?"

"And then Graham will come down to hell and resurrect us and do it again," Cal agreed. "Ghost can do it."

Ghost nodded. "Just show me what I need to do."

I stared at the men around the table. There was no use fighting against the resolve I saw on all of their faces. They wanted me to stay home.

Fine. I'd let them think that. But there was no way I was going to leave this up to someone who didn't know these drones. I didn't doubt Ghost's ability, especially once I put the kill codes in his hands, but it was the principle. I wanted to help. I wanted to show Vetticus that when you mess with one of us, you got all of us.

"Sure." I pasted a strained smile on my face and while Knight looked at me suspiciously, I pushed my computer closer to Ghost to show him what I was doing.

Several hours of planning and coding later, Demetrius looked at his watch and stood up.

"We have to get going." He nodded to Viktor and Kon. "Vetticus is expecting us shortly."

Cal and Knight stood up and shook his hand.

"Good luck in there," Knight said.

He did the same with Viktor and Kon. I stood up and nodded to Demetrius but I gave Viktor a hug.

"Be careful." I looked up at him in concern. "You too," I said to Kon, grabbing his hand.

"We will, *lisichka*," Viktor said. Kon tapped me on the nose with as much of a smile as he usually had which was more of a twitch of his lips.

"Be safe," Demetrius said as he passed me.

The look on his face was one of knowing and he had a sly glimmer in his eyes as though he could see the plan I had to sneak off and join the fun. He placed a hand on my shoulder and winked. Nyx met him in the doorway.

"Thanks for the save," he smirked. "I owe you one."

"Just make sure you find Atlas before he finds us," Demetrius said in amusement as he shook Nyx's hand and then he was gone.

"Alright team," Knight said. "Let's get organized. We leave in a few hours."

I raided Theron's room, finding another shoulder holster as well as ones to go on my thigh and boot. Along with my gun, I snuck down to the armory and loaded up on another two handguns, a few knives and enough ammo in case I ran into trouble. I covered it all up with a leather jacket, threw my hair up and made sure I stashed my drives where I wouldn't lose them. I didn't necessarily need them, but it would make everything faster if I had them.

I'd made a show earlier, going on about how I was mad I didn't get to come. I stormed off in a rage and locked my bedroom door so the men would think I was holed up sulking. Instead, I'd hopped the fence and was currently in an Uber to the airport.

Thankfully when we pulled up to the airstrip, I didn't see any of the men's SUVs. The pilot was busy doing pre-flight and it was the perfect opportunity to sneak onboard. I hid in the closet in the back cabin and waited.

It felt like forever, but it couldn't have been more than an hour before I heard the SUV approach and the men got out. I could hear Knight bantering with Nyx and Cal's occasional laugh but otherwise they worked quickly to load the plane.

Once we were airborne I tried to relax for a bit, knowing the flight would be a few hours. The airport we were flying into was small, private and remote so I'd called in a favor to an associate and had him leave a car for me. Perks of having contacts with PMCs—they didn't ask questions.

The flight went off without a hitch and soon I was off the plane and in the car. I pulled up the men's trackers and followed them at a comfortable distance in order not to be noticed. A mile out from the staging area, I ditched the car and hiked the rest of the way in. My plan was to stay hidden nearby until the last second and go in without anyone noticing, but that all went to shit a few hours after my arrival.

Creeping through the trees in the dark, I went into the woods to take care of business. It was on the way back a hand closed around my mouth and I was yanked hard against a very solid chest of muscle. I quickly realized who it was and elbowed him lightly in the side.

"I knew you'd pull some shit like this," Knight complained.

"I couldn't let you guys have all the fun," I said, once he'd dropped his hand.

He huffed a laugh and let me go. When I turned to face him, I could see the humor in his eyes.

"I don't blame you," he said. "You're gonna get me in trouble though."

"T doesn't have to know," I said, folding my arms across my chest.

Knight scoffed and nodded his head for me to follow as he exited the treeline and made his way towards the main tent. "That's cute—this is his deal, of course he's going to find out."

I entered the tent behind Knight.

"We have a stowaway boys," Knight announced.

Cal looked up from the gun he was cleaning and groaned.

Ghost just laughed and West didn't even turn around from his computer.

"And you're surprised she's here, why?" West grumbled.

"You're off the hook, Ghost," I smirked.

"How'd you even get here?" Cal asked, then turned to Knight. "She's not going in there."

Knight ran a hand over his face and threw up his hands. "Then you'll probably have to tie her to something, Cal, because there's no way she's going to listen. It's probably better if she comes, that way we can keep an eye on her."

"Or we could put her right back on that plane," he grumbled, fixing me with a look.

"Now that's just silly," I scoffed. "I'm here and I'm not that girl you found in the forest, Cal," I said.

We stared at each other for a long moment. I'd been a wreck when they'd found me and Graham. That had been a dark time for me. Nearly two years later I was stronger and much more capable than I was back then.

"Fine—but you stick with one of us at all times," Cal said.

Nyx walked into the tent and stopped in his tracks when he saw me. "Oh hey, baby girl, fancy seeing you here." A slow smirk took over his features. He chuckled and looked at Knight. "He's definitely going to kill you."

102

KAELIN

Cal led the way towards the house. It was the grey before the dawn and everything had a muted quality to it. A heavy fog rested across the landscape with the dark green treetops poking through. It was haunting and beautiful—the calm before the horror that would inevitably ensue.

Knight had received the signal from Demetrius. The games would start in an hour and our job was to help him clear the mansion and find a man named Albatron. Well, their job. Mine was to find the server room and plant the kill codes for the drones so that when the games started, the drones would first be transferred over to West's control and then rendered useless. We carefully made it into the house where we parted ways with Nyx who went off to find the others, specifically Atlas. He kissed my cheek.

"Give 'em hell," he said with a wink.

We entered the first room and ran into trouble immediately. Cal and Knight had to go after one of the guards who tried to get away and Ghost was just finishing knifing a second when a third rushed out from the back room. I didn't want to use my gun yet...so far the men had been silently using their knives—so I pulled mine out and intercepted him.

"Intruders in the—" I didn't let him finish his report over comms. I brought him to his knees and shoved the blade into his neck. When I looked up Cal, Knight and Ghost were watching me.

"Shit," Ghost muttered. "Gigs up." He pulled the comms unit off one of the dead men and put it into his other ear. Cal and Knight did the same.

"Get to the server room," Cal ordered. "Ghost, go with her."

Ghost and I made our way through the house. The server room was off the main control center so when we got to the doors, there were two guards posted outside. Ghost leaned out into the hallway and using his handgun with a silencer, shot both men. He motioned for me to follow him and we settled on either side of the door. He opened the door just enough to peek inside and signaled to me.

Two men. Take right.

Ghost shoved open the door and he shot the left. I didn't hesitate but shot the guard on the right and we moved into the server room. While Ghost watched my back, I pulled out my phone and the drives and got to work.

A short time later, I heard Ghost curse.

"Shit, they're sweeping this wing, we need to go," Ghost said.

"Alright—almost done," I muttered. "Just transferring control over to West." I set the countdown on the kill code and pocketed my phone and the drives. I nodded to Ghost. "Let's go."

We made it as far as the door of the server room before guards streamed in and immediately started to fire at us. Ghost returned fire, shoving me around a corner. Both sides were pinned down with bullets flying everywhere.

"We need to move," Ghost growled. He leaned out and delivered a barrage of bullets, taking that moment to look towards the exit.

"On my go, run," he glanced at me briefly.

"What about you?"

He didn't answer, simply poked back out and yelled at me to go. I didn't hesitate, knowing better than to ask questions. Staying low I sprinted to the door, flying through just as bullets bit into the wood frame. I slammed into the bank of security monitors, barely catching myself on one of the chairs. I turned back to run and help Ghost when an arm wrapped around my neck from behind.

My gaze connected with Ghost and then I was fighting to get out of the hold. Somehow I got out of the man's grip—whether it was training or a miracle, I didn't know—and quickly put a bullet in his head. I tried to get a second one off as another guard came at me but he was too fast and knocked the gun away. A hard hit stunned me long enough for him to disarm me entirely. A second hit sent me to the ground. My ears rang, the gunfire sounded muted and I heard yelling. I looked up and the last thing I saw were the guards standing over an unresponsive Ghost before everything went black.

FLASHBACK

THERON

ROME, ITALY

It killed me to leave Kaelin. But the thought of finding my daughter overrode everything—even though I knew I was probably leaving Kaelin in some asshole's careless hands. I wanted nothing more than to take the men I had with me and take her from Cooper by force but I didn't have time.

My team picked me up at the Warren and Nyx immediately filled me in on a message Deathwing had sent. He'd scheduled a raid and he'd heard someone matching Emersyn's description may have been there—may still currently be there. So that's where we were headed.

We landed in Rome, and Deathwing was waiting for us with a blacked out SUV on the airstrip.

"How was the Warren?" He asked as we greeted each other.

"He found himself a girl," Nyx said over my shoulder.

Deathwing raised his eyebrows at me, something close to a smile pulling at his lips as he greeted Nyx and Atlas next, before nodding to West and Lachlan behind them.

"That's unexpected," he said.

"Tell me about it," Nyx continued. "Apparently we have to extract her though. Cooper is holding on a bit too tight."

"Well, if you need help, let me know," he gestured to the SUV, and we all piled in. "What else did you find?"

"I laid the groundwork with Greg and should have an invitation to the next Red Auction."

"First name basis already?" Deathwing glanced over at me as he pulled out of the airport. "You move fast. You sure you don't want to come work for me?"

We got to the safe house and Deathwing led us immediately into a large room for a briefing.

"Gentlemen," he said, addressing his team of men already gathered around. He pointed to two floor to ceiling screens where Rune had the mission specs pulled up. "This specific operation distributes to Palmero and Mahoney, however there are also a few middlemen we've seen come and go. North and his team are here to assist—it's rumored his daughter may have been sighted in this den."

Deathwing went over the mission plans and the directives which were to sweep the warehouse, take one or two of the men captive for questioning and then send the recovery and clean-up crew to take care of the girls and sweep the place for all information.

"We move out tomorrow at 0600," Deathwing said. "Dismissed."

The next morning, I stood at a table in the safe house aggressively cleaning and loading my guns. I was trying to keep myself under control when all I wanted to do was to storm the place immediately. Screw guns, I wanted to get at these people with my bare hands. Just the thought of how Emersyn could be in there right now was driving me insane. But this was Deathwing's operation, and I knew better than to let my emotions dictate my actions. As much as I wanted to go rogue, that would only get me and my men killed.

The rest of my team had arrived late last night and I nodded to Tex, Sakari and Knox who were inventorying their own weapons and making friends with Deathwing's crew. I felt Nyx's eyes on me from across the table where he was cleaning and readying his own guns—a lot less aggressively. I looked up, and he raised his eyebrows, a ghost of a smile on his lips.

"You good?"

I finished with my AR and started loading bullets into a mag.

"What do you think?" I growled.

His face grew hard, and he nodded. "I can't imagine how you must feel. If it was my sister I thought was in there—" He shook his head.

I sighed and put everything down, resting both palms flat on the table and leaning over it.

"My nerves are shot," I admitted.

"I know, that's why you have Atlas and me at your back," he said, his grin back in place. "We'll be there in case you need to unleash hell."

Atlas walked up and slung an arm around Nyx's shoulders. He leaned in and whispered something to Nyx that made his eyes shadow and the barest hint of *color stain his cheekbones.*

"Fuck," Nyx breathed. "Promise?"

He turned to Atlas and bit his lip as he looked at him. Atlas brought his thumb to Nyx's lip and pulled it out of his teeth.

"Don't do that," Atlas said gruffly. "Makes me want to do naughty things and we don't have time."

"We always have time," Nyx said.

"Jesus, you two," I teased. "Get a room."

Atlas chuckled and looked over at me. "Don't worry, we'll grab your girl on the way home. Then you won't be so salty."

"You think she'd let us join in?" Nyx perked up, looking way too excited about that prospect. He held up his hands. "Or watch, I'm not picky."

"She's known him for five days," Atlas said. "Let them get to know each other more before we insert ourselves."

"I mean, T did say he wouldn't be opposed to finding a girl we could all share. It was pretty hot with Red," Nyx insisted. "With T ordering us around and everything—"

His grin was contagious, and I shook my head, unable to hide my own anymore.

"We'll see how it goes," I muttered.

Somehow both of them always got me back on track and calmed me down which I knew was their intent all along.

We swept through the dingy warehouse. It was dark and stuffy and smelled like sex, fear and death. Deathwing and I were in lead pushing through the main door. There were also two teams going through the back. Rune was in our ear with a play-by-play from the cameras he'd hacked. When we entered, we were in a long narrow hallway where part of the warehouse had been sectioned off into rooms. There were girls of various ages chained inside.

Deathwing and I quickly took out two men in the hallway and Nyx and Atlas entered the first room, pulling a man off the girl chained to the bed. I didn't wait around but heard Nyx unload a clip into the man's face.

Deathwing and I continued down the hallway as the teams behind us swept through the rooms. We reached a door at the far end and I lifted my gun and gave Deathwing a nod. He pushed open the door, surprising a group of men who jumped to their feet, grabbing for their guns. I shot two in my sector before I was on the third. I slammed my gun against his face and shot the man coming up behind him. A Glock was aimed at my face, I shoved his arm down at the last second and the shot hit his friend across the room. The anger surged up inside me as the thought of these men putting their hands on my daughter took over every rational space in my mind. It took all of my self control not to beat these men to a pulp with my bare hands. They didn't deserve the quick death my bullets were giving them. With the room secured, Deathwing and I moved to the next door. This time I pushed it open, and he entered, but the room was clean.

"Sector one all clear. Report in," Deathwing said over comms.

All teams reported all clear.

"Two taken alive. We have them restrained in Sector three."

"Copy that. Hold there for now."

One of Deathwing's men appeared. "Boss, you need to see this."

He led us to the back of the warehouse and into a room that must have been their command center. All along one wall were printed headshots of girls. There had to be at least a hundred of them lined up and labeled with a number. I walked up to them, my eyes scanning each one, only to land on a pair of raging grey eyes so like mine, it made my heart stop.

Emersyn.

I hadn't seen her in so long. In my mind she'd stayed a child, frozen in time. Always my little girl. But a father knows his daughter and there weren't any doubts this was her. When I learned she was alive, West and Rune had tried everything to find an image of her but they weren't successful. Now, here she was, staring at me with eyes as hard as steel and so haunted it made me sick.

I ripped it from the wall to get a closer look. My thumb traced over her face and the scar. Pain seared through me at the sight and the guilt threatened to drown me. It had faded over the years and did nothing to take away from her beauty, but just the thought of how she'd gotten it by my hand made me hate myself.

"North." Nyx and Atlas were at the door. "She's not here."

I barely heard them. I stormed out of the room, shoving past them and heading towards where I knew two of these scum of the earth were being held. Someone called my name, but I was beyond stopping now.

I'd been so close.

I rounded the corner and saw the two men tied in chairs in the center of a large open area of the warehouse. I had eyes only for them as I stalked over. I grabbed the first man's shirt and shoved him backwards so hard the front legs of the chair tipped up. I put the photo in his face.

"Tell me where she is!"

"I don't know." I could see the fear in his eyes as his pupils expanded. I pulled out my .45 and shot him in the knee. The man howled in pain.

"Wrong answer," I snapped. "Again—where is this girl?"

"I-I don't-know," the man whined. "She—we distribute to-to several—"

I shot him in the other knee. "Where the fuck is she?" I yelled.

The man was outright sobbing now.

"Where is she?" I struck my gun across his face. "Useless piece of shit," I growled. I pressed the gun against his groin.

"Wait-wait, she's either—"

"Shut up," the other guy hissed.

My eyes immediately jumped to him. He tried to look tough but I must have looked unhinged, I certainly felt it, because he tried to lean away from me as I stepped over to him.

"Oh no," I purred. "If you're not going to let him answer me, then you're going to."

I shoved the photo in his face. "Where is she?"

"I don't know," he snapped.

I shot him in the thigh. I shoved the gun between his legs as he groaned in pain. The threat was clear.

"Yes, you do. You know," I rasped.

He opened his mouth, and I shook my head. "You better think carefully about your answer. My trigger finger is real itchy today."

"We sent t-two shipments yesterday," the man gritted out. "One to Palmero—the-the ot-other to Quarry."

I straightened and took the gun away, only to backhand him across the face with it just because I felt like it. I turned to see I had an audience. Nyx and Atlas stood near Deathwing's two men, looking like they'd stopped them from intervening. Deathwing was casually smoking a cigarette out of the way, not looking the least bit concerned.

"You finished?" He dropped his cigarette and stomped it out.

"Who's Quarry?"

"Middleman," Deathwing answered. "Let me wrap up here and we'll regroup at the house and plan next steps. My recovery and clean-up crew are already en route."

He walked off, talking into his comms unit and directing his men. I walked over to Nyx and Atlas scanning them like I always did to make sure they were *in one piece.*

"We talked to a few of the girls," Nyx added. "Your daughter is apparently just like you."

When I looked at him with a question in my eyes he chuckled.

"Causing trouble, has an insane temper—killing people," Nyx said dryly. "Yet at the same time there were a few of the little ones who said she'd tell them the story of Little Red Riding Hood when they got scared."

My breath stalled in my lungs and I blinked away the emotions threatening to spill over. I could just picture the chaos and destruction she'd been leaving in her wake. But I could also see her telling whatever version of Little Red Riding Hood she thought the little ones would resonate with. She always did like the different ways I'd tell it although she would let me tell it the traditional way whenever she knew Cole was having a difficult time. The traditional way had been his favorite. I cleared my throat as I folded up her picture and carefully put it into a pocket.

"That sounds just like her," I said finally. "Although I don't know how I can say that after all this time. She was only a child—" I couldn't continue.

I shook my head and walked away, needing to move and clear my head. Being this close and then still not having found her was torture.

104

THERON

After freeing my men, I'd sent Lachlan and Graham off to find Cal and Knight. I needed them to search for Albatron. I sent Tex, Sakari and Knox to sweep and secure the rest of the house and hopefully find Atlas in the process. I was concerned about him.

Having Nyx get taken away from him now, so close to the end—I shoved those emotions down because I couldn't think about how after all of this, he wouldn't be there to see it. Listening to the chatter over comms, I knew Vetticus had Kaelin so that's where I headed.

I limped my way towards the end of the hallway. As I neared the middle, I heard two guards come up behind me. I threw myself at them, just barely avoiding a gunshot to the face. The sound was deafening but I slammed the gun against the wall and turned my own handgun on the other. Two gunshots later, they were down.

After that, the guards kept coming.

Where I got the adrenaline from, I didn't know. By the time I made it out of the hallway, I left a pile of corpses behind me and I was bleeding from more than Vetticus' handywork. After the hallway, I found myself in a large hall. It was similar to the one Vetticus had held the party in. I could tell he hadn't lived in this estate for quite some time. There was dust on everything and cobwebs decorated the corners and window sills. Nice of him to bring us back to where it all began.

I wiped blood out of my eyes in time to shoot a man who appeared in the far doorway, then dove out of the way to avoid the gunshots from his partner. I shot back as I hauled myself to my feet. Footsteps came up behind me and the bite of a bullet hit my side before I was moving again. My breath sounded ragged even to my own ears as I launched myself at two of the men. My momentum took us all to the ground where I rolled on top of one, crossing my gun with his and killing two at once.

I turned and dodged a knife to my neck, only to pull his arm forward and shove my gun under his chin. Blood sprayed across my face and I pushed the body to the ground. I used the nearby windowsill to pull myself to my feet and staggered towards the door.

I'd just made it into the next hallway when four men appeared. It was close quarters as they all tried to use their guns. Bullets thudded into the wall near my head. My gun went off three times, with three kill shots. The forth went wide as my arm was knocked aside and the man tackled me to the ground. A knife came for my throat and I dropped my gun just in time to shove my arms up to block it. The man ground his teeth, panting as he threw his weight forward, attempting to drive the knife home.

Somehow, I found the strength and with a shove, unbalanced him enough to daze him. I got to my knees and drove the knife towards his own throat. My chest heaved as I watched his life blood drain onto the floor between us.

This time when I tried to get to my feet, I stumbled and went down on one knee. My own blood mingled with the dead man's and I was momentarily mesmerized by it.

We all bleed the same in the end.

Getting to my feet took more effort than the last time but I managed and moved on.

Towards Kaelin.

Towards Vetticus.

Towards the end.

FLASHBACK

THERON

ROME, ITALY

After the raid on the warehouse, we went back to the safe house. I barely had the patience to clean up but somehow I did and then paced impatiently around the war room while I waited for the others. Food and beers were brought in and soon everyone was assembled and Rune was throwing up the evidence boards on the massive monitors.

"Who is Quarry?" I asked.

Rune pulled up all the information they had on the middleman.

"He often pulls inventory from different sources and they end up in the auctions," Rune said. "We're not sure if he specializes in grooming certain kinks, certain women, or what, but they use him as a secondary often."

I pulled out Emersyn's photo. "We have her number now," I said, paying attention to the writing under the image for the first time. "And apparently they nicknamed her Hurricane."

Rune quickly pulled up a list and highlighted the matching number.

"There she is," Rune said. "She went to Quarry."

"This is good," Deathwing nodded. "Now that we have her number and even a nickname, we'll be able to track her as long as there is documentation."

"I pulled up the cameras around the area," West said. "Look at this."

He threw a few video feeds up on a monitor and we watched a large work truck drive down a street near the warehouse. He paused the video and froze the image.

"There obviously aren't any camera feeds near the warehouse, but I scanned the footage of the nearby streets and this truck is the only vehicle during the timeframe of the sale that could have been used to transport a group of people."

"Can you follow it further?" I asked.

"On it now," West answered.

West followed the truck until it left the city and then lost track of it as soon as there weren't any more cameras.

"I'm already checking any available cameras outside town and in the next few cities accessible by that road," Rune said.

The silence stretched as Rune and West searched through the area for any footage they could find. A few minutes later Rune shook his head.

"All I found is a gas station camera that caught them as they passed by," he said. "The cities off that road don't show them entering so they must have taken a side road somewhere into the hills out there."

"What's out there?"

"Just farmland until the Apennine Mountains."

"How many other roads off that one could they have turned down?" I looked at the map of Rome and the surrounding countryside and mountain range.

"Not many but it will still take us time to check all of them," Rune said.

He clicked a few things and the roads on the map lit up in yellow. Frustration rose in me. It was going to take time to search such a large area especially with the roads traveling deep into the mountain range.

"I'm going to call in additional resources," I said.

I heard Deathwing coordinating his own teams as I walked out the back door to make the call. Northern Tactical had offices all over the world which meant I had tactical teams ready to go anywhere I needed them.

"Theo, please tell me you have a team available for me," I said as soon as the line picked up.

"Of course boss, where are they going?" Theo was my Chief Operating Officer in this sector with an office in Florence. He dealt only with legal NorTac contracts working with security details and other private military companies. My teams in Italy flew all over Europe doing security, extractions and other missions related to high-profile business and political names.

"Have them fly into Rome," I said, already texting him the coordinates and flight information.

"You're here?" Theo asked.

"Yeah, flew in yesterday for a job. Off the record."

"Anything else I can do for you while you're here?"

"No, I'll send a mission brief. I need them in the air ASAP."

"Consider it done," Theo said. "I'll text you the ETA shortly."

We ended the call, and I stared at the screen, suddenly thinking of Kaelin. This was going to further delay extracting her from the Warren.

I dialed a number and ran a hand over my face as I listened to it ring.

The line clicked. "Cooper."

"It's North."

"What's up, brother?"

I bristled at the casual tone he used like we were friends but pushed it aside.

"I want to make an offer on Kaelin," I said.

There was silence on the other end of the line.

"She's not for sale," Cooper said.

My jaw clenched. "I believe you said you had a business deal you wanted to discuss. I'm willing to negotiate terms that include Kaelin in the contract."

"Kraven, she's not for sale," he insisted. "Do you know how much money she's already made me?"

"Come on, everyone has a number," I pressed.

Silence again. "Afraid I can't do that."

"I'll double what she's made you."

I heard Cooper's incredulous huff. "Why do you want her so badly? Her pussy is great, don't get me wrong, but she's only a woman—a commodity. One that's making me a shit ton of money—did I mention that?"

He'd fucked her. I clenched the phone so hard I was afraid I'd snap it.

"Just name the price, Cooper," I said tightly.

This was not a shining example of my negotiation skills, but I couldn't back track now. I didn't have the time nor the patience. Cooper didn't speak for several long moments and finally he chuckled.

"Forget about her, Kraven," he said. "I told you she wasn't yours and I meant it. Don't call me again unless it's to really talk business."

The line clicked dead, and I nearly threw the phone across the yard. I didn't have time to deal with Cooper or spend the time I needed to successfully break into a place like the Warren and steal her. That was no small operation. Cursing viciously under my breath I walked back inside. The minute I could head back to the states, I would get her back.

I just hoped she could hold on for long enough.

106

KAELIN

Vetticus' men dragged me into a room with a bank of monitors along one wall. The screens showed the game and all the angles of the action. Demetrius and several other men in rich looking suits stood on one side of the room watching a larger monitor with localized action and running bets on the side.

"Escort these men out," Vetticus snapped. The guards led the men out, all except Demetrius. He lingered, his face carefully blank.

"Trouble?"

"Nothing to be concerned about," Vetticus said, his attention still on me.

"My men are here—let me help," Demetrius continued. "They know North—they know his men—"

"Very well," Vetticus said impatiently with a wave of his hand. "North's men are missing from the cells. Have your team help find them. Unfortunately, we couldn't include them in the game, but have them taken alive—I still have something planned for them."

Vetticus walked over to me and without warning, threw his fist into my stomach. I doubled over and fell to my knees, coughing. Vetticus bent down.

"You'll give me back control of my drones now," Vetticus hissed.

He grabbed me by the hair and yanked my head up, only to slam his fist into my jaw. He let go and I fell onto one hand. I tasted blood and when I looked up, I could see Demetrius' fury like fire in his eyes. Vetticus hauled me up by my neck and I saw Demetrius' hand twitch towards where his gun was under his suit.

Vetticus turned to him. "What are you still doing here?"

I discreetly gestured to Demetrius to leave, hoping he wouldn't react. He needed to maintain his cover a little longer. Just until we had the situation under control. Demetrius' attention flickered from me to Vetticus and he stared at him with a calm coldness I would have been frightened of if it had been directed at me. I knew the only reason he was staying his hand was because of his respect and trust in Theron. Otherwise, I was under no illusions that Vetticus would have been a dead man. As it were, Vetticus just stared, an annoyed look on his face.

"Very well," Demetrius said. "My men will take care of your...problem."

He gave me one last lingering look before he headed for the door. Once he was gone, Vetticus shoved me towards the computers.

"Fix it," he barked.

"It's not that simple," I ground out, touching my split lip.

I looked at the screens, watching the game in play. The drones had all fallen out of the air and were laying around the map.

"I don't care—just do it," Vetticus snapped.

"It was a kill code," I insisted. "I can't just wave a magic wand and restart them." Vetticus shoved his gun against the side of my head.

"You have fifteen minutes," he threatened. "I trust you'll figure it the fuck out." As soon as I started typing again, Vetticus pulled up his security cameras around the estate. It was obvious he didn't care about the game anymore. All over the screens were dead bodies littering hallways, the grounds and other areas of the house. Vetticus threw a chair across the room in rage. When I jumped at the violence, he came and stood over me.

"How much longer?"

I didn't answer and Vetticus growled impatiently under his breath but my fingers were still going across the keyboard so he didn't react. I was busy searching for the backup I'd stored just in case I wanted to use the drones later. West and I decided they were better off dead just in case there were other access points for controlling them. However earlier as I was planting the kill code, I'd decided to back things up just in case I needed to restore them to life.

"Find him!" Vetticus shouted in his comms unit, turning away from the monitors to pace around the room. "I don't care—he's injured and bleeding—you're telling me he's taken out half the guards?" He seemed to be listening and then cussed out whoever was on the other end. "I don't care about the game! His men are loose in the house—you need to find them!"

Vetticus paced behind my chair, which only added to my nerves. I was trying to stall, code and watch the security feeds to see what was going on. As soon as fifteen minutes was up, Vetticus grabbed me by the hair and yanked my head backwards.

"Time's up," he snarled.

The drones twitched on the screen in front of us and I took my hands off the keyboard.

"It's done," I said.

"Good—there!" He pointed to one of the security feeds. "Send the drones there." It took me a minute because of the tactical gear but I could see it was Graham and Lachlan. Dread settled in my gut.

"What part of that didn't you understand?" Vetticus ground out. "Send them." I pulled a few drones and sent them towards the house. Soon they were flying through the hallways. I pulled them up short in front of the men. I stalled, hoping they would move. Graham looked up at the drone warily while Lachlan watched the other end of the hallway.

"Shoot him," Vetticus demanded.

"No," I balked and tried to push away from the computer.

Vetticus slammed my head forward on the desk and pulled me back up. Blood poured from a cut on my nose.

"Do it, now!" He roared.

"I can't—" I whimpered.

I could feel the anxiety creeping up. It became hard to breathe. My hands shook as I placed them on the keyboard.

"Do it now!" He pressed the gun to my head again. "Don't overestimate what you're worth to me."

I typed in the code as slowly as I could.

"Now!" Vetticus demanded.

"Fuck..." I cursed quietly in frustration.

My finger hovered over the execute button and a sob escaped. I was full on crying now.

"Do it!" Vetticus shoved me forward again. My shoulders shook, the screen blurred. I brought my finger down on the button, but before I could push it the door slammed open.

FLASHBACK

THERON

NEW YORK CITY

A few months after the Warren and the first raid with Deathwing, we were back in New York. The investigation into Quarry had been a dead end and we weren't any closer to finding Emersyn then we were before we raided the middleman's operation. There was evidence she'd been with him but somehow Quarry had gotten spooked and disappeared before we got to him—taking all of his inventory with him.

Unfortunately, I couldn't stay abroad any longer. I was needed back home—several aspects of my business could no longer be ignored—and so I begrudgingly flew back to the states. Deathwing promised he'd continue having eyes on the operations there and in the meantime, he told me it would be beneficial to work on getting close to Mahoney.

Greg and I had stayed in touch after the Warren and gotten together for drinks a few times. Before I left he'd told me he was due for a trip to New York and just this morning he'd called me saying he was in town. I hoped this would be when he extended the invitation to the Red Auction he'd promised me.

"Oh good you're here," West said.

I was in the kitchen at the house making coffee. I looked him over. He was brimming with excitement and anticipation.

"What is it?"

"You need to see what I found," he said.

I poured another cup and handed it to him and we walked down the hallway towards his rooms. The minute I walked in, Kaelin's picture was up on a monitor. Except, it wasn't just any picture.

"Why is she on the cover of a tech magazine?" I asked.

The title was CTO of Phox Enterprises Develops Latest in Military Drone Technology.

The date was from six years ago.

"Yeah, your girl is a techie," West grinned. He clicked through some screens. "Kaelin Bennett. She has several patents, is an active philanthropist—" he pulled up a screen with several tech magazine articles. "And as you can see, she's a world renown military tech developer and the CTO of Phox."

When I didn't say anything West chuckled. "I never thought I'd see you speechless."

I ran a hand through my hair, staring at the image of her on the magazine cover. She looked a thousand times better than she had in the Warren and her resume was incredibly impressive. I would be lying if it didn't make me even more intrigued than I already was if that was even possible.

"This is all from a few months ago," West said.

He clicked a few more things and article after article popped up all talking about the missing CTO of Phox. There was everything ranging from conspiracy theories to worries about the company's stock but the bottom line was no one knew where she was or even how she had disappeared.

"It looks like all they know is she was somewhere in the Arctic Circle visiting a friend. She never made it home when she was scheduled to. They also questioned her fiance—"

"She has a fiance?"

"Looks like you have some competition," West snickered.

I studied the pictures West pulled up and scoffed. He looked just like every other law firm asshole.

I pulled out my phone and called Cooper.

"Cooper," he answered.

"It's North—"

"Ah, I was going to call you," Cooper cut in. "My partner is interested in contracting for a few hundred thousand rounds."

"That's fine. I can draw something up but the deal will need to include Kaelin."

Cooper was silent, then I heard him sigh. "Jesus North, you're like a horny teenager going after your first crush. I told you to forget about her."

I was quiet, composing myself before I spoke again.

"I can't do that," I said firmly.

"Well, I have some bad news anyway," Cooper sighed. "She's gone."

"What do you mean gone?"

"I mean, she's not here anymore, okay?" Cooper snapped. "Do you want the contract or—"

I hung up before he could finish his sentence.

"She's not at the Warren anymore," I said to West.

"Does that mean she's—"

"He didn't say—just that she was gone," I replied.

I ran a hand over my face and stared at Kaelin's picture on the screen.

"I'll keep an eye out for her. Let me know if you want me to dig into anything else," West said.

I went back to my office to do some work but when I sat down at my desk, I found myself putting her name into Google. An hour later, I'd gone deep down the rabbit hole of Kaelin Bennett. Everything in the Warren made sense now. The things she talked about during cocktail hour, knowing the book on biotech I'd brought—I knew she was a force but knowing what I did now, I had a hard time believing she was dead. She was a survivor, and I hoped she'd found a way out of that hell.

Nyx knocked on the half-open door and when I gestured for him to come in, he plopped down in one of the chairs in front of my desk. I turned the monitor towards him and showed him the image of Kaelin on the magazine cover.

"Who is—no," he said, eyes wide. "That's not—she's actually—T, she's a big deal! And in the same industry? What are the fucking odds, man?" He grinned. "So, we still going to grab her at some point?"

"She's missing. Cooper doesn't know where she is."

"Dead?"

I shrugged. "Unclear. West is keeping an eye out but the news of her missing has caused a stir on the internet. We must have missed it in all the chaos recently and being abroad."

"Damn, well, she's gorgeous," Nyx smirked. "I'm sure she'll surface and then we'll get her—wait—she wants to be with you too right? Or is this a kidnapping situation?"

I shrugged. "She has a fiance. Could be a kidnapping situation."

Nyx waved his hand. "Who is he and do you want me to take him out now?"

I chuckled even knowing he was serious. "If she's alive, she's mine. Let's wait and see what happens before pulling any triggers." Literally.

"You should have just taken her when you left," Nyx said.

"And then what? It's not like I could have given her the attention she deserved—no, needed after coming out of a trafficking situation. Plus, if she really does like this asshole fiance, she probably would run back to him and I wouldn't have time to do anything about it."

"Yeah, but she would've been safe," Nyx shrugged.

I sighed because he was right and I still questioned myself for not just grabbing her and stealing her away while I had the chance.

"Cooper would have come after us," I said. "Just too many variables and my daughter takes precedence."

"Over a girl with a fiance who you've only spent five days with? Definitely," Nyx chuckled.

108

THERON

THREE DAYS AGO
EN ROUTE TO ELYSIUM

The phone call came through my Aston showing an unknown number.

"Yeah?"

"North—it's Gabriel—" The phone cut out.

"Where are you?" I demanded. I hadn't heard from him in months. His team had gone completely radio silent and no one knew where he was, not even Knight. I searched and searched, even going so far as to hint around Mahoney but there was nothing. It was like he'd completely disappeared.

"—in deep, can't talk—her—"

"What? Tell me where you are so I can send a team in!"

"—she's here—"

For one brief moment, his voice came through crystal clear.

"We found her, North—" Then it cut out again. "Trust—be in touch—"

The line went dead.

"Gabriel!" The call was dropped.

"Fuck!" I shouted.

This could not have been worse timing. For one brief moment I debated stopping everything and putting all of my resources into finding Deathwing. But the thought disappeared as quickly as it came. This was a means to an end—too much work had gone into it to stop now. Besides, I had to trust Gabriel. This was his deal, if he'd found her, I trusted her to be in good hands. Once this thing with Vetticus was done, I wouldn't stop until she was finally standing in front of me.

109

KAELIN

I yanked my hand away from the button. Both Vetticus and I whirled at the sound of the door. Relief washed through me when I saw Theron standing there. He looked like a demon straight from hell. He was covered in blood—literally covered in it.

He slouched against the doorframe as though it was the only thing keeping him on his feet. But the fire and rage in his eyes was beyond this world. It was searing in its intensity and I momentarily forgot how to breathe altogether.

"Just the man I was hoping to see!" Vetticus said.

Theron lunged for Vetticus and I stood up from the chair so fast, it tipped over behind me. Vetticus and Theron collided. Theron managed a few quick hits before Vetticus threw him into the bank of computer monitors, sending it all crashing to the ground. While Theron struggled to get back to his feet, Vetticus tried to get to me. He grabbed my arm but I managed to get a punch to his jaw and Theron dragged him bodily away from me.

"Go!" Theron shouted.

I froze at the doorway. It was obvious he was in bad shape, even though he didn't look any less dangerous. I wanted to help but I didn't want to be another weakness or a distraction for him.

"Kaelin, go!" Theron barked again.

I internally cursed then climbed over a fallen table to grab a gun and a tablet as I ran out the door. The last thing I saw was Theron take Vetticus to the ground with a knife in his hand.

I raced through the hallway and found myself in an empty sitting room. I pulled open a screen on the tablet. If I couldn't help Theron by being there with him, I'd find another way. I quickly began the process of transferring control of the drones to the tablet. It was difficult on a touch screen and painfully slower than I was used to. I was still breathing heavily, my adrenaline out of control and every creak and sound around me made me jump. The loading bar appeared on the screen, initializing the transfer to the tablet.

"Come on," I muttered as it inched its way to one hundred percent.

I heard movement at the door and saw two guards pop around the corner. I dropped the tablet. I didn't have time to pull my own gun so I threw myself at them, barely avoiding a gunshot to the face. I knocked the gun away, dragged his wrist around and shot his friend. The guard landed a hit that dazed me and shoved me hard into the wall. My vision dimmed dangerously.

I drew my gun and turned, only to have it batted away and deflected before a knife was swung towards me. I avoided him stabbing me in the neck, only to block and have him stab me in the side. We locked together—his larger size forcing me backwards and the pain took my breath away. My gun was useless trapped between us. He shoved the knife in further with a snarl, his breath hot in my face.

I headbutted him savagely, gaining just enough space to bring my gun up to shoot him in the thigh. He stumbled back, taking the knife with him. With a hiss of pain, I leveled the gun at his face and pulled the trigger.

In my anger, I unloaded the clip into him. The memory of the forest with Vandal suddenly the only thing on my mind. All I could see was him, feel his hands on me and hear his voice in my ear. With a cry of rage, I fell on the guard. I grabbed the knife that he'd stabbed me with and viciously drove it into him over and over again. All that existed was blood and fury and all of the pent up rage I still didn't know I had. It all needed to go somewhere.

My breath came in wheezing gasps and my arms gave out. Chest heaving, I leaned heavily over the bloody mess of a body I was straddling, nausea coming up strong when I looked down at my handiwork.

"Kaelin."

I scrambled off the guard and grabbed my gun, leveling it at the door. I lowered it when I saw it was Graham and Lachlan. I closed my eyes in relief and picked myself up off the floor.

"Are you okay?" Graham asked, looking me over with concern.

I grabbed my side as the movement jarred the stab wound.

"I'm fine," I ground out.

I stumbled across the room to where I'd dropped the tablet and picked it up. The status bar said one hundred percent and the interface for the drone controls appeared. I typed in some commands, my hands bloody and shaking.

"Are you sure?" Lachlan asked. "I really hope that's all his blood."

I didn't have the breath to answer. I heard the rip of fabric tearing, but I wasn't paying attention until the pain of the stab wound flared violently.

"Jesus—" I hissed.

Graham pressed the bandage to my side. I cursed viciously again, glaring at him briefly as he finished tying it off.

"I'm not having you bleed to death on me," Graham said dryly. The hum of drones filled the air and Lachlan and Graham turned quickly, ARs raised as they swarmed into the room.

"It's okay—they're mine," I said. I looked up with a smirk of satisfaction, then typed in a few more commands, grouping a swarm outside on the grounds. "I'm in control now."

110

NYX

Atlas and I hooked up with Cal's group and made our way through the house, searching for Albatron. Demetrius said he was here, all we had to do was locate him. We entered a massive ballroom. Across the space along one wall were platforms. This must have been where North was taken for the fight he told us about when he killed Kai. But my attention quickly shifted from the room, to the man standing in the center of it. Even though the room was massive, the man seemed to take up the space—his presence large and intimidating.

His suit was immaculate and he stood with his hands clasped behind his back as though he didn't have a care in the world. As though he was maybe even waiting for us to find him. He didn't even flinch as we quickly killed the five men guarding him. He slowly turned to regard us—a look somewhere between smugness and disinterest on his face.

"This him?" Cal asked.

"Yeah," I nodded. "That's him alright—Albatron."

Albatron looked me over, his head tilting slightly.

"I would think very carefully about your next move, gentlemen."

"I don't think you're in a position to negotiate," Atlas said with contempt.

A smirk pulled at his lips as his intense gaze jumped between all of us.

"Oh, I would have to disagree, Atlas," Albatron said.

Atlas was taken aback. "Do you remember me?"

A sound very close to a laugh escaped Albatron although his expression didn't change.

"I know all of your names," he said. "And I have something to discuss with Theron North."

"What makes you think he wants to hear what you have to say?" I scoffed.

"He told you to take me alive," Albatron said. "I think you'll all benefit from my little chat. And here's the thing—I have something of yours—" He looked at Knight pointedly. "—and I have something of North's and if you kill me, there won't be anything you can do to get them back."

"Them?" Knight raised his eyebrows.

When Albatron didn't answer, Knight grunted in irritation and waved his hand. Atlas took out zip ties and walked behind Albatron so he could jerk his wrists tightly together to secure him. I didn't know what to make of the threat, but regardless he was right—North did want him alive.

"Then let's go," he said. "You're lucky he wants us to take you alive, cause I remember what you did to his little girl."

Albatron didn't reply as Atlas grabbed his upper arm and jerked him towards the door. I fell into step with them and made our way back through the house.

111

🔥 🔥 🔥

THERON

My body was screaming at me. I'd forced it way beyond when it should have failed. But I wasn't done. Vetticus and I had fought our way out to the large terrace along the front of the house. It was lightly raining and the ground was slippery with water and blood. I'd lost all of my weapons. My knife was behind Vetticus and my gun was inside the double doors. I had only my fists. Vetticus walked over to my knife and picked it up, shoving his hair out of his face, he leered at me.

"You never did know when to stay down," he taunted. "Just can't get enough of me, even now."

He beckoned me to come at him and I growled and attacked. The knife came for me but I quickly landed a hit to his jaw, slammed my knee into his face and he went down dazed. I disarmed him and fell to one knee, heaving in air and unable to keep my feet.

"It's over, Vetticus," I said in a ragged gasp.

Vetticus lurched to his knees but fell back onto his hand.

"No..." He snarled.

"Your men are dead..." I stood and grabbed him by the hair, turning his head up to me with a yank. I pressed the knife to his throat, for a moment living off the high of seeing him on his knees. I saw movement out of the corner of my eye and watched a smug look take over Vettitcus' face.

"Looks like not all of them," he said. "Shoot him!"

But no gunfire came.

"I don't think so."

I recognized the voice. It was Viktor.

"Shoot him, you fools!" Vetticus shouted, but there was an edge to his voice this time. "You work for me, now!"

"Actually, we don't," Demetrius said, the contempt heavy in his words. He stood in the doorway of the terrace, his cold eyes glimmering with satisfaction. I bared my teeth in a bloody grin.

"You're playing my game now, Vetticus," I said. "And I'm looking forward to showing you just how far I can break you."

My fist connected with his face in a knockout blow and he collapsed onto the stone. I couldn't help but hit him a few more times. Again, and again and again. The pleasure of it intoxicating. The rain was falling in earnest now and I shifted off of him and sat back on my heels. I stared at Vetticus unconscious before me and fought to catch my breath.

The victory overshadowed my pain. He was mine. He was finally mine.

Demetrius came over and held out his hand to me. I nodded my thanks as I let him haul me back to my feet. Before I could speak, I heard a shout from the doorway.

"North!" I glanced over to see Atlas hurrying over to me and behind him... Nyx. I stumbled towards him, relief taking my breath away.

"Nyx—" I grabbed onto him, convinced I was hallucinating.

He grabbed my shoulders, wearing that wicked smile of his.

"Turns out the devil didn't want me this time either," Nyx said with a wink.

I nodded in relief and tapped him lightly on the cheek with a bloody hand. I was still breathing heavily all the while gripping his shoulder to steady the world that was trying very hard to spin out of control around me.

"Cal and Knight have Albatron," Atlas reported as he zip tied Vetticus' wrists behind his back. "Tex, Sakari and Knox are rounding up the other Atrox patrons and coordinating a team to free the men playing in the current game."

"Where's Kaelin?" I asked hoarsely. "Lach and Graham?

Atlas shook his head, unsure.

"I wouldn't be worried," Nyx said lightly. "If the drones flying around right now are any indication, I think your girl is just fine," Nyx said.

We all congregated out in front of the estate. Nyx and Atlas went to check on Albatron and secure Vetticus for the flight home. I could see Tex, Sakari and Knox helping organize all the other people we'd found on the estate. Although Vetticus hadn't lived at the estate in awhile, he'd still brought quite an entourage, including a small wait staff who had hid through the entire thing.

Lachlan, Graham and Kaelin were still missing but I'd spoken to West and apparently she had control of the drones. The drones were currently all over the property, sweeping the forest, the house and hovering above keeping watch. I was just about to go in and tear down the place looking for her, when I saw three people descending the front steps.

Kaelin was covered in blood, holding a tablet surrounded by a small fleet of drones. Lachlan and Graham were a few steps behind, but I only had eyes for her—I'd never seen anything so beautiful. I quickly met her at the bottom of the stairs and took her into my arms.

"I should be mad at you but seeing you come down these steps covered in blood surrounded by drones is doing something to me," I rumbled against her hair. She huffed a laugh and clung to me for another moment before pulling back to look at me. Concern flickered across her face but she didn't say anything. Her hand came up and grazed across my jaw, a small smile tilting the corner of her mouth.

"I love you," she said abruptly.

My grip on her tightened and I opened my mouth to reply. I think I was fully prepared to tell her the same—it was on the tip of my tongue. But she pressed a finger to my lips and shook her head.

"I don't want you to say it now because I said it—I want you to finish all of this first. Then I want you to come home to me," she murmured. "Come home to me, Theron—and when you do, I want it all. Your mind—" she trailed her finger down my cheek. "Your body—" Her tone was seductive as her finger trailed down my neck and collarbone. "And your soul."

Kaelin pressed a light kiss to my lips, nothing more than a brush of skin, before she walked off.

"I'll take her home," Graham said next to me. "We'll be waiting for you."

He flashed me a quick smile and clasped me on the shoulder, then followed after Kaelin.

112

🔥 🔥 🔥

THERON

A few hours later, everything was nearly wrapped up. The grounds were empty of people and most of the team was already on their way home. I stood staring at the house that had held so many horrors for me for so long. It sat empty and dark, nothing more than a building with memories I was ready to leave behind.

Demetrius walked up with Viktor and Kon in tow.

"You look like hell," Demetrius said. "But I'm glad to see you mostly in one piece."

I grinned and shook his hand. "You too, my friend. Thank you for saving Nyx by the way."

"Think nothing of it," Demetrius said. His eyes took on a mischievous light. "On second thought, I think you owe me a favor."

I barked out a laugh. "It's about time. You hold on to that—make it count."

"I probably won't make you wait ten odd years," he said dryly with a smirk.

I shrugged. "We have the time."

Demetrius chuckled and clasped me on the shoulder. "That we do, Theron. I'll see you at home."

Tex, Sakari and Knox were the next to approach. They stood by me looking at the building and Tex shook his head.

"Now what are we gonna do?" He asked.

"I think you all deserve a vacation."

"I don't know what that word means," Knox said.

"I think you need one, boss," Sakari smirked. "Take your girl and your man somewhere tropical or something—just somewhere with no guns."

"No guns?" Tex frowned. "That doesn't sound fun."

"He'll be too busy holding a mai tai to care," Knox chuckled.

"Come on degenerates," Tex threw an arm around Sakari. "Let's go home and prep the torture chamber. See ya soon, boss."

I nodded to them and they headed off towards a waiting car that would take them to the airstrip. They were headed home to help ready the house for everything I was going to do to Vetticus. Because this wasn't the end. Not quite yet. I still had to make him suffer.

I looked at the building again and saw Knight emerge and give me an all clear sign. He walked off towards where Nyx and Atlas were on a small rise, heads together as they talked. Seeing Nyx alive had been shocking but I was so glad Atlas didn't have to suffer again. I couldn't imagine coming out of this without either one of them. This revenge was for them as much as it was for me. I walked towards the helo and climbed aboard to wait for the others. I rested my forearms on my thighs and said goodbye to the past. This nightmare was over.

The ghosts in this place were dead.

It was time to go home.

113

ATLAS

I have a surprise for you," I said. I came up behind Nyx as we stood in front of the building that was our home for the hellish years we'd spent in captivity. He turned quickly, his lips pulled into a smirk as he stepped closer.

"I like the sound of that."

My hand slid up to his neck, holding him back even though desire pulsed through my blood.

"Not that kind of surprise," I rasped, my voice betraying me.

"Hey lovebirds," Knight called. "Did someone call for an RPG?"

"No way," Nyx breathed, a smile lighting up his entire face. "You brought it?" Knight laughed and handed it over to Nyx who looked like a kid who'd just been handed a puppy.

"I recall I told you I'd be aiming one at that house one day," I said.

Nyx's gaze locked on mine and it grew heated, the air suddenly thick between us.

"Whoa, okay, this is definitely some kind of foreplay so I'll leave you guys to it," Knight said, socking Nyx in the arm and winking at me. "The house is clear, by the way. Fire when ready."

Nyx looked over at Knight. "Thanks man."

Knight saluted him casually before heading off towards the waiting chopper. Nyx looked eagerly at me, and I laughed.

"Well, let's do this thing!"

We quickly set everything up and Nyx rested the RPG on his shoulders, leveling it at the building.

"Count me down, Atlas," Nyx said.

"Three, two, one—fire in the hole!"

Nyx fired the grenade, and we watched it fly off towards the house, landing a direct hit into one of the massive first-floor windows. The sound of glass shattering echoed in the space as the fire exploded inside. Nyx giggled—actually giggled as he loaded another one. Each one he fired, I could see the tension start to ease away from him. After the fourth one, he handed it over to me.

"Your turn," he said.

The front of the house was nothing more than a fiery smoking mess by the time we were done pummeling it with grenades but I felt more closure than I ever had. I lowered the grenade launcher to my side then turned to Nyx and pulled him into me by the back of his neck. My lips slammed into his and his fingers twisted into my hair, yanking me closer. The kiss left me wanting more but not here. Never here.

"Let's go home" I whispered against his lips. "It's time to leave it all behind."

We walked back to the helo hand in hand and once we climbed in, the bird took off only to hover nearby.

Knight handed his phone over to North with a smirk.

"Care to do the honors?"

A slow smile spread across North's face as he took the device.

"Figured Nyx and Atlas shouldn't have all the fun," Knight chuckled.

"Yeah right—you just wanted to blow something up," North said dryly.

Knight just shrugged and sat back. "That's what I call a win-win," he said smugly. North looked down at the house. The rain had cleared up and the house lay in a broken ruin below us. I gripped Nyx's hand and with great delight, watched North press the button.

We flew away to the fireworks of the explosion, leaving behind nothing but a hole in the ground.

The perfect grave for the past.

114

THERON

I sat in a chair, idly toying with a knife as I leaned forward on my forearms. In front of me Vetticus dangled naked and unconscious from a chain, strung up by his wrists. I hadn't touched him yet. I wanted him awake first.

I heard the door open and Nyx and Atlas appeared. Nyx circled Vetticus with a dark look on his face before coming over and hopping up on the counter behind me. Atlas came and stood next to me, folding his arms across his chest.

"Are you ready?" I asked.

"Let's finish this," Atlas nodded.

"Nyx, wake him up," I said.

Nyx hopped down and brought the smelling salts over to Vetticus, waving them under his nose. Our captive jolted and jerked awake, blinking rapidly as he came back to reality. When he saw me sitting in front of him, he smirked.

"You know if you wanted to tie me up, you could have said something," he mocked.

I shook my head. "You just don't understand do you?"

I rose to my feet and walked over to stand in front of him.

"This doesn't change anything—I claimed you long ago," Vetticus smirked. "You wear my brand, I've taken your body, nothing can change that."

"Delusional," Nyx scoffed.

Vetticus' gaze sharpened on Nyx behind me and he frowned. "I should have killed you myself."

"Yeah, you should have," Nyx agreed. He held out his hands. "But you didn't...and now the Reaper is here for you."

Vetticus scoffed. He looked back at me and let his gaze trail lazily down my body and back up.

"You can't change the past, Kraven. You're mine and you always will be."

I poised the knife on his face above his eyebrow and saw the first flicker of fear appear in Vetticus' eyes. I reveled in it.

"No, Vetticus, that's where you're wrong," I slid the blade down, digging it deep. A cry of distress left him as I dragged it through his eye, down his cheek and ended at his jaw. A deeper, more violent version of the cut he made me give Emersyn. "I was never yours in the first place."

Nyx, Atlas and I took turns brutalizing Vetticus. When he passed out, we revived him. Soon we were covered in blood and the entire space looked like a slaughterhouse. After the first cut, Vetticus didn't have anything smart to say again. In fact, the only words out of his mouth for the next two hours were curses and screams. We tortured him for every loved one he'd taken and we made marks and inflicted pain for everyone we lost in that hell—for Preacher, for Kane—even Red and all the kids whose names we knew and those we didn't.

At the moment, Nyx was in the process of cutting off Vetticus' pinky finger. Atlas held a smoking iron ready to cauterize it. We wanted him alive as long as possible. Vetticus' screams echoed off the walls only to die off a moment later when he passed out.

"Oh no you don't, pussy," Nyx growled, waving the smelling salts under his nose again. Vetticus jerked awake and moaned, then screamed again as Atlas pressed the iron to the stump where his finger used to be. The smell of burnt flesh filled the room. Nyx tossed the finger away in disgust and patted Vetticus on the cheek.

"Sucks doesn't it?" He chuckled.

There wasn't a spot on Vetticus that hadn't been abused. He was missing several fingers, one of his eyes and I was pretty sure most of his blood was on the floor instead of inside his body. His once cocky features were vacant and dull. He was finally resigned to his fate. Atlas handed the iron to Nyx.

"Heat that up again," Atlas said.

"With pleasure," Nyx answered. "What are you going to do?"

"I'm going to make him choke on his cock," Atlas muttered.

Vetticus screamed, his struggles pathetic and weak when Atlas placed the knife at the base of his dick and started cutting. He made an animalistic sound of anguish and passed out halfway through. Nyx let out an unhinged laugh.

"Man, that's satisfying," he said.

Atlas held out his hand for the iron and when Nyx handed it to him, he shoved it into Vetticus' skin over the wound. Vetticus woke up again, his screams piercing as he panicked and struggled, sobbing as he struggled to breath. Atlas dangled Vetticus' appendage in his face and grabbed his jaw, forcing his mouth open.

"This is for all the times you terrorized the two people I love the most," he growled. He shoved the dick into Vetticus' mouth.

"I shouldn't be turned on by that," Nyx chuckled. "But I like it when you get all possessive."

Atlas came over and grabbed Nyx by the throat. "You're mine, not his," he growled.

"Forever, baby," Nyx smirked and Atlas yanked him into a kiss.

I watched them and a wave of peace swept over me. I looked back at Vetticus, hanging broken and bleeding—a barely breathing corpse. All the years of planning, hustling, and the torment of knowing he was still out there—all came down to now. Everything seemed more clear than it ever had before. I always wondered who I'd be once the smoke cleared and the blood that was owed was paid in full.

Who am I if not a hunter?

That was the question I asked myself, worried I'd get in too deep and lose any shred of humanity I had left. I worried I wouldn't know what to do with myself once the hunt was over. Who was I without Vetticus driving my every breath? Even in the darkest moments, I'd never been his. I'd sat in wait, collecting my shadows and my pain and honing it all into a storm of vengeance. I'd bent to his will—all so I could get me and my men out alive. But in the end, it was always my game.

Powerful under the guise of being powerless.

Kaelin.

She'd wanted me to put the past to bed and come home to her.

To give all of me to her.

It should have felt strange, it should have felt wrong, to give instead of take. I wasn't sure if I could really love someone or not, but I knew I would damn well try.

For her. For Graham. For the life I'd built.

The thought of her had me tossing the knife at my feet and heading towards the door.

"Where are you going?" Nyx asked, tearing his face away from Atlas momentarily.

"To find Kaelin," I said.

"What about him?"

"He's the Devil's problem now."

Who am I if not a hunter?

I suddenly wasn't afraid to find out.

115

THERON

I didn't care that I was tracking blood in the house. I didn't care that I was running on fumes after the fight or how much pain I was in. I didn't care about anything but finding Kaelin. My body protested every step as I hurried up the stairs. I knew I was going to have to rest soon, but I had something I needed to do first.

I threw open the bedroom door and heard the shower running. I slipped inside, not even bothering to remove my clothes. She turned and gasped, only to inhale sharply when I grabbed her neck and forced her back against the tile wall. Blood ran in rivulets down my body, turning the shower red but she'd turned her wide green eyes on me and I knew—she was mine—forever.

"What are you doing?" She breathed.

"You told me you wanted all of me," I rumbled. "My mind—" I brought my hand up and pushed a stray lock of wet hair off her cheek. "My body—" My fingers tightened around her neck. "And my soul." I brushed my lips over hers, nothing more than a skate of breath. "But you forgot something, darlin'."

"I did?" She asked, sounding breathless.

"You did," I growled low, my cock already painfully hard in my jeans.

"What did I forget?" She whispered, barely audible over the shower. I took her hand and placed it over my heart, a dark smirk pulled at my lips.

"This," I said. "As dark and tattered as it may be—this heart is yours."

Her fingers curled against my chest, digging into my skin.

"Did you come home to me?" She whispered.

"I'm home, baby girl, and everything I am belongs to you."

"I want to hear you say it" she murmured.

My hand slipped up to grip under her jaw and I pulled her towards me.

"I love you," I rasped, my lips brushing hers. "Relentlessly. Completely. Ferociously. You set fire to my soul and call me home from the shadows—my darling wildfire."

The air took on a fervorous edge and I captured her lips in my own. She tore at my jeans that stuck frustratingly to my skin now that they were soaking wet. With the passion came the pain of my injuries as we molded our bodies together, but even that wasn't close enough. I crushed her against the tile wall, my hand around her throat now gripping the back of her neck. She hissed in pain against my lips but when I looked down at her own injuries she made a sound of protest and jerked my chin back to hers, kissing me once more.

Kaelin's hand closed around my cock and I gripped her thighs and pulled her up into my arms. Her back slammed against the tile and as she wrapped her legs around me. I slowly slipped inside her and we both moaned in pleasure, her fingers digging into my shoulders as I watched the ecstasy play across her face with each stroke of my cock. Her soft pants caressed my face and as our eyes clashed I knew I'd never be the same. My lips crushed hers again, biting her lip, the need to claim what was mine a nearly insatiable urge.

A few more strokes and the pain became too much. I set her down and turned her, shoving her into the tile. She pushed her hips back, her breathless moans a silent plea. I drove back into her with a growled curse and slapped her ass, then grabbed her hips and set a relentless pace that soon had us both on the edge of unraveling.

My hand went around to rub her clit and I leaned into her, sinking my teeth into her neck. She cried out and arched into me, the look of divine pleasure on every inch of her face.

"Yes, oh god—yes—" She gasped.

"It's not god who makes you shatter so beautifully," I growled against her neck. "I don't want his name on your lips—only mine." My words were ragged as I fought through the pleasure and the pain. One hand continued to work her clit, the other wrapped once more around her neck. I may have given her all of me, but I would always take what was mine.

"Theron," Kaelin breathed—a plea or a prayer—her pussy gripping my cock as the wave of pleasure crashed over us. Maybe it was both. A plea for release, a prayer for rapture. I hit the edge and the energy between us sparked, collided and pulled me in. The burn was everything—the pleasure immeasurable. There was no beginning and no end as the intensity rippled through us.

My hands left her body and slammed against the wall as I began to come down, sucking in air as I pressed against her. We came back down to earth, our skin still molded together still burning to the touch. I rested my lips against her neck and she turned her head to me, sharing air and those green flames I'd fallen in love with burned through the storm in mine.

"I love you," she murmured.

Such small words for something so vast but I could see the breadth of her conviction and all the question marks bled away.

"I love you too, darlin'," I growled and I knew in my soul I meant it with everything I was.

Who am I if not a hunter?

Maybe, just a man in love.

I looked down at the wildfire in her eyes and claimed her lips once more.

EPILOGUE

THERON

After showering with Kaelin and showing her exactly what I meant by my words, I knew there was one more thing I had to do before I could put this all behind me.

Albatron.

My men had said he wanted to talk and that he had something of mine. I walked down into the basement where I'd put him in one of the holding cells. He was leaning against the back wall, calm and collected. I opened the door and stood in the entrance.

"You have two minutes," I demanded.

Albatron met my gaze.

"I appreciate a man that is direct and to the point," he said. "So I will be too." There was a pause and when I didn't speak, Albatron continued.

"I have Gabriel Griffin," Albatron said. "And...your daughter."

Time stopped, then I was on Albatron, grabbing him by the shirt and shoving him back against the wall. He regarded me as calm as ever.

"If you've hurt her—" I snarled.

"I propose a trade," Albatron said.

"You're not in a position to bargain," I growled.

His lips twitched. "You don't want me as your enemy, North. I admire what you've built over the years. I will even admit to letting Vetticus have too much rein. But I am not so easily snuffed out and if you kill me—well, I don't advise it."

"Is that a threat?"

"I don't deal in threats," Albatron stated. "It is simply a fact. What I'm proposing is beneficial to all parties."

All I was seeing was the suffering of the past decade. Of thinking my daughter was dead. Watching him pull the trigger and killing her so nonchalantly. As if he could hear my thoughts, he sighed and looked at me with a sympathetic, yet condescending look.

"I didn't kill your daughter, North," he said. "She is alive. Griffin is alive. You let me go, they get delivered to you still breathing and we both go on with our lives."

"Why?" I ground out.

"I see opportunity and I capitalize on it—regardless of the means to get there. But, killing is messy and despite appearances, I'm a businessman first. Besides, I actually admire you—"

I scoffed and shoved off of him, stepping away.

"I do," Albatron insisted. He smoothed out his jacket as though he wasn't covered in dirt and blood. "You've overcome much and were quite innovative in your thirst for revenge. The dedication is staggering honestly. I prefer to keep men like you alive."

"What's the catch?"

"No catch," Albatron said. "A simple trade. Me for them."

I stared at him, but I already knew what I was going to decide. I pulled my phone from my pocket and held it out to him. "Make the call."

"No need," Albatron smirked.

Nyx appeared in the hallway.

"A car just pulled up. The driver is asking for you," he said.

I looked at Albatron and headed towards the stairs.

"I hope you're a man of your word," Albatron called after me as Nyx relocked the cell. "You'll find I'm a man of mine."

I didn't answer. Nyx followed me through the house and out the front door where a blacked out SUV sat idling.

The driver got out and nodded to me. "Courtesy of Albatron—" he said. "In good faith." He opened the door and Gabriel climbed out. He looked exhausted and a little rough around the edges but he nodded to me then turned back to the car and held out his hand.

A feminine hand gripped his and a woman stepped out.

Blond hair fell forward and she brushed the chaotic curls away from her face—the gesture sending me back decades. Those storm filled eyes latched onto mine, and I finally heard the words I'd been dying to hear for years.

"Hello, dad."

THE END

THE SILENT STRUGGLE

Suicide is the silent struggle.
If you, or someone you know, is struggling,
there are resources to help.

Your mental health matters. **You matter.**
You are not alone. You are not a burden.

1-800-273-TALK (8255)
988 Suicide and Crisis Hotline

1 in 6

Researchers have found that at least 1 in 6 men have experienced sexual abuse or assault, whether in childhood or as adults. Males who have such experiences are less likely to disclose them than are females. **It can happen to anyone**. If you know someone who might need support, or would like to learn more about how you can help break the silence, visit: **https://1in6.org/**

A FEW NOTES

Kraven is one of those polarizing characters—you either are feral for him and fall in love, or you absolutely HATE him and can't understand why anyone would like him. This book is for the ones who adore him as much as I do. This book is for the people who wanted to try and understand him better and lastly, this book is for the people who wanted all of their burning questions about the Warren answered. I hope this book sheds some light on most of the mysteries of *Red Rabbit*.

This book was a JOURNEY. I wasn't planning on making it into a novel, but Kraven just kept telling me his story and I just knew I needed to tell it all. I apologize for all of the time hops—I know those can get annoying and throw people off, but I felt it was necessary since his story covers such a wide span of time. Per usual, this book will raise questions, just like *Red Rabbit*—and you just have to trust I'll answer them in the next ones.

But let me tell you, I was nervous about this book. I set the bar so high with *Red Rabbit* that I was worried this book would let you all down and not be what you expected or hoped it would be. If that was the case, I'm so sorry—please read the other books that come out next—they won't be this... insane? Convoluted? I don't know—but I hope you'll still stick with me.

All that to say, Kraven is one of my all time favorite male characters that I've written. He's just so raw and sociopathic—the ultimate *take-what-I-want-man*. I hope it's now pretty clear why he was in the Warren. He was looking for his daughter, Emersyn, and needed to manipulate Greg. Now, I'll be real, some of the Warren was definitely Kraven's feral side coming out to play. He became so immersed in his manipulations, it was inevitable it would bleed over to his interactions with Kaelin. Also, let's face it, he does like the control. Kraven also didn't know Kaelin very well and wanted their interactions to be genuine in front of Greg, ie: to fear him, submit to him in public, etc.

Nyx and Atlas were a fun surprise in this book. I wasn't expecting them to have a romantic relationship but as their time in captivity progressed, it felt so natural for me to have them fall for each other. I love bi-awakenings and while Atlas was in a polyamorous relationship previously, Nyx--as far as he was concerned, has always been straight. Writing those two characters was a joy and I think they balanced Kraven out in the best ways. I didn't want to take over the book with those two—so maybe there will be some bonus scenes? *wink*

Speaking of bonus scenes—I referenced a night in Austria where the men had a sixsome, (I don't think that's even a word) or as Lachlan called it, a straight up orgy, with Kraven, Lachlan, Nyx, Atlas, Knight and Mads. There will absolutely be a wild bonus scene detailing that yummy action because how could I not?

I purposefully had Kraven go by many different names in the book—Theron, North, Kraven, T, boss, etc—because I wanted to show his different personalities depending on who he was with. IE: Sometimes Graham would call him North, usually in a public setting, while when they were in private with Kaelin, he would call him T, alluding to the closeness they were cultivating.

Kraven is a true sociopath. He manipulates people, his surroundings, his reality, in order to get what he wants. He generally views people as possessions and does not react emotionally to situations the way most people would. He can be erratic, contradictory and violent.

I want to make it clear, there is no relating to Kraven. You may not understand why he reacts a certain way, or does certain things, because he does not care about being a good person, or doing the right thing. The "right thing" to him is whatever gets him what he wants.

I hope you've been enjoying meeting Cal, Knight and Ghost in these books because their story is coming next! I adore Knight and I can't wait for him to get the chance to tell his story. I love how he's connected to Graham and Kraven AND Deathwing—another character you get to know more in depth in this book. And don't worry, Deathwing's book is coming too.

I'm so sorry I left you on a cliffhanger of sorts—if you hadn't guessed already, Emersyn and Deathwing will have a book and all your questions about what happened to Emersyn and how Deathwing found her, will be answered—including what the hell the Red Auction is.

Finally, I apologize if you were expecting a book that focused more heavily on Kaelin, Graham and Kraven. But that just wasn't what this book needed to be (Kraven was VERY adamant about that, and you know how he can be!) so please understand it was intentional to have them be important, but also not front and center. I mean, no surprise Kraven wanted his book to be mainly about him, right?

A fun fact: I love words and in all my books, I like to play on words and/or names so here are just a few: Kraven's name is indeed a Spider-Man comic book villain. The character is a big game hunter. The name Theron also means hunter. Kraven is hunting for his daughter, hunting for revenge, etc.

Atrox and Vetticus both have hidden meanings. *Atrox* is a Latin word meaning: *fierce, terrible, cruel, savage, atrocious, grievous, horrific, unrelenting or abominable*...which is what that company represents. And Vetticus is a play on a Roman name because of how the *Atrox* games resemble gladiator fights.

I incorporate wolves in a lot of my writing. Volkov means wolf and I liked the idea of having the connection between the Volkov Brothers and Graham's last name being Wolfe. When Demetrius meets Graham, he says, "Ah, *another wolf...*" The *NorTac* logo also has a wolf in it. And finally, Emersyn's favorite story is *Little Red Riding Hood*.

Another fun fact: the two Special Forces groups I mentioned—GGK (Malaysia) and the Jagdkommando (Austria), are in fact real. If you get a chance, look up the GGK—the exercise Atlas and Kane were talking about, the live firing drill, yeah—that's a real thing. It's wild.

I did heavy research into all of my military terms and watched a ton of videos on clearing kill houses, how to pie your corners, etc. so if something is inaccurate, I apologize—I tried. As with all of my books, now and in the future, sometimes you just have to suspend reality for a bit and go with it.

THE AUSTRIAN GOLD

The Nazi gold they went after in Austria? Also a real thing. Well, a very probable historical myth, I guess I should say. It is rumored that Nazi commanders dumped billions (around $5.6 billion to be exact) of stolen gold and other valuables into Lake Toplitz, a lake in the Austrian Alps located in a narrow, steep sided valley covered in dense forest. It can only be accessed via a mile-long private dirt track and is about 60 miles from Salzburg.

Diving for the gold is indeed treacherous and lethal because of a layer of sunken logs floating halfway down this over 300 ft deep lake. Only the upper 60 feet of the lake water is fresh – below this level the water is very salty and contains almost no oxygen. This means that fish and other marine life cannot exist in the deeper areas of the lake, and anything that falls into the water and sinks below this level does not rot or decompose.

The first deaths seemingly associated with the Lake Toplitz area occurred in February 1946 when two climbers pitched a tent on the shores of the lake.

Their bodies were discovered on the mountain around a month later—both had been murdered.

In 1947, a team of US Navy divers was sent to the lake, but the difficult and dangerous conditions made it impossible for them to find anything, and the attempt was abandoned when one of the divers drowned.

In the summer of 1952 the body of a visiting French geography teacher was found close to the shore of the lake where he had been camping. There were signs of digging, though nothing was found. While investigating the death of the Frenchman, Austrian police also discovered two other bodies on the opposite shore of the lake. Both had been shot in the head, and neither was ever identified.

There were also multiple deaths over the years associated with divers attempting to dive past the layer of sunken logs, only to drown. Diving in the lake is now illegal, however treasure hunters still flock to the area and an average of ten divers are arrested every year.

THE VOLKOV BROTHERS

The story that Kraven told about how he met the Volkov brothers, Viktor and Konstantine, was actually based on a real event. There are conflicting reports on what actually happened, but I just took the general idea and ran with it.

In 2018 around 500 pro-Syrian government forces, including Russian mercenaries from the Wagner Group, launched a nearly four-hour attack on a small group of 40 American Special Operations troops and their Syrian Democratic Forces (SDF) allies at a Conoco natural gas refinery in eastern Syria.

REAL VS FICTION

As always with my books, the reader needs to sometimes stretch reality for the sake of the story. I will keep things as close to real as possible because this is contemporary fiction, but at the end of the day, this is fiction and quite frankly, I want to have some fun with it! If that is difficult for you, then my books probably aren't for you. I will reference real cities, I will make up fake ones—I will reference real technology, I will also stretch science.

The sex will always be real and things I've either done or seen done. The only thing I won't describe is probably real life stuff like how you should pee after sex or use protection. Which are both things you should do when it comes to sex. But I just don't want to write about those things!

You best believe I do heavy research into everything (I even Googled how much $5.6 billion in gold bars weighs in order to know how many trips in the helicopter it would take) and if I can't make my story fit perfectly into the confines of what is real, I will take some liberties. If you ever have questions about something—I welcome the polite discourse in my DMs or email—and would love to answer your inquiries.

ACKNOWLEDGEMENTS

Whew, Kraven definitely had a story to tell. This book was a challenge, let me tell you, but I told his story as best I could and I'm proud of it. It should come as no surprise now, but my books always hold heavy themes such as sexual assault/abuse, suicide and human trafficking but because my main character is a male, I wanted to bring to light how men suffer these situations just like women.

It doesn't make either experience less valid, or take away from the fact assault can happen to any human being, regardless of gender. If you have a body—you can go through these traumas. My point being: no one is alone.

I write about these deep themes because I think it's important to talk about them. I want my characters talking about them together, dealing with them together and coming out the other side with hope and healing.

I WANT TO GIVE A BIG THANK YOU...

To everyone who read *Red Rabbit* and has come along on this writing journey with me — **THANK YOU**. From the bottom of my heart, I cannot thank each and every one of you enough. I thought RR would oanly be read by a few of my friends but boy was I wrong! The way RR took off in the dark romance community was a dream come true. I get giddy just thinking about it and I cherish every comment, story share, private message, custom made graphic/post, etc. that comes my way. RR changed my life and was such a validating experience for me as a writer who has written her whole life but never finished anything until that book.

So thank you, thank you, thank you — your support means the world to me.

I also want to thank a few key people who have been a constant support and sounding board for when I needed to just unload plot points or talk through this story. J and L for my constant hounding of tactical and psychological questions regarding LEOs. You both are just as deviant as I am and I love you for it.

Noelle, my fellow author friend. I cherish our hang outs because talking shop with another author is so important. Even though she writes less dark books than I do, her help with my plot points has been invaluable. I cherish our coffee dates!

Finally, and arguably the most important—my mother. Because honestly, she's my biggest fan and the first one to read all of my books—even *Red*

Rabbit which I was terrified to give her. She's my alpha reader and unofficial ARC reader all in one.

I'm so lucky to have such an amazing support system in my family who when I came out with arguably one of the darkest romance novels out there, they not only read it (yup, even my grandpa), they simply said: "I'm proud of you!" And you know what? I'm proud of me too.

ABOUT THE AUTHOR

Devyn Rivers is an author living in Northern California. She writes primarily dark contemporary romance and dark fantasy romance novels. Emphasis on the dark -- she enjoys jumping back and forth over the thin line of morality in her novels and says her books are for people who love the antiheroes, morally grey men and spicy sex scenes.

When she's not writing, she's working her full time job in the photography industry, daydreaming about her next novel or hanging out with her family, friends and dog.

www.devynrivers.com